# The Shadows of Nemesis

A Story of the Fall of Rome
Book 2 of the Amulet Series

## Malcolm David Logan

Found Missing Publishing
Chicago

Found Missing Publishing
1449 N Bell
Chicago, IL



May 2022 Edition

ISBN: 978-0-9989695-2-7 (Paperback Edition)
ISBN: 978-0-9989695-3-4 (Ebook Edition)

Cover design by Rebekah Haskell

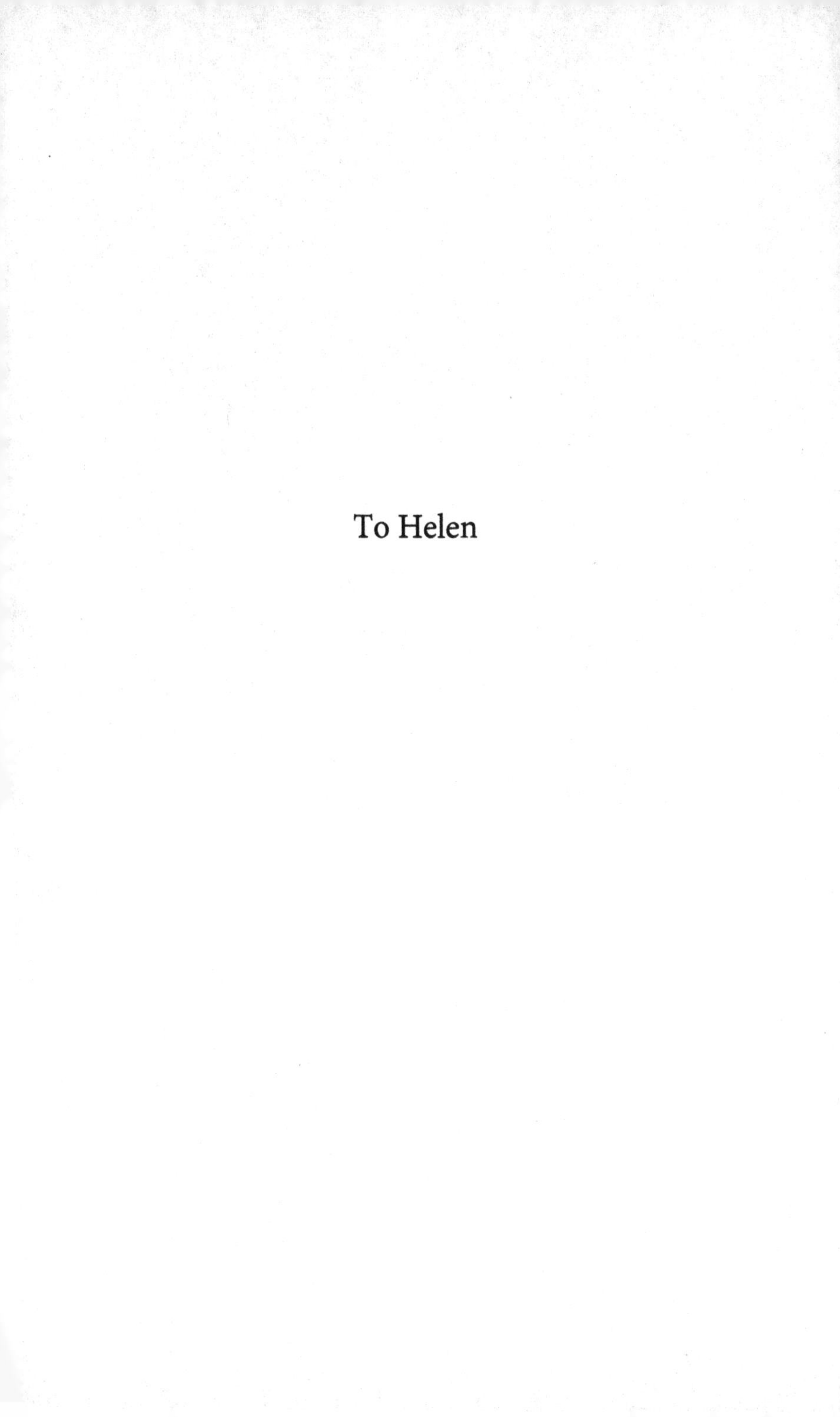

To Helen

# Author's Note

Throughout this novel I have tried to balance historical accuracy with the sensibilities of the modern reader. To that end it's worth noting a few of the measures I've taken.

Readers may notice the occasionally confusing similarities of characters' names. In the late Roman Empire, sons and daughters were named after parents and grandparents. The daughter of the Roman Emperor Placidius, for example, was named Placidia, while his mother was named Galla Placidia. I have tried to differentiate these characters as much as possible to avoid confusion.

What's more, many Roman names were similar in pronunciation. For this reason, I have taken some liberties to ease the reader's burden. The historical character of Palladius, the son of Petronius Maximus, I have renamed Junius to avoid confusion with Placidius, the Emperor. The wife of Petronius Maximus, I have fashioned as Agnus rather than using her historical name, Lucina, much too close to that of the main character, Licinia. As for Petronius Maximus, according to Roman naming conventions, his personal name would have been Petronius, and his family and friends would have called him that, but in the novel I have them refer to him as Maximus to avoid confusion with other characters whose names begin with P.

The Emperor in the novel is named Placidius, which is the personal name of the actual historical figure. It is the name family and friends would have called him. But history knows him by his ceremonial name, Valentinian III.

Pronunciation of Roman names can be difficult for the modern reader. Of the novel's main characters, Placidius is pronounced Pla-sid-ee-us. Aetius is pronounced Ee-tee-us. Licinia Eudocia is pronounced Lis-sin-ee-ah You-doe-see-ah.

Readers will notice some anachronistic elements in the story. For example, the use of contractions in speech and language did not come into being until much later in history. However, I have employed them to convey the sense that the Romans had a casual way of speaking as we do and did not converse in the stilted language of a nineteenth century stage play. For the same reason, I have occasionally employed a modern turn of phrase, but never one whose referents would have been unknown to the people of the time.

I have also used modern imperial measurements for the sake of clarity and to relieve the reader of the burden of translating the Roman system of measurement. For any other anachronisms I may have included unintentionally, I beg your indulgence.


Malcolm David Logan

# List of Characters

**Aetius (ee-tee-us)**
Master of All Soldiers of the Western Roman Empire,
the highest ranking general in the Roman army

**Agnus (Ag-nus)**
Wife of Petronius Maximus

**Albinus (Al-bye-nus)**
Praetorian prefect of Gaul

**Attila (uh-till-uh)**
King of the Huns

**Bassus Herculanus (bass-us herk-ye-lay-us)**
A Roman senator. Husband of Justa Grata Honoria.

**Eudocia (yew-doe-see-uh)**
Eldest daughter of Placidius (Emperor Valentinian III)
and Licinia Eudocia

**Galla Placidia (gal-ah pla-sid-ee-uh)**
Mother of Placidius (Emperor Valentinian III). Formerly regent
during her son's minority and de facto ruler of the Western
Roman Empire for twelve years prior to her son's ascension.

**Genseric (gen-sair-ick)**
King of the Vandals. Father of Huneric.

**Heraclius (Her-ack-lee-us)**
The keeper of the sacred bedchamber, a high
ranking servant, and a eunuch

**Huneric (Who-nair-ick)**
The Vandal prince. Eldest son of the Vandal king
Genseric. A hostage in the Imperial Palace in Rome.


**Junius (jew-nee-us)**
Praetor responsible for the production of public games
and festivals. Son of Petronius Maximus.


**Justa Grata Honoria (just-uh great-uh on-oar-ee-uh)**
Sister of Placidius (Emperor Valentinian
III). Daughter of Galla Placidia.


**Licinia Eudocia (liss-sin-ee-uh yew-doe-see-uh)**
Officially Licinia Eudocia Augusta, wife of Placidius (Emperor
Valentinian III). Daughter of Emperor Theodosius II of the Eastern
Roman Empire. Niece of Pulcheria. Mother of Placidia and Eudocia.


**Olybrius (oh-lib-ree-us)**
Adoptive son of Petronius Maximus


**Onegesius (oh-ne-guess-ee-us)**
A highly placed Hun official


**Orestes (oh-rest-ees)**
Secretary of Attila


**Petronius Maximus (pe-trohn-ee-us max-e-mus)**
A wealthy and influential aristocrat. Formerly urban
prefect of Rome. Father of Junius. Husband of Agnus.


**Placidia (plu-sid-ee-uh)**
Youngest daughter of Placidius (Emperor
Valentinian III) and Licinia Eudocia.

**Placidius (plu-sid-ee-us)**
Officially Flavius Placidius Valentinianus Augustus, known
to history as Emperor Valentinian III of the Western
Roman Empire. Husband of Licinia Eudocia. Son of
Galla Placidia. Brother of Justa Grata Honoria.

**Pope Leo (lee-oh)**
Head of the Roman Church. Successor to Pope Sixtus.

**Pope Sixtus (pope six-tus)**
Head of the Roman Church. Friend of Galla
Placidia. Predecessor to Pope Leo.

**Pulcheria (pull-care-ee-uh)**
Sister of Emperor Theodosius II. Aunt of Licinia Eudocia.

**Theodosius II (thee-oh-doh-see-us)**
Emperor of the Eastern Roman Empire. Father of Licinia Eudocia.

**Theodoric (thee-oh-dor-ick)**
King of the Goths

**Thorismund (thor-is-mund)**
Prince of the Goths. Son of Theodoric.

# Theodosian Family Tree

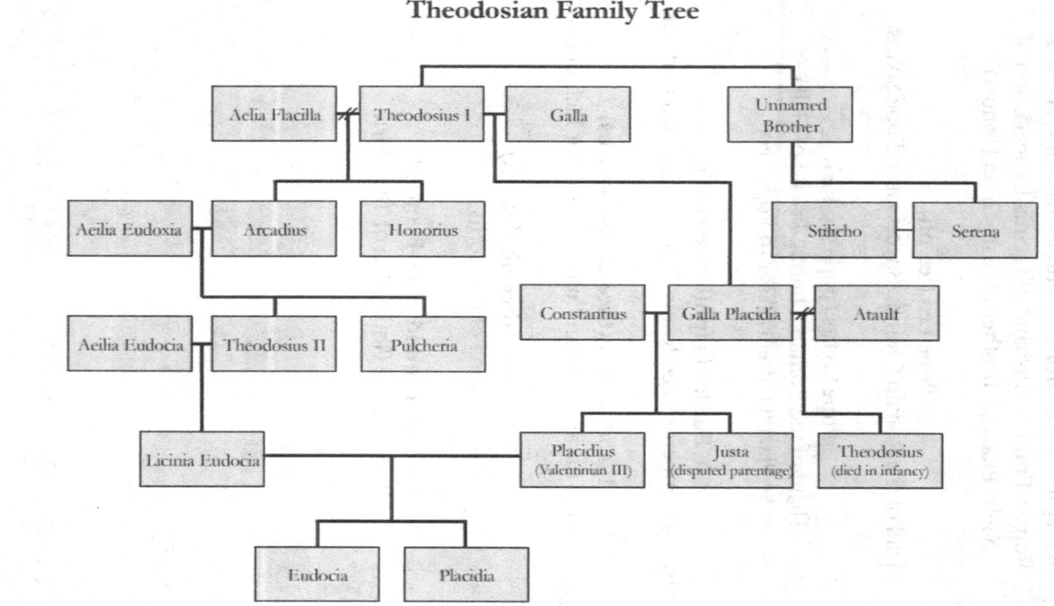

# Roman place names and their modern equivalents

| | |
|---|---|
| Agrigentum | Agrigento |
| Arelate | Arles |
| Armorica | Brittany |
| Augusta Treverorum | Trier |
| Augustonementum | Clermont-Ferrand |
| Aurelianum | Orleans |
| Carthago | Tunis |
| Colonia | Cologne |
| Cyrnus | Corsica |
| Dertona | Tortona |
| Divodorum | Metz |
| Gallaecia | Galicia |
| Illyricum | The Balkans |
| Lusitania | Portugal |
| Lutetia | Paris |
| Mediolanum | Milan |
| Narbo | Narbonne |
| Noviodunum | Soissons |
| Pánormos | Palermo |
| Pavitium | Padua |
| Placentia | Piacenza |
| Salona | Split |
| Sardus | Sardinia |
| Servitium | Gradiska |
| Sicilia | Sicily |
| Tolosa | Toulouse |

5th Century AD Roman Provinces

Pivotal 5th Century AD Cities, Towns and Villages

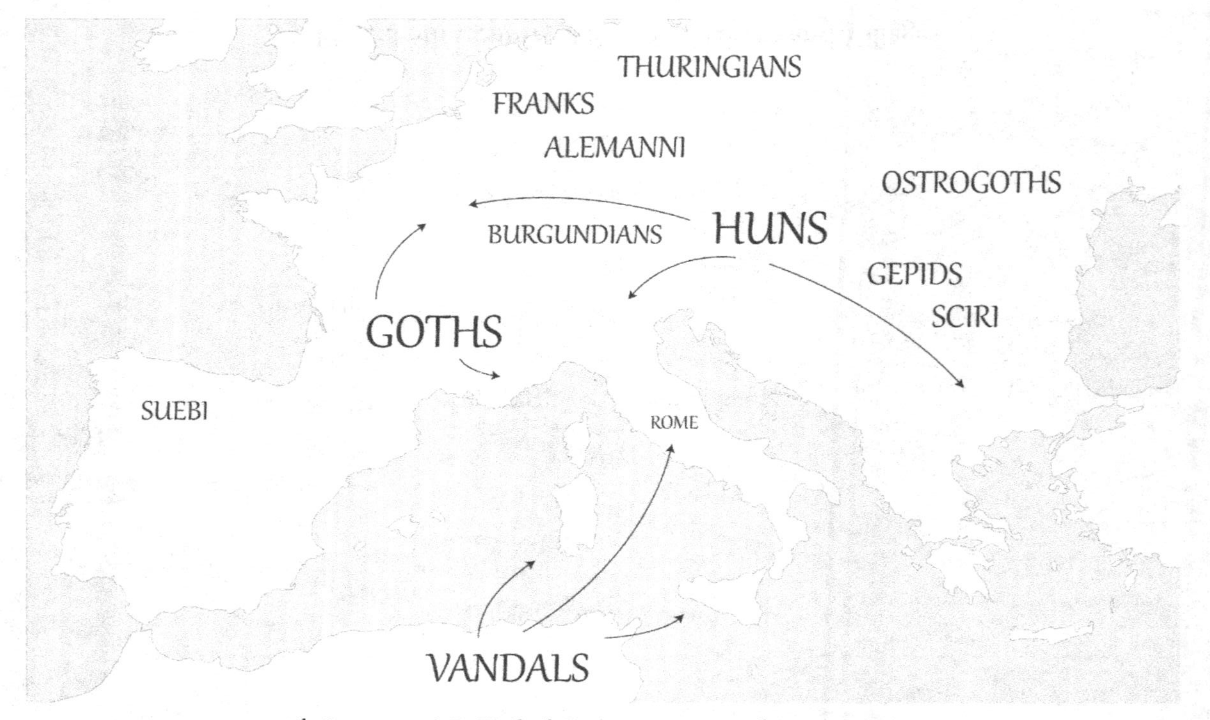


5th Century AD Tribal Dispositions and Invasion Routes

# Prologue
## August AD 437

He was between my legs again. I could see the shadow of his hunched figure on the wall, pushing and straining, cast there by the glow of the coals in the brazier and the tiny flames of the oil lamps that surrounded the bed. It was the second time he had come to me, his second attempt, with no more success than the first. I had just turned sixteen, and no one had told me it would be like this. I tried to be submissive, to let him know I was agreeable, even though it was awkward. At first, I held him high up on his torso, my hands clutching the muscles at his sides, and tried to pull him into me. But it was no use. He made a little grunt of frustration and pulled away. After that I just lay there with my head turned, looking at the black bowl of the brazier festooned in gold, trimmed in Greek meander, smelling the smoke of the rose and grapevine trimmings above the odor of his sweat.

He lay in the dark, playing with it, jiggling and pulling on it. My initial fear subsided. Unlike the first time, earlier that evening, when he had come to me, telling me to take my clothes off and taking in the sight of me for the first time, it did not thicken and enlarge, not even briefly. It did not threaten to push into me, to stretch and fill me in that God forbidden place, in that place I had been cautioned never to explore, that place reserved only for my husband and in the service of God in obedience to His directive to multiply. The first time I wondered if it was always like this, if all men fussed and wriggled before growing stiff and forcing it in. But this time I understood. He had a problem.

I heard a stirring at the door and saw the eunuch hovering in the shadows. It was Heraclius, who had been given to my husband as a gift by my parents, a part of my dowry, along with jewelry, gold, and land. His presence was proper, but he should have been more discreet. His sly intrusiveness was no accident. He had always been artfully insolent, and I loathed him.

My husband stopped and lay on top of me. I could feel his breath on the nape of my neck. Then with a miserable sigh he stood up. Except for a few drops of sticky fluid on my thighs, I was dry. He muttered an apology and started away.

"Oh, Placidius," I said, but it was too late. He was already gone. Even then I sensed this was the beginning of a long pulling away, the commencement of our estrangement so fast upon the heels of our wedding day. I could not help but conclude that I had failed him.

I slid down off the couch. I got to my knees. Maybe I should have listened to my aunt. Maybe I should have taken the vow of celibacy as she had asked. As to what I was supposed to do now, I hadn't the slightest notion. This sort of thing was beyond me. I bowed my head and prayed.

But my mind wandered. It was all my mother's fault. She was the one who had put the idea into my head, telling me a woman should not be other than she knows herself to be, insisting a woman must be honest with herself and not fight the inherent parts of her character. I should have known her advice was wrong after all the trouble she had caused, after the scandal she had brought down on our house, on my father. I should have rejected her advice and listened to my aunt.

Celibacy is not for everyone. My aunt had never been anything but perfectly frank about that. It was only for the strongest and most pious, which was why it was so widely esteemed. And if I did not feel equal to it, I should not try it. She had told me that, but in the same breath she had assured me I was capable of anything and reminded me how a woman of high privilege who remained celibate was the most admirable of God's creatures, an inspiration far and wide, a paragon of virtue. And she ought to know. She was just such a woman.

But I told myself I would be admired in any case. To be married to the Emperor of the West, to bear him a son, would make me one of the most admired and celebrated people in the world. Our union would bring together the two halves of the Empire, and our son would be the first Emperor to rule over a unified Rome since Constantine a century ago. Together Placidius and I would restore the glory of the Empire and reestablish its dominance over its rivals. I needed only to wed Placidius and bear him a son, and I would be venerated. It seemed a simple thing. By comparison, celibacy seemed more challenging. I took what I thought would be the easier path.

Now, I wasn't so sure. If Placidius and I were unable to consummate our marriage, the criticism would be intense.

We had to make it happen. There was no other way. But I was at a loss about what to do now. No one had ever talked to me about sex, other than the bishop, who had only discussed it in the most rudimentary terms and given me to understand that my part in it was strictly submission. I prayed to God for understanding, but got nothing back, nothing I could interpret as guidance. But why? Perhaps I had fallen short. Perhaps I had offended God and earned His indignation. Perhaps my rejection of celibacy had made Him angry.

I raised my eyes and looked around the room. In the murky darkness I could make out the frescoed images on the walls, pagan images, appallingly salacious. One was of Priapus the pagan god of fertility cavorting naked in a garden, his erect manhood on full display. My breath caught in my throat, and I turned away. We had no such paintings in our palaces in the East, but here in Thessalonika, where nostalgia for the old Greek gods was all the rage, change was slower to come. The original fresco was half painted over by a stirring new image: Salome accepting the head of John the Baptist on a platter. In the background sat King Herod weeping over his weakness, a tragic lesson in unintended consequences and the dangers of being ensnared by a woman.

Then my eyes wandered to an image on the opposite wall. Another pagan painting, uneradicated but without the blatant carnality of the garden scene. This was an image of the winged goddess Nemesis wielding a whip, hovering above a cowering miscreant, threatening him. Nemesis, the ancient instrument of divine retribution, a woman meting out justice to men.

How I knew any of this was beyond me. The lessons arranged for me by my aunt had never delved into the pantheon of pagan deities, those often ludicrous figures whose bizarre antics formed the basis of the old religion. But there were plenty of people, particularly among the servants and slaves, who still worshipped the old gods, and I probably learned about Nemesis from them, without ever intending to, the way one picks up bits of gossip or the scraps of old songs. To me it seemed particularly odd that a woman should have been granted such power. According to the truth revealed by Christ, women should be subservient to men. God was male, and only He could wield retribution through his representatives on earth, bishops and generals and Emperors. Women never entered into the discussion. Even the Virgin Mary was subservient and amenable, a distributor of grace, not justice.

I stood and looked at the fresco. Then I realized I was naked. My face turned red. I had been praying to God without my clothes on. *What a fool*, I thought. *No wonder God is angry with me.*

* * *

Women were weak when we were not altogether wicked. This was a truth that had been drummed into me from childhood. Men were the conduit through which God conducted his business on earth. Consequently, if I wanted an answer as to what to do about my husband, I was going to have to get it from a man. The bishop might have helped if we were in Constantinople, but we were not. We had stopped in Thessalonika on our way to Ravenna. It was a lovely seaside city with a wonderful old palace where we had paused to enjoy our honeymoon.

5

We had been awkward with each other at first, which was to be expected, given that we had just met three weeks before. Placidius had been gentle and kind; he had not rushed me, which had allayed my fears and made me warm to him, but then he had awakened me unexpectedly one night and told me to undress, and everything had gone sour from there.

It couldn't go on like this. I was going to have to figure things out. Then I remembered the books my aunt had given me, and I went to the door and called for them. When they arrived, I bent over the volumes, paging through them beneath the flickering light of an oil lamp. They were written by the Church Fathers, those acclaimed theologians whose interpretations of scripture were inspired by God, and thus infallible: Tertullian, Origen, Augustine, and Jerome. The works of men, the Word of God. If I had hoped for some encouragement from them, I was disappointed.

The Church Fathers were not men to indulge in empathy for anyone, much less for the sexual failings of a couple trying to consummate their marriage. Still, I was not to be deterred. I kept on reading until I came upon this passage from Augustine: "It is the natural order of things that women serve their husbands, the lesser must serve the greater, the weaker the stronger. This is the natural justice of things. As with slaves and masters, those who excel in reason, also excel in power."

Like a man wandering in a desert, I had circled back to the place where I had started. My role was to be subservient, and that was all. Like a slave, I was a tool to be wielded by my master.

*Very well,* I thought, *I must go to him and serve him. I must do whatever he requires of me.*

I hurried from my cubiculum[1] through the peristylum[2] to his bedchamber.

Heraclius was standing just outside the door. He gave a little start when he saw me, followed by the faintest hint of a smirk. I told him to go away. Then I went to my new husband, took of my clothes, and slipped in beside him.

I whispered in his ear, "Tell me what I must do."

He turned to me, searching out my eyes in the dull light of the brazier. He said, "Resist."

I didn't understand. It didn't make sense. I asked for an explanation, but he grabbed me by the wrists and shook me.

"Stop me," he snapped. "Don't let me."

He raised his hand as if to strike me. Reflexively, I tried to block it. He batted my arm away and wrestled me onto my back. He was very rough. He mounted me. I struggled and fought. He overcame me. The pain was harsh. I tried not to scream. It was brutish and ugly, but in the end, he left his seed in me. Then he rolled off me and went to sleep.

I turned on my side, clutching myself, tears streaming down my cheeks. And then I saw it for the first time. It was lying among his discarded clothes by the bedside, a curious amulet cast in lead, circular in shape and bearing a three-line inscription: "God be with you". I reached out and touched it.

"Leave it there," he said. "It's not for you."

Naturally, I obeyed, but I couldn't take me eyes off it. Long after he fell asleep, I kept looking at it, my tears vanished, and my pain mysteriously subsided.

———————————

1  Small, private room in a Roman house- often a bedroom.
2  An architectural space formed by a row of columns surrounding a courtyard, usually a garden within the home.

# Chapter 1
## September, The Year AD 437

"The disputes will stop. But that's just the beginning, Licinia. With the two halves of the Empire at peace, we'll be able to pursue more pressing matters, things long overdue. We'll bring the Goths under control and drive the Vandals out of Africa. We'll repel the Huns. Don't you see? That's why I did it. That's why I gave Illyricum to your father."

His eyes glimmered with excitement. This was a side of him I hadn't seen before. During most of the six-week journey from Thessalonika, he had been distant and guarded. Maybe it was because of the way he had treated me that night; perhaps he regretted it. In any case, suddenly now, as we were nearing Ravenna, he opened up as if we were old friends, boon companions. He seemed unable to contain his excitement. He bubbled over with the things he wanted to tell me. I was grateful for the opportunity to improve matters between us.

We hardly knew each other in spite of the fact that we were second cousins; his grandfather and my great-grandfather were one and the same. He was my father's first cousin. We were family. Yet we had been brought up in different worlds.

I was the only child of the Eastern Roman Emperor Theodosius II and had grown up in the Greek-speaking East where a silky orientalism pervaded everything. He was the newly invested Emperor of the West, Flavius Placidius Valentinianus Augustus by convention, Valentinian III to those who would chronicle his reign, and simply as Placidius to those of us who knew him intimately. Placidius had been raised in a Latin-speaking world where boots-and-leather militarism were the order of the day, a gritty, no nonsense place reflective of its frequently embattled condition. It was only natural that he would feel a little uncomfortable around a pampered, privileged person like me. But now, as we neared his home, his reticence slipped away, and he became more voluble.

He was talking about Illyricum.

"Why quarrel over it? Soon enough it will be ours—ours and our children's."

There was a glint in his eye when he said that. I couldn't help but giggle.

"We have been given a great opportunity," he said. "It has been given to us to reunite the Empire." He gathered my hands in his and kissed them. "You and I, together." I felt the thrill of his affection and favored him with an adoring look.

He got up and began to pace, tapping his finger on his lip, contemplating the possibilities. "I will go at once to Rome and convene the Senate. I will not presume to instruct them. I will show them the respect and dignity that is their due. I will listen. I will learn. The same with the generals. I will surround myself with learned counselors and advisors and draw knowledge from them as a thirsty man draws water from a well. That's wise, don't you think?"

I agreed.

He knelt on one knee. "Listen, Licinia, I have my flaws, God knows. I don't mind telling you. I have not always been so . . . well, self-possessed. I intend to change all that. I intend to change how I am and become a better person, a better leader, and you can be a part of it. Will you help me with that?"

I told him I would.

"If you see me acting unwisely, I want you to remind me. Will you do that?"

I nodded. I was excited. I assured him I would. Then I offered a suggestion.

He seemed taken aback, as if he had not expected me to have any thoughts on the matter, but he recovered and put on a good face. "What is it?"

"You should pray," I said. "You should ask God to help you."

His expression went from ridicule to bemusement to uncertainty in the course of a moment. "Really?"

"Well, of course. If you are asking everyone else for help, why not ask God?"

"Okay," he said. "I'll do that."

"Now," I said, taking him by the hand.

He flinched imperceptibly. "What?"

"Now," I said. "Let's pray."

There was the vaguest hint of resistance as I knelt down beside him. I bowed my head and closed my eyes. I could feel him looking at me. When I turned to meet his gaze, he bowed his head and clasped his hands. Together, we prayed. His devotions were unfocused and distracted. He went about them mechanically, without conviction. After a while I took pity on him.

"That's enough," I said. "I'm sure God has heard you."

He stood up, blushing. "I'm sorry," he said. "My piety is not what it ought to be."

"I can help you with that," I said.

Again, that look of barely contained astonishment. "How?"

"I've got an idea," I said. I went and got the books my aunt had given me, the ones written by the Church Fathers. I pressed them into his hands. "Read these," I said. "They will tell you everything you need to know."

"Thank you," he said, examining them as if they were a handful of squirming rodents.

"Don't worry," I said. "They won't bite."

His face brightened. He smiled. "Books don't scare me," he said. He had a funny look on his face like the whole thing was the set up for the punch line of a joke. His good humor disarmed me. I found it charming. It was then I realized I might grow to like him, which is a wonderful blessing for a woman who has just met her spouse and knows she must spend the rest of her life with him. It's not always true. It certainly wasn't that way for my mother. Yet except for the awful way we had to go about sharing intimacy, Placidius and I seemed to be warming to each other, and I had every reason to hope for a long and fruitful marriage.

* * *

In the days that followed, my new husband opened up to me. He spoke of his family, of his mother, Galla Placidia, and his sister, Justa Grata Honoria.

His mother was a formidable woman. She had been the ruling Augusta of the Western Roman Empire for more than twelve years and had only just stepped aside on our wedding day to bestow complete authority on Placidius. His praise of her was tempered by a note of distrust. He warned me not to be taken in by the face she showed the public. She might appear to be mild and unassuming, he said, but it was all an act. There was nothing unusual in that, he was quick to add. Women in positions of power often pretended to be meek and agreeable, even when they were as treacherous as snakes. If I ever had any questions about the women I would be dealing with in my role as Augusta, I should ask him. I should rely on his experience. I should not try to find out for myself. It was too dangerous. Besides, he liked my innocence and didn't want to see it wrecked.

It seemed a harsh indictment of powerful women in general, and his mother in particular, and I felt compelled to ask a question that was nagging at me.

"I heard your mother was a woman of great piety," I said. "How could such a person can be considered treacherous. Aren't pious women virtuous by nature?"

He looked at me in disbelief. "She has endowed many churches," he said. "She is on the very best terms with the Pope. If that's what you call piety, then she's a pious woman, but that doesn't mean she's trustworthy."

I was shocked. I had never heard anyone speak of their mother in such harsh terms, at least not explicitly. Didn't God command us to honor our mother and father? His boldness unsettled me. But I had to admit it was not the first time I had heard unflattering things about Galla Placidia. My aunt had warned me about her. She had called her devious and cunning and cautioned me to steer clear of her.

"And my sister Justa," Placidius went on. "She's a bare-faced bitch. There's nothing subtle about her. She will drag you down like a hound takes a stag. Stay away from her."

I was taken aback by his vehemence, and I asked him what his sister could possibly have done to earn such a hostile judgment from him. "She tried to sabotage our marriage," he said. "She was a part of a wicked plot designed to keep us apart. Others were involved, others who shall remain nameless. But you needn't trouble yourself with that. Just do as I tell you. I will keep you safe."

I was itching to learn more, but his last words had a finality to them, and I decided not to test him. It was just as well. Discussing his mother and sister cast a shadow over him, and it took him a while to regain his former humor.

Our entrance into Ravenna was a convivial affair. Well-wishers lined the roadside, waving and cheering. Drums and trumpets sounded. Exuberant supporters ran alongside our litters, ringing bells and clapping cymbals. We were showered with wheat and rice and candied nuts. Flocks of doves were sent aloft in celebration. I turned and smiled at him. He smiled back, clearly touched by the warmth of his people.

We were carried through the gates of the city and down the Via Porticata past low-slung buildings with orange tiled roofs, residential structures for the most part, well appointed, but with none of the splendid ornaments so common in Constantinople. Along the way we passed overgrown lots thick with weeds and reeking of garbage. We traveled over sickly-looking canals filled with stagnant water. The mosquitoes rose around us in swarms. The city was built on a marsh, which made it easy to defend but hard to live in especially in the summer months. From afar, it appeared as a squat, ugly town hunkering down in the swamp like a toad, and I was dismayed at the thought this was to be my home. Mercifully, my first impression was softened by the graciousness of the inhabitants, but I could hardly ignore the sense that I had come down in the world. Compared to Constantinople, Ravenna was a sad, ramshackle affair.

The city was devoid of monuments. No triumphal arches. No obelisks. The only fountains were simple sluice tongues pouring water into communal basins. If there was a grand central plaza somewhere it was not observable anywhere, and it was not situated before the palace, the entrance to which was a simple arched doorway in a long, featureless wall.

Our litters were lowered, and we stepped out to greet the cheering throng. Placidius feigned an imperious dignity, chin up, eyes forward, not deigning to make eye contact with his admirers, but I smiled and waved. Placidius gave me a disapproving look. I went over and stood by his side and waited until a pair of soldiers took up a position in front of us. They preceded us down a long gray corridor to an open doorway at the other end. The voices of the crowd rang in the passageway as we went. The walls dripped with moisture. A fetid odor hung over everything.

We emerged into a large octagonal chamber with a vaulted dome and mosaic floor. Drapes were suspended from the ribs of the vaults and hung in the dead air like faded laundry. Seated on a raised dais at the opposite end of the room was a handsome woman cloaked in ceremonial robes and surrounded by attendants. As we entered, she got up and moved aside, revealing an ornate throne trimmed in gold and studded with colored marbles. Placidius cut me a look, crossed the room, climbed the steps to the dais and lowered himself onto the throne. He pressed his back against the backrest and situated his arms on the armrests.

"We are glad to see you so comfortably installed," the woman said. "You look well. Your contentment radiates from you."

His eyes shifted to her though his shoulders remained squared, and his hands did not move from the scrolls at the ends of the armrests. The two held each other's gaze for a long moment. Then the woman turned to me.

"And here is the reason for all this contentment." She descended the steps and greeted me. "I am Galla Placidia," she said, "and I would know your pretty face anywhere. If you came to me as a stranger, I would know you. Your resemblance to your mother is astounding." She gathered my hands in hers and searched my face. "Welcome to Ravenna, Licinia Eudocia."

"Thank you," I said.

She studied me a moment longer. Then she turned to Placidius. "Shall your wife sit beside you?"

Placidius looked at the empty chair beside him. "Very well," he said.

Galla nodded in the direction of the chair. "It is well that you sit beside him. Placidius requires the company of women."

Something moved in my husband's eyes, something dark and resentful. "And where shall you sit, Mother?" he asked.

Galla waved this off. "I have sat for long enough. It's long past time for you to take the seat that has been prepared for you. I hope you'll find it to your liking."

"You have made it so, have you not?"

"You know full well that I have, if you took the time to read my letter."

"I read it."

"Did you? I was never really sure. The man tasked with delivering it never reported back to me."

"I'm afraid a misfortune befell him," Placidius said.

"A case of misunderstood motives?"

"You might say that."

I crossed the dais and sat down beside my husband. Galla remained standing. She smiled at us. "Such a lovely couple."

"I have come to claim my rightful inheritance," Placidius said. "I know you would have preferred I remain in Constantinople, but I will have to disappoint you. I have come home to assume my full powers. I will be Emperor now."

Galla folded her arms. The smile was gone from her face, but her eyes were inscrutable.

"Don't look at me like that," he said. "I've made my decision. The East is at peace. They're comfortable and prosperous. But here in the West there's so much to do, so many problems. It would be irresponsible for me to stay away."

"You spoke to Pulcheria," Galla said.

I was startled by the mention of my aunt's name. The sour look on my husband's face was even more unexpected.

"I met her," he said. "We talked. She had nothing to do with my decision. I came to it on my own."

"A judicious decision, well considered," Galla said.

"The West is my birthright," he said.

"It is," Galla said, "as was Illyricum."

I saw Placidius's knuckles go white. He looked down for a moment and gathered himself. "If you think Illyricum is lost to us, you are mistaken. I surrendered our claim to it in order to keep the peace. It has been a bone of contention for years, but there is no reason to keep quarreling over it. Illyricum is Licnia's birthright. When her father dies, he will leave it to her as an inheritance. Then it will be ours again."

"So, you lent it to them?"

"I saw no reason to keep quarreling over something that will be ours in due time anyway."

"Unless you should meet an untimely demise."

Placidius scoffed.

Galla went on. "It's not the first time Illyricum was lent to our cousins in the East, you know. We lent it to them before, to help fight the Goths. It was agreed the territory would be returned to us once the crisis was over. Instead, the Eastern troops occupied it. They've been there now for more than half a century. For so long, in fact, they think they're entitled to it. But it's ours. The prefecture of Illyricum represents a substantial portion of our sovereign territory. We cannot and should not negotiate over it. I advised you not to do so in my letter. But apparently you ignored me."

Placidius started to object, but his mother cut him off. "It would be different if you never read my letter," she said, "but you claim you did. Unless, of course, it wasn't really my letter at all. Unless it was a forgery designed to trip you up."

Placidius reached into his robes and produced the amulet, the extraordinary piece of jewelry I had seen it among his things at the bedside. He leaned forward and held it out to her. She came forward and took it. She looked down at it for a long moment. "You had this with you when you made your decision?"

"I did."

"And yet you made it anyway?"

He gave her an apologetic shrug.

Galla shook her head. "Did Pulcheria see this?"

"She saw it. I believe she would have liked it for herself, but it was not to be."

"I'm glad you didn't give it to her."

"It wasn't entirely up to me. Besides, I thought it only right to return it to you. You seemed so enchanted by it."

"I had hoped you would see the value in it."

"I'm not like you, Mother. I don't see the point of attributing mystical motives to every little thing. Sometimes people just make bad decisions. Sometimes that's all there is to it."

"So, what's the solution? To replace those who make the bad decisions?"

"Maybe."

Galla held his eyes for a moment. Then she looked away.

"Oh, come on, Mother. The value of your piety is not lost on me. I understand the importance of being on good terms with the Church. Which is why I intend to work on it. Licinia will help me. She has given me several books on theology to instruct me, and I am praying twice a day now, some days as many as three or four." He turned to me. "Isn't that right?"

I concurred.

"I intend to meet with Pope Sixtus as soon as possible. He seems like a reliable ally. I hope he is as devoted to me as he was to you."

Galla said nothing.

"To tell you the truth, there are a lot of people I want to meet with," Placidius said, "magistrates and prefects, governors and generals. I want the very best men to guide me, to advise me, so my judgments are sound, and I act with prudence."

He was speaking to her, but she wasn't listening. She was staring at the amulet as if her mind was miles away. It was immediately clear that her indifference to him was painful. I decided to come to his rescue.

"He wants to improve himself," I told her, "to become a better leader."

Galla looked at me in surprise.

"He knows he made mistakes in the past and he wants to do better."

"Be quiet. That's enough," Placidius said.

"But I was only—"

"Be silent!" He turned to his mother and leaned forward. "Where is my Master of Soldiers today?"

"Aetius is in Gaul concluding a treaty with the Goths."

"In Gaul? Well, Gaul is not far. He should have come. I am the newly anointed Emperor. He should be here to celebrate my ascension."

"Well, technically you have been the Emperor since you were six-years-old," she said slipping the amulet around her neck and arranging the horsehair strands. "So, there is really nothing to celebrate."

"Oh, please, Mother. You, of all people, know that you have been my regent all this time. I have been little more than an Emperor in waiting, forbidden to assume full power until I reached full adulthood and was wed. Well, now I have, and the throne is mine. It certainly is a cause for celebration. Just ask all those people out there cheering for me."

Galla was unimpressed. "The adulation of the public has no substance, Placidius. It's like a fog. Don't be taken in by it."

"Aetius should be here," he said. "This is just more of his intolerable insolence."

"In case you weren't informed, Narbo has been under siege for months. The city was eventually forced to surrender, and the Goths took it. They destroyed the local garrison and expelled the prefect."

"Because he failed to defend it."

"He saw the situation for what it was. They had the harbor blockaded. He couldn't get enough troops ashore to break the siege. But he had an army approaching from the north. He considered trying to trap the Goths between the army and the city, but the people of the city were weak, depleted; they couldn't have held out much longer. On the other hand, the navy was strong, and the army was strong, so he let the Goths take the city. Then he turned the tables on them. Now they were the ones under siege, from both land and sea. What's more, the people of the city, under his direction, sabotaged their defenses. Within a fortnight the Goths found themselves backed into a corner. They were forced to sue for peace. Aetius is there now, working out the terms of the agreement. He is negotiating from a position of strength, not weakness."

Placidius made a snorting sound. "The mighty Aetius, hero of the Empire."

"You should not underestimate him."

Placidius offered a bland smile. "I intend to become fully conversant on all matters pertaining to military strategy. I will not become the puppet of our Master of Soldiers."

I detected a flash of anger in her eyes, but it was gone as soon as it appeared, and she remained calm if somewhat brittle. "When you say foolish things like that, I'm inclined to believe you didn't really read my letter, or, in any event, didn't finish it."

Placidius rolled his eyes. "Do we have to go on and on about that letter? I spent the better part of two months reading it. It was monstrously long. I read it and reached my conclusions. Do you want me to keep going back to it like a theologian consults the scriptures? I'm here now. I'm the Emperor. If you have something you want to say to me, you can say it to me directly."

"Give me back the letter," she said. "I want to see it. I want to know it was mine and not some fake meant to misguide you."

He was momentarily disconcerted. In that instant I saw the awkward, agitated teenager he had been. "I don't have it anymore. I threw it away."

Galla dropped her eyes and shook her head. "Why would you do something like that?"

"I was done with it. It was time to move on."

She assumed the exasperated tone of a mother admonishing a child. "Let me tell you something, Placidius. You are going to have to rely on Aetius. He is a formidable military commander who has won the undying loyalty of his troops. Do not attempt to diminish him. You're going to need him. In any case, you're going to have quite enough on your plate dealing with domestic issues. The Senators and their patrons can be quite challenging; keeping and maintaining their loyalty is a fulltime job. Then there's the Church. Let Aetius look after your military affairs. Don't interfere with him. He knows what he's doing."

Placidius lifted his chin and said, "Maybe I'm not as informed as you on these matters, but I fail to see how surrendering valuable territory to a hostile enemy can be characterized as a shrewd military strategy."

"You are speaking of the Vandals now, and the deal we struck regarding Africa."

"Yes."

"You realize, of course, that the territory was already lost. We had no chance of retrieving it. Formally acknowledging their dominion cost us nothing. In return we received a promise that Carthago wouldn't come under attack. Lives were saved, hostages exchanged, bloodshed averted. What's more, settling with them freed us up to deal with Burgundian aggression on the Rhine Frontier and Gothic intransigence in Gaul. It may not have been ideal, but it was sound policy."

"That's your opinion. We shall see if anyone else has a different view. I intend to consult with alternative advisers."

"I'm cautioning you against that."

Placidius smirked. Then turning to me he said, "My mother considers Aetius a god. She thinks he's infallible. In the meantime, Rome keeps losing territory. With his help she's been ruling over an empire that's slowly falling apart.

I intend to reverse that. We are going to return Rome to its former glory, aren't we, Licinia?"

I gave him warm smile.

Galla kept her gaze locked on his face as she fingered the strands of the amulet.

Thinking he had won the round, Placidius laughed. He looked around at those in attendance. "As long as we are on the subject of absent subordinates, where are the rest of the dignitaries who should be attending my arrival? It seems you have done a poor job of welcoming the new Emperor, Mother. One might think you are less than enthusiastic about my return."

"A formal ceremony has been arranged for later. All the right people will be in attendance. You will be received with the proper reverence, I assure you."

"And what of my sister, where is she?"

"Justa is away in Sicilia."

"Well, isn't that convenient? What could possibly have called her away at such an auspicious moment?"

"She was feeling low. She asked permission to go, and I granted it. She will be back in the autumn."

"Feeling low, eh? Perhaps she was suffering some grievous disappointment, some carefully laid plan gone awry."

Galla narrowed her eyes. "What are you getting at, Placidius?"

"Justa orchestrated a plot to sabotage my marriage, a conspiracy that went wrong and resulted in casualties. It was a mess, Mother, and Justa was behind it."

To my surprise Galla didn't reject his accusation, neither did she come to her daughter's defense. Instead, she said, "Do you know who else was in on it?"

"Who would you expect?"

"I see."

"You realize she cannot escape punishment."

Galla sighed. "Your anger is well justified. What do you have in mind?"

"She shall be whipped. Thirty strokes."

"You cannot whip your sister. She is a member of the House of Theodosius."

"She is a traitorous wretch. Thirty strokes are a pittance. She will recover in a week, but she will remember the sting long enough to think twice before attempting something like that again."

"I won't permit it."

Placidius pursed his lips. "I'm acting with restraint, Mother. The punishment is lenient given the crime."

"You have to think of public opinion. They won't understand. They'll speak ill of you."

"It will be done discreetly. No one will know."

"People will know."

"By people you mean Aetius."

Galla's voice hardened. "Your newfound prudence and restraint would serve you well in this regard."

Placidius opened his mouth to retort but thought better of it. He took a deep breath. "I have your advice on the matter," he said. "Go now. Leave me alone. I'd like time to think."

Before she withdrew, Galla turned to me. "You deserved a warmer reception from us. I'm sorry about that. But I'm glad you're here with us now. Welcome, Licinia."

I gave a nod of assent, and she withdrew.

Placidius sat silently on his throne for some time and stared into space. I sat uncomfortably by his side. I stared at my hands. After a while, he excused himself and got up and went out. I was left alone.

I thought someone might come to show me to my quarters. I was wrong. After a while I went out into the corridor and found a servant who located the chamberlain who assigned a eunuch to lead me to my rooms.

That night Placidius forced himself on me and I resisted. I would much rather have given myself to him willingly. I wanted to show him how much I sympathized with him and shared in his frustrations. Poor fellow.

* * *

There were many things in the conversation between Placidius and Galla that sparked my curiosity, but it was better not to ask. A wife's place is to forbear and remain silent, so I didn't ask my husband what his mother had meant by implying he could be in danger over his decision to cede Illyricum to the East. Nor did I question his reaction to the mention of my aunt's name, and, although it was difficult, I resisted the urge to ask him who he believed to have conspired with his sister to sabotage our marriage. It was none of my business. I had better things to do. There was so much to learn about my new place here. I needed to arrange my wardrobe and jewelry. I needed to get acquainted with my servants. And I needed to learn how to dress properly for dinner. Everything was so new.

Still, I couldn't stop thinking about their conversation. My sympathies were all with Placidius, naturally, and against his mother, who struck me as quite certain she was correct and unwilling to give her son the benefit of the doubt. Later, when we were alone and he asked my opinion of her, I told him as much, which had an interesting effect. He opened up to me as if he had been on guard against the possibility that I might take her side against him. He told me more about the letter she had written, a long, convoluted chronicle of her life with pearls of wisdom scattered throughout, the upshot of which was a request by her that he remain in Constantinople and permit her to remain on the throne in Ravenna.

"She didn't want me to come back," Placidius explained. "She doesn't believe me equal to the job." He lowered his head. "The truth is everyone is against me. Even those who support me only do so because they're hoping I will fail."

I gathered his hands in mine and vowed my unwavering support. Then I ventured an observation, something to cheer him up. "Not everyone is against you. My father championed our marriage. He welcomed you as his co-emperor in the West. That is certainly a meaningful endorsement."

"But your aunt wasn't very enthusiastic. Was she?"

I was surprised he would come back at me with my aunt in that way. If my aunt had been less than enthusiastic about our marriage, what difference did it make in light of my father's approval? I tried to clarify her motives to him.

"My aunt was disappointed because I had not chosen celibacy. It had nothing to do with you."

"You think not?"

"Of course not. She barely knows you."

I could see something move behind his eyes. Then, apropos of nothing, he said, "I need you to get pregnant. I need you to give me an heir to strengthen my claim to the throne."

"Your claim is beyond dispute," I said. "You are the grandson of Theodosius I, the same as my father. If you are not the rightful Emperor of the West, then my father is not the rightful Emperor of the East. Who could question your legitimacy?"

"It's not about legitimacy," he said. "It's about vulnerability. If I were erased from the picture, the succession would become hazy. Anyone could seize the throne."

"But who would be so bold?"

"Plenty of people," he said. "Aetius for one. Our Master of Soldiers. He's always felt himself entitled to it." He brooded for a moment. "He manipulated my mother for years," he said. "Now that I'm in charge, he knows it won't be easy, and he's not going to like it. By getting rid of me he can get what he wants without interference."

"But how can he do that?"

"The army will back him. He's their leader."

"But you're the Emperor."

He looked at me as if I were a dimwitted child. He started to say something but thought better of it. "You're on my side, aren't you?"

"Yes."

"Then you must get pregnant. That's all I ask of you."

He turned away; the conversation was over.

But there was something I wanted to ask him. "Wait," I said.

He turned back to me with a flicker of annoyance.

"You say plenty of people may try to take the throne from you. Are you really so vulnerable? You're the Emperor, after all. It's the duty of the people to honor and uphold you."

He vacillated for a moment. Then he smiled. "You're a sweet girl, Licinia," he said, "but you're too inquisitive."

I started to protest, but he cut me off. "Your innocence is charming. Let's try to keep it like that."

I bit my tongue. But it wasn't easy. My curiosity was bubbling just below the surface, threatening to boil over at any moment.

* * *

There was in those days a strange boy who lived in the palace at Ravenna. At first, I assumed he was the child of one of the servants, but I realized I had never seen him doing a menial task. I often observed him lolling about in the window embrasures, looking out pensively at the marshes, or wandering aimlessly through the palace gardens trailing a handful of reeds. It came to my knowledge that he was a hostage, the son of the Vandal king. He had been sent to Rome as a surety against future aggression. He had been there for the better part of three years. His name was Huneric.

He was slight of build and looked younger than he was. At first, I thought he was eleven or twelve when in fact he was fifteen, just one year younger than I. His loneliness touched my heart, and I pitied him.

One day I sent him a honeyed cake, thinking it would lift his spirits. He ate the cake, never asking who had sent it, and picked disconsolately at the crumbs while gazing off into the distance. Another time, I sent him a partridge to amuse him, but he refused it. I asked Placidius whether he was being well treated or whether anyone had taken the time to inquire into his wellbeing. Placidius, consumed by matters of state, looked coldly at me, and told me not to concern myself with him.

"He is being adequately attended to," he said, looking up from where he was gathered with his counselors around a map of Gaul.

He was acquainting himself with the political geography of the region. The meeting was taking place in a state room that opened onto a courtyard where the walls were thick with vines. The vines had turned orange with the coming of autumn, and freshly fallen leaves littered the ground. There was a chill in the air.

Placidius went back to studying the map, but when he caught sight of me hovering in the doorway, he said, "Licinia, it surprises me you're so concerned about the wellbeing of that boy when you should be concerned about yourself. You have not given me what I asked of you."

I had by then received his seed on several occasions, but I had not gotten pregnant, which concerned him. When Galla got wind of his apprehension, she took him aside and explained that it didn't always happen immediately, that it often took time. After that, his nocturnal visits became more frequent, and I had the bruises on my wrists to show for it.

"Tonight, the moon is full," he said. "I will come to you later. Go now and wait for me."

I was a little peeved that my solicitation for Huneric had been brushed aside so easily. "But he's so lonely," I said.

"Who's lonely?" Placidius asked.

"Huneric, the Vandal boy."

He looked back at the map. "Send him a ferret or a monkey to play with."

"I think he wants human companionship," I said.

"A eunuch will be assigned."

"Really, Placidius? A eunuch?"

My opinion of eunuchs was not high. They were considered safe as servants for women and children because they had been neutered, ideal as privy attendants or chamberlains, but as companions they fell short. To a man they seemed to harbor a simmering resentment, a bitterness, perhaps, at having been castrated without consent at an early age. When they were not distant and inscrutable, they were devious and cunning, and I did not trust them. The one I trusted least of all was Heraclius, who happened to be standing nearby when I expressed my dubious assessment of them. He shot me a quick, angry look, which dissolved into an obsequious smile as soon as I locked eyes with him.

"Eunuchs can be good company," Placidius said. He traced the course of a river with his finger on the map. "They're good conversationalists."

I didn't want to have this argument, not with Heraclius standing there, so I steered the subject back to Huneric. "He's lonely and wants good company."

Placidius was a little irritated at my persistence. "He's a hostage, Licinia. He's not a visiting dignitary. Now, I've heard enough about him. I'm meeting shortly with the praetorian prefect of Gaul and must acquaint myself with the situation before he arrives, so do as I tell you and go lie down."

But I was not yet finished. "Just because a boy is a hostage doesn't mean he has to be miserable."

Anger flashed in my husband's eyes. "Don't argue with me. Do as I tell you. Go and wait." He pointed at the door.

I begged his pardon and started to withdraw, but as I did so I noticed a subtle look pass between him and Heraclius. When I had reached the door, Placidius called out to me.

"Yes, dear?"

"Don't even think about befriending that boy," he said. "It's not appropriate."

I lowered my head and promised my obedience. When I withdrew, the fallen leaves crunched underfoot.

# Chapter 2
Autumn, The Year AD 437 – Winter, The Year AD 438

Placidius's meeting with the praetorian prefect of Gaul had been calculated to deliver a subtle message to the Master of Soldiers. Twice Aetius had refused the Emperor's summons to appear. Placidius intended to show him that such insolence would not be tolerated. For the past three weeks Placidius had been meeting with high-ranking administrative officials, both civil and military, to develop an understanding of the current state of affairs in the West. For the most part, those meetings unfolded in a similar fashion. First, there was the formal greeting followed by a discussion of broad generalities of their respective jurisdictions. Finally, they got down to specifics, whereupon Placidius pressed for answers. They almost all replied in the same manner: If he wanted to know how things worked, he would have to ask Aetius.

He tried. God knows from the beginning, he tried. He sent a note to Aetius the day after our arrival in Ravenna requesting his presence, but Aetius rebuffed him with a brusque note explaining he was too busy and could not appear. A few weeks later, Placidius tried again. This time the Master of

Soldiers cited a pressing need to conclude a peace treaty with the Goths. But it wasn't just the Goths who were demanding Aetius's time. The Franks and Suebi were up in arms too, and then there were the Bagaudae, those roving bands of peasant insurgents who were a persistent challenge to civil government in Gaul, as well as the Huns in the east, who were quiet at the moment but always a menace.

When his request was refused a third time, Placidius took stock. Rather than lashing out, as he was wont to do, he inquired more deeply into a matter that had come to his attention, a dispute between Aetius and the praetorian prefect of Gaul, a man named Albinus. Most officials were unstinting in their praise of Aetius, crediting him with suppressing the many military uprisings and usurpations that had bedeviled Rome for years, but there were those who despised Aetius, including a good many members of the aristocracy who resented his incessant demands for taxation to feed and clothe his army. Among them was the urban prefect of Rome, a man named Maximus, who informed Placidius about the dispute between Aetius and Albinus and urged him to look into the matter.

The disagreement was over a question of access to the imperial mint at Arelate. Aetius believed he was entitled to withdraw funds from it under the emergency powers granted to him by the Senate to combat the Goths. Albinus, the Prefect of Gaul, disagreed, arguing that if military necessity was the standard by which the army gained access to the mint, he might as well hand over the entire contents and wash his hands of civil governance, since the army's hunger for money was bottomless. At last, at the urging of Maximus, the dispute was brought before the Emperor for adjudication. That was when Placidius saw his opportunity. He had no doubt how Galla would have handled it; she would have given Aetius whatever he wanted. But Placidius was not his mother, and he intended to teach Aetius a lesson.

Placidius met with Albinus and decided the matter in his favor. He made a public pronouncement to drive home the point, which won him the praise of the aristocracy. But Galla was not happy with him, and the silence from Aetius, when next Placidius commanded his presence, was both recalcitrant and worrying.

* * *

A couple of months later Placidius and I were sitting together on a couch in the triclinium[3] of our private quarters, contemplating the flames of a fire. It was well after dark, and we were sharing a heavy cloak draped across our shoulders to shield us from the chill. Placidius had one hand on my belly. I was smiling. There was a rap at the door.

"Who is it?"

The eunuch Heraclius appeared, hands clasped before him, the firelight shimmering across the folds of his silken robes. On his feet were embroidered slippers that curled at the toes. A bright orange conical cap was perched on his head. He bowed and begged our pardons. He had come to report that the Emperor's vestiarios, his keeper of his wardrobe, had fallen ill and would not be available to dress the Emperor that night.

"I trust a substitute has been arranged," Placidius said.

---

3  A formal dining room in a Roman home.

"I will take over his duties, if you please," the eunuch said in a high, reedy voice. His face was hairless, his mouth small, pinched and red.

"Fine," Placidius said. "Is there anything else?"

"Your cup bearer as well, and two of the kitchen slaves." The eunuch shifted his eyes to me. "And the boy."

Placidius looked askance at me, and then returned his eyes to the eunuch. "What's going on? Is everyone sick?"

"Many are. The symptoms are similar, a fever followed by a dry cough and a rash. It started with the stable hands. Two of them have since perished. The physician sent to treat them also fell ill. He's not expected to survive." The eunuch's creepy falsetto and preternatural calm gave him a haunting air.

"This is most alarming," Placidius said, "and ill-timed. The Empress has just now reported to me that she's pregnant. Arrangements must be made to remove her from the city at once. The child must not be endangered."

"Of course not," the eunuch said. He shifted his eyes to me. "I'm very glad for you," he said, but his voice was flat; his eyes were expressionless.

I gave him a bland smile.

He withdrew, the swish of his silks trailing behind him.

All at once the palace was in an uproar. Servants rushing to and fro. Preparations were made to carry me off to Rome first thing in the morning. Galla appeared, looking agitated but in command as usual. She was not wearing the amulet. She took me in her arms with kisses and congratulations. She asked Placidius what plans had been made to safeguard the government against the possibility of plague. He had not given it much thought; he had been too concerned about my wellbeing. She instructed him to remove his chief counselors and administrators. Then she asked about the boy Huneric.

"He's fallen ill," Placidius informed her.

"Send a physician to him at once," Galla said.

"But the disease is contagious. The physician could become infected too."

"Send one anyway."

"I'm not going to do that," Placidius said. "We're going to need all the physicians we can get to prevent the spread of the disease."

Galla's calm gaze reflected her years of experience. "Think about it, Placidius. Huneric is the son of the Vandal king. He's crucial to the maintenance of the peace. If he dies, they'll accuse us of being negligent—or worse. If the Vandals strike, we may not be able to withstand them. Carthago is vulnerable, as is Sicilia. With Aetius away, they could cross the Strait of Messina and invade Calabria. We cannot allow the boy to die. We must save him."

Placidius sat down, stunned. Clearly, he had not considered the implications of his responsibility for the hostage.

Without thinking, I spoke up. "Send the priests. They'll pray for him. God will save him."

Placidius gave me a sharp look.

"They won't come," Galla said. "Sending for them will be an exercise in futility."

I didn't understand.

Galla explained, "Huneric is an Arian. No priest will risk his reputation to save him. We needn't waste our breaths asking them."

It was sad but true. The doctrinal rift between the Nicenes and Arians had poisoned Christianity with a longstanding feud that showed no signs of abating. Two centuries earlier the Church had split over a dispute about the personhood of Christ. On one side were the Nicenes who believed in the concept of the Trinity, the idea that the Father, the Son, and the Holy Spirit were one and the same and co-equal. On the other side were the Arians who believed God the Father and his son Jesus Christ were not equal, that God stood above Christ. After much heated debate within the Church, a statement of faith was articulated to express the Nicene view, a creed that became the orthodoxy of the Church, the Nicene Creed.

The Arians were ordered to renounce their beliefs and embrace the new creed, but they refused. The Nicenes declared the Arians heretics and excommunicated them. The whole process had taken several decades, so by the time the Arians had become pariahs, their version of the faith had been spread far and wide, particularly among the barbarian tribes where it had taken hold among the Vandals and the Goths. Young Huneric was an Arian Christian through no fault of his own. It was the tradition in which he had been raised, but his faith was anathema to our Catholic Church.

"Can we not locate even one priest to minister to him?" I asked.

Galla frowned and shook her head.

Placidius shot to his feet. "Send Pope Sixtus. He has no patience for these ecclesiastical squabbles. Send him. He can pray for the boy."

Galla sighed. "Of all those with reputations to protect, Pope Sixtus is the most at risk. If the Church Fathers were to find out he had prayed for the life of an Arian, they would use it as an excuse to strip him of power. No, we will not do that. We will not make Pope Sixtus susceptible."

This came as a surprise. It was the first time I had heard anyone suggest the Church Fathers were anything less than infallible. Those bishops and theologians whose teachings I had pressed on Placidius with such fervor were powerful men, but the idea that they might usurp the Pope or try to discredit him simply because he prayed for a poor, sick boy saddened me. We had to find some other way to save Huneric.

"Maybe we can find an Arian priest to pray for him," I said.

Galla gave me a pained smile. "The Arian clergy of this town were long ago purged and driven out. If there is an Arian priest anywhere in Ravenna, he would not risk exposing himself. We must accept the fact that there is no one here who will pray for the boy."

"I'll send a physician," Placidius said.

"Do it quietly," Galla said, "and don't let it get out. If the doctor becomes ill, and the others find out about it, it will be impossible to find another one."

Placidius agreed.

Galla turned to me. "I'm sorry this has spoiled your happy news. Your pregnancy is the best thing that's happened here in a long time. We must keep you safe. Go to Rome. The plague will pass in a month or two. When it's over, we'll send for you and make a formal announcement to the public. Then you will receive the congratulations you are due."

I agreed, of course, but congratulations for my pregnancy were my last concern. I was worried about Huneric. He was such a sad and lonely boy, and now it looked as if he might die without a friend to his name, and with no one to pray for him.

I took my concerns to God. I went to the chapel and got down on my knees. Then it came to me with the force of revelation. I must go to the boy. In spite of the danger, in spite of my husband's injunction against befriending him, my Christian duty was clear. If no one else would pray for him, I must do it.

I waited until late at night when the palace was quiet. I dismissed my servants and waited. Then, I slipped out. The guard at the end of the hall was absent. I encountered no one in the corridors. Even the soldier who had been assigned to stand guard a Huneric's door was nowhere to be found. I suppose I should have been wary of this, but I was so full of my purpose I paid it no heed.

Huneric was lying on his side, facing the wall, clutching himself, and shivering. When I entered, he did not acknowledge me. I went to his bedside and knelt down. A dull light cast by a moon shrouded in clouds shone through the darkness from a high clerestory window. I lowered my head and clasped my hands. Huneric turned to me. He muttered something I didn't understand. He was as pallid as parchment, glistening with sweat, and spotted with rash. I prayed with great intensity, calling on God to save his life.

When I was finished, I got to my feet.

"Thank you," he said in Latin. It came out as a croak.

"God save you," I said and left the room.

As before, the guard was absent, and I did not see another living soul until I got back to my room. But as I was letting myself in, I noticed something move out of the corner of my eye. Standing at the opposite end of the corridor beneath a stone archway, was Heraclius, head bowed, hands folded in front of him. He lifted his chin and took note of me, his face expressionless. Then he drifted back into the shadows.

* * *

I went to Rome to escape the outbreak, but it was no use. Within a fortnight I became ill too. It started with a fever and advanced to cold-like symptoms followed by a rash. Unlike poor Huneric, there were plenty of people to minister to me, and I was assiduously attended by a physician who himself became ill after the worst of my ordeal has passed. I lost the baby.

First came a brownish discharge followed by heavy bleeding, and then it was over. I felt drained and dejected. A few days later I was overcome by a sense of sadness so profound I could not stop weeping. Galla Placidia tried to comfort me, telling me about her own experience with losing a child, a bright little boy, the joy of her life, who had lived less than a year. The fact that I had lost mine so early could be interpreted as a sign of grace, she said, as it may have spared me the agony of having grown attached to it only to see it taken away later. I wondered why God would have given me such hope if He intended to snatch it away as soon as my heart became set on it. There seemed to be an element of cruelty in it. Yet God did not act without reason. Perhaps I had offended Him. I just didn't know how.

Placidius was devastated, but the worst of his grief was mitigated by his concern for my survival. He begged and pleaded to come to my bedside but was restrained by those worried he might fall ill as well. When the disease had finally passed, he knelt beside me and prayed, making a great show of thanking God for sparing me.

When he was finished, he said, "You see, Licinia, I have become a proper Christian."

I touched his hand and commended his progress.

He said, "I've been studying the books you gave me. They speak of obedience and the temptations of sin. In the same vein they talk about the relationship between husband and wife. They say that the wife owes obedience to the husband in the same way that man owes obedience to God, because one is over the other, one is superior to the other. I know you have read the books. I'm not wrong about that. You have. Haven't you?"

I assured him I had.

"Because it would be one thing if you had never actually read them—if you said so only to impress me—but if you actually did read them, then I'm confused."

"Confused?"

"Why you disobeyed me."

My heart sank.

"You went to see him. After I told you explicitly not to, you went to see him. Didn't you?"

I could not hold his gaze. I averted my eyes.

"Oh, Licinia. Why?"

"He was dying. No one would pray for him, so I went."

"But he was sick. The disease was contagious. You knew that."

"I recalled our Lord's words, 'As you have done it unto the least of these, you have done it unto me.' If it had been me, I would have wanted someone to pray for me."

"But you were pregnant, Licinia."

"I trusted in our Lord to protect me."

Placidius shook his head.

I was mortified by his disappointment and put my face in my hands and wept.

He waited for the tears to pass. Then he said, "You may not realize it, but you are my only friend in the world, the only one I can trust."

I looked up, astonished, my eyes glazed with tears. "Is that true?"

"Of course," he said.

"Oh, Placidius," I said, throwing my arms around his neck. "I'm so sorry I disappointed you. Please forgive me."

"I forgive you," he said, stroking my hair.

Then I heard the servants slipping away, the guards closing the doors behind them. He stopped stroking. I felt my hair being gathered into his fist.

"That was our son," he said. "Our heir." His grip tightened. I could feel my hair being pulled out by the roots. "You killed him!" His voice was the bark of an angry dog.

I screamed. Suddenly he released me. He was glaring at me like a wild beast. He lunged at me and began to tear my clothes off.

I knew what I was supposed to do. We had played this out many times. I was to run to the door to escape him, I was to fight him. But this time it was different. There was something savage in his eyes I has not seen before, and it scared me.

"Please, Placidius. I don't want to do this. Not now. Please."

He struck me. The blow stunned me, and I fell back. He grabbed me by the hair and hit me again. When he raised his hand a third time, I tried to fend him off, but he batted my arms away and threw me to the floor. He mounted me. I screamed. It was awful. I begged him to stop but he kept going, thrusting away with brutal intensity.

When it was over, he lay on top of me covered in sweat and panting for breath. I could feel his seed dripping down the creases of my buttocks. I couldn't stand the smell of him. I wanted to be sick.

He got up to go and stood over me, glaring down at me where I lay curled on the floor. "The boy lived," he said. "But it was the wrong boy."

When he was gone, I crawled into the corner and vomited.

# Chapter 3
Spring-Autumn, The Year AD 438

In the spring we returned to Ravenna amidst news that my father had issued a series of edicts with the force of law. They had been compiled by a commission constituted of members from both the Eastern and Western Empires and were intended to apply across both halves of the realm, but Placidius opposed them, insisting he had not been informed of the commission and wanted to review the edicts before approving them. Galla reminded him that he had no background in the law and therefore had no qualifications by which to review them. But Placidius saw the edicts as an encroachment on his authority and refused to endorse them until he had given them due consideration. Exasperated, Galla gave in, and the edicts were issued for the eastern half of the Empire alone.

Buried in the news of the edicts was another story. My mother, Aelia Eudocia, who had returned to Constantinople to attend my wedding, had not returned to Antioch afterwards but had gone to Jerusalem on a pilgrimage where she had collected a number of holy relics, which she had brought back to Constantinople as a demonstration of her faith. I knew in an instant what she was doing. It was a cheap attempt to win back the approval of the public after she had brought shame and scandal on our family.

But Galla didn't see it that way. When I mentioned it to her, she looked at me with a bemused expression and said, "What makes you think your mother has anything to be ashamed of?"

I opened my mouth to protest, to point out that anyone who had done what she had done ought to be ashamed. But Galla gave me a look of skepticism that made the words curdle on my tongue. Was there something I didn't know, something that would make my mother's behavior more comprehensible?

That spring Justa returned home. After months of waiting, Placidius was eager to deal with her. He called for a formal reception in the audience hall, hoping to use it as a showcase to excoriate her and demonstrate to others that no one could escape justice, not even his sister.

We assembled in the hall with Galla and a dozen or more attendants and dignitaries. But Justa kept us waiting. Instead of entering at the Emperor's summons as she was required to do, she lingered in the corridor and chatted with the guards. We could hear her laughing and joking. Then we heard the whimpering of a dog followed by a short, sharp bark and a chorus of laughter. Placidius looked askance at his mother and his face clouded with anger. He was about to tell her to go and get her, to inform her in no uncertain terms that the Emperor was waiting, when Justa swept into the room, shoulders back, head high, flanked on either side by two powerful mastiffs. She presented a proud, imperious figure. She crossed the broad mosaic floor and stood before the dais, looking up at us with a smirk.

She was not beautiful but there was something about her, something in her narrow, sculpted face and large soulful eyes that was arresting. She wore a saffron colored palla[4] over a white stola,[5] a combination usually reserved for virtuous brides, and a silver diadem that expressed a higher majesty than she actually possessed. Her dark hair was loose and lustrous and cascaded out from under her headscarf in a manner that might have been considered indecent in some circles. She nodded to her mother and then bowed to Placidius.

"Your Excellency," she said in a mocking tone.

Placidius looked at her in contempt. "What do you mean by bringing those animals in here?"

Justa looked at her two dogs. She gave a little laugh. "Wonderful, aren't they? I picked them up in Sicilia. They're like a pair of little gladiators, only more hygienic. They don't drool as much."

Stifled laughter escaped the company. Placidius looked around and the laughter stopped.

Galla interceded. "Perhaps you ought to remove them, dear. They are not appropriate under the circumstances."

"But Mother, I brought them here as a symbol of my obedience. Dogs are submissive, an age-old symbol of fidelity. I'm surprised you didn't know that."

Galla glared at her.

---

4  A loose outer garment formed by wrapping or draping a large square of cloth over the shoulder

5  The traditional garment of Roman women, like a female version of a toga.

"Oh, all right," Justa said with a petulant toss of her hair. She handed the leashes to some servants. "It's never my intention to be inappropriate, although sometimes I stumble into it unintentionally."

The servants led the dogs away.

Placidius wasn't having it. "You never stumble into anything unintentionally. You're the most calculating creature in the world."

Justa pretended shock. "Really, Placidius? I only just arrived, flanked by two expressions of my fidelity, and the first thing you do is attack me. Now who is being inappropriate?" She turned to her mother with eyes that pleaded for understanding.

Galla shook her head. "Try to treat the situation with the proper gravity, Justa. Your brother is making some serious charges against you."

"Serious charges?" Justa asked in faux consternation. "I'm all ears."

Placidius scowled at her. "Let me remind you. You are speaking to the Emperor. I won't stand for your insolence."

Justa went down on one knee and bowed her head in deference. "Forgive me, Excellency."

"Get up!" Placidius's voice was clipped and snappish. "I won't allow you to make a travesty of these proceedings. You are here to answer for your crimes, and you are squandering any chance you may have had for leniency."

For a fleeting moment something like fear could be detected in Justa's eyes, and then she was herself again. "Before we get started, maybe you should introduce me to our new Empress. It's really quite rude of you to overlook her." And before Placidius could respond, Justa shifted her eyes to me. "Hello," she said. "My name is Justa Grata Honoria. You may call me Justa." She gave a little bow.

I didn't know how to answer her at first. I didn't want to get into the middle of a family squabble, and I certainly didn't want to interfere with a legal proceeding, but she had addressed me directly.

"I am Licinia Eudocia," I said. "It's a pleasure to meet you."

Justa gave me a warm smile. "A pleasure to meet me. How nice. At least someone around here knows their manners. You know, we have actually met before. It was a long time ago. I was just seven and you were a babe in arms. I remember looking at you and thinking how vulnerable you seemed. I hope you've grown out of that. You're going to need a thick skin to survive around here."

"Justa!" Galla hissed. "That's enough."

Justa gave me a mischievous wink.

Placidius drew himself erect and looked around at the assembled dignitaries. "We are here to confront a conspiracy, a conspiracy to subvert my marriage. Innocent people lost their lives. The perpetrators were discovered and arrested. Under interrogation, they revealed the names of their organizers. One of them was my sister." He turned his gaze to Justa. "I hereby charge you with conspiracy to subvert the Emperor. How do you answer?"

Her eyes went wide. Her jaw fell open. She stepped back and put a hand to her mouth. "Oh, my Lord. I'm exposed. Forgive me. I was duped by villains."

Placidius watched her performance with mounting anger. Galla shook her head in weary exasperation.

Seeing their reactions, Justa threw back her head and laughed. "Just look at yourselves. You should see your faces. So stern. By God, one would think you were serious!"

Placidius glowered at her. "Let it be recorded that the accused offers no defense."

She snorted in contempt. "Come off it, Placidius. What is this? Are you trying to make me look bad in front of these people? Are you trying to destroy my reputation?"

Placidius sneered. "You'll never need any help for that, Sister."

Justa appealed to her mother. "See what he does? See how he denigrates me? He's never liked me. He's always resented me because I'm older and smarter than he is."

Placidius did his best to maintain his dignity. "I will take your refusal to answer the charges as an admission of your guilt."

"I admit nothing. Whoever said such a thing was obviously lying. But of course, you ran to it like a dog to a bone. Nothing would delight you more than if it were so. Your whole life is consumed by your jealousy of me."

"Jealousy?"

"Yes. Jealousy. It's deplorable. With all the troubles afflicting the Empire, you're fixated on pursuing your petty grievances against me. Why don't you grow up for once?"

Placidius glared at her, trembling with anger.

But Justa wasn't finished. "Why don't you concentrate on something useful? The Goths are on edge. They're bound to rise up again. Why don't you attend to that? Or how about the Bagaudae? They're running riot through the countryside, turning whole villages against us. Or the Vandals. God knows the Vandals are scheming some horrible bloodshed. A real Emperor would be focused on that, not pursuing a petty vendetta against his sister."

Placidius spoke through clenched teeth. "I have it in mind to have you whipped."

"Oh, for God's sake, do whatever it takes to make you feel better. After that, maybe you can get back to doing your job. Face it, Placidius. You can't go on ducking your responsibilities forever. Sooner or later, you'll have to start acting like a real emperor."

He was on his feet. His voice thundered through the hall. "I *am* a real emperor!"

She laughed. "You're weak. You're ridiculous."

His face went crimson.

"Stop it!" Galla shouted. "Enough!"

The assembled dignitaries looked at each other, squeamish to find themselves in the middle of a family row.

Justa lifted her chin. "Go ahead, brother. Beat me. Whip me. But don't expect me to come slinking back to you in contrition when you're done. I'm not a dog to be beaten every time you come face to face with your own inadequacies; I will not be a proxy for your self-contempt. No man will beat me and get away with it."

Placidius thrust his chin forward. "Do you dare threaten me?"

Justa smiled. "It seems to me, brother, you're the one threatening me."

Placidius stabbed a finger at her. "Arrest her! Take her in hand!"

Everyone froze. Several pairs of eyes shifted to Galla.

"The Emperor has spoken," Galla said.

The guards came forward and stood on either side of Justa, but they did not put their hands on her. She smiled around at them as if to say, "I'm sorry to have to put you through this." Then she looked at Placidius and sighed, "Same old Placidius. You never could control your temper."

She smiled at her mother and withdrew, a guard on either side.

* * *

"What are you going to do with her?" I asked.

We were in Placidius's tablinum,[6] which opened on to the peristylum. At the moment, the open-air garden was being drenched in a heavy rain.

"She's lying through her teeth," he said. "She's as guilty as sin, and she knows it. And she has the audacity to mock me." He sat with his chin on his fist, staring out at the rain. "She should pay with her life."

"Placidius!"

He gave me a churlish look. "Oh, please. Don't tell me you're coming to her defense now too."

"Never! You know I will always support you. But really, aren't you being too severe? She denies it."

"She's lying."

"Explain it to me. I want to understand."

With a heavy sigh, Placidius explained how Justa had stolen his mother's letter, the one she had written to instruct

---

6  In a Roman home a room situated on one side of the atrium and opposite to the entrance; it opened in the rear onto the peristylum

him, and sent it to her co-conspirators in Constantinople to be altered in an attempt to manipulate him, to get him to abandon the marriage.

"She had co-conspirators in Constantinople? Who were they?"

"Look, Licinia, these matters needn't concern you. The only thing you need to worry about is giving me an heir."

For some reason this got under my skin, even though I knew it was my duty to bear him children, especially after I had failed him so spectacularly. Still, my request was a simple thing. I only wanted to know who had conspired against us— and why.

"But I don't understand. Why would Justa try to sabotage our marriage? What was in it for her?"

"Nothing. She's jealous of me. That's all. She thinks because she was born first, she should be the Augusta. She thinks she should be in charge. She has never accepted the fact that as a woman she is inferior and can never rule."

"Even so, you cannot execute her, Placidius. The public will think ill of you."

"I cannot let it go unanswered. It makes me look ineffectual."

"If you show her clemency, you can turn it to your advantage. Frame it as a demonstration of your wisdom and restraint. Look, you've already condemned her to the lash. By granting her a reprieve, you show yourself to be benevolent. The people will admire you for it."

He brooded out at the rain. It was coming down in sheets, pummeling the new spring flowers.

"She'll only be emboldened by that. She'll see it as weakness and try to take advantage of it; I know her."

"If she does, you can drag her out into the light of day, put her sedition on display so everyone can see it, and punish her. Then they'll understand. But this—this just looks spiteful."

He scowled.

I took his hand in mine. "Beloved, never avenge yourself, but leave it to the wrath of God, for it is written, 'Vengeance is mine, sayeth the Lord.'"

He looked at me.

"It's in the Bible."

He snatched his hand away and turned his face to the rain. 'A woman should obey her husband.' That's also in the Bible."

The rain came down.

* * *

The summer passed in relative peace and contentment. Little did I know it would be the last untroubled time for many years to come.

The Goths were contained in Aquitaine having signed the armistice imposed upon them by Aetius. The Vandals were placated by the peace agreement of 475, which had sent Huneric to us as a hostage; their aggression was subdued by the knowledge that Aetius and the cream of the Roman military were no longer distracted by the Goths and would react to any hostility with overwhelming force. The Franks and Suebi were, for the moment, mollified, satisfied with their acquisitions along the Rhine and in the Pyrenees. Farther east, the Huns, had been bought off with promises of tribute and had contented themselves with subjugating rival tribes to the north.

All of this freed Aetius to go after the Bagaudae, those roving bands of peasants who plagued Gaul and the Ebro Valley with their insurgency. He smashed them, eradicated their leaders, and dispersed them. It began to look as if Rome would finally reestablish civil authority in northern Gaul. There was even talk of recovering Britannia.

Two events happened during this halcyon interlude that would have lasting effects on my future. In May I became pregnant again. Placidius was delighted. This time he made sure I was well looked after and could not slip off without anyone's knowledge to do something risky. He assigned three extra eunuchs to keep an eye on me. In spite of the scrutiny, I was able to deepen my relationship with Huneric.

Now sixteen and rapidly losing his boyish features, Huneric came upon me quite by accident one day while I was admiring a pair of prized steeds in the Emperor's stable. Placidius was a fan of chariot racing and kept a stable for that purpose. He made no secret of the fact he wanted me to adopt his passion for racing and required me to sit with him in our private box overlooking the Hippodrome as he cheered on his favorites. Truth be told, I was not very interested in racing, and I disdained the wagering, which the Church condemned. On the other hand, I liked the horses, their strong, sleek bodies and powerful agility. I often found myself escaping the fetid heat of the palace to travel out to the imperial stables to watch them being trained. On this day Huneric was there as well. He appeared beside me where I stood leaning over the rail.

"That one won't persist," he said. "He eats too much. His appetite outweighs his ambition. Whip him as you will; he will flag before the finish."

I turned to him. "How do you know so much about horses?"

"Before we were masters of the sea, we Vandals were expert horsemen. It was a matter of survival. We had to know how long a horse could carry us. We had great ambitions. We had to adjust our appetites to match our ambitions."

"Not a bad policy," I said.

"It was necessary," he said, "if we were to survive."

I was surprised at how much he had changed since I had last seen him, back when he had been lying consumed with fever on his deathbed. Not only had he grown taller since then, but he was broader through the shoulders. He had grown whiskers, and he held himself with an air of steady confidence. "They have carried you far, your horses."

"To your borders."

"And then some," I said.

"Yes," he said.

We watched the horses. After a spell, he said, "You prayed for me. When no one else would, you prayed for me. Why?"

"I am a Christian," I said.

"So are the rest."

"Yes," I said, "but not in the same way."

He nodded. The horses pranced and cantered. Then he said, "Maybe your religion is more like mine."

I didn't know whether to be offended or flattered, but I knew it was wrong of me to be talking to him about such things. I tried to act aloof, but for some reason I couldn't. My curiosity got the best of me. "In what way?" I asked.

"Well," he said, "we don't persecute those who disagree with us, and we don't look down on our women."

I was taken back. "What do you mean? The Nicenes don't look down on their women."

He gave me a skeptical look. "Don't they?"

I wanted to refute him, but words failed me. I looked away. I made some bland remark about the horses. Then I excused myself and hurried away.

* * *

I would not seek him out. To do so would be to defy my husband. But should he approach me, that was something else altogether. I had not been instructed how to behave should he initiate contact, so I allowed myself the liberty of conversing with Huneric whenever our paths crossed. He was a pleasure to talk to. He was never ill-tempered or disagreeable, which, under the circumstances, he had every right to be, stuck in a foreign court, dismissed and ignored, biding his time like an overprotected criminal. I expected him to complain about his captivity, but he never did. Still, he made it clear he would rather have been at home honing his skills as a Vandal warrior and getting ready for the day when he would assume leadership from his father.

He spoke wistfully of past when his people had migrated from Hispania, the excitement and enthusiasm they had all felt crossing beneath the Pillars of Hercules and landing for the first time on African soil. He was only a child back then, but he remembered it well. The tribe had had a long history of migration, going from Pannonia to Gaul in the decades before he was born. But this was something new, their arrival in a place so long prized by Rome, a place vital to her interests, the source of her grain, and the font of her enduring preeminence. This was where Rome had vanquished the Carthaginians, her greatest rivals, driving them down in ignominious defeat after years of struggle, razing their glorious city and sowing the ground with salt so they could never restore it. It was a tale every Roman schoolboy knew by heart for it spoke of the invincibility of Rome—and the Vandals knew it too, as they had been schooled by Roman missionaries and indoctrinated with ideas of Roman supremacy.

Down the generations as their numbers grew, the Vandals shared it amongst themselves, marveling at Rome's heroism, her dominance and power, which, ironically and quite unintentionally, inspired the Vandals' own drive for power. But they had never dreamed they would find themselves on hallowed ground so soon, and it filled them with heady zeal. Perhaps they could rival their heroes. Perhaps they could defeat them. Some among them were for pressing on, advancing through Mauretania and Numidia to Carthago and emulating what Scipio Aemilianus had done by torching the city. But Genseric, Huneric's father, had counseled restraint. Now was not the time. They had to be patient. Their opportunity would come.

We were sitting atop a little hillock overlooking the meadow where the Emperor's white stallions were grazing on the high summer grass. The sky was blue. Here and there a fluffy white cloud drifted past. I came here often to listen to the birdsong and commune with nature. Huneric sometimes approached me, timidly at first, and then with growing confidence as he realized I would not report him. He was careful not to give offence and studiously avoided any mention of the differences in our religions. Instead, he concentrated on the horses, about which he knew a great deal, and increasingly on the circumstances that had brought him here, which was how we came to be discussing his people's invasion of Africa.

"There were many who argued we should have attacked while we were still full of confidence and hungry for glory having just crossed the sea unopposed. But my father disagreed. He said, 'The best time to strike is not when you are at your strongest but when your enemy is at his weakest.' He was concerned that the Romans would send Aetius to oppose us. As it turned out, your mother-in-law did the inexplicable and ordered Aetius to remain in Gaul. She sent some lesser generals, which emboldened those who were eager to attack. Then we got word the Romans were squabbling among themselves. It was all we needed to know. My father gave the orders, and we swept through Mauretania virtually unopposed, conquering the city of Hippo and pressing on to Carthago. It was then the Romans offered terms. My father Genseric worried that if we pressed any further Aetius would come. He thought it best to stop and consolidate our gains, so we negotiated with the Romans and reached an agreement. We would retain what we had, including Hippo, which gave us a port on the Mediterranean, but we would leave Carthago to the Romans. As a part of the deal, and to ensure the peace, I was sent here as a hostage. I have been here now for four years."

My heart went out to him. "You must miss your family. I know I miss mine. Placidius promised we can return to Constantinople to visit my parents after the baby is born."

"You are fortunate. I will never see my family again."

"Oh, don't say that."

He picked pensively at the grass. "There are only two possibilities," he said. "Either the peace will hold, and I will make a political marriage to someone here to solidify the alliance, or the peace will be broken, and I will be executed."

"Maybe your people will retreat to Hispania, and you will be released as a condition of their withdrawal," I said.

He shook his head. "We will never withdraw. We will only advance. Among the Vandals there is a saying, 'Those who do not advance perish.'"

"But surely you can enjoy the fruits of your conquest. Surely you can be satisfied with what you've got and live peacefully where you are."

He looked at me for a long moment. Then he shaded his eyes and peered out at the meadow and pointed. "You see that horse over there?" He indicated an animal grazing apart from the others. "He will not live out the week. He was once the bravest animal in the stable, but he has been on four losing teams in the last eight weeks. He is past his prime. He is in decline. He will be slaughtered, and his meat will be used to feed the charioteers. The men who drive his rivals will grow stronger from devouring him. They will prosper from his loss." He turned to me. "It's a law of nature. If you are not advancing, you are retreating. If you are not flourishing, you are declining. The Vandals understand that. We must press forward, or we will die."

I didn't know how to respond. At some level he was making a threat. I said, "God will determine our fates."

"God takes His time," he said. "God doesn't expect us to sit idly by while He makes up His mind. There is a proverb. 'The sluggard craves and gets nothing, but the desires of the diligent are satisfied.' God wants us to be decisive. Forward or back. To remain in place is also a decision, a decision to be on the defensive. The Vandals will not do that. We will press forward, and in that the Romans will either be with us or against us. Whatever happens, I will not be returning to Africa. I will be here until I die."

"But you're the prince. You're destined to be king."

"My personal status is of no consequence," he said. "My only purpose is to help my people. If I must sacrifice my life, I will."

"You are truly brave," I said.

He smiled. "So are you," he said. He looked down at my belly. I was just beginning to show.

The shadow of a cloud crept across the meadow and fell on the horses. Only the retired horse, the one destined for the knackers, looked up. The others went about their grazing, oblivious.

# Chapter 4
## Autumn, The Year AD 438 – Winter, The Year AD 439

In the autumn I grew large with child, and Placidius forbade me to travel. My weekly visits to the stables were curtailed, and I was confined to my room. I was still a good two months from delivery, but I was sequestered like a prisoner. It was not lost on me that Huneric, who actually *was* a prisoner, was free to move about, while I, the Augusta of Rome, was detained.

Boredom, always a challenge for a woman of my status, became a burden. Placidius sent musicians and jugglers to amuse me. Dwarves were mocked and idiots tormented. A priest read to me from the Bible. Still, I longed to escape. Galla Placidia was generous with her time, sitting with me for hours while we sewed and chatted. From her I learned the latest news from Gaul.

The Goths were restless again, and Aetius was trying to appease them. Unhappy with the terms imposed upon them after the siege of Narbo, they were demanding modifications to the agreement. Aetius was willing to negotiate but he would not be dictated to. Galla Placidia was of two minds. On the one hand, she understood the need to appease them. On the other hand, she didn't trust them. She knew firsthand their appetite for territory. She had been kidnapped by them as a young woman and had spent several years with them, even marrying their king.

In those days they had been a landless people, wandering from place to place. They had been betrayed more than once by the Romans who had promised them a homeland only to renege. The Goths had learned not to trust the Romans and vowed never to live under the Roman yoke. After she left them and returned home, she advocated for their independence as a client state, insisting they would be peaceable if appeased, but the Goths had been insulted once too often and were not of a mind to cooperate.

When at last she got her way and the Goths were granted territory, they did not behave peaceably as she had hoped, but demanded more, declaring the land they had been given— most of Aquitaine—was inadequate. In the ensuing years they kept trying to expand, mounting raids into Roman territory, and forcing negotiations. It seemed Aetius was forever buying them off. Their most recent aggression, the siege of Narbo, was particularly galling to Galla Placidia. She had long sympathized with their need for a port on the Mediterranean, and during the course of her regency had arranged for them to have access to Narbo, but it wasn't good enough; they wanted Narbo for themselves. It was churlish, she said, and she had written to Theodoric, the Gothic king, expressing her displeasure and calling him ungrateful. Theodoric had not written back. As a result, Aetius had been dispatched to deal with them. There had been a fight, and the Romans had prevailed. The Goths had sued for peace and a settlement negotiated.

But now they wanted more. It made Galla furious, but she understood the need to stay calm. Rome had too many other problems. To get bogged down in a fight with the Goths was dangerous. It was better to buy them off—again.

I found Galla's explanations fascinating. I could sit and listen to her for hours, and when she spoke, my boredom vanished. But she was a busy woman, acting in her role as chief advisor to Placidius, so my time with her was limited, and when she was gone, my ennui reasserted itself.

Justa also visited me in my confinement. She was animated and earnest and wanted to get to know me. I found her agreeable if a bit too strong, like un-watered wine. I had to keep reminding myself that she was not to be trusted. She had visited Constantinople a few years back and spoke glowingly of my father and aunt. If she met my mother, she did not mention it. I found it odd that I was not introduced to her at that time. It was the second time she had come, and I was certainly old enough to meet her then. She explained she was quite busy while she was there, and, for one reason or another, the opportunity had not presented itself. She had come to take orders in a nunnery on the advice of her mother and priest. She tried but had found the life too restrictive and had given up.

"The truth is," she said, speaking behind her hand, "I like men too much."

Her words made me blush. She drew back and laughed. "Why, Licinia, I've embarrassed you. My goodness, you are a delicate flower, aren't you?"

She offered the opinion that my piety had made me overly sensitive. Then she said it didn't have to be that way; a woman could be reverent and still exude strength and confidence.

"Your aunt Pulcheria is the most pious woman I've ever known, and she's also the strongest. You should follow her example. She's extraordinary."

I agreed. I had always looked up to my aunt. Everyone who knew her said she was a formidable woman.

Justa changed her tack. "Look at you sitting there," she said. "What a pale, dreary looking thing you are. If you want to exude confidence—which, after all, is the first step to achieving it—you must use all the tools at your disposal. Have you ever used cosmetics?"

I pointed out that my aunt Pulcheria had never used cosmetics. Justa ignored my comment and plowed ahead. "Proper use of cosmetics can heighten your best qualities and make people stop and take notice of you. Proper use of cosmetics can make people admire you."

I told her I felt admired quite enough as it was.

"Do you?" she asked. She gave a rueful little chuckle.

I began to take offence, but she headed me off. She took me by the wrists, her eyes alight with enthusiasm. "Let me do this for you," she said. "Let me make you up. Everyone will stop ignoring you and give you the attention you deserve."

"I don't crave attention," I said.

"Don't you have a meeting with the Pope next week? Placidius will want you to look your best for that. Let me show you what a big difference it can make."

She was right. Placidius did have a meeting scheduled with Pope Sixtus. It was to be the first formal meeting between the two most powerful men in Italia. The Pope would have his full retinue with him, and Placidius would surround himself with his chief counselors and dignitaries. It promised to be extravagant. Placidius wanted me at his side for the ceremony, in spite of the fact that I was six months pregnant. I had been looking forward to it as it would afford me a respite from my confinement.

Justa was insistent. "Oh, please, Licinia. Let me do it. I'll do a good job. I promise." She was grinning.

Her enthusiasm was charming. "Oh, very well," I said with a laugh. "Let's meet here before the ceremony."

She flitted out of the room, giggling as she went.

* * *

On the day of the big event Justa showed up with her cosmetic case. It was brimming with face whiteners, eye shadow, lipstick, and rouge. Laid in beside them were spatulas, tweezers, pins, combs, bowls, jars, and spoons. She moved close and went to work. She dabbed and buffed and primped and smoothed all the while wearing a look of intense concentration. When she was finished, she drew back and smiled.

"Perfect!" she said.

"Can I look?" I asked.

But when she went to find the mirror it was gone.

"I'm sorry," she said. "I must have forgotten it." She offered to run and get one, but it was too late; the escort had arrived to take me to the ceremony. "Don't worry," she said. "You look gorgeous."

The eunuch who was to take me looked at me with a curious sidelong expression. Justa sidled up to him and said, "Doesn't she look great?"

He gave her an ambivalent nod and gestured toward the door. "We should go," he said.

Justa announced that she would accompany us to the ceremony, so with Justa on one side and the eunuch on the other, we made our way to the audience chamber.

We approached by way of a rear corridor that opened onto the raised dais above the main floor. As we approached, we could hear the sound of a crowd. There must have been a hundred people in the reception hall. Only the Pope, Placidius and I were yet to appear. In keeping with protocol, I was to enter first and take my place, after which the Pope would make his grand entrance. The Emperor would appear last accompanied by the sound of blaring of trumpets and pounding drums. Justa squeezed my hand.

"Show them what you're made of," she said, and gave me a little nudge.

I walked out onto the dais.

All eyes turned to me, but the reactions were not what I expected. Mouths fell open. There was an audible, collective gasp. As I approached the throne, the attendants who stood behind it drew back in astonishment. Some looked away. Others smiled and tried to hide their expressions. I knew in an instant what had happened. The makeup was caked on my face like a garish mask. In the heat it had begun to melt and crack. I wanted to be sick. But I held myself together and tried to appear as dignified as possible. I sat down and folded my hands in my lap.

The Pope's grand procession entered the reception hall with the great man himself at its head. He was dressed in a green pallium over a white dalmatic with a single stripe down each sleeve. In his left hand he bore a golden crosier with a curled top. With his right hand he waved his blessings. He came forward to his seat, an ornate chair—a throne by any other name—arranged to face the dais. With great solemnity he lowered himself into it, still waving. By all accounts he had once been a broad-shouldered man, strong and muscular, but the man who sat before me now was frail and gaunt having suffered a series of setbacks to his health, which had reduced him dramatically. When he saw me, his eyes opened wide. His hand hung in the air, frozen for a moment, before he lowered it onto his armrest and pulled his eyes away from me.

The trumpets blared, and the drums rolled. At the back of the hall a pair of golden doors swung open and Placidius entered. When the drums fell silent, a crier stepped forward and shouted at the top his lungs: "Flavius Placidius Valentinianus Augustus, his excellency Valentinian III!"

Men went to their knees with heads bowed. Placidius strode past the assemblage with an imperious air not deigning to look at them. He was wearing a long white belted tunic that fell below his knees and a purple trabea trimmed in gold flung over one shoulder. On his feet were jewel-encrusted shoes, and on his head a diadem of gold. Trailing him to his left was Galla Placidia in a position of prominence due to her former role as his regent. Trailing him on his right was the primicerius sacri cubicula, the keeper of the sacred bedchamber, Heraclius. No one dared betray their surprise, but the installment of the eunuch in such a position of importance was a shocking breach of protocol.

The Emperor and his entourage proceeded down the aisle, gazing straight ahead of them with proud self-possession.

Galla Placidia caught sight of me first. Her expression went from shock to dismay in an instant. Heraclius noticed me next. His face registered disgust. When Placidius saw me, he stopped and nearly stumbled. He recovered himself and continued, his face clouded with anger. He sat down beside me and refused to acknowledge me for the rest of the ceremony. The proceedings unfolded with the requisite decorum. The two men exchanged vows of loyalty and humility. The meeting ended with the Pope's blessing of the new emperor. Then everyone withdrew with dignity and comportment.

Placidius was waiting for me in my chambers when I returned. His face looked like an approaching storm.

"Don't tell me," he said. "I know my sister's handiwork when I see it. I thought I told you to stay away from her."

"But she was only trying to help," I said.

"Silence! I don't want to hear your excuses. You deliberately disobeyed me."

The door flew open and Galla Placidia came pounding in dragging Justa behind her. I had never seen her so mad.

"Here she is," Galla said. She shoved Justa forward.

Justa turned up her hands. "What's the matter? I only did what she asked of me. She is the Empress, after all. How could I disobey?"

I was stunned by her dishonesty. "I never asked you to," I said. "You begged me. It was your idea."

"Semantics," she said.

Placidius flew at her and seized her by the throat.

I screamed.

Galla got between them and called for the guards, who pulled them apart, but not before they were both injured.

Placidius was scratched above the eye and bleeding. On Justa's neck the imprints of Placidius's fingers had left angry red marks. Galla looked at them both in revulsion.

"You disappoint me. Both of you."

"I want her sent away!" Placidius said. His eyes twitched; his breath came in short spurts. "I want her gone! Send her to the Franks! Send her to the Huns! I don't care. Just get her out of my sight before I kill her!"

Galla tried to placate him. She steered him into the corner and spoke to him in hushed tones.

Justa sidled up to me, rubbing her neck.

"Sorry," she said. "I have a problem controlling myself. It's a shortcoming."

I gaped at her in disbelief. She shrugged an apology and moved away.

Galla sent her to her room and forbade her to leave it on pain of arrest. Justa started to object but the look on Galla's face stopped the words in her throat. Muttering about the injustice of it, she withdrew. Then Galla turned to me.

"And you, young lady. You were told to stay away from her. What were you thinking? Listen to me. Sweetness and innocence may be charming to some, but around here it will only get you into hot water. Stay away from her. Do you hear me?"

No female in my life had ever spoken to me in such a temper, neither my mother nor my aunt, and I bristled at the effrontery. I threw back my shoulders and prepared to hurl a retort but caught myself up short and subsided into submission.

"All this excitement is not good for the baby," Galla said in a gentler tone. "Go lie down. Try to relax. I'll send someone to wipe that mess off your face."

I didn't argue, but I also didn't budge. With a look of exasperation, Galla went out.

When she was gone, Placidius came over, looking testy and mean.

"You disappoint me," he said. "I thought were a woman of substance who could be molded into a good Christian wife. Instead, you are weak and stupid."

I started to come back, but he cut me off. "Unless it's all just an act." He shook his head in disgust. "Maybe I should be more careful around you. Maybe you're not who you appear to be. God knows, you wouldn't be the first woman in your family to put on an act."

At first I thought he was talking about my mother, but in the next instant I realized he was talking about my aunt. For some reason he didn't like my aunt. In any case, it was hurtful to be insulted by him, and I began to cry. He scoffed at my tears and left me alone. I sat and wept.

A little while later I saw the eunuchs peeking in at the door. I told them to go away, and they did at once, except for Heraclius who lingered a moment longer, a tight smile on his face, before disappearing into the shadows.

* * *

Preparations were made to send Justa into exile. Where she was to go was a matter of conjecture; for Placidius was undecided. Two weeks after the ugly incident with the cosmetics, however, Placidius changed his mind. Justa would be allowed to remain in Ravenna but would be relegated to a separate part of the palace where she couldn't be seen or heard by the rest of us. Essentially, it was to be an internal exile. It was an odd reversal, but I understood it to be related to events unfolding in Gaul. No one had to tell me. After a year in Ravenna, I was beginning to understand how things worked.

The Goths were at it again. They had made another attempt on Narbo. They had broken the treaty they had signed with Aetius eighteen months earlier and attacked. Aetius was furious and dispatched his best general, Litorius, to oppose them. By all accounts, Litorius was making good progress against them, so Aetius felt no urgent need to go there himself and remained at his headquarters in Arelate.

But Placidius was concerned. Without Aetius's troops, he feared Litorius might falter, which could lead to a wider war and draw Aetius in only after things had gotten out of hand. If that happened, he would be unavailable should trouble flare up in other parts of the Empire. Wanting the Gothic intransigence dealt with at once, Placidius ordered Aetius to march without delay to Litorius and crush the Goths once and for all. Aetius never acknowledged his directive.

If it had been any other general, his silence would have gotten him sacked. But Aetius was not like any other general. Not only was he the Master of Soldiers, but he was also twice a consul and a patrician. He was more knowledgeable about foreign affairs and military strategy than any other person in the Empire. He had been Galla Placidia's right hand man throughout her twelve-year regency; his cooperation and support had been vital to her survival. Yet this new obstinacy combined with his continued refusal to answer the Emperor's summons to come to Ravenna, smacked of insubordination and reflected badly on the Emperor.

The possibility that Justa was Aetius's daughter complicated things further. I had heard this not from Placidius, who might have been expected to tell me, but from one of the household servants, a slave girl, the daughter of a colonus[7] whose duty it was to draw my bath. She was gossiping with a eunuch just outside my bed chamber, not knowing I was within earshot, insisting that what she had heard was true, having heard it from multiple sources. This made perfect sense to me as it explained why Galla was so adamant that Placidius restrain himself from punishing his sister even when Galla admitted Justa deserved it. It also explained Placidius's change of heart over sending Justa into exile. Seen in the context of Aetius's stubbornness, it could be understood as an attempt on Placidius's part not to alienate Aetius when his main goal was to get him to come to Ravenna and answer his summons.

But Placidius's charity only went so far. When, after a couple of weeks, Aetius continued to rebuff him, Placidius threatened to withhold his funding. But not explicitly. Instead of implementing cuts to the military budget—something that would have delighted certain members of the aristocracy—he slyly threw his support behind the prefect Albinus in the matter of the army's access to tax revenues in Gaul. Placidius had reckoned such a move would bring Aetius running as the army needed the money in the mint at Arelate to keep its troops fed and ready, but Aetius would not budge. Now Placidius considered going further, reducing the tax burden on

---

7  A tenant farmer bound to the land and required to pay rent.

the senatorial class thereby drying up the army's main source of revenue and essentially starving Aetius into cooperating.

Galla objected. Not only would it weaken the army at a time when it needed all its resources, but it would create an impression in the minds of the aristocracy that they had won a great victory in their never ending battle to get their taxes abated. Galla was against it, and in this she had the support of the Emperor's other counselors and advisors.

Placidius was disappointed. He had thought it an inspired idea, and he had been eager to try it, but it had been summarily rejected. Now he was no closer to bringing Aetius to heel, and Justa continued to mock him. At some point someone had to pay. Mischief left unpunished was mischief invited. About this last part, he was absolutely correct.

*  *  *

In my eighth month of my pregnancy, I nearly lost the baby. I became deathly ill. One minute I was strong and healthy, and the next I was plunged into misery. Poisoning seemed a possibility. No one was more convinced of this than Galla Placidia. In her life she had seen enough treachery to recognize its lineaments. She sat at my bedside and grilled me about what I had eaten and when. Sick as I was, I reviewed what I had taken. The culprit seemed to have been a cup of mulled wine infused with herbs, the most prominent of which was spearmint, the aroma of which stood out above the others. When Galla heard this, her face went white. She demanded I induce vomiting at once by sticking my fingers down my throat. I did as she directed and kept retching until my stomach was tied in knots and my head was pounding. Then I lay down and passed out. When I awoke, several priests were at my bedside, among them the Pope. Beyond them, in the back of the room knelt Placidius who was as ardent in his prayers as any of them.

When the praying was over and all the men had left, I found myself alone with Galla Placidia. She went to the door to make sure no one was eavesdropping, and then she explained. Someone had poisoned me with pennyroyal, a known abortifacient. When I asked her what *that* was, she said, "Someone was trying to make you lose the baby."

I was flabbergasted. Who could have done such a thing?

She didn't answer. Instead, she said we must keep it a secret. We must pretend I had been stricken by an illness common to women in their final months of pregnancy. She would enlist a physician to confirm this, and we need never speak of it again.

"Was it Justa?" I asked.

"I don't know," she said, but she wasted no time in sending a servant to search Justa's apartments. Sure enough, they found a vial of crushed pennyroyal leaves

I was horrified to think that my sister-in-law was capable of such a thing, but Galla wasn't altogether surprised. Justa was a deeply disturbed young woman. Even as a child she had been insufferable, throwing tantrums and demanding things. Where her brother was concerned, she was especially vindictive, believing he had cheated her of her birthright as the first-born, never accepting that, as a female, she could never rule. Now, with my arrival, she was being marginalized yet again, this time by an outsider.

"She resents you," Galla said. "She knows that when your child is born, you will be granted the title of Augusta, and it makes her angry."

"What should I do?" I asked.

Galla thought about it for a minute. "Appease her," she said. "It's the only way."

I wasn't entirely satisfied with her answer, but I knew Galla understood the situation better than I, and, in any case, the attempt to make me miscarry had failed. The baby was still inside me and moving around, giving me the occasional kick.

"What do you propose?"

Galla leaned in and whispered. "We should encourage Placidius to give her the same title."

"You mean make her an Augusta too?"

Galla nodded. "She would no longer feel threatened by the birth of your child."

I was reminded of Placidius's concern about rewarding bad behavior, but Galla interpreted my hesitation as something else. "Don't worry," she said. "It's not without precedent. Your mother and your aunt both ruled as Augustas in the same household. Nothing bad ever happened to them."

Galla was being disingenuous, and we both knew it. The rancor between my mother and my aunt was familiar to all, a deplorable state of affairs that had caused my mother to lash out against my father. In consequence she had committed an immoral act for which she had been exiled, and which she was now at pains to compensate for.

Galla saw my skepticism and quickly changed tack. "The main thing is to protect your unborn child, and this is the best way to do it."

I already knew the answer to the question I was about to ask, but I felt it was important to pose it anyway. "Why not just exile her as Placidius wants?"

Galla shook her head. "It's not that easy. Justa has her advocates. There are people in powerful places who may not take kindly to her being abused."

I could have pressed her to name names, but I knew full well who she was alluding to, and I didn't want to cause a rift between us. I could see she was struggling to do the right thing, and she truly did have the welfare of my unborn infant at heart, so I said I would pray on the matter and let her know my decision in a day or two.

Truth be told, I already knew what I was going to do. If Justa was really as dangerous and vindictive as she appeared to be, there was no point in antagonizing her. I cared not a whit for the title. I was already the Empress, so sharing the title of Augusta was of little consequence to me. As long as Placidius remained the emperor, Justa's status as a co-Augusta was little more than window dressing. So, I would go along with it.

When I told Galla, she was relieved, but it only served to alienate Placidius further. He was furious with me for siding with his mother, but when Galla suggested that a ceremony to confer the title on Justa might be just the thing to bring Aetius to Ravenna, he capitulated, under one condition. Afterwards, Justa must leave Ravenna. He didn't care where she went. It could be anywhere in the Empire. But he didn't want to see her again. She could flaunt her worthless title someplace else, but she could not use it to influence policy in the capital. Hers was to be an empty distinction. Like mine.

Justa acquiesced. She promised to remove herself to Alexandria after the ceremony. So, plans were made, and the ceremony took place. The title of Augusta was conferred with all the pomp and circumstance of a real coronation. Justa paraded around in a jeweled gown with rubies and sapphires sewn into the sleeves and an elaborate necklace of silver and gold. She sported her tiara and made mock pronouncements. She even laughed at her own jokes, much to the chagrin of Placidius, who watched her antics with a grim expression. He felt cheated. Aetius did not come as expected but remained in Gaul, stewing over what to do about the Goths.

After all, Aetius's reluctance to leave Arelate had everything to do with his financial situation. The soldiers he held in reserve had not been paid in months, and he could not count on their loyalty in his absence. For the same reason, he resisted Placidius's demand to send them to reinforce Litorius. Without more money, Aetius's hands were tied, and Placidius's decision to back Albinus in the matter of access to the mint had only made things worse.

Finally, Aetius could wait no longer. The stirrings of discontent among his troops were mounting. He needed to act to avoid a mutiny. Six weeks after Justa was granted the title, two weeks after my baby was born, he took matters into his own hands and raided the mint.

Predictably, the praetorian prefect Albinus was outraged. He wrote to the Emperor demanding consequences for the Master of Soldiers. Placidius was immediately faced with the first major crisis of his administration at the center of which stood his most dangerous adversary, Aetius.

* * *

Eudocia was born on the coldest day of the year. I remember it well because I could see my breath coming in clouds as I sat propped up in bed nursing her. The first floor of the palace was kept comfortable by a hypocaust system that circulated warm air from a furnace beneath the floors. My rooms were on the second floor near the corner of the building where they were exposed to the cold damp winds blowing in from the marshes. I asked Placidius if the two of us could be moved to a downstairs room where we would be warmer. He promised to arrange it but got distracted, and it never happened.

Looking back, he was not completely indifferent. He was happy enough at the birth of our daughter. But it seemed obvious to me that he would have been more attentive if she had been a boy. It was a terrible thing for a wife to think about her husband, and I didn't like having such thoughts, but there they were, nevertheless. I didn't banish them from my mind using penance and prayer, as I should have, but let them linger. If my aunt were around and knew what I was thinking, she would have instructed me to kneel down and remain in an attitude of repentance until my knees ached. She would have encouraged me to suffer, knowing God would see my suffering and take pity on me. But, as it was, I considered the discomfort of my cold room adequate penance for my uncharitable thoughts and tried to leave it at that. It was a mistake.

The discomfort went unrelieved, and I began to worry about the welfare of the baby, so I decided to take matters into my own hands. I padded down the corridor to find some warmer place to nurse her and happened upon a closed door

I mistakenly believed led to an interior staircase. I opened it and fell back in shock.

Inside were two servants engaged in an act so outrageous and disgusting I nearly fainted. The man's trousers were down around his ankles, and the woman was on her knees before him. The man's eyes were closed and his was head tilted back in pleasure. The woman was sucking on his penis. I gasped in horror and shut the door. My heart pounded in my chest. My face was flush. Perspiration prickled on my forehead and neck.

*Such a thing must be against the law*, I thought. I had to sit down.

I went around the corner, found a bench, and sat.

*Maybe I should call someone*, I thought. *Maybe I should have them arrested. It was appalling what they were doing. It was wrong.*

The baby began to fuss, and I realized she was cold. I had to find a place to warm her. I continued down the corridor and ran into Huneric coming around the corner.

The sight of him so soon after witnessing that awful sight filled me with confusion. I stammered and blushed. He asked me what was wrong, and I assured him it was nothing. When he saw that I was shivering, he took off his outer garment and draped it over my shoulders. He rubbed my hands. There was real concern in his eyes.

"What are you doing out here? Shouldn't you be in your room?"

"I was looking for a place to warm the baby."

"Where is your guard?"

He saw my hesitancy, but he didn't press me. "May I see the baby?" he asked.

I showed her to him.

"She's beautiful," he said. "What do you call her?"

"Eudocia," I said.

"Oh, that's lovely."

"Yes," I said struggling to make polite conversation. "It's my mother's name."

"Your mother must be a very special person to deserve such a distinction."

I didn't tell him I had not wanted to name the baby after my mother and preferred to name her after my aunt instead, but Galla reminded me it was customary to name a first-born girl after her maternal grandmother and that my mother would be hurt if I eschewed the practice.

Huneric continued rubbing my hands. "You're so cold," he said. Then he noticed my bare feet. "Wait here," he said. "I'll run and fetch your slippers."

While he was gone one of the eunuchs happened upon me. This particular eunuch was known to keep company with Heraclius and was surprised to see me out of my room. He asked me what I was doing there. I made some excuse about needing to get some air and told him I didn't need his assistance. But he lingered, and he was still there when Huneric came back. The look on his face told me all I needed know. My association with Huneric would be reported to Heraclius, and, through him, to Placidius.

I suppose I could have headed things off by telling Placidius myself—it was innocent enough—but Placidius was so prickly of late I didn't want to start a fight. Later, I would come to think God was punishing me for being so timid. Perhaps Placidius had been right when he had called me weak and stupid. In the course of time, my decision not to come clean right away would come back to haunt me.

* * *

Placidius's first reaction on hearing that Aetius had raided the imperial mint at Arelate was to sack him, but Galla, along with his most trusted advisors, cautioned against it. Aetius could not be alienated they told him. He had the loyalty of the army and could call on formidable allies, most notably the Huns. Making an enemy of him could end in disaster. Better to countenance the reasonableness of his actions and try to reach an accord. After all, he had only been trying to pay his soldiers.

Placidius dug in. He thought making excuses for an act of subversion made him look weak and would just invite more of the same. He wanted to send a message. He wanted Aetius punished. He slammed his fist on the table.

The counselors looked to Galla with helpless expressions. She raised her hands and called for calm. She recognized Placidius had a point. The optics of letting Aetius get away with such a thing would reflect poorly on the Emperor. On the other hand, antagonizing Aetius was dangerous. What was called for, she said, was a compromise, something that would give Aetius what he wanted but allow the Emperor to look like he was in control.

Placidius's face flushed. "I want to do more than *look* like I'm in control!"

Galla told him to calm down. The edge in her voice surprised him, and he relented.

"Look," she said, speaking to the group. "If anyone understands the importance of appearances, it's Aetius. He knows the Emperor must do something to demonstrate his authority. By the same token, he must show that he has the best interests of his army at heart. By refusing to give him the means to do so, we have put him in a difficult spot, which has led him to commit this unlawful act. Fortunately, Aetius is a reasonable person. If we speak to him reasonably, he will return the money and clean up the mess he's made, but we have to give him the funding he needs to compensate his army."

"So, we have to pay his extortion," grumbled Placidius.

Galla cut him a scathing look.

One of the counselors spoke up, "But where will we get the money? Our finances are depleted. We've been fighting multiple wars against multiple enemies for decades, and now the Goths have risen again. Our coffers are not bottomless. Where are we to get the funds?"

Galla sighed. "If we are to be honest with ourselves, we must acknowledge that certain parties have not paid their fair share of taxes. As unpopular as it may be to admit it, we must face facts. We must demand more from the aristocracy."

The counselors looked at each other uneasily. "They won't like that. Their support for the Emperor is contingent on maintaining things as they are. We dare not antagonize them. Perhaps we can squeeze more out of the common people."

Galla shook her head. "That would be unwise. Our heavy taxation of the Commons in Gaul led to the uprisings in Armorica and elsewhere? Unless you want the Bagaudae on our doorstep, we must refrain from taxing them any further."

"I won't tax the aristocracy," Placidius announced firmly. "It's out of the question."

Galla shot him a dismayed looked. She addressed the others. "Perhaps we can enlist the aid of the Church. What the aristocracy denies to us, they may furnish to the Church without objection. If the Pope were to ask for contributions to help save the starving children of Gaul, for example, the aristocracy might be generous."

The counselors made approving noises. Even Placidius appeared to be in agreement.

Then Galla said, "Once we have the money, we must be prudent about how we disburse it. We must not give it to Aetius directly. That would raise too many eyebrows. Instead, we must give it to Albinus so he can replenish the mint. That way everyone is pacified, and no one can claim he is the worse off."

Placidius shook his head in disbelief. "Are you proposing we allow Aetius to keep the money he stole?"

"It's a whole lot easier than asking him to give it back. The injured party here is Albinus. By providing him what he needs to replenish the mint he is made whole, and the whole ugly business is behind us."

"But that's unjust," Placidius said. "Aetius robbed the mint. He shouldn't be allowed to get away with it. He should be compelled to give the money back."

"And just how do you propose to do that?"

"Demand it of him, and if he refuses, punish him."

Galla laughed. "You're not going to punish your Master of Soldiers. It's out of the question."

"Then I want an apology," Placidius said. "My mint was raided, and my money was stolen. If Aetius is going to keep it, I want an acknowledgment that it was improperly taken."

Galla looked exasperated. "I will ask it of him."

"Demand it."

"I will demand it of him."

"I want a public apology," Placidius said. "I want an admission of wrongdoing."

Galla turned to the counselors. "Shall we move on to other business?"

The conversation turned to other subjects. Placidius sat fuming throughout. He glowered at his mother beneath lowered brows.

The plan to replenish the mint with the help of the Pope was a sound one, but it ran into trouble almost at once. The plan had been to have Pope Sixtus deliver the funds to Albinus in person, giving it the imprimatur of official Church business. But before the plan could be implemented the Pope fell ill again, and it was decided someone else would have to go to Arelate in his place.

Most senior clergymen in Rome were loath to leave the Pope at a time when his health was in a precarious state, so the Church had to look elsewhere for a surrogate. An unlikely candidate came to the fore, an owl-faced deacon from Tuscany with a cheerful mien and buoyant disposition. His name was Leo, and before long he would factor heavily into the events about to unfold.

# Chapter 5
Spring, The Year AD 439

As a negotiator, the affable Leo came highly recommended by the well-connected and aspiring prelates that surrounded the Pope. Pope Sixtus was usually circumspect around such men as the politics of the church were as fraught and factional as those of any civic government, and Sixtus was as vulnerable as any political leader. But Sixtus was ill, and Leo's bona fides were supposedly above reproach, so Sixtus accepted the recommendations, and Leo was given the assignment.

When the new emissary came to the palace to meet the Emperor and learn the details of the offer being made, something rubbed the Emperor the wrong way. Leo struck Placidius as glib, almost flippant. His manner seemed a little too unctuous, his enthusiasm a little too forced. Placidius didn't trust him.

Galla accused her son of being against him just because everyone else was for him, but Placidius maintained his misgivings were valid. Galla refused to believe him. From what I could see, Placidius would have been a better ruler if his mother had countenanced his good opinions. As it was, the only positive feedback he received was from sycophants and flatterers. It was a shame. Galla could never quite see him as the capable, independent, nineteen-year-old he was, a young adult striving to be a good leader. Instead, she saw the spoiled, peevish adolescent she had sent off to Constantinople a year and a half earlier, the one to whom she had written a long letter as a way of moderating his worse impulses. The letter had succeeded; Placidius had learned from it and was trying to correct his shortcomings. But Galla couldn't see the progress, which only made him more frustrated and petulant. His reactions confirmed her low opinion of him.

One day I came upon him in the cloister of the peristylum looking out at the garden. It was the first week of March and the cool, damp temperatures, while good for the early spring flowers, made it uncomfortable to sit outside for any length of time. Placidius wore a heavy robe. He opened the cloak and invited me in beside him. I snuggled against him. Together we sat looking out at the garden.

"You look like something is on your mind," I said.

"It's my mother. She doesn't think me capable of making good decisions." He went on to explain the situation with Leo. "I don't know what to do to convince her. I don't like the man. I don't trust him. Why won't she listen to me?"

My heart went out to him, but this was between him and his mother. I worried that offering my opinion might be seen as presumptuous. I contented myself with the fact that he was opening up to me. I rested my head against his shoulder and murmured something sympathetic.

"I'm not stupid," he said. "I understand she's more experienced than I am. But I have valid opinions too. My opinions are worth something. I am the Emperor, after all."

I pulled the robe tighter around us and snuggled closer.

He gnawed his thumbnail as he sat looking out at the rain. "I could put my foot down. I could demand they do as I tell them, and they would have to do it. But that wouldn't make them think any better of me. I don't want them to listen to me because they're afraid of me. I want them to listen to me because they respect me." He looked at me with the face of a wounded child.

I cocked my head and pushed out my lower lip to demonstrate my commiseration. I placed a hand on his cheek.

He sighed. "If I take a hard line, they'll say I'm being obdurate. They'll accuse me of being peevish and contrary, the same old Placidius. I hate that, Licinia. I'm not that kind of person anymore. I've grown."

"I know you have."

"I've tried to cooperate. I've gone along with everything they've asked of me. But what has it gotten me? They continue to ignore me. And nobody has to answer for it. It's insolence, what they're doing—insolence plain and simple, which breeds defiance if left unchecked. Before long, they'll be plotting to overthrow me. It's dangerous, Licinia. I tell you, it's dangerous."

I told him I understood.

He looked at me. His expression was tender and loving. "Only you respect me, Licinia. Only you demonstrate the virtues of your station. Humility and obedience, that's what a man wants from a female, and that's what I get from you.

That's what you owe me. It's the will of God." He pulled me closer. "You've been well bred, Licinia. You've read the Church Fathers. A lot of people say they've read those books, but you actually have. You understand, Licinia. You really do. You're a good woman. You're a good wife."

My heart swelled as he took me in his arms. I melted into him. Then he led me to one of the small rooms off the peristylum and began to undress me. My heart hammered in my chest. It was a delicious feeling. We hadn't lain together for months, not since before the baby was born, and I could barely contain my desire. The books were explicit on the subject. Sexual congress between husband and wife was strictly forbidden except for purposes of procreation. To take pleasure in it was a sin. But I couldn't help it.

He stood behind me and nuzzled my neck. He rubbed his hands down the length of my body. He stroked my arms, my waist, my breasts. I was on fire. He spun me around and slid his tongue between my lips. He ignited something in me, something primal and needy. I pressed myself against him. I put my hands behind his neck and his drew his mouth against mine. I wanted to devour him. He lowered me to the floor, pushed up my dress. We had never been like this before, surrendering to each other without violence, and it was a wonderful feeling.

Yet something deep inside me, a faraway voice, kept telling me that what we were doing was wrong. Placidius must have had the same thought for he hesitated, and then he said, "Give me a son."

It shouldn't have mattered, those innocuous seeming words. But it did. The spell was broken. The desire quickly drained out of me. What only a moment before had been a delicious euphoria became the dry, obligatory exercise that characterized all of our lovemaking. Placidius pinned me to the floor and rubbed himself between my thighs trying to bolster his erection. I surrendered to him and gazed up at the ceiling. But then a thought entered my mind. I don't know where it came from. Perhaps from somewhere wicked. It was the memory of what I had seen between those two servants. It was appalling. It was disgusting. Yet it was titillating. I reproached myself for even contemplating such a thing. It was horrible and wrong. To commit such an act would be offensive to God. But Placidius was getting no satisfaction, and neither was I.

"Resist me," he said, and took hold of my wrists.

I didn't want to fight him. I didn't want to go through this again, not after things had begun so lovingly.

"Do it!" he snapped, jerking my hair.

"Wait," I said. "Let's try something different."

He stopped. "Something different?"

"I think you'll like this. Stand up."

He got to his feet with an air of distrust. I got on my knees before him. He stood above me, his arms dangling at his sides. I took his penis in my hands and stroked it. He grew rigid. I thought maybe this would be enough, that I could stroke him this way, and he would become more tender toward me, and we could go back to kissing again. But it was not to be. After a minute, his erection flagged, and he grew anxious. So, I braced myself, shut my eyes and took him into my mouth. The effect was immediate. He grew as rigid as a fencepost. It was not nearly as disgusting as I thought it would be. In truth, the feeling of him growing large in my mouth aroused me. I sucked him with vigor, trying not to think about what I was doing, trying to enjoy the sensation, which was pleasurable—for as long as it lasted.

The excitement was too great for him. He tried to mount me. But I didn't want to be ravaged. I braced myself against his chest and pleaded with him to enter me slowly. To my surprise, he did. He filled me. He moved languorously. It was glorious. Together we rocked to the rhythm of our bodies, kissing and caressing. Then I began to feel it, a series of palpitations like nothing I had ever felt before, each one a pulse of transcendent color like a rain soaked flower opening, and then a gorgeous burst of nectar that spread through my body, tingling my skin, and rippling along my fingers and toes. I shuddered and moaned.

Placidius went on for a long time as if in a trance. By the time he had finished, I had known the pleasure twice more. It was magnificent. And yet it was a thing forbidden, a sin. These two thoughts intertwined in my mind like the warp and weft of threads fashioning the fabric of my being.

When he asked me why I was crying, I said, "I love you. I want to be your wife. Always."

He said. "You will be."

The way he said it was like a cold wind on a warm autumn day. And I knew this thing I had done would come back to haunt me.

* * *

The shame of what I had done hit me like a hammer. I was overwhelmed heart and soul, and I wept with remorse. The devil had used me like a tool to pervert my husband. I had polluted my master and offended God, all the while wallowing in my own carnality. I was a despicable woman, and I deserved to be punished.

It was disgusting. I could barely stand to think about it. I had to get the stain off me. I tried fasting and praying and giving alms, but nothing seemed to work. I went to Placidius and apologized. I begged his forgiveness. Then I saw the look in his eyes. I had awakened something in him. He was hungry for more. Even as I agonized in repentance, he demanded a repeat of my sin.

I tried to refuse. I tried to tell him it was the work of the devil. I pleaded with him to admit the sin and pray to God. But he wouldn't hear of it. He called it love. He called it affection. He made it clear that if we didn't do it again, we would have to go back to the old way. I begged him not to do that to me, not to make me choose, but he kept pressing. Finally, when I told him I would not do it again, he threw me down and took me. This went on for weeks. It was agonizing. At last, when it became clear that I had become pregnant again, he stopped coming to me.

Other things began to demand his attention. I was grateful for the reprieve, but his absence was a problem. If I were to offer him the solace he needed, I had to know what was troubling him. Since he had stopped sharing his feelings with me, I had to find a different way, so I began to sit in on his councils. I stayed in the back of the room, unobtrusive, in the shadows where he would not notice me. It was there I learned the ugly truth.

Leo returned from Arelate at the end of May and assured everyone that his envoy had been a success. The money contributed by the aristocracy had been dispensed to the poor, suffering children of Gaul through the mint at Arelate. The praetorian prefect Albinus, a former member of the Roman senatorial class himself, was appeased, the mint was restored, and Aetius was able to pay his army out of the money he had taken. It seemed the crisis was behind us.

But it became clear within a fortnight that something was off. General Litorius, who had pursued the Goths to Tolosa and put them under siege, suffered an unexpected setback. The Goths had put up a staunch defense and driven him back. We all awaited news that Aetius had marched from Arelate with reinforcements, but no news came. Then word arrived that Litorius had been captured and taken prisoner. We were stunned. Where was Aetius? Why hadn't he gone to the aid of his colleague?

Placidius sent Aetius a sharply worded message demanding an explanation. But Aetius didn't respond. Then word came that Aetius had marched at last after a long delay. He had engaged the Goths at Carcassonne some sixty miles south of Tolosa. But it was too late. The Goths had been reinforced. They drove him back. The Romans were in disarray. Worse yet, Litorius was dead.

Placidius demanded that Leo be brought before him to explain what had happened. But Leo was gone having departed on a pilgrimage to Jerusalem to visit the holy sites. Placidius convened his counsel and railed at them. What was going on?

What had happened? Nobody knew. They were as clueless as he was.

Then the unthinkable happened. The Vandals struck.

Violating the peace agreement they had entered into four years earlier, they overran the province of Africa Proconsularis and put pressure on the vital seaport of Carthago. Suddenly it was glaringly obvious what Genseric the Vandal king had been plotting all along. He had never intended to make a lasting peace. He had used the pause in hostilities to build up his navy, which was now a formidable fleet in search of a deep-water port. Carthago was perfect for them. But he dared not act, not while Aetius could still oppose him. So, he waited. Then, as soon as Aetius was pinned down by the Goths, he struck.

Placidius persuaded his mother to reach out to Aetius to get him to come to Ravenna to discuss a strategy for dealing with the crisis. Aetius's answer was a long time in coming, and when it arrived, it was terse. He said he would appear once the situation in Gaul had stabilized. He had nothing to offer regarding the Vandal threat to Carthago. We would have to wait.

Placidius suggested moving troops from Pannonia to Carthago, but his counselors warned against it as it would leave Pannonia vulnerable to the Huns. He suggested moving troops from Hispania but was told this was unwise as it would leave Lusitania and Beatica vulnerable to the Suebi. That's when Placidius realized our armies were spread too thin. We needed more troops, but where to get them? Gathering my courage, I stepped out of the shadows to make a suggestion. Why not reach out to my father in Constantinople?"

Placidius told me to leave, but I was not so easily discouraged. The answer seemed obvious to me, and I wanted him to hear it.

"My father would be glad to help. We could go to Constantinople and make the case to him in person. He would not refuse us. We are family."

But Placidius wouldn't hear of it. The Western Roman Empire could stand on its own. He didn't need any need help from the East. He turned back to his counselors and ignored me.

But I wasn't finished. The whole purpose of our marriage had been to bind the two halves of the Empire together, and now that we were facing a crisis, he was refusing to ask the East for help. What was going on? I demanded an explanation, but he continued to disregard me.

Truth be told, I had another reason for wanting to return home after two and a half years. I missed my family. I missed Constantinople. What's more, I was struggling with the enormity of my sin. It was grinding me down, and I needed someone to make me feel better.

I had turned to God already. I had prayed innumerable times. I had made a pilgrimage to the Lateran Basilica in Rome. I had fasted. I had flagellated myself with a horsehair whip. But I could not escape the overpowering sense of remorse that weighed down on me. I wanted the guidance of my aunt. She would know the proper penance to expunge my sin, but it was not something I could write about in a letter. I needed to see her in person. Yet it was not to be. Placidius would not call on the East for help. He would wait for Aetius instead.

As the days dragged on and the tension mounted Placidius became snappish and irritable. One afternoon in a fit of pique he ordered Huneric executed. Under the circumstances, it was not a surprise. As the firstborn son of the Vandal king, Huneric had been sent to Ravenna as an indemnity against the Vandal threat. By breaking our trust, Genseric had condemned his son to death. As a matter of strict diplomatic protocol his execution was required, but for Placidius it was an act of revenge. He had been embarrassed and frightened by the Vandal uprising, and he needed someone to punish. Huneric was the obvious choice.

I didn't like it. Not at all. The political rationale was one thing, but Huneric was innocent. He was not involved in his father's treachery. He was a lonesome boy far from home in a foreign land and friendless—except for me. His execution would solve nothing and might make things worse. To let him become the victim of my husband's wrath seemed irresponsible, and there was something else. It occurred to me that saving Huneric might be just what I needed to do to compensate for the enormity of my sin. Rescuing the boy might appeal to Christ's forgiving nature and provide me some form of absolution.

Huneric tried to talk me out of it. He understood what it would mean if I were caught. He didn't want me to risk my life to rescue his. He was a brave young man. He was willing to accept his execution as a matter of principle. He had known from the start what might happen and accepted it. Anyway, a Vandal nobleman's duty was to his people, he said. Sacrifice was the highest virtue. If he had to die to advance the condition of his people, he would do it.

But I saw only waste, the squandering of a good man's life to settle a political score. It accomplished nothing. Surely God would not be pleased. So, I steeled myself for whatever lay ahead and planned his liberation.

I brought him a horse from the stables, the aging one he had predicted would soon be dispensed with and arranged for the gates to be opened. He rode off before they came to arrest him.

Before he went, he said, "Licinia Eudocia you have saved me, not once, but twice. I shall never forget you."

He sat astride his mount and looked at me with a warm smile. Then he pulled his horse around and rode off with the carriage of a man who knew how to ride and had always done so with great confidence, wherever he was going.

When word got around that Huneric had escaped, Placidius lost his mind. He demanded to know who was responsible and threatened to punish anyone who had a part in it. It was my intention to tell him—eventually. I thought I might tell him in a way that would make sense to him. Maybe then he would understand. But not when he was acting like this. I would tell him later, after he had settled down. I would tell him when he was calm and rational. But the time never came, and that was unfortunate, because had he learned the truth later it would look very much like I had been trying to keep a secret.

# Chapter 6
Summer, The Year AD 439

After two years of fruitless requests, unheeded demands, and spurned cajolery, Aetius finally showed up in Ravenna. He arrived unannounced and demanded an audience with the Emperor. Placidius was so put out he seriously considered refusing it, but Galla told him he was being ridiculous. The Master of Soldiers had a great deal to tell him, she said. He would report on the situation in Gaul and provide vital information on how to deal with the Vandals. Finally, Placidius gave in, but he wasn't happy about it.

The meeting, which was to have taken place in the audience chamber, was moved at the last minute to the imperial basilica adjoining the eastern end of the palace. Placidius ordered the move because the room was outfitted with an ambo, a high marble pulpit, from which he could tower over Aetius from a position of prominence. Placidius ordered that Aetius be given no place to sit and be made to stand before him like a supplicant. Behind him on the ambo, Placidius would array his council of advisors who would stand like a tribunal looking down on Aetius in judgment. Among them would be the eunuch Heraclius with his cone-shaped hat, rouged cheeks, and pale complexion, as well as the Emperor's wife and mother, a motley collection of lower status individuals sitting in judgment on the most powerful figure in the land.

It was the height of summer, and the sun was pounding down relentlessly. The air was hot and sultry. Whatever respite the stone and marble chamber might have provided was nullified by the clustering together of so many bodies. I was six months pregnant. The child was heavy in my belly, and I kept shifting my position to try to get comfortable. A mosquito buzzed in my ear. A trickle of sweat ran down my face and dripped off my chin.

When Aetius entered, he strode forward purposefully but was intercepted by a body of soldiers who closed around him and prevented him from going any farther. He looked from one to another in bemusement. When he heard their muttered explanations, he smiled as if he had just been let in on a joke and made his way to the center of the room where he stood like a man waiting for a conveyance.

Placidius sat erect on his throne with his advisors clustered around him, chin raised, glaring down at Aetius. "To what do we owe the favor of your presence," he said. His voice dropped a full register in an attempt to sound commanding.

Aetius lowered his head. "Forgive me, Imperator. I was under the impression you wanted to see me. If I was mistaken, I beg your pardon. I will not waste your time."

"Halt!" Placidius shot back. "I did not give you permission to leave my imperial presence."

Aetius looked around in feigned bewilderment. "I'm sorry. Did you mean that I should stay? Instruct me, Excellency.

I stand ready to fulfill your wishes. I am your most humble servant."

Placidius turned an exasperated look at his mother. She made a subtle nod in the direction of Aetius, encouraging her son to carry on. Aetius watched this pass between them.

"You are here to report the situation with the Goths," Placidius said. "We have been waiting for months to hear from you. You are aware of this."

"I am aware," Aetius said. "I have received your entreaties. Let me assure you I have not been remiss, although it may appear that way. On more than one occasion I sat down to write to you, to report our situation, but the circumstances were changing so rapidly that by the time I had finished writing it was no longer relevant. I might have sequestered myself and ignored the crisis, but that would have required me to turn a blind eye to the many looming threats. I had to weigh the responsibility of keeping you informed against the need to prevent the situation from spinning out of control. I had to rely on your good judgment to perceive the wisdom of my decision and hoped you would understand when we met."

Having delivered this irreproachable account of his actions, Aetius stood with his arms folded like a seasoned gambler awaiting his opponent's throw. He was lean and muscular with an upright bearing. His face was narrow with a strong jaw line. He was not attractive in any conventional sense, but his charisma was striking. It was easy to see how he commanded armies.

Placidius started to say something, stopped and reconsidered, then fell silent.

After an uncomfortable moment, Aetius spoke again. "Perhaps you would like a report now, on our current status—or at least the status as it existed when I set out."

Placidius nodded.

"Very well. As you know, the Goths are pressing us at Carcassonne. We don't possess the troop strength to hold them back. When they break through there, they will almost certainly carry on to Narbo. Within a month we will be back where we started. The Goths will be investing Narbo, and we will be putting them under siege, only this time they will have the upper hand."

"What are you talking about?" Placidius asked. "We are Romans. Ours is the greatest military the world has ever known."

"Be that as it may, the Goths are an especially fertile people; their numbers increase daily, while we grow weak from attrition. What's more, they are becoming ever more sophisticated in their tactics. The situation is changing rapidly. As much as it pains me to admit it, I think it may be time for a different approach."

Placidius raised a brow. "A different approach?"

Aetius wore a somber expression. "Not to put too fine a point on it, I think we ought to recognize their sovereignty in Aquitaine and negotiate their harbor rights for Narbo."

Placidius woofed like he had been punched in the gut. "Recognize their sovereignty in Aquitaine! Grant them harbor rights! We did that before and look what it got us. They turned against us and laid siege to Narbo. You speak of doing things differently and then you propose to make the same mistakes again."

Aetius remained calm. "Before, they were only granted federate status. This time we should face the facts and grant them full independence."

Placidius's mouth fell open. "Are you are proposing to surrender a large portion of our territory to the Goths?"

"Aquitaine to be exact, from the Pyrenees to the Loire River. They are de facto rulers there anyway. Our insistence on treating them as hospitalitas, as nothing more than billeted soldiers on the land, denies the reality of their situation, and provokes them to acts of violence. If our purpose was to reinforce their obligation to us, we have failed. Not only do they refuse to fight for us, but they also actively fight against us, mostly as a way to resist the imposition of that hated label. They know they are free and independent, even if we pretend otherwise. I propose we dispense with the fiction. Grant them the sovereignty they already possess, and they will gladly contribute to our cause as allies and equals. But force them to play the part of subordinates, and they will resist to the last man."

Placidius was not having it. "You are certainly free and easy with the dismemberment of our Empire. I wonder if you have considered the many sacrifices it took to acquire it."

Aetius measured him. "I am a soldier. I have learned a thing or two about sacrifices."

Placidius looked at Galla in exasperation. "Tell me, Mother, what do you think of this? I know you have a soft spot for the Goths, but are you prepared to give away half of Gaul to purchase their fealty?"

If he thought Galla would support him in his opposition, he was disappointed. "I think you should listen to your Master of Soldiers."

Placidius gave a snort of contempt. "So that's it then. We are all of one accord. Let's carve up the Empire. To the Franks goes Belgica. To the Suebia goes Hispania. The Huns will get Pannonia, and Aquitaine is for the Goths." He laughed, but I could detect the strain in his voice.

Aetius watched him impassively. After a moment, he said, "If you are so against surrendering territory, sir, then I don't understand why you turned over Illyricum to the East."

Placidius stiffened. Aetius went on, "Your mother wrote you a letter. She sought to explain everything. But something tells me she did not communicate the importance of Illyricum. Either that or you ignored her."

Placidius set his teeth.

Aetius went on. "Illyricum was vital source of revenue for us. We relied on her taxable estates to fund our armies. When the West lent her to the East, it was supposed to be temporary, an act of generosity to help her fight off the invading hordes. But when the East refused to return her to us, it was not just an indiscretion; it was a theft. We needed that money, and the East did not. Their treasuries were overflowing. Ours were depleted. Their armies were well compensated. Ours were starving. You gave them Illyricum to placate them, but in so doing you surrendered a key source of revenue to which we were lawfully entitled. Now you criticize me for placating an enemy—an enemy who will become a friend and ally if treated fairly, a friend and ally we must rely on if we are to defeat the Vandals and drive them out of Africa. We must face the facts. This is not the Rome of a hundred years ago. This is the Rome of today. The idea that we can continue fighting multiple enemies on multiple fronts without adequate funding and no outside help is a fantasy. We need the Goths. We cannot afford to alienate them."

Placidius was seething, but before he could say anything in response, his mother came to his rescue.

She directed her comments to Aetius. "May I remind you, sir, that you are speaking to the Emperor?"

Aetius lowered his head in humility. "I am sorry. I understood you to seek a candid assessment. Forgive me if I have been too forward."

Placidius struggled to contain his anger. I prayed he would find the wherewithal. It could not have been easy in that heat and humidity. My own discomfort was building. The mosquito that had been afflicting me was joined by two or three others, and I could feel them feeding on my neck and back. I fought the urge to swat them because to do so would make me look fussy and undignified.

As for Aetius, he seemed immune from the discomfort. He regarded the Emperor with a cool dignity. "Permit me to explain further. The Vandals pose a formidable threat. They have not sat idle while we have been at peace. They have built a mighty fleet, and now they are seeking an anchorage from which to launch it. They are driving for Carthago. If we do not stop them, they will take it and use it as a base from which to launch an assault on Italia. We must make a demonstration of strength. I'm going to need every available soldier to achieve that. We cannot be tied down in Aquitaine fighting a pointless war with the Goths. We must make peace.

Placidius was dismissive. "And what will *that* cost us?"

Aetius looked skyward for a moment. "As I said, we must acknowledge their sovereignty in Aquitaine and negotiate their access to the port at Narbo. In exchange they will fight as allies on our behalf."

"So, we have to give up one part of our territory to safeguard another."

"Let me spell it out for you. We must give up part of Gaul to safeguard Italia and recover Africa."

Placidius frowned. "I don't like it. My ancestors never had to trade territory to purchase peace. It makes me look weak. I don't want to look weak. I am not weak."

Aetius watched him dubiously. He said nothing.

The mosquitos were insufferable. The Emperor was obviously afflicted too. Placidius slapped the side of his face and then looked at his hand to see if he had gotten it. His hand was empty. Aetius was smiling at him. Placidius thought he was being mocked. He lost it.

"Where are your troops! You have plenty of troops. You should be using them to fight the Goths, to destroy them, so you can turn your attention to Africa!"

Aetius looked surprised. "My troops? You want to know where my troops are? I have all the troops that money can buy—or at least all the troops that I can buy with the money I have. A man will only risk his life for a pittance for so long. Eventually he gets disillusioned and deserts. Half the men I had at Arelate have gone. My Hun mercenaries were especially restive. Mercenaries will not lift a finger without compensation, you know. It's too bad. They were a vital component of our success. Now they are gone. That's why I didn't march to support Litorius. I didn't have enough soldiers to make a difference. When I finally scraped together enough money to pay the men who remained, I ran to his assistance, but it was too late. It would have been different if I had had the money earlier. It would have been different if I had been able to pay those men what we owed them."

Placidius was incredulous. "What happened to the money you took from the mint? That should have been enough to pay your men. What happened to that?"

Aetius shook his head. "You are mistaken, Excellency. If you will recall, you directed me to give that money back. You instructed me to wait for reimbursement from the Church. I did as you directed. The praetorian prefect Albinus is the steward of those funds now, and, as you know, he is not inclined to share them. The Church has still not reimbursed me. I waited and waited, but time ran out. Circumstances now force our hand. We must move at once to deter the Vandals, and we cannot do it without the Goths."

Placidius recoiled as if he had been slapped. "Wait, what?" he said. "Go back. What did you say about Albinus and the treasury?"

"You directed me to give the money back. The Pope's emissary spoke to me on your behalf. What was his name? Oh, yes. Leo. He told me the Church was collecting funds from the aristocracy to buttress our forces. He promised me it would equal or exceed the funds I had taken from the mint. He assured me it had been arranged and endorsed by you, with the ratification of your mother. Are you saying that was not the case?"

"Most assuredly not," said Placidius. "Leo was to tell you to keep the money you took. The funds provided by the aristocracy were to go to Albinus, to replenish the treasury. We all agreed on that."

"I should have known better," Aetius said. "The aristocracy. How can you trust men who have nothing to do all day but sit around plotting ways to hoard their money?"

Placidius drew himself up. "Well, you'll just have to go back and help yourself to the mint again."

Aetius shook his head. "It's too late for that. They were well aware I was coming here to meet with you. Albinus will have resigned his post by now and handed the keys to someone with even more powerful connections to the senatorial class, and this Leo, let me guess, has disappeared.

"Gone to Jerusalem on a pilgrimage."

"What a surprise. I'm afraid you've been bilked, Imperator. The mint has been shuttered, and the treasury is empty. The money has been channeled to the aristocracy to repay them with interest for the money they lent. The aristocracy never contributes anything unless they can profit from it. You should know that. But you can be forgiven your ignorance. You are young and inexperienced, and these men are seasoned charlatans."

A scowl creased Placidius's brow.

"We find ourselves in a difficult situation. Our resources are strained, and we have a formidable enemy bearing down on us. With your permission, I will approach the Goths with a generous offer to end hostilities, and then I will prepare our forces to fight the Vandals."

"In Africa?" Placidius asked with tightness in his voice.

"Well, of course, in Africa. You don't intend I should fight them here, do you?"

"Ah, Africa," Placidius said with a mocking tone. "Beloved Africa, the breadbasket of the Empire. Everyone wants Africa.

Especially you, Aetius. You have been trying to get Africa ever since Mother first named you Master of Soldiers. If my grasp of history doesn't elude me, you implored her to send you there when Bonifacius was your predecessor. But she didn't trust you and denied your request. Isn't that true, Mother?"

Galla narrowed her eyes at him.

He went on. "So desperate were you to be posted to Africa that you engaged in a little chicanery, something to do with a false letter, ostensibly written by Bonifacius, but actually written by you, Aetius. This misled my mother into thinking that Bonifacius was plotting against her. As a result, she sent troops to Africa to arrest him, which would have been enough for most schemers, but it wasn't enough for you, was it, Aetius? There was more to your little ruse, wasn't there? You also sent a letter to Bonifacius informing him that my mother suspected him of treason and meant to have him executed. You advised him that his only chance was to resist the troops sent to arrest him and fight to the death, if necessary. Your selfish little gambit caused a rift in our forces at precisely the moment when the Vandals were preparing to strike. It is not too much to say that you created the vulnerability that led to their crossing over into Africa. It is not too much to say that their invasion can be laid to your account. Isn't that right, Aetius?"

Placidius was obviously relishing this. He didn't wait for Aetius's answer. "So now you stand before us demanding to be sent to Africa to deal with the Vandal threat, to solve the problem you created." He gave a rueful chuckle. "That strikes me as wrong. That strikes me as rewarding bad behavior. To my way of thinking, there has been way too much of that sort of thing lately." He shook his head. "No. I don't think I'm going to do that. You see, I'm not as stupid as you think I am. I actually did read my mother's letter. And one thing I learned from it is that rewarding bad behavior only invites more of the same. So, no, Aetius, you are not going to Africa. Not now. Not ever."

Galla began to protest, but Placidius cut her off. "I have made my decision. I am the Emperor."

Aetius grinned. He clapped his hands. "Well done, Imperator. That was a bravura performance. I must say your recollection of the past is flawless. I stand convicted. My ambitions got the best of me. I confess. I was a little too power hungry when I was younger. What can I say? Youth is like that. It lacks self-restraint. Wouldn't you agree?"

Placidius glared at him.

"Let's drop the histrionics and face the facts. We are facing invasion by a powerful enemy. If you will not permit me to stop them, then how do you plan to deal with the situation?"

Some of the smugness drained out of Placidius. He seemed to falter. Then he drew himself up and said, "I will take it under advisement."

Placidius smirked. "Oh, you will, will you? Well, you had better hurry up, because my intelligence informs me the Vandals are outfitting their ships and preparing to set sail."

Placidius struggled to maintain his composure. He squared his shoulders. "I will not be coerced into an ill-considered decision. I will take it under advisement."

Placidius looked to Galla with an expression that said, *Are you kidding me?*

Galla gave a little shrug.

It was then I spoke up. It was not planned. It just sort of came out of me. It was a combination of the mosquitoes, the heat, and the heaviness in my belly. It was impelled by my feelings of sympathy for poor Placidius, who wanted so desperately to do the right thing and was not being given the proper consideration.

"We should call on the East," I said. "We should call on my father. He will help us. I'm certain of it."

They all turned to me in astonishment. I knew in an instant I had overstepped. I blushed and tried to recover.

"The reason Placidius and I got married was so that the two halves of the Empire could come together and support each other, for the good of both. Why is that such a bad idea?"

They looked at me for a few seconds, and then they turned away and resumed talking amongst themselves.

"I will wait in Ravenna for a few days more," Aetius said, "to give you time to reconsider. After that, I will assume nothing has changed and I will return to Gaul to fight the Goths with whatever resources are available."

Placidius started to endorse this idea but stopped short. "It's not for you to decide. I am the Emperor. I will decide when you come and go. A few days is too short. One week. You will remain in Ravenna one week to hear my decision. Is that clear?"

"Distinctly," Aetius said with an exaggerated bow.

Placidius turned up his nose.

Galla announced that the audience was over. Everyone began to withdraw. Placidius first with his advisors behind him. Then Aetius and the others. Galla lingered till the end. She caught me at the steps.

"Come to me in my rooms," she said, her voice tight with repressed anger.

I couldn't imagine why she was so upset. I had done nothing but make an innocent suggestion. When she was gone, I headed out of the basilica unaccompanied. The last person I saw as I was going out was Heraclius. He was standing with his back to me in the arched recess of one of the alcoves near the entrance gazing up at one of the high narrow windows where a bolt of sunlight was angling down to the floor. He reached up and put his hand in it, wiggling his fingers, turning his hand this way and that. Slowly, he turned to me, his high conical hat tipped slightly forward on his head. He gave me a measured look.

"Hot," he said in his high, reedy voice, and grinned.

* * *

"It's time you understood a few things," Galla Placidia said. We were in her private apartments at her request. "Placidius will never call on the East for help, not while Pulcheria is still alive."

I was confused. "You mean my aunt?"

"That's right. Your aunt. In spite of everything he did for her, she still intimidates him."

I shook my head, befuddled. "But why would Placidius be afraid of my aunt?"

Galla gave me a pitying look. "Oh, my poor child. You really don't know anything. Your mother once said she would shield you from all this, but now I see she succeeded only too well. You have no idea who your aunt is or what kind of person she is, do you?"

I bristled. "My aunt is a good person, generous and devout."

"She is both of those things, and other things as well."

The windows of Galla's first floor room faced the Adriatic where cool sea breezes helped ease the heat. I was still feeling tired and overheated from my ordeal in the basilica, and I wanted to be left alone. I asked to be excused.

"I know you don't want to hear this," Galla responded. "It cannot be pleasant for you. But you are not a child anymore. You are eighteen. You have some important decisions to make."

"Some important decisions?"

"You are going to have to decide what kind of woman you want to be."

I didn't know what she was talking about, and I certainly didn't see how any of this had anything to do with my aunt, but she went on. "Will you be one of those women who covers their ears and whistles cheerful little tunes to shut out the world? Will you be ignorant? It's a choice many women make. It has its benefits. You do not have to grapple with uncomfortable truths. Hypocrisy and nuance need not discomfit you, and the Church prefers you that way; it wants you to be naïve and submissive, as most men do. It's easy enough. But there's a cost. You will have to endure a life of tedium, an endless cycle of routine and ritual, your every thought and action prescribed by custom and expectation. And be prepared to extinguish any glimmer of curiosity in your mind, for in that way lay only anxiety and confusion. Is that the sort of woman you want to be?"

I really didn't know. I hadn't given it any thought.

"Or do you want to be a woman who is not afraid to indulge her inquisitive nature? Open it up and let it shine? It will reveal things you never thought possible. It will make you courageous and quick of mind. But it is not without its costs. It will force you to look at ugliness. It will make you struggle with puzzles with no solutions. It will show you dark things that lurk in the shadows, things you may not want to see. I have observed you, Licinia. You are clever and brave, and you have a good heart. You remind me of your mother. But you have been taught to be ignorant. You have been taught to be ashamed of the part of you that longs to look at things and understand. But you don't have to be ashamed. You have a choice."

I was skeptical. Are you saying that my aunt has misled me?"

"Pulcheria has shown you one way. There's another. That's all I'm saying."

I shook my head. "You started out by saying that my aunt was bad, that she was a threat, someone of whom Placidius is afraid. Why did you say that?"

Galla closed her eyes for a moment. When she opened them, she spoke with great earnestness. "Your aunt is a powerful woman, more powerful than you realize. She presents herself as demure and humble, but her influence reaches everywhere. The Church she pretends to venerate is actually a weapon she uses to pursue her enemies. Her brother, your father, who is a good man at heart, has been prodded and manipulated by her to undertake policies that fulfill her agenda, even though they often reflect poorly on him. Your mother, who tried to resist her, has been hounded and persecuted, driven from her home, her reputation destroyed."

I didn't want to hear this. I looked away.

"Pulcheria does not like people she cannot control. She perceives their independence as a threat. When, many years ago, she found out we had betrothed you two children, she tried to stop it. Later, when Placidius set out for Constantinople to marry you, she planted spies in his caravan to sabotage him. She did not want this marriage. She understands only too clearly that when the two of you have given to birth to a male heir, her days are numbered, her power weakened. You are a threat to her, so she is a threat to you."

"That's not true," I said under my breath.

"Placidius tried to appease her. He struck a deal with her. He gave her Illyricum and promised not to oppose her claim. In exchange she agreed not to stand in your way. Whether or not it works remains to be seen. If it were me, I would not have done it, and I counseled him against it. My letter to him, the letter you have heard so much about, was my attempt to persuade him to remain in Constantinople after the wedding. Aetius and I anticipated there would be times like these when we would need to call on the East for assistance. With Placidius on the ground there we could have made sure the help would come unencumbered. Without him there, we can never be sure. Plucheria's influence makes it too risky. Anything we ask from them will come with strings attached, if not an outright trap. Your aunt is not to be trusted, Licinia. That's why we cannot ask for help from the East."

I was stunned. It was as if the world had shifted under my feet. "But my aunt has always been kind and decent to me."

"By design. She has kept you naïve and innocent. In that she has been of one accord with your mother. But they did it for different reasons. Your mother did it to protect you. Pulcheria did it to manipulate you."

This had gone far enough. It was one thing to insult my aunt, to accuse her of wickedness, but it was another thing to cast aspersions on the Church.

"You will have to excuse me now. It is oppressively hot, and I'm not feeling well. I'm going to my room."

Galla took me by the elbow as if to steady me. "You're not faint, are you? I'm sorry if I kept you too long."

"I am all right. I just need to go."

She helped me to the door and called for the servants to escort me back to my room.

At the door I turned back to her. "I have only one question. If this is true, why didn't Placidius tell me about it?"

Galla sighed and looked down. "I'm afraid Placidius is overwhelmed. Troubles are mounting up for him, and he's afraid. Unfortunately, he does not accept the advice of others. He is reactive and argumentative. He digs in and resists, which only makes things worse for him. As a result, he is deeply unsettled. The last thing he needs is someone else telling him what to do. He wants you to remain as he found you, innocent and sweet, so you do not become another thorn in his side. All he requires from you is blind, unthinking support. He prefers you to remain ignorant."

I stood in the doorway, pondering this. She was not wrong.

She gave me a kindhearted look. "You can give your husband what he wants, but not if you are going to keep intruding into his affairs. If you mean to be silent and submissive, then be that. But if you intend to be brash and outspoken, embrace it and accept the consequences. But you cannot be both. You are a woman. You have to make a choice."

I went to my room and lay down. I was feeling dizzy and a little sick.

* * *

It wasn't as if what Galla had told me was inconceivable. I knew my aunt Pulcheria could be cold and forbidding. I had seen her that way with others, although never with me. With me she had always been patient and forbearing, if a little distant at times, as if she were listening to a far-off voice. I had always assumed it was the voice of God, but Galla was suggesting it was something else.

In any case, I wasn't about to let my aunt be maligned without giving her a chance to defend herself. I would write and tell her what Galla had said and ask for an explanation. Perhaps what Galla had perceived as cunning was actually something less nefarious. Perhaps what she had read as a plot to disrupt my marriage was nothing more than my aunt's zealous need to control every little thing. That's just the way my aunt was – a stickler for details. But it wasn't ill intentioned.

What's more, the idea that she had been trying to shape me into something bland and servile, something against my better nature, struck me as wrong. She had only wanted me to be a good Christian, to be obedient to God and to the men who held sway over me. Certainly, there was nothing sinister in that. It was decreed by the Bible and encouraged in the teachings of the great theologians whose works formed the foundations of our Church.

But try as I might I could not put Galla's words out of my head. She saw something encouraging in my outburst in the basilica, a hidden potential buried beneath years of my aunt's teachings. The most remarkable thing of all—the most unsettling—was I shared my well-intentioned inquisitiveness with my mother.

My aunt had called it "irreverence." She had thought it sacrilege and interpreted it as the impious residue of my mother's pagan upbringing, the prideful overreach of a brazen woman who thought she could rely on her own intellect rather than the Word of God. She held it responsible for the terrible sin that had brought my mother to shame, an awful crime that drove a wedge between my parents and condemned my mother to exile. This was the thing Galla recognized in me too, and it was worrying.

I had been presumptuous and spoken out in the basilica. Regardless of my good intentions, I had been wrong. I didn't want to be a woman like that. I didn't want to offend and overreach. I owed Placidius an apology. Certainly, he would understand. He had accused me of disobedience before, but had forgiven me. He knew me to be weak. He understood I was merely a woman and therefore prone to frailties. I would go to him and express my profound regret. I would explain that I had misinterpreted the intimacy with which he had shared his apprehensions as license to speak freely. I would ask his forgiveness for my impertinence, and he would give it to me. I was sure of it.

I found him strolling along the ambulatory beside the exterior wall of the palace. He was walking with his head down, his hands folded behind him, four or five eunuchs keeping their distance behind him. When I came upon him, he glanced up. His eyes were red-rimmed as if he had been crying. He looked down again.

"What do you want?" he asked.

"Are you all right?" I said, reaching for him.

He pushed my hand away.

I looked at the eunuchs in distress. They dropped their eyes. Among them was Heraclius. Of the five, only he met my gaze, but his eyes offered nothing. His expression was as blank as the gray stones of the palace.

It didn't take a scholar to realize why Placidius was so upset. Ever since his meeting with Aetius he had been struggling with a way to counter his proposal to surrender Aquitaine. He did not want to give it up. No other Emperor had ever surrendered such a large chunk of territory in exchange for peace. It would blot his record. It would make him look weak. Yet he could see no alternative. If we did not have enough troops to beat back the Vandals, Italia was doomed. Rome itself would fall. The Vandals were an existential threat. They had to be stopped.

His brash proclamation forbidding Aetius to lead the army to Africa was unsustainable. He knew Aetius had to lead the army. With Litorius dead, there was no one else who had as much experience or could command so much respect. And there was no one else who could strike as much fear into

Genseric, the Vandal king. So, Placidius had to reverse his decision, which would make him look petulant and juvenile. The only way to soften the blow would be to offer an alternative to surrendering Aquitaine to the Goths. No matter how he racked his brain, he could not think of one, so he felt embarrassed and trapped; the emotion welled up inside of him, the tears stung his eyes, and he showed me his back.

"Go away," he said. Leave me alone."

I couldn't stand to see him like this. He wanted to succeed, to make the right choice and be honored for it.

Then I had an idea, and it was out before I had a chance to reel it back. "Why not offer them a return to the status quo?" I said. "In exchange for peace, offer them a return to the way things were before."

As I said it, I realized I was offering my opinion without being asked for it – once again. But Placidius did not correct me. On the contrary, he seemed intrigued.

"Before?"

"Yes. Before they assaulted Narbo. Tell them their status will not change; they will remain hospitalitas, soldiers billeted on the land, and their aggression will be forgiven. We will not punish them. Everything will go back to the way it was before."

I could see my suggestion had struck home. He thought it over and seemed on the verge of embracing it when his eyes shifted to the eunuchs and his expression clouded. His voice became brittle.

He said, "You are too forward, Licinia. It's not your place to advise me."

I was shocked at the change. It was as if he had become a different person. I tried to explain myself, but he interrupted.

"You're an unruly woman, Licinia. Your behavior is a disgrace. Your interruption in the basilica made me look inept. I cannot have that. I'm your husband, or have you forgotten?"

I began to splutter an excuse.

"You assured me you were a good Christian," he said. "You told me you had read the books, but I see you've misled me."

This last part caught me by surprise. "Why, whatever can you mean?"

"You told me you had read them, but plainly you have not."

"But I have!"

"Silence!" he said. "Don't contradict me." Again, he looked past me, as if taking his cues from someone behind us. I began to turn around, to see who it was, but he demanded my attention. "Look at me!" he said. "Pay attention to what I'm saying."

"Yes," I said. I lowered my head.

"You do not recall the words of Origen, the great Church Father, the flawless theologian who cautioned against impropriety. He said… he said…"

A figure came forward and handed him the book he was struggling to quote from, the very book I had given him, one of those gifted to me by my aunt. The person handing it over was Heraclius.

Placidius paged through the book until he found the place he was looking for. He read:

> For it is improper for a woman to
> speak in an assembly, no matter what

> she says, even if she says admirable
> things, or even saintly things, that is
> of little consequence, since the words
> come from the mouth of a woman.

I vaguely remembered the passage, but it had not seemed terribly important at the time, and I had not committed it to memory.

He was glaring at me. "Do you mean to tell me you read this passage and didn't heed the warning in it?"

I stammered out an excuse.

"You are not a good woman," he said. "You are wicked."

I felt a sickening dismay. He was right. I had failed him. My eyes welled with tears. A single drop grew weighty and streamed down my cheek, then another, and another.

Somewhere in Placidius's expression was a hint of pity, and then Heraclius pressed another volume into his hand and opened it to the relevant passage. Placidius read.:

> Woman does not possess the image
> of God in herself but only when taken
> together with the male who is her
> head.

He looked at me. "Do you not know these words? These are the words of Augustine. Have you considered them?"

I didn't know what to say. I was stricken.

"You are prideful, Licinia. You claim great piety. You presume to instruct me. Yet you do not even read the books you champion. Either that or you willfully ignore them, choosing only the parts that suit you."

I tried to explain, but he wouldn't permit me.

"I have been lax with you. I fear my permissiveness has emboldened you. It is obnoxious in a woman. I will not have it. You must be chastised for your insolence. Turn around."

I didn't understand.

He repeated himself. "Turn around and lift up your dress."

I was stunned. "Out here in the open? In front of the servants? But I'm an Empress!"

"You're a sinner," he said. "Turn around."

I grasped at the last flimsy straw. "But I'm pregnant!"

"Now!"

Sick at heart, I turned around and started to pull up my stola. It was vulgar. It was wrong. I turned to him. "But the servants, they are men!"

"They are eunuchs. They care nothing for your nakedness. Now expose yourself so I can whip you properly."

I bent over and hiked up my dress. I felt the hot air on my buttocks. My face burned with embarrassment.

Placidius moved around behind me. He paused. Then I heard Heraclius coming up beside him. I craned around, not willing to submit to the violence of a surrogate. Heraclius was a mere servant. I was an Augusta.

"Turn back! Bend over."

I heard the whistle of the leather thong as it cut through the air. It struck my skin with a snap, and I cried out. It stung, and my tears splattered the pavement.

But who was beating me? If it was Heraclius, I would not stand for it.

The whip struck again, and the thong bit deeply into my skin. I felt blood trickle down the back of my leg. I looked between my knees and saw the legs of two people: my husband and the eunuch. My resentment boiled over. I whipped around as Placidius was rearing back to strike. Heraclius was standing beside him, watching the proceedings with clinical detachment. The others were looking on in anxious embarrassment.

The thong whistled through the air. I put up my arm to block it. The thong lashed across my face, cutting my cheek. I was roused to anger.

"Stop!"

Placidius took a step back, shocked at my impudence. Here in addition to everything else was his pregnant wife standing before him in defiance—he, a man who had had been defied by almost everyone. And now another. His face became purple with rage. He raised the thong and lunged at me. I parried the blow and ducked away. He came at me again, bringing the thong down again and again. I shrank back, cringing and cowering. He lashed and grunted with his teeth clenched. I went to my knees, feeling the slash and sting of each blow. I curled into a ball. Still, he did not stop. He stood astraddle me and kept swinging, spittle flying from his lips. There was a look in his eyes. I knew it only too well. He was becoming aroused. He touched himself through his clothes and began to lower himself on me.

"No, Placidius! Not here!"

Suddenly he stopped. He panted for breath. I could see his tumescence against his trousers.

I cradled my head and sobbed.

He stepped away. "Go to your room and don't come out until I tell you to," he said. He walked away, complaining to his servants, "Everywhere I turn I am confronted by defiance."

I heard their muttered concurrence. They left me bleeding on the pavement while they headed to the chapel to worship the God who loved them, who elevated them, even as He humbled me.

I, a woman, deserving of scorn.

# Chapter 7
Autumn, The Year AD 439 – Summer, The Year AD 440

In late November I gave birth to a girl. Placidius was gracious enough to see her, but that was about it. His disappointment was palpable. He wanted a son and heir, which he believed I had denied him by miscarrying my first pregnancy. I named her Placidia after her grandmother.

Now with two babies to occupy me I had less time to concern myself with the issues of the day. Placidius almost never spoke to me, making a determined effort to keep me apart from current events lest I make myself obnoxious. But Galla knew what was going on, and she informed me.

We would not surrender Aquitaine as the Master of Soldiers wanted but would negotiate a return to the status quo. The Goths would resume their former status as hospitalites, soldiers billeted on the land, which meant they would be required to fight on our behalf in the upcoming war against the Vandals. In exchange we agreed not to punish them for the damage they had caused in three years of conflict and struggle. In every respect this was my idea, but I did not share that with Galla, especially as she opposed it.

Aetius didn't like it either and warned that the Goths would rise again when they got the chance. But Placidius had made up his mind; the Empire would not swap territory for peace. Chafed, Aetius extracted a price. In exchange for his agreement, he demanded the right to lead the Roman army against the Vandals in Africa, something Placidius grudgingly conceded considering there was no other way; but Aetius had more. He wanted the truce with the Goths presented as a victory to the public, and he wanted a statue erected in his honor, along with a triumphal procession through the streets of Rome. It was to be a message to those who had conspired against him, the senatorial class and the Church that forced him into this distasteful situation. Aetius wanted to show them he had not been beaten, that he was still the champion of the people, and that he could call on them if needed to pressure the monied classes for the funds required to prosecute their wars.

And so, it was done. Aetius returned to Gaul to make peace with the Goths, his initial urgency exposed for what it was: a negotiating gambit intended to press Placidius to make a decision. Now Aetius was unhurried, confident, as winter set in, that he would have until late spring to assemble the kind of army he would need to fight the Vandals.

Placidius finally relaxed as well. The anxieties of the past months receded. But he kept his distance from me. What's more, he seldom came around to see his daughters. Instead, he spent his time in prayer and contemplation, poring over the words of the Church Fathers. I should have been pleased as this was what I had wanted, but it worried me that he would find something in their words to condemn me further.

After several months, my aunt replied to my letter regarding the charges Galla made against her. My aunt was straightforward. She admitted that she had been against my marriage. She worried that as Placidius's wife I would be compelled to reside in Ravenna and feared I would fall under the influence of reprobates and sinners, chief among them my mother-in-law Galla Placidia. She was surprised it had taken me so long to write. She thought Galla would have begun her mischief sooner. My aunt had contemplated warning me, but she knew my goodhearted nature would have made me dubious, so she thought it best to wait until the evidence revealed itself before making her point. Now I could see for myself; Galla was schemer. She plotted against everyone, but chief among her targets was my aunt. I read the letter with horror.

> She fears my piety. Galla is a licentious
> woman who disdains the teachings of
> God and hates the church. Watch her.
> See how she presumes to put herself
> above men. Observe how she encour-
> ages you to succumb to those parts
> of your nature that lead you into sin
> and error. She did the same to your
> mother. She encouraged her to wick-
> edness, leading her down a dark path
> that destroyed her.

This was news to me. I knew Galla and my mother had been friends, but I had never heard that Galla was in any way responsible for my mother's disgrace. I read on:

> Your poor mother was seduced and
> beguiled by Galla Placidia. I fear the
> same for you. That's why I tried to
> stop the marriage before it happened,
> but I failed. Now she is attempting to
> create a breach between us, as I knew
> she would. She wants you to doubt
> the pious instruction of your youth, to
> turn away from the teachings of God
> and embrace a life of sin and rebellion.
> Don't let her. Deny her. She is a sinner,
> and you have God on your side.

She went on to confirm that Placidius had indeed conceded Illyricum to the East, but not to appease anyone's thirst for power as Galla had contended—a claim my aunt deemed ludicrous on its face—but because Placidius understood that Galla's obsession over it was creating a rift between the two halves of the Empire and driving a wedge between them.

> Your husband wisely chose to end
> the dispute, comprehending that in
> due course it would be yours anyway.
> Galla would have preferred endless
> discord, which is not surprising, given
> the kind of creature she is.

That Placidius had given up Illyricum as a matter of common sense was something he had always maintained. Yet my aunt's letter made no mention of the value of Illyricum to the West as a vital source of revenues to fund her armies. Nor did she acknowledge the loss of those revenues might eventually weaken the West, forcing it to turn to the East for help, much in the role of a supplicant, who might be exploited. She probably believed me ignorant of such details and incapable of drawing the conclusions implied by them. Indeed, her final words seemed to underline this point.

> Galla Placidia will try to encourage you to think for yourself, to rely on your intellect and embrace your curiosity. But as a woman you can know nothing that is not given to you by your betters to know. Learning is not an ornament on a woman. It is a blemish. You must reject this error and turn to prayer.

I put the letter aside and considered it over for a moment. Then I went to the chapel and prayed as she had instructed.

* * *

Aetius returned in the early spring with his full army behind him, an army comprised of a good many Goths required by the terms of the new treaty to act as federates on our behalf. With them were the remaining soldiers from

Arelate, mostly Gauls, willing to fight for half pay, as well as a mixed bag of Hun, Burgundian, and Frank mercenaries. It was remarkable. Even those who disliked him were forced to admit that Aetius was adept at assembling a powerful army out of the ragtag remnants of other peoples' forces. Soon the army would march to Ostia and launch for Africa to confront the Vandals. But first Aetius had to receive his triumph.

The whole city of Rome turned out to cheer him, the mighty victor, the conqueror of the Goths. It was a designation that would not sit well with the thousands of Gothic soldiers in his employ. They viewed their service as a condition of the armistice brokered by a chastened Rome after a military stalemate, and not the result of an unconditional surrender forced on them by a superior foe. But Aetius went ahead with it anyway. He was intent on proving to his political enemies that he was not a man to be taken lightly. Yet even as he rode through the streets on his golden chariot pulled by a team of handsome white steeds, the laurels of victory on his brow, terrible news arrived to cast a dark shadow over the festivities.

The Vandals had struck. Not bothering to wait until Rome had finished reveling in her own unwarranted glorification, they had crossed the Mediterranean and started raiding along the coast of Sicilia. Panormos was under siege. A hush fell over the crowd as the news spread like a plague. The aristocrats and churchmen who despised Aetius for his arrogance glared at him in contempt as he mounted to the rostrum to observe the unveiling of his statue. He spoke at length, pontificating over Rome's inevitable victory while the faces of the crowd studied him in contemptuous silence. Only a smattering of applause met his wrap-up.

As he stepped down, Aetius received the news that had already blighted his audience. His face turned red, and his jaw tightened. He wasted no time in ordering his army to mobilize. They marched out of the city within the hour.

The Emperor sat on his throne beneath the colonnaded portico perched above the Forum of Trajan. The crowd gathered on the plaza below him turned their eyes to him with mingled expressions of incredulity and disgust. Their attitudes unnerved him. After a few awkward words meant to reassure them, he withdrew. He hurried from the city with his retinue in tow and returned to Ravenna to await word from the front.

The news was not good. Within a fortnight Aetius was in retreat, his army much reduced. It was the Goths. Offended at the way they had been slandered by Aetius in his remarks, they had deserted. Without them, Aetius lacked the strength to turn the Vandals back. Sicilia was lost.

A collective dread settled over Italia, the heartland of the Empire. The barbarians were on our doorstep, and we lacked the strength to stop them.

* * *

Oddly, and to our great good fortune, Genseric did not press his advantage but contented himself with plundering Sicilia. Spring turned to summer and the expected invasion never materialized. Everyone was on edge. They knew the Vandals could strike at any moment. The tension increased the public's resentment, and they spoke bitterly against the Emperor. They blamed him for the disaster. Placidius lashed out privately at Aetius for having brought him to such a pass. He was desperate to regain the good opinion of the people, no matter the cost.

Aetius remained in Rome and tried to drum up the finances to rebuild his army. He knew he could not tap the lower classes for fear of provoking a rebellion. The upper classes despised him and would resist him at every step. So, he reached out to the Church through the auspices of Pope Sixtus to locate the money he had been promised by Leo but never received. Sixtus was sympathetic and promised to do what he could, but his poor health prevented him from pursuing the matter personally. He was forced to rely on a deputy who, after two weeks, found nothing. Two weeks later Pope Sixtus died, and the idea of enlisting the Church's aid in locating the missing funds expired with him.

Pope Sixtus had been unfailing in his devotion to the royal family. His relationship with Galla went a long way back, and he stood by her in all circumstances. But with Sixtus gone, the loyalties of the clergy could not be relied on, so Aetius took a different approach. He went to the Emperor and demanded a new tax against the aristocracy. He offered to enforce the new levy with his troops.

Placidius balked. He didn't want to incur the wrath of the upper classes at a time when the lower classes despised him. He blamed Aetius for his predicament and demanded he come up with a different way to get the money they needed. Aetius had a ready answer.

"If you will not compel the aristocracy to pay their fair share, then you must take the advice of your wife and call on her parents, your cousins in Constantinople."

Placidius was taken aback. This was something new for Aetius. The Master of Soldiers had always been opposed to the idea of involving the East in the West's affairs. He had even joined Galla Placidia in urging Placidius to remain in Constantinople after our marriage as a check against Constantinople's intentions. Now he was telling Placidius to go to my father in all humility and ask for his help in repelling the Vandals.

"I won't do that," Placidius said.

Aetius responded with a knowing smile, "I'm afraid you have no choice, Imperator. It is either that or you will lose the Empire to the Vandals."

Placidius winced as if afflicted by a sudden pain. He turned away from Aetius.

"I'll consider it," he said.

* * *

I could count on one hand the number of times Placidius had come to me since the birth of our second child nine months earlier. I had sat beside him at audiences and at ceremonial functions, but he rarely acknowledged me. I had seen him around the palace, occasionally with Galla Placidia, sometimes with his other counselors, and often with Heraclius, but he had never bothered to greet me. I considered his chilliness a part of the penance I had to pay for my impertinence and accepted it unhappily, but it didn't mean I didn't love him or long to be permitted back into his good graces. I still wanted to be a good wife to him.

One day shortly after his meeting with Aetius, I was breast-feeding little Placidia in the peristylum with one-year-old Eudocia playing at my feet when he came upon us suddenly. Seeing my exposed breast, he faltered and averted his eyes.

"Cover yourself," he said.

I did so at once and smiled as sweetly as I could.

I said, "To what do I owe the pleasure of your visit, husband?"

Placidius crouched down beside little Eudocia. She was grappling with a little wooden horse on wheels, holding it in her pudgy little hands, and gnawing on it. He tenderly stroked her head.

"You must do something for me," he said. "It's important."

"Anything you wish," I said.

He kept looking at the baby. "Write to your father. Ask him to send a fleet. We need their help."

I felt a surge of joy. At last, Placidius was getting over his mistrust of my family. Now he would see there was nothing to fear. Now he would see they only wanted the best for us and would not try to take advantage. In spite of whatever twisted idea Galla Placidia had put into his head, he would see that my Aunt Pulcheria meant us no harm.

Placidius glanced up in time to see my expression "What are you grinning at?"

I didn't want to tell him what I was thinking; I didn't want him to think I was trying to advise him. "I'm not grinning," I said.

He gave me a dark look. "Are you laughing at me?"

"Never!"

He scowled. "You think you're pretty smart, don't you? Offering policy advice where it's not wanted and then gloating when you see it adopted." He got to his feet. "You're no different than the rest of them. You think I'm stupid."

"I don't think that at all," I said.

He pressed his hands to his face and dragged them down with a groan of frustration.

"This is not my fault," he said. "This is Aetius's doing. We would not be in this spot if he had done what I had wanted. I was against his stupid triumph from the start. Obnoxious self-glorification, that's what I called it. But no one would listen. They took his side against me. They said he had to be given a chance to show the senators and aristocrats who was boss. They said he had to be given a chance to rub their noses in it. Stupid. Stupid. Stupid. The Goths were not defeated. It was a negotiated peace, an armistice. But he had to don the laurels anyway, and the Goths got mad. You could see it in their faces. Naturally, they deserted at the first opportunity. It was a disgrace. If they had listened to me, none of this would have happened. But oh no! 'We cannot listen to Placidius. Placidius is inexperienced. Placidius is thin-skinned and short-tempered. Placidius is a child.' They don't respect me, Licinia. They think I'm a spoiled brat!"

Throughout this tirade his voice had been rising. Now he was practically shouting. Little Eudocia gaped in terror and began to wail. I picked her up and tried to soothe her. Then Placidia started crying. With a baby in either arm, my stola slipped, exposing my breast. He stared for a moment.

"What are you doing?" he asked.

"It slipped."

"Cover yourself."

I struggled to pull myself together. The babies squirmed. He came forward and took Eudocia from me. I covered myself.

He bounced Eudocia lightly on his knee and made cooing sounds at her. Very quickly her crying subsided, and she looked up at him in curiosity. He laughed. "Look at her," he said. "I think she likes me."

"Of course, she likes you. You're her father."

He looked at me for a long moment, and then broke into a smile. It was the first time he had favored me with a smile in months. "I need you to write to your father," he said.

"I will do whatever you ask of me."

He put the baby down. She crawled over and picked up the wooden horse and put it in her mouth. I went back to nursing Placidia beneath my robes. Placidius was deep in thought.

He said, "I opposed the idea of sending Leo to Arelate. You were there. You saw it. I didn't trust him. But my mother persuaded me, and the council backed her. They're not infallible. They're wrong more often than they're right. And Aetius… Aetius is supposed to be a genius, a military mastermind, but he's gotten us into a mess. The Empire is falling apart. Who are they to advise me? I can assemble my own team of counselors, people more in sympathy with my way of thinking."

I didn't dare say it, but I didn't think this a good idea. I smiled benignly at him and bit my tongue.

"My mother ruled the Empire for twelve years," he said. "She and Aetius. All that time I was the Emperor in name only, a child too immature to rule. But I am a child no more.

I am the Emperor now, and it's about time I start acting like one."

I said nothing.

Then he surprised me. "I'm not wrong, am I? I mean, it does make sense, doesn't it? There comes a time when a man must stand on his own."

I started to express my actual opinion but caught myself. "You can rely on my support in whatever you choose to do."

He didn't seem entirely satisfied with that and opened his mouth to say something more when I cut him off. "Let's talk about the letter to my father," I said. "What shall I write? How do you want me to frame it?"

He began to contemplate the letter and to compose it aloud. He was at pains to suggest that in exchange for the East's help the West would feel a duty to reciprocate should the East ever find itself in a similar crisis. It was a transparent attempt to communicate that neither money nor territory would be offered as payment for their services. When he was finished, I made bold to offer a suggestion.

"Why don't we go to Constantinople to make the appeal in person? I think it would help. We could bring the babies. My father would love to see them."

He looked at me like he had been insulted.

"Didn't I just tell you I intended to rule alone? Didn't I just say I wanted to free myself from Aeitus and my mother? If I leave here to go to Constantinople, what do you think will happen? Who do you think will rule while I'm gone?" He shook his head and sighed. "I asked for your view, and you evaded the question. Now it's clear what you're up to. You're trying to get me to go to Constantinople, so I'll be out of the way, so they can rule in my absence." He glowered at me. "I'm the one who took exception to Leo. I'm the one who called out Aetius's triumph as the blunder it was." He began to pace back and forth, working himself into a pique. "I pray, Licinia. I pray to God every day. I ask for His help, and He gives it to me. My decisions are sound, but no one trusts me. They keep looking to Aetius and my mother to save the Empire, and things just keep getting worse." He pointed his finger at me. "Write the letter the way I told you. Use all your persuasive efforts but offer him nothing in return. Tell him if he doesn't want to see his grandchildren carried off by barbarians, he must send help at once. We don't have to be standing in front of him for him to get that."

It was crass and ugly, putting it that way, but I was in no position to object. Placidius would read the letter when I was finished it. If I didn't write it exactly as he instructed, he would perceive it as disobedience.

"As you wish," I said.

He seemed satisfied. He picked up Eudocia and kissed her. He set her down and left me with these parting words: "You should pray, Licinia. Pray to God for guidance. He will tell you what to do. He will tell you whose side to be on."

I knew all about praying to God. I had been doing it long before I met him. He had forgotten that I was the one who had taught him.

I held up Placidia for him to kiss, but his mind was elsewhere. He walked off. The baby began to cry, and I put her to my breast. She was still hungry. To a certain extent she always would be.

* * *

Even before Pope Sixtus passed away, Galla realized what his death would mean for the imperium. An agreeable replacement would have to be found quickly. Rival clerics were already springing into action, and Galla knew only too well the danger they represented. Clergymen steeped in reactionary politics dominated the Church. The chauvinistic pugnacity of the Church Fathers considered any dissent a threat to their authority. Persecutions and oppression were routinely used to silence critics. Incitement to violence was common. The threat to civil society was real and palpable.

In this environment calm, forgiving, benevolent men like Sixtus were an exception. Finding another churchman of similar character was going to be tough, but Galla had already begun the process. Within hours of learning about the Holy Father's death she was before the Emperor with a list of names. She urged Placidius to review them without delay so he could choose one to his liking. Having done so, he was advised to contribute a substantial sum to ensure his candidate's election. This last part left Placidius cold.

The Empire was strapped for cash. It could not even afford to pay its army. To think it must devote precious resources to the Church in the form of a bribe struck Placidius as misguided. But Galla was adamant. On this score she was as passionate as I had ever seen her. If a pope were elected who did not share their agenda, it could cost them dearly. She reminded Placidius of the persecutions of Sixtus's predecessor, Pope Celestine, who had pursued heresies like a hound. He had persecuted Jews, Arians, and small, harmless sects with tenacity, sowing bigotry and hatred, creating instability and discord in a population recently riven by civil war. Only the deft political maneuvering of Galla had gotten Sixtus elected on Celestine's death and prevented bloodshed and rioting. Now they had to do the same or risk a domestic crisis that could weaken them internally at the same time they were teetering abroad.

Placidius dug in. It was the Church, he reminded her, that had absconded with the money earmarked for Aetius's army. To give it more now would be reckless. It would be rewarding bad behavior.

While Galla conceded it might look that way, there was no evidence Leo had been acting on the Church's behalf, and it was not clear where the money had gone. In all likelihood it had been returned to those members of the senatorial class who had donated it in the first place. Placidius could not assume the Church had profited from it.

Placidius was unconvinced. He told her he would examine the list and get back to her. That evening he picked a name at random, and publicly announced it the next day. He told his mother there would be no further endorsement, and there would be no payoffs to purchase support. Galla objected, but Placidius would not be moved.

A week later he faced the consequences of his actions. The assembly of bishops placed another name in nomination, a name that Placidius and his mother knew only too well: Leo. Suddenly it became clear where the money had gone. It had been given to the senatorial class to purchase the votes necessary to make Leo the pontiff. The quid pro quo was clear. In return Leo would do the aristocracy's bidding and use the power of the Church to favor them in any dispute with the Emperor over the military.

Now Placidius would have to deal with a person he neither liked nor trusted. There was no other way. Having become Pope, Leo was now effectively beyond the reach of the Emperor. Placidius could not arrest the Pope without causing a major upheaval in Church-State relations. The Emperor had to accept the new status quo.

He ranted and raved at the injustice, pacing up and down the council chamber while his counselors looked on dumbfounded and Galla sat with her head in her hands. After a while, she got up and left, appalled that things had come to such a pass.

# Chapter 8
Autumn, The Year AD 440

As summer turned to autumn the Vandal threat waned. Instead of progressing west along the coast of Sicilia to the Strait of Messina where they might have threatened the Italian mainland, they turned east into the Mediterranean and sacked Cyrnus[8] and Sardus.[9] While it was agonizing to see these Roman possessions laid waste, it was not nearly as catastrophic as it might have been had they tried to invade us.

The threat was so reduced that by late October Aetius felt secure enough to withdraw from Italia and return to Gaul where the Bagaudae insurrectionists had risen again in Armorica and were attempting to overthrow the Roman authorities there. He left the capital after assuring the Emperor he had nothing to fear from the Vandals at least until next summer, by which time the Eastern fleet would have arrived from Constantinople and provided us the reinforcements we needed.

Placidius didn't like it, but he could not reasonably demand that Aetius remain in Italia when so many other trouble

---

8  Corsica
9  Sardinia

spots demanded his attention. Aside from the Bagaudae, the Suebi were threatening in Hispania, and the Goths, having turned their back on Aetius, were an unknown quantity again in Aquitaine. As a side issue, the Huns had attacked Castra Constantias, a Roman fortress on the banks of the Danube. This was properly the concern of the Eastern Empire as it lay within the Prefecture of Illyricum, but it was nevertheless troubling as it presented a distraction for Constantinople, which otherwise was at peace.

The toll of all this weighed heavily on Placidius who could be seen moping around the palace in the company of Heraclius and the other eunuchs. The Emperor took some solace in the pleasure of the chariot races, which he attended regularly, and he could be seen at daily prayer in the chapel, but he was cold and distant when we met for dinner in the tricilinium, and he rarely spoke to me outside of formal events where my company was required. I longed to reach out to him, to offer him some comfort and support, but I was still doing penance and dared not speak to him.

If Placidius was brooding and restless, I was bored. With little to engage me, I found life in the palace tedious. Sure, I had my babies to occupy me, but they were also attended to by a flock of servants who amused and entertained them and tended to all of their needs, save breast feeding, which I jealously retained for myself in spite of the fact that I employed a wet nurse. It was one of the few pleasures I enjoyed during the long days. Otherwise, I worked on embroidery, recited poetry, and took long walks around the grounds. I occasionally went out to the stables to watch the horses as I had when Huneric was around, but without his bright, engaging conversation, it wasn't the same. Much as I hated to admit it, I missed him. Other than my immediate family, he was the only friend I had in Ravenna.

Our friendship and my role in aiding his escape remained a secret. More than a year had passed since that fateful day and nothing had happened, so it appeared it was behind me. For that, at least, I was grateful. But it did not relieve me from the grinding tedium of my day-to-day existence.

Before I married, I had learned to play the lyre, but I had not played it since coming to Ravenna. Now I took it up again. My aunt hadn't liked musical instruments. She warned me against them, regarding them as sensual indulgences that distracted from devotion to God. But my father was all for it. He loved music and encouraged me to play. Eventually he got his way. It was proof positive that he was not the pushover Galla insinuated he was.

One afternoon I sat in the atrium strumming my lyre. I delighted in the sounds coming from the strings. It was wonderfully uplifting, and I wondered why I had not returned to it earlier. It was a warm autumn day. Outside a light breeze was blowing. Leaves were falling through the opening in the ceiling and landing in the shallow decorative pool, the impluvium, in the center of the room. Our impluvium was inlaid with blue tiles that gave the water a cerulean glow, offset by a black and white floor mosaic rendered in geometrical patterns: compasses, zigzags, cuboids, and swastikas. In the center of the impluvium was a pedestal, bare now, where once had stood a statue of some pagan deity long since removed. The frescoed walls of the atrium depicted garden motifs, curling branches, and flowers. There were also renderings of the Good Shepherd, the Virgin Mary with Child, and Christ ascending.

The hard surfaces of the room lent a warm resonance to the sound of my lyre, and for a moment I was transported. I closed my eyes. When I opened them, I saw Galla standing before me. She gave me a sweet smile and gestured for me to continue. She sat down beside the pool with her legs curled under her and trailed her hand in the water, a pensive look in her eyes.

When I finished, she looked up. "That was lovely," she said. "I had no idea."

"My father says music has charms to soothe men's souls."

Galla smiled, "I thought only religion could do that."

I gave a non-committal shrug. She asked me to play something else. I plucked and strummed. Galla continued gazing down at the blue water, the orange leaves spinning slowly on its surface. When I finished, she remained in the same pensive attitude.

"Are you all right?"

She hesitated a moment. Then she said, "It's nothing really. I don't want to trouble you."

"It's no trouble," I said. But the moment I said it I regretted it. This was exactly the sort of thing I should not get involved in if I wanted to stay in my husband's good graces.

"It's the new Pope," Galla said. Then she stopped as if pondering whether to continue.

What about him?" I asked.

"He wrote a letter to the Bishop of Aquileia. I'm afraid it's starting all over again."

I was completely in the dark. "What's starting all over again?"

"The persecutions," Galla said. "He's targeting the Pelagians. I'm pretty sure it's a warning to me."

"The Pelagians?" I said trying the word on my tongue. I had heard it before, although I could not say where.

"They're a Christian sect whose beliefs have been declared heretical," Galla said. "They believe human beings are capable of choosing between good and evil without divine intervention."

"I believe that," I said.

"No, you don't," Galla said with a gentle smile. "Believe me, you don't."

I really thought I did, but I didn't argue with her.

"Regardless of what they believe, they're harmless," Galla said. "On this small matter their beliefs are unique. In every other way they're devoted acolytes and faithful followers of the Nicene Creed. For the past ten years they've been permitted to worship among us unmolested. Sixtus saw no reason to harass innocent people or create divisions in the Church, but all that is at an end now. Leo won't have it. He sent a letter to the Bishop of Aquileia warning him not to admit Pelagians into the communion unless they make a formal repudiation of their errors. Ultimately, I'm afraid this is aimed at me."

"At you?"

"It's a warning not to interfere with the Church. It's a warning to the Emperor as well. By this method the new Pope is telling us that the Church will act as it sees fit without interference from the State."

I was bemused. "Really? A letter from the Pope to a bishop over an obscure ecclesiastical matter is telling you all that?"

She recognized my skepticism. "Perhaps I should explain."

Part of me wanted her not to, yet I held my tongue. She went on. "Years ago, before Sixtus was Pope, I intruded into Church affairs—or at least that's how some saw it. To my mind it was not a Church matter but a civil one. The former Pope, a man named Celestine, was a cat's paw for the African Fathers, whose teachings have come to dominate our theology. Their dominance was achieved through persecution, declaring heretical any ideas that challenged their own. They punished through exile and excommunication. They deliberately caused bitterness and discord. We had just been through a civil war. The society was trying to heal, and here was Celestine try to drive it apart again with persecutions. I put a halt to it. Using various methods, I discouraged him from carrying out his agenda. He was not happy. He and his sponsors took note. But I managed to stay one step ahead of them, and, when Celestine died, I moved quickly to replace him with a clergyman who thought more like I did, a Pope who cared more about people than politics."

"Sixtus," I said.

"That's right. Sixtus who was an old friend of mine. He was a gentle giant with a big heart, but he had a secret. He had begun his career as a Pelagian in the days before it was declared a heresy. As he rose through the ranks, he tried to hide this from the others. But they knew. They all knew, and they lay in wait, ready to use it against him should he ever displease them. Fortunately, Sixtus was a clever man. He charted a middle course, which, while not ideal for the long term, at least kept his enemies at bay during the course of his lifetime. But now they have struck again. Leo is their agent. He means to expand the power of the Holy See, extending its authority over all those who question him, making them subservient to Rome and threatening them with excommunication if they resist. This is tyranny backed up by coercion. What's more, it's a blatant attempt to seize power for the Church at the expense of the State. Leo is a threat to us, Licinia. He is a threat to Placidius and the imperium. This letter to the Bishop of Aquileia is actually a message to us. He is telling us that if we dare to interfere with him, he will accuse us of heresy."

"But Placidius is not a heretic," I said. "He is devout. He studies the Church Fathers daily, the African Fathers. He contemplates their writings piously, as he should.

"It makes no difference. If Leo decides to point his finger at us, it will be difficult to convince anyone otherwise. Leo is the Pope. He judgments are considered infallible. Now you understand why it was so important to get another man elected, so this wouldn't happen."

"Did you tell Placidius that? I mean, before the election took place?"

"Yes. But he wouldn't listen. Now he's compounding his error by refusing to meet with Leo. He's still angry over how Leo seized the papacy and is determined to teach him a lesson. But I'm afraid he's the one who will be taught a lesson if he doesn't relent." Galla heaved a sigh and looked down at the water. "Oh, Licinia. I'm so tired of this. I've spent a lifetime trying to keep things from falling apart, and now I'm being forced to fight the same battles all over again. Play me another melody, will you? Take me away from this."

I cradled the lyre against my shoulder and prepared to pluck the strings, but I hesitated. "Can the Pope really be so venal?" I asked. "He is a man of God."

Galla trailed her hand in the water. "You saw what he did to get elected. What do you think?"

I didn't like to say what I thought. It was against God to speak ill of any bishop, much less the Pope. I began to play, but the whole time I was wondering about the Pope. If he was really so determined to discredit Galla Placidia, maybe it was she who had wandered from the true path. Maybe it was she who was trying to hide something by accusing him of duplicity. After all, her barely concealed contempt for the Church was obvious. I faltered and stopped. She glanced up.

"I don't understand something," I said. "How can the Church accuse you of heresy if you haven't done anything wrong?"

She regarded me evenly. "By supporting Sixtus I harbored a Pelagian from persecution. I protected a heretic against the Church. Then I made him the Pope. It will be enough, should they choose to come after me."

"And what about Placidius," I pursued. "He is sincerely devout. What could they possibly do to him?"

"They could destroy his mother, for one thing."

I found this unsettling, even if she seemed resigned to it. I spoke up, "You should go to Placidius. Explain everything. Tell him he must meet with the Pope."

She sighed. "He wouldn't listen to me. You know how he is. I'm afraid I would be wasting my breath."

"But what about the Empire? What about Rome?"

She gave me a sad, indulgent smile. "I have tried to do what I could for the Empire for forty-seven years. I'm tired. It's time for someone else to take over." She let eyes linger on mine for a moment, and then she looked away.

I hardly knew what to say. I didn't want any harm to come to Galla Placidia, but it was not my part to get involved. I was merely a woman, the wife of the Emperor, the mother of his children. I could not presume to advise him. I knew that much, even if I didn't know anything else. I had learned my lesson.

"Play me another tune," Galla said.

I shouldered the lyre, but just before I plucked the strings, Galla mused aloud. "Maybe if I spoke to Heraclius. Maybe if I spoke to the eunuch, he could get through to him."

The first note I played was sour.

* * *

One gray morning in November I went to collect the children from the servants, and Eudocia was gone. Alarmed, we looked for her in the rooms immediately adjoining the playroom and the garden, which lay just beyond, but she was nowhere to be found. She was nearly two years old then and had been walking for months, but this was the first time she had wandered off. The servants charged with tending her were beside themselves. We widened our search, going from room to room. Finally, I went to the Emperor's quarters and found her on her father's lap where she was being bounced on his knee and letting out shrieks of delight.

I smiled at this scene of domestic bliss, and when Placidius looked up and returned my smile a feeling of familial warmth swept over me. It gave me hope. I looked forward to putting the estrangement of the past year behind us and reestablishing our relationship. I chided him gently for his thoughtlessness in taking her without notifying the servants and knelt down beside them. I took Eudocia's little hands in mine and made baby talk to her. Placidius gently stroked her head. We smiled lovingly at each other.

It was a great relief for him, of that I had no doubt, to realize there were those who still cared for him. It was something he needed. Ever since the Pope's ascension, public opinion against him had sharpened. The shame and embarrassment caused by our failure to confront the Vandals was absorbed by every citizen as a personal affront. Illusions of Roman superiority had been shaken. The people were humiliated, and they wanted someone to blame. The aristocracy and the Church left no doubt who was responsible. From the pulpit, in homilies laced with subtle invective, the Pope and his priests denounced the Emperor and Aetius. By refusing to meet with Leo, Placidius had only added fuel to the fire. As the weeks dragged on, the criticism became more uninhibited, and members of the aristocracy began to speak out, men like Symmachus, Bassus and Petronius Maximus, esteemed members of the senatorial class whose patrons numbered in the thousands. Graffiti appeared on walls around the city disparaging the Emperor in vulgar language. Rotten fruit was hurled at the imperial litter as it passed.

Placidius wanted the Pope arrested. He wanted the senators imprisoned. His counselors cautioned him not to react. They said it could incite a rebellion. He ignored them and began to set the wheels in motion when he was checked by the council of Heraclius whose advice may or may not have been influenced by Galla Placidia. At last, the Emperor relented, but he wasn't happy about it. More than anything else he wanted the public censure against him stopped. He didn't think what had happened with the Vandals was his fault, and he resented being blamed for it.

When I came upon him with little Eudocia in his lap, he was hungry for the good opinion of anyone, so widespread was the public outcry against him. He took my hand so that we were linked together, husband to wife, and wife to child. We were a family.

He said, "I've decided. I'm going to meet with the Pope." He looked for my reaction.

I was careful to restrain the urge to offer my opinion. I gave him a non-committal smile.

"I can bring him great news which he can take to the people," he said, "news to quell their fears and lift their spirits. I've received a letter from your father. He's agreed to send a fleet. They'll be on their way by spring." He grinned. "And do you know the best part? He demands nothing in return. He's prepared to do this for you, Licinia, because you're his daughter, and for the children, because they'll be the future of the Empire."

I gleamed up at him.

"Isn't wonderful?" he asked.

"Marvelous," I said.

He leaned down and kissed me.

Relief washed over me. Was this it? Was my long penance finally at an end? Would he finally accept me, treat me as a wife, embrace me as a partner?

"I know it wasn't easy for your father," he said. "Pulcheria was against it. She tried to persuade him that they couldn't spare the resources. But your father overrode her and ordered it done anyway. That's how I knew he was on our side when he mentioned Pulcheria's resistance. I would have expected nothing less from her. She's against us. Always has been. But your father is going to help us."

"My father is the Emperor," I said.

"Pulcheria tried to convince him the Huns were a threat to them. Apparently, they're massing on the Danube border as they always do when they return from their summer hunting grounds. They're probably hoping to be recruited as mercenaries. But she wants him to believe they're contemplating an invasion, so she can hold the troops back and deny us the help we need."

"My aunt has a cautious nature."

"Your aunt is wicked."

I had no response.

"I will report the happy news to the Pope," he said. "He will report it to the people, and they will be overjoyed."

"You're a clever man, Placidius."

He seemed pleased. He bounced little Eudocia on his knee. He looked at me with a tender expression and laid his hand on my cheek. He said, "I will come to you tonight."

I told him I would look forward to it even though I was less than thrilled about the prospect of being forced again. I would have preferred to stay where I was, lingering in that sweet moment, feeling his love.

Placidius said, "Your father's letter has removed a great burden. The credit must go to you, Licina. You wrote the letter. You're a good wife. I'm proud of you."

I wanted to embrace him, to kiss him, to let him know how relieved I was to be reconciled with him. But Heraclius had suddenly appeared in the doorway. He cleared his throat and announced in his high, reedy voice that the Emperor was needed elsewhere. Placidius stood up and handed Eudocia to me.

"You're a good woman," he said. He patted my head, and then left.

After he was gone, Heraclius remained standing in the doorway, watching.

"What do you want?" I asked.

He did not grin. His eyes did not change. They were cold and black.

"Leave me alone," I said.

The baby began to cry, a strange, jagged wail. I tried to soothe her, and when I looked up, he was gone.

I felt my skin crawl. Oh, how I hated that creature.

The baby cried and cried. She could not be comforted.

* * *

When I was just ten years old, a strange incident occurred in my household that stood out to me now. I had a playmate, a boy of twelve, who had descended from a noble family. His name was Anthemius. He was a rambunctious child, always up to some mischief, but curiously endearing, with a bright smile and a nimble wit. We shared the same tutor who scolded him one minute and laughed with him the next. Anthemius had a way of winning over all those who knew him. He would do great things one day, everyone agreed.

Anthemius was named after his maternal grandfather, the legendary prefect and consul Flavius Anthemius, who had been regent for my grandfather Arcadius when he had been a boy and too young to rule. As the regent, the elder Anthemius had done marvelous things for the Empire. He had reorganized the grain supply, made peace with the Persian Empire, and built the formidable walls that made Constantinople the most indomitable city in the world. On his father's side, young Anthemius could trace his bloodline all the way back to the Emperor Julian. He was a member of both the House of Procopia and the House of Flavia, two of the most powerful gens in the aristocracy. He had an irreproachable pedigree.

One day when I went to take my lessons, young Anthemius, who had always greeted me with an impish grin and a ready jibe, was missing. When I asked where he had gone, my tutor averted his eyes to hide his tears. Anthemius had been arrested. He had been taken to the imperial dungeons and locked away.

I was appalled. I couldn't understand what a boy of twelve could possibly have done to incur such a harsh punishment. I went to ask my father for an explanation, but he was tied up in council meetings and couldn't see me. I went to my rooms and tried to sort it out. I couldn't comprehend it. I prayed. I asked God to enlighten me. But I got no satisfaction. I suppose I should have prayed for relief from my unrelenting inquisitiveness; I should have prayed to become oblivious to the facts, but instead I prayed for answers, and when I didn't get any, I decided to find things out for myself.

I went to the dungeons and, as the daughter of the Emperor, had no trouble in gaining admittance to his cell. I found Anthemius curled up on the floor and weeping. He told me he had been selected for a very special privilege. When I asked him what he was talking about, he tried to be evasive. But when I made it clear that I wasn't going to leave until I got some answers, he gave in. He confessed that he was going to be made into a eunuch.

I had been surrounded by eunuchs all my life and had never thought much of them—to me they were just sallow, humorless things with brightly colored clothes and high-pitched voices. I had never given much thought to where they came from. I assumed they were foreigners, and such was their natural condition. But now Anthemius was implying something else.

"What do you mean you are going to be *made* into a eunuch?"

The corners of his mouth drooped as he explained. He was to have his testicles removed. When he saw the look of confusion on my face, he lowered his trousers and showed me. I had never seen male genitalia before, and I drew back in horror. That men should be so different down there, so weird and freakish, made me woozy, and to think that it was to be violently cut away made me sick. Anthemius caught me by the arms and held me up. When I had recovered a little, he sat me down and explained.

His popularity had done him in. His winning personality made him a threat. Combined with his noble credentials, his charismatic appeal rubbed some people the wrong way, and they had selected him to become a eunuch. It was supposed to be a privilege.

"A privilege?"

"Well—yes. Eunuchs are given favored places in the imperial household. They are well treated and are permitted to be near power. They often become close confidants to those they serve."

I tried not to show my revulsion.

"You are getting older, Licinia. You will become a woman soon. You will no longer need nursemaids and governesses. You will need a different kind of servant. Some of them will be men, but none of them can ever look on you with desire. Eunuchs are deprived of the part of themselves that make them want to sleep with a woman. The role I am to be given is indeed a privilege. We will be closer than ever before. I am to become the keeper of your bedchamber, Licinia."

This was almost too much for my mind to absorb. This horrible thing was to be done to my friend on my behalf. It left me stunned and speechless. Anthemius was fighting back tears. His hands were trembling. His face was ashen. I told him I would not let it happen, that I would speak to my father and stop it. He fell to his knees and kissed the hem of my dress.

"I will serve you in any capacity you wish," he said through his tears, "but not this!"

I went to my father and demanded admittance. When I entered, he was surrounded by his servants, some of them eunuchs. My aunt was sitting across from him. They were playing a game of latrunculi,[10] moving the pieces around the

________________

10  A two player strategy board game popular in the Roman Empire, similar to chess.

board. The servants were standing behind them, looking over their shoulders with interest. My aunt appeared to have the upper hand in the game.

I didn't wait to be acknowledged. I plunged right in. I told them I had been to see Anthemius. Before they could interrupt, I pressed ahead. I told them I knew what they were planning to do, and I didn't like it. In my haste I mispronounced the word "castration" and my aunt corrected me. I told them I didn't want it to happen, that I had no need for another servant of my bedchamber. I insisted that I had enough servants, and I particularly did not want a eunuch. I spit out the last word in disgust.

Among the servants standing there was a eunuch new to court at the time, a slender pasty-faced fellow with rouged cheeks and a strange, empty look in his eyes. His name was Heraclius. They waited until I had finished, and then my aunt addressed me calmly. She told me that Anthemius didn't understand, to be made into a eunuch was not a punishment but a privilege. Plenty of young men aspired to it. Then she turned to Heraclius.

"Isn't that right?" she said. "Tell the princess how you came to be in my service."

Heraclius addressed me in slow, measured tones, as if he was in a trance, his high, reedy voice devoid of inflection, his cold black eyes riveted on me. He told me he had pleaded with his father to offer his services to the Emperor. He knew that doing so would bring honor and prestige to his family. His father had resisted at first, worried about the pain it would cause him, but he had pointed out that, as the youngest of five boys, his inheritance would be a pittance, and he had few other prospects. As for the pain, he was not afraid. Life was full of pain, he said. Even the best people felt pain. But only a few could have the honor of serving the royal family.

Pulcheria grinned. "So brave," she said. "And so dedicated."

But the whole scene made me sick, and I exclaimed loudly what was in my heart, repeating the words Anthemius had screamed as I left him alone in his cell waiting for the knife.

"It will make him less of a man! It will disgrace him among his peers and make him an object of scorn!" I broke down and sobbed.

My father came over and gathered me in his arms, tut-tutting me and stroking my hair. He promised he would not make Anthemius a eunuch. It was not necessary. He would find another way for my friend to serve the Empire.

My father was always so good to me. I clung to him, hitching with sobs, trying to control my emotions. I kept my face buried in his shoulder for a long time.

When I looked up again, the others were gone. The room was empty as if they had vanished into thin air. But the game board was on the floor, the pieces scattered everywhere.

* * *

Ultimately Pope Leo was the beneficiary of Placidius's buoyant frame of mind. If he came into his first meeting with the Emperor expecting a fight, the Pontiff was disappointed. Placidius was upbeat and amiable, willing to let bygones be bygones. To be sure, he still had his demands. He wanted the Pope to publicize the fact that he had won the cooperation of the East in coming to our aid, and he wanted him to use the pulpit to convince the public there was nothing more to fear and that the Vandals were no longer a threat. In exchange Placidius was prepared to look the other way regarding the misappropriated funds from Arelate.

Leo was only too happy to oblige. He would sing the Emperor's praises, and he would see to it that all his subordinates did the same. The aristocracy would come to understand the importance of the Emperor's great achievement and give him their approval. The people would be unstinting in their acclaim. But he could only answer for Rome and those bishoprics within his reach. Those outside of his authority could do as they saw fit. He could not compel them.

At this, Galla Placidia, who was present at the meeting, narrowed her eyes.

Placidius scratched his head. He was confused.

The Pope explained. There were ecclesiastical jurisdictions outside the authority of their local diocese. He could name a few, but a case in point was Mauretania, which was under the bishopric of Carthago. Carthago, however, had fallen to the Vandals. Mauretania was cut off. In reality the subordinate bishop there could preach anything he wanted. Here the Pope stopped for effect. He gave the Emperor a sad smile.

"Given the privations the bishop there has had to suffer he might be inclined to speak out against those in power for permitting it to happen."

Placidius's expression darkened.

Galla started to get out of her chair.

Leo backed her down with a smile. "I am only speaking the truth," he said. "It's nothing to get agitated about. They can be brought under control easily enough. Let me explain."

Galla eyed him with distrust.

"Everyone knows that Rome is the center of the Church, the Holy See. As the Head of the Roman Church, I can assert my authority over any upstart jurisdictions, even those beyond the pale. But I cannot do it without your permission."

"Well, then do it," Placidius said. "What's the problem?"

"Not so fast," Galla said. "Are you telling us the provincial bishoprics are a threat to us unless you are granted power over them?"

Leo gave her a pleasant smile. "There are those who will resist, who will claim they have the right to operate independently even if it threatens our unity. The Church in Mauretania, for example, isolated as it is and surrounded by Vandals, might decide to embrace Arianism. They would have an incentive to do so since that heresy has been adopted by our enemies. If they are free to operate independently, they would fear no consequences for taking such an action. It would be a tragedy if that happened. It could prefigure other such lapses in areas where the barbarians make up the majority of the diocese. But not to worry. I can prevent it from happening by asserting my authority over those bishoprics to bring them into the fold. But only with your permission."

"Do it," Placidius said. "You have my backing."

Galla shook her head in resignation.

Leo smiled. He thanked the Emperor and stood up. "When the people hear of this, they will rejoice at the name of Emperor Valentinian III! Perhaps they will even erect a statue in your honor. I'm sure the aristocracy would gladly pay for it."

Placidius blushed and pretended to wave off this naked attempt at flattery. The Pope looked at his entourage and raised his hands. The audience chamber filled with applause.

Placidius grinned.

Galla sank back in her chair, defeated.

# Chapter 9
The Year AD 441

All through the winter and the spring, Placidius was good to me. We talked and worshipped and spent time with our children. We even made love. It was as if the horrible estrangement of the past two years had never happened. Occasionally, he even asked for my opinion, but I was careful not to appear too forward in answering. I charted a middle course where I would draw him out on his views, praising those I preferred a little bit more than those that I didn't. It seemed to work.

As happy as we were, our lovemaking remained awkward and painful. I was often sore, my wrists and arms bruised from being pinned to the floor, my vagina sore from the dry pounding I was forced to endure. I prayed to God that we could find another way, something that would permit me to enjoy the act, but then I felt guilty to be praying for such a thing and begged God's forgiveness for having permitted the thought to enter my mind.

Placidius and I spent hours reading and contemplating the works of the Church Fathers. Placidius often lingered on the passages about the inferiority of women. He even once made a ludicrous attempt to read them aloud to our two-year-old daughter and her infant sister, neither of whom could be made to concentrate on them, much less absorb them.

The Church Fathers were stern men full of dire admonitions, bleak warnings about the fates of those who did not obey God, a God made angry by our stubborn refusal to live by His example. And what was that example? Asceticism, self-denial, a life of abstinence, sobriety, and frugality, or, failing that, a life endured in shame and humiliation over our inability to live up to His expectations.

Perhaps it was my unruly female mind, but I observed the hypocrisy of an institution that preached abstemiousness but wallowed in wealth, donned silken robes, sat on silver thrones, and bore vessels of gold. I wondered how such blatant extravagance could be squared with their own convictions. Why had they not offended God at least as much as some poor woman who had chosen motherhood over a life of abstinence?

But these things were beyond my comprehension. I was just a woman, and my questioning of such things was part and parcel of my feminine nature, one struck through with vanity and pride.

Because I was weak and chose to marry rather than to remain a virgin, I had one principal duty: I was to give my husband a son. Bearing daughters was insufficient—some would say detrimental—as it brought more females into the world who would themselves have to struggle with the challenges of piety and humility and all the attendant damage those could bring. The fact that I was the Augusta tasked with bearing an heir magnified my responsibility immeasurably. Yet I continued to fall short.

Although Placidius and I had laid together a number of times that spring, I did not get pregnant. He began to wonder if there were something wrong with me, so he had me examined by a physician, who poked and prodded and found nothing. The only plausible explanation for my failure to bear him a son was that I had fallen out of favor with God and must pray and do penance. I fasted and prayed and gave alms. I made repeated pilgrimages to Rome under grueling conditions. Nothing worked.

Placidius grew anxious. He grilled me about things I might have done, things I had not told him about. Certainly, I had my secrets—there was the poisoning that had nearly cost me the baby, and there was my involvement with Huneric. But I failed to see how either of those things could have made God so furious that He would deny me a son. In any case, nothing was as heinous as my having taken my husband in my mouth, and I began to believe it had to be that. Clearly, whatever suffering I had experienced had not been enough. I needed to endure more, so I began to flagellate myself with greater intensity. But whipping myself with a leather thong until my skin broke and bled was but mild chastisement compared to the punishment I was about to suffer.

It came in the summer of that year and began in Illyricum where the Huns had crossed the Danube and sacked the cities of Margus, Viminacium, and Singidunum. The ramifications of those attacks would have far-reaching consequences for my marriage and my life. Things were about to get a great deal more painful.

* * *

The Huns had always been an unknown quantity. As much as Roman leadership had, at various times, convinced itself that it had their measure, the Huns always managed to surprise. They were first and foremost a venal, grasping people forever on sale to the highest bidder, willing to compromise loyalty and honor in pursuit of personal profit. As a result, they were found on both sides of every conflict, having sold themselves as mercenaries, willing to fight each other as much as any other. They were fearsome combatants, known for their brutal savagery, torturing the wounded and desecrating corpses, raping old women, and murdering infants. Terror was their specialty, and it was widely coveted by those seeking to intimidate their enemies. Aetius had employed them in every campaign he had been on, sometimes in great numbers.

They first burst onto the scene sixty years earlier when they chased the Goths out of their ancestral homeland at the foot of the Carpathians and sent them spilling across the Danube in search of refuge in the Empire. The Goths sudden appearance within our borders in such great numbers set off a series of events culminating in the battle of Adrianople, which witnessed the death of the Emperor Valens and resulted in the ascension of my great-grandfather, Theodosius the Great.

Since then, the Huns had ranged along the Danube, passing back and forth over that porous border, at times sacking defenseless villages, at other times agreeing to a fragile peace purchased from them with cartloads of gold. In recent years they had agreed to a binding treaty giving them trading rights and an annual tribute in exchange for assurances they would direct their depredations elsewhere. Specifically, it was hoped they would attack the Persian Empire, which would relieve pressure on the Empire's eastern flank. And for the past five years it had worked, so much so that the Huns had become an afterthought in the litany of problems besetting us. In the past few years, under their leaders Attila and Bleda, the Huns seemed to have disappeared altogether and were all but forgotten. Now, suddenly, they were back.

Without provocation, they attacked the Roman trading post of Castra Constantias. The reason given was our breach of the Treaty of Margus. In a minor postscript of that treaty the Romans had agreed to give up Hunnic refugees who had fled to Constantinople to escape execution. Government officials in Constantinople had handed over at least a hundred such men, but the Huns accused them of holding out. When the Romans failed to hand over more, the Huns attacked. In retaliation my father ordered the cessation of tribute, which only provoked them further.

By that time, however, the winter had set in, and the Huns returned to their winter camps north of the frontier. All remained quiet for eight months – so long that trade resumed between the Huns and the Eastern Empire. Then came the welcome news the Huns were preparing to march east again to attack Persia. Whatever revenge they had sought for the violation of the Treaty of Margus had apparently been forgotten. In consequence, my father felt no compunction about removing large numbers of troops from the border to help fill out the army he was preparing to send west to help us against the Vandals. When the fleet finally set sail in June, the Eastern Roman Empire was at peace. There was no sense of an impending attack. But, as I said before, the Huns were an unknown quantity.

One of the reasons my father was so complacent was a long held perception by the Romans of the Huns that they were a fractious and impulsive people given to senseless outbreaks of violence that yielded short-term gains but few long-term rewards. The Huns were not like the Vandals, a well-led and cunning people capable of strategic planning. The Huns were too venal and corrupt. They lacked proper leadership. They were basically bandits, albeit on a large scale.

So, the fleet set sail in blissful ignorance and by mid-July had landed at Sicilia and handed the Vandals their first major setback. Placidius was overjoyed. The Vandals were on the defensive and Aetius had yet to join the campaign. What's more, Pope Leo had made good on his promise and praised the Emperor for having arranged an alliance with the East. Public opinion was now squarely in the Emperor's favor, and the Senate voted to erect a statue in his honor. For once, everything was going his way – until the Huns ruined everything.

They poured across the border into Illyricum, burning and looting. The feeble garrisons left behind to contain them were overrun. Within a week they surrounded Margus and put it to the torch. A few days later they razed Viminacium. Then they advanced on Singidunum, a vital military outpost containing our last line of defense. The Huns destroyed it in two days and sold its inhabitants into slavery. My father was appalled. He called the fleet back from Sicilia. Our offensive against the Vandals ground to a halt.

Placidius howled as if gouged. He ordered me to dash off a letter to my father at once, begging him to reconsider, but it was no use; our fastest couriers could not outpace the Eastern fleet, which was racing for home. Then things got worse. The Persians, seeing the Eastern Empire under attack from the north, took advantage and struck. Suddenly my father was under attack from both the east and the west.

We had to face facts. Our allies had deserted us and were not coming back. In a panic, Placidius called on Aetius to rush to Sicilia and fill in where the Eastern armies had withdrawn, but Aetius didn't have enough men. He had only assembled a large enough army to support the fleet, not to replace it. The Vandals immediately began to regain the territory they had lost. Placidius was stunned.

Within a fortnight the Vandals had regained control of Sicilia. Roused to martial anger, they seemed unlikely to remain there. An invasion of Italia appeared imminent. Seeing no other option, Galla proposed an idea that made everyone heartsick. It was the last thing any of us wanted to do, least of all Placidius.

* * *

"It's out of the question!" Placidius shouted when he heard his mother's advice. "Never!"

Galla looked in my direction, helpless.

He raked his eyes over his advisors. "Come up with something else!" he said. "Think! That's what I'm paying you for."

They blanched and looked away.

"And what about you!" He whirled to face Aetius. "You are the legendary general, the master strategist. How do you propose to get us out of this mess?"

Aetius studied the ground. He looked up. "I could offer you plenty of alternatives if we had the time, but we do not. Under the circumstances, I think your mother's solution is best."

Placidius grumbled under his breath. He paced back and forth, kneading his brow. "This is your fault, Aetius. You caused this. In so many ways, this is your doing. You're the one who settled the Huns along the Danube in the first place."

True. After using the Huns as mercenaries in earlier wars, Aetius had compensated them for their services by granting them a stretch of land along the Danube, which they used as a base of operations to make raids into Illyricum. The instability they caused helped create the current crisis.

"And it was you who allowed the Vandals to seize Sicilia by alienating our Gothic allies with your condescending performance in the forum."

Also true.

"I ought to sack you," Placidius said.

Galla looked up in alarm.

Placidius went on. "You have backed me into a corner. You have tied my hands. You think yourself smart. You think yourself superior. Yet it is you who have brought about this crisis, not me." He gave a rueful little chuckle. "But you will not accept responsibility, will you? Oh, no. Not the great Aetius who never has to answer for anything. Not the irreproachable hero of the West!" He got to his feet and shook his fist. "Someday you will answer for this, Aetius. Mark my words. Some day."

Aetius didn't flinch. He was not about to throw fuel on the fire by reacting to this provocation.

Placidius glared at him. "And you can forget about giving them my daughter. It's out of the question. Eudocia will not be betrothed to a Vandal. She is not a bargaining chip you can use to buy peace."

Galla opened her mouth to object, but Placidius silenced her with a look. "I will not reward the Vandal king for his deceit. We have tried dealing with him fairly before and look what happened. Offering Genseric another treaty in which we purchase his forbearance by rewarding him for his duplicity is out of the question. Not again. Think of something else."

"But Imperator." It was one of his advisors. "The Vandals are massing troops along the Straits of Messina. We don't possess the strength to resist them."

"I don't care! Think of something else!"

The advisors looked at each other. Aetius hung his head. Galla fixed her eyes on me. It was clear what she wanted me to do. But I couldn't. I couldn't take a stance against my husband, and I couldn't commit my three-year-old daughter to be married to some unknown Vandal nobleman, in all likelihood an adult. I dropped my eyes.

Placidius was still staring at them. With a sneer at their lack of response, he stormed out. By fits and starts, they trailed after him.

I was left alone in the room where I wrestled with my conscience. Maybe I should have spoken up. In spite of what it might have cost me, maybe I should have thought of Rome. Maybe I should have put the Empire first. But it wasn't up to me. It wasn't my role. I was a wife and mother. I would do as I was told. I would be obedient – a dreadful inconvenience at the moment.

* * *

After the tense meeting in the council chambers, I received a message from Galla inviting me to her rooms. I thought about declining but decided to go anyway. Galla was a formidable woman, but she couldn't force me to do something I didn't want to do. Were she to try, I would simply tell her that any imposition of my opinion in these matters would cause Placidius to put me aside. He would refuse to see me. He wouldn't lay with me, which meant that any hope of conceiving an heir would be lost.

But when I arrived in Galla's room, she was anything but demanding. She seemed weary and downhearted. She was lying on her couch with her feet curled up under her, staring blankly at the flickering of an oil lamp. It was dark in the room. She didn't acknowledge me at first, but when I stepped into the light, she raised her eyes with mild surprise.

"Oh, Licinia," she said. "Where is your lyre? They were supposed to tell you to bring it. I wanted a little music."

I confirmed they had neglected to ask me, but it didn't matter, I was no longer playing the instrument. I had given it up.

She raised an eyebrow. "Why is that?"

The truth was I had given it up as a part of my penance. Pleasure in music was contrary to my purpose if I was supposed to be suffering. But I didn't tell Galla that. Rather, I told her I had grown bored with it.

She watched my expression for a moment and then she patted the couch next to her and asked me to sit down. I did, facing forward with my back to her. After a moment, my eyes adjusted to the darkness, and I could make out the shapes of the figures painted on the walls. They were mostly biblical, but not all. I saw Diana, the goddess of the hunt, with a bow in one hand and a deer beside her.

"There used to be another image next to it," Galla said, "a picture of Polyphonte and the bears. Do you know the story of Polyphonte and her two sons, the boys who were half-human, half-bear?"

I knew a few pagan myths but not many. My aunt had seen to that.

"Polyphonte admired Diana for her virginity and longed to be like her," Galla said, "so she turned her back on her responsibility to marry and have children and fled to the forest to join Diana in a life of celibacy. Diana was pleased, but Venus, the goddess of fertility, took offense. She cast a spell on Polyphonte and made her fall in love with a bear who took her and left her pregnant. When Diana found out, she was furious, but not at Venus, as you may have thought, but at Polyphonte who was just the innocent victim of a jealous god. Diana expelled her from the forest, and Polyphonte returned to the home of her parents where she gave birth to twin boys, half-human, half-bear. You might have thought that Polyphonte had suffered enough for her failure to remain a virgin. But our pagan forebears had no more love for a fallen woman than our honored Church Fathers do. No, Polyphonte had to suffer more. Her sons grew into large men of great strength and bestial tendencies. They were cannibals who devoured humans. So offensive was their behavior that Jupiter decided to punish the entire family. He turned them all into flesh-eating birds. Poor Polyphonte became an owl, the ancient omen for treachery and war. For the remainder of her days, men looked upon her with fear and dread. And what was her crime? Her crime was to have failed to be a virgin."

Galla gazed at the images on the wall, a smile playing around the corner of her lips. "An image of Polyphonte and the bear used to be there. You know what the funny thing is," she said. "The picture that was painted over it is an image of the sacred virgin." She laughed.

Galla had a glass of wine on the table in front of her. She took a sip.

"There's something I've been meaning to tell you," she said. "Something you ought to know. I have had a letter from your mother. Your aunt isn't in Constantinople anymore. She's been sent away to Antioch. She's been exiled."

I nearly fell off the couch. This was mindboggling. My aunt, the Augusta, the most powerful person in the East, had been exiled! What could she possibly have done to deserve such a fate?

"Your father announced that she was being exiled for her cruel treatment of the Jews, but you may be certain that is not the real reason. Your aunt has a long history of persecuting the Jews. There is nothing new in that. Your mother says it was something else. She says it was your aunt's opposition to sending the fleet to us. When your father made the decision in spite of her objections, she began plotting against him. When your father found out about it, he acted."

This was almost too much to absorb. My head was spinning. How would my mother know anything about it? My mother was exiled herself.

"Not any longer," Galla said. "Your mother has won her way back into your father's good graces. They are reunited."

I looked at Galla with an open mouth.

"Pulcheria has fallen out of favor. At last, your father has placed the blame where it belongs. She has been exiled as she should have been long ago."

Out of reflex I came to my aunt's defense. Galla listened to my objections, and then said, "I know you love your aunt, Licinia, but it's time you understand. Pulcheria is not someone you should defend. She tried to prevent your marriage, and then she tried to stop your father from sending the fleet to save you. She pretends to love you, but she doesn't. The only thing she loves is power. You are a threat to her, you and Placidius. The birth of an heir means her days are numbered. Think about it. She would rather you had died at the hands of the Vandals than lose her grip on power."

I put my hands over my ears.

Galla watched me impassively until I removed them.

"May I speak?" she asked. "Will you listen?"

I shook my head. I had to think. I wanted to leave the room. I didn't want to hear any more.

Galla propped herself up on one elbow and waited.

I had to consider the possibility that Galla was lying. After all, she hated Pulcheria. She wanted to see her influence over me broken, so she could control me, so she could turn me into a sinner like her.

Galla called for a servant and whispered in his ear. He withdrew and returned a moment later with a piece of paper. He handed it to me. I recognized the handwriting at once. It was my mother's. There it was in my mother's hand, exactly what Galla had told me. I grew dizzy. I had to lie down.

Galla got up and invited me to recline. I lay down on my back with my head on a cushion and stared at the ceiling. There was a picture up there, an image of Christ ascending to heaven and surrounded by a dozen holy men in robes. There were no women. There were never any women except for the Virgin Mother. It occurred to me that Galla had kept the image of Diana just to have another woman on the wall.

"I want to assure you of something," Galla said. "I want to assure you it's all right to be who you are. You should never be ashamed. Being a mother is one of the most sacred things a woman can do, and anyone who tells you differently is lying."

I was confused. I didn't understand.

Galla continued. "Your aunt taught you that God favors a virgin. The books she gave you say the same thing. She wanted you unmarried and without children; she wanted it for her own reasons, and in the course of things she made you feel guilty about who you are. It's not wrong to be a mother. God does not look down on you. It's the most natural thing in the world for a woman to love a man and bear his children. You do not have to suffer for it."

I tried to tell her she was wrong, that I had never felt guilty about being a mother, but her eyes told me she didn't believe me. She said, "I've seen you in the chapel. I know you've been fasting. I've seen the blood spots through the fabric of your stola. And now the lyre. You've given up the lyre as penance. Admit it."

I confessed the truth, but insisted it was not for the reason she thought.

"Then what is it, Licinia? Why are you punishing yourself?"

I couldn't tell her. What was I to say? Should I tell her I had committed a sexual act of such shocking depravity that even the most indifferent child of God would know it for a crime worthy of punishment. I said nothing.

She heaved a sigh. "Oh, Licinia. I see such potential in you. Of all my children you are the one with the most promise. But you must stop telling yourself that you are less than you are. You must stop accepting the lies Pulcheria has put into your head."

I didn't know what to say. I didn't hate my aunt, no matter how Galla tried to frame it. And I had no desire to be anything more than a mother and a wife. But there was one thing I knew for sure, I wanted this conversation to end, so I sat up.

"I have to go now."

Galla looked disappointed. "Before you go, let me ask you something."

I told her I was listening.

"The eunuch Heraclius, I have to rely on him to get my message through to Placidius, to persuade him to do what is right and save us from the Vandals. But there is something strange about him, something—off. Do you feel the same way?"

It was a trap. She was trying to get me to admit my distrust of Heraclius so she could appeal to me to help her. "Not really," I said. "He seems harmless."

Her expression went blank. She sat down on the edge of the couch and resumed gazing at the flickering lamp.

I started to go.

"Licinia," she said. Her voice was strangely hollow.

"Yes?"

"I'm thinking about bringing Justa back. She is my daughter. I miss her."

I reminded her how Placidius might react.

Her expression was dark. "Things are not going well, you know. The danger we face is real. If Placidius cannot be persuaded to do what is necessary, I will have to consider other options."

Other options? She couldn't possibly be suggesting removing Placidius in favor of Justa. Nothing could be bad enough for that. I looked at her in disbelief.

Galla never took her eyes from the flame. "Aetius always said, 'If you can't get help from the friends you have, you have to make new friends.'" She looked up at me standing in the doorway. "I consider you a friend, Licinia."

Her meaning was not lost on me. If I didn't do something to help her, she would consider throwing Placidius aside for Justa.

From that day forward, I saw Galla in a new way.

* * *

I went to my room and sat in the light of the oil lamp. I wrote two letters, one to my father, and one to my aunt Pulcheria. While I was writing I heard a stirring at the nursery door and looked up to see baby Placidia, nearly two-years-old now, toddling toward me. She rubbed her eyes with balled up fists. She was learning to talk and had begun to string words together in pairs.

"Mama sing."

I had always sung to the girls at bedtime, and they liked it. Placidia climbed up into my lap and nestled her head against my breast.

"Mama sing."

I began to sing, and she dozed off at once. When I looked down at her, my heart felt like it would burst with love for her. I picked her up and carried her back to bed. She stirred.

"Ire."

I didn't understand.

"Ire!" It was not a request.

Then I understood. Placidia had trouble pronouncing the letter L. She was asking for the lyre.

"No," I said. "It's time for you to go to bed. Mama will sing to you."

But Placidia was stubborn like her father. "Ire," she said again. There was a whine in her voice. "Ire."

It was a small thing. The lyre was propped against the wall. I could pick it up and pluck out a tune and she would fall asleep. But I had given it up, denied myself its pleasures, made myself feel its absence. To take it up now would violate my penance.

"Ire!" She was agitated.

"No, Placidia. You go to sleep now. Mama will sing to you again."

Now the tears started. "Ire!"

Eudocia woke up and looked around in consternation. She too began to cry. Suddenly I was in the midst of a full-fledged uproar. The nurses came and offered to take Placidia from me, but she shrank from their outstretched hands and buried her head against my chest. Eudocia scrambled from bed and clung to my legs. The nurses were at a loss.

I raised a hand. I told them it was okay. I asked them to bring me my lyre. As soon as they did, the girls began to settle down.

We put them in their beds, and I began to play. They were asleep before I finished the song. One of the nurses offered to take the lyre from me, but I refused. I would hold it a little longer, I told her. The nurses returned to their rooms. I slowly plucked the strings and watched the sleeping faces of my children in the dim glow of the oil lamp.

Then I put the instrument aside and went back to my writing.

* * *

For reasons unknown, the Vandals did not attack. They remained mustered on the Sicilian coast, their ships at the ready, poised to cross, but they did not move. Weeks went by and then months. The waiting was awful. Preparations were made to meet the onslaught, barriers erected, soldiers dug in. Aetius transferred as many of his troops as he could from other hot spots, but he knew it wouldn't be enough. If something was not done to buy the Vandals off, the homeland would be invaded, and Rome would be sacked for the second time in thirty years.

The Emperor's newly acquired popularity vanished like a vapor on the wind. As before, voices could be heard speaking out against him. Graffiti appeared on the city's walls denouncing him in the most vulgar terms. Placidius summoned the Pope and demanded to know what was being done.

Pope Leo was unperturbed. He was smiling. He explained there was only so much that could be accomplished with sermons and homilies. The people were like cats and apt to hiss at sudden shocks. Calming them would take more than soothing words; they would have to know that a firm hand was in charge, that their world was not about to be destroyed. He pointed to the example of Mauretania. The people there had been terrified after the Vandals had seized Carthago and the diocese cut off.

"They didn't know what would become of them," he said. "They began to quarrel among themselves, to point fingers at each another, even to speak ill of you, your Excellency. But you quelled their fears. You permitted the Holy See to extend its authority over them, and they were mollified. In times of upheaval, it is comforting to know that there's a higher authority who will protect you."

A frown puckered Placidius's brow. "Your point?"

"A consolation, a way to reassure the people, to show them that even though the state may be under threat, the foundation of their spiritual existence is firm. Augustine said it best when he counseled us not to fret over the City of Man, but to devote ourselves to the City of God. You must show them the Church is strong and reliable. They will thank you for it. These negative opinions, though they may not be completely quieted, will be offset by more favorable sentiments." The Pope smiled.

Placidius eyed him distrustfully. "Specifics, please. Come to the point."

"Campania and Picenum," the Pope said. "They are errant. Their bishops defy the precepts of Rome. They are arrogant. They believe themselves beyond her reach. They think themselves independent. But they are mistaken, are they not? As you know, Your Excellency, papal authority is descended from St. Peter. Only the papal throne lies in the direct line of succession from Jesus through Peter to me. To declare otherwise is to err, which demands correction. They must acknowledge the Holy See as superior. Dissent in times like these can be dangerous. We must not have division. Unity is essential. Wouldn't you agree?"

Placidius chewed his lip. "And if I endorse your proposal, the people will be placated?"

"They hunger for stability," the Pope said. "That's why they are apt to flare up. By doing this, you will provide a measure of peace. They will thank you for it."

"Go ahead then," Placidius said.

"And Tuscany," Leo said. "Tuscany errs and must be brought to heel as well."

"Fine," Placidius said. "Tuscany as well. But I want this slander against me stopped. Do you understand?"

Pope Leo inclined his head. "You shall have it."

Of course, there was nothing to it. Placidius was grasping at straws, and the Pope was using the opportunity to grab more power for himself. Nothing was going to stop the outcry against Placidius as long as the Vandal threat hung over everyone's head. His counselors pleaded with him to offer the Vandals terms, but he would not. He demanded they come up with something else. They turned up their hands.

It was around then I received a reply from my father. It was just as Galla had reported. My aunt Pulcheria had committed treason.

All my illusions were shattered. She was not the simple pious woman she pretended to be, but a treacherous schemer bent on grabbing power. And if this were true, then likely everything else Galla had told me was also true. I didn't want to believe it, but it was right there in front of me. I knew my father's handwriting well enough.

It was devastating—but more so for my father. He had always trusted his older sister. As a young man he had looked up to her and followed her advice, and his deference to her had carried over to his time on the throne. Pulcheria was his closest counselor. She helped shape his policies. It was not too much to say that they ruled in tandem. Yet for all the power he had granted her, it was never enough. In the matter of sending the fleet west she had opposed him, and when he had ordered it done in spite of her objections, she had conspired against him. She left him no choice but to make an example of her, and it broke his heart.

He wrote:

> It is a cruel thing when someone close
> to you betrays you. If those we depend
> on for love and guidance cannot be
> trusted, then who can we trust...

> ...My deepest regret is the pain I have
> caused you for my failure to see her
> for what she is. Because of her, your

mother was separated from you and driven from home, and, as a result, Pulcheria was free to raise you in any way she saw fit. I fear she tried to suppress your natural spirit—a trait you inherited from your mother—and steer you into a life of self-denial. Worse yet, she tried to make you choose abstinence over marriage, which would have served her purposes well, but would have left you childless and unhappy. Thank God she did not succeed. The Empire needs an heir, and you are the one to provide it...

...As rulers we are surrounded by sycophants and schemers. Vigilance is required. But vigilance takes effort. For that reason, when we are alone with family, we are finally free to relax and let our guard down. It is our only respite. Sadly, your aunt took advantage and betrayed us. Always be honest and true, Licinia. Don't be like her. Don't hide your true feelings. Always be yourself. Your family requires it of you. Your people require it of you. Rome requires it of you.

I waited a month for my aunt's reply. I wanted to give her a chance to respond to the allegations against her. She didn't.

As a result, I decided it was wrong of me to withhold my opinion from Placidius. I owed it to him to tell him what I thought, no matter the cost. The fate of the Empire hung in the balance. I would speak to him about the Vandals. I would urge him to take his counselors' advice. It was the only reasonable choice. Surely, he could see that.

He only needed someone he could trust to tell him the truth.

# Chapter 10
## The Year AD 442

When I entered the triclinium for dinner, Placidius was already there. He was reclining on his couch, twisting a piece of yarn in his hand. Several of his eunuchs, heads bowed and motionless, formed a semi-circle behind him. Heraclius stood in the middle. They all wore brightly colored silk robes, each of a different color, orange, green, yellow, and blue, high conical caps, and shoes curled at the toes. As I came in, they didn't stir. Placidius glanced at me and held up the piece of yarn.

"Look," he said. "It came out of my tunic. My clothing is falling apart—like everything else."

I gave him a sympathetic nod, came forward, and stroked his cheek like a mother to an anguished child. He took hold of my wrist and held it for a moment. He looked at me, then kissed the back of my hand and released me.

I sat down on my couch. One of the eunuchs detached himself from the others, went to the door, and came back with a platter of oysters. He offered it to me. I selected one and slurped it out of its shell. Placidius ignored the platter and continued to wind the yarn around his finger. After a moment, the eunuch with the platter moved on.

Placidius said, "I remember the first time I saw you, Licinia. I was so pleased. You were so pretty. Later, when we dined together for the first time, I saw how poised you were. I thought you were going to be a great asset, a pillar I could lean on. I thought you would calm me. God knows I hoped so. You know how I get sometimes."

I maintained my equanimity. "What's the matter? Do I not calm you?"

He remained silent for a moment. He fiddled with the yarn. "Licinia," he asked, "do you believe God is angry with me?"

The question caught me off guard. "Of course not," I said. "Do you think God is angry with you?"

He sighed. "I pray and pray but nothing changes, nothings gets better."

"You need to be patient, Placidius. God will answer you in His time."

He gave me a beleaguered look and went on playing with the string.

"On the other hand," I said, "God will not think ill of you if you help things along a little."

"What do you mean?" Placidius asked.

A second eunuch came around with a bowl of eggs. I took one, cracked it open, and spooned its contents into my mouth. I was still swallowing when I noticed Placidius watching me.

I gulped and answered. "I should probably not say. You will think it impertinent of me."

"And yet the thought is in your head," he said. "You might as well say it if you have gone to the trouble of formulating it."

The eunuch bowed before him and offered the bowl of eggs. Placidius took one and cracked it open.

"Well, I was just thinking," I said, "that it might accrue to your benefit to take the advice of your counselors."

He spooned the contents of the egg into his mouth. "In what regard?" he asked. His mouth was full.

"With regard to the Vandals."

He selected another egg. Again, he spoke with his mouth full. "You think I should recognize Vandal sovereignty in Carthago in exchange for their withdrawal from Sicilia."

"And the ceasing of hostilities," I said.

He nodded, swallowed, and waved the servant away. "And you think this will persuade God to answer my prayers?"

"I think it will bring peace, which will restore the good opinion of the people and give you the breathing space you need to devise a new way of dealing with your enemies."

"You want me to surrender Africa."

"Temporarily. Until you can devise a new strategy for winning it back."

He pondered my comments while he studied mosaic floor. It featured an image of the three Fates seated before their looms, a pagan image I had never particularly liked.

Another eunuch lowered a dish of splayed hare with pears and quince. I took it onto the couch before me and began to pull the meat from the bones.

"And you would give them our daughter," he said. "You would give them Eudocia as a surety."

I framed my answer with caution. "I would promise them the hand of our grown-up daughter in marriage if they do not offend the peace in the meantime. Her betrothal will be a promise in exchange for the performance of a duty, which is to keep the peace. In any case, she remains with us until she is grown up, another fifteen years. Then she will be sent to them to be married."

"So, you would marry her to him," he said. He considered the dish of hare. "You would marry her to that young villain who agreed to remain in our custody and be a warranty against the treachery of his father, but who ran away like a coward and deprived us of what was rightfully ours."

The name caught in my throat. "Huneric?"

He nodded.

It had never occurred to me that Huneric would be the Vandal chosen to marry Eudocia. He was fifteen years her senior. But it made sense. Eudocia was the daughter the Emperor. Huneric was the son of the Vandal king. Their union would do more to guarantee the peace than a stack of treaties.

Placidius found the whole idea distasteful, albeit for all the wrong reasons. I sought to placate him.

"Yes, he fled," I said. "He feared for his life. It should not surprise us that a man would run for his life."

"He owed us a duty," Placidius said again. He gnawed the meat from the bone. "He should not be rewarded for his treachery."

"Don't think of it as rewarding him," I said. "Think of it as buying time. If you do this, you will secure the peace for the foreseeable future. Genseric won't dare attack if it means losing an opportunity to marry his son into the imperial family."

"He attacked us once before when it meant he might lose his son altogether. Make no mistake, he will do it again if it suits his purposes."

"He wanted Carthago. He already possessed Africa, but he could not secure it without Carthago. Now he has Carthago. All you have to do is betroth Eudocia to Huneric, and our problems are at an end. The Vandals will withdraw from Sicilia, and the people will praise you for your wisdom and discretion."

He ate his hare in silence. He did not touch the quince and peaches. He finished chewing before he spoke again.

"What I want to know," he said at length, "is why these things keep happening to me. I strive to do the right thing. I pray to God for guidance, and I try to do what He wants from me, yet I am continually frustrated. I don't want to give up territory for peace. No emperor has ever had to give up territory for peace. Yet I'm expected to do it, and if I object, I'm called childish and stubborn. God is angry with me. I'm sure of it."

"That's not true," I said.

"I did some things in my youth, he said, "some things I'm ashamed of. I killed a man. I tortured him to death. It should never have happened. It was an accident, really. Sometimes at night I still dwell on it. Do you think God is punishing me for that?"

"I don't think so."

"Maybe I have not prayed enough. Maybe I have not humbled myself sufficiently."

"You are a good man at heart, Placidius. Anyone in your position would have similar difficulties."

"Even Aetius? Even my mother?"

"Even them."

He brooded for a moment. "So, you think I should agree to the treaty?"

I took a moment to deliver my response. It was important to get this right. Another eunuch was standing before me, holding out a platter of fruits and pastries. I began to reach for one when I noticed it was Heraclius. This was against protocol. He was the chamberlain. He should not have been serving me. He was above such things. Yet, there he was.

I took a pastry.

"Yes," I said. "I think you should agree to the treaty. I think it will reflect favorably on you."

Heraclius narrowed his eyes at me. Or maybe I imagined it. He offered the tray to Placidius.

Placidius mused aloud. "Augustine was wayward in his youth. He was guilty of sin. Yet God forgave him. Why do you suppose that was, Licinia?"

"He reformed," I answered.

Placidius took a pastry. "It was a matter of sacrifice," he said. "Augustine surrendered his appetites to win the favor of God. A man must be willing to surrender things, Licinia, if he expects to earn God's grace."

"I think you have surrendered enough," I said.

He put the pastry down. Now, he was staring at me. "Do you, Licinia? Do you really?" There was a strange edge to his voice, and he looked unconvinced.

I stopped chewing and looked at him. For the life of me, I could not figure out what he was getting at.

* * *

A few days later to everyone's amazement word arrived that the Vandals had agreed to our terms. They would surrender Sicilia, Mauretania, and their conquests in the Mediterranean and pay an annual tribute to the imperial government in exchange for formal recognition of their sovereignty over Africa including the vital seaport of Carthago. The only thing remaining to be affirmed was the betrothal of three-year-old Eudocia to the eighteen-year-old son of the Vandal king, Huneric. With the Emperor's permission, the deal would be finalized.

Much as I cringed at the thought of promising my daughter to anyone, I was glad it was Huneric, a good and decent person who would not harm her. Taken altogether, I was pleased that Placidius had taken my advice and gone forward with the treaty. I went to congratulate him, but as I approached the audience chamber where he was in conference with his counselors, I had a rude awakening.

The Emperor's tirade could be heard ringing in the corridor as I approached. The target of his wrath was his mother who was struggling to get a word in edgewise. It was obvious what this was about. Placidius had not offered the Vandals terms. Somebody else had, probably Aetius, and without his consent. He was apoplectic.

As I drew closer, Galla Placidia was expelled from the Emperor's presence. She appeared in the doorway, her expression equal parts anxiety and despair. She tried one last time to appeal to him, but he cut her off and thundered for her to leave.

She passed me with an apologetic frown and a tinge of anguished pleading in her eyes as if I were the only one who could save the situation.

Placidius was still raging when I rounded the corner. His counselors were getting the full brunt of his it. He was accusing them of all manner of conspiracy and duplicity. Only Heraclius avoided his ire. The eunuch stood apart, impassive. When I came into the room, Placidius turned to me.

"Ah, here she is. Now all my betrayers have come."

"I did not betray you. I had no part in this."

"No part! Wasn't it you who persuaded me to accept the treaty? Wasn't it you who came offering your unsolicited advice—again!"

"I gave you my opinion," I said. "I knew nothing of any outreach to the Vandals without your consent."

He quoted Gregory of Nazianzus. "Fierce is the dragon and cunning the asp; but women have the malice of both."

My face stayed passive.

"Of course, you have your own reasons for deceiving me, don't you?" he asked. "You have your own agenda."

"I don't know what you're talking about."

He threw back his head and laughed. "Ha! Your expression betrays you. Guilt is written all over your face. You were cheating on me! You and Huneric! That's why you helped him escape!"

The color drained from my face. I struggled to get my words out.

"Oh, vile woman. Oh, serpent's disciple. You would surrender my daughter to this sneering rogue so you can be closer to him."

I was so stunned I couldn't speak.

"Get away from me," he said, "before I kill you."

I turned away but as I did so I cast a glance at Heraclius who was watching me with a devilish glint in his eye. A feeling of such abhorrence came over me that I might have flown at him had he been within reach. As it was, I was so shaken I had to get out of there before I did something I would regret.

This was not like me. I was not the sort of person who hated. I was good-natured and sweet. I did not wish anyone ill. But somehow Heraclius would have to pay for his treachery, or I would risk more of the same.

*  *  *

If my estrangement from Placidius was bitter before, it was ten times worse now. He refused to see me, and for a time he even restricted me from joining him at formal functions and ceremonial events. I was totally cut off from anything to do with the court. But what really broke my heart was the way he treated our children. He stopped coming to see them, and when their nurses asked if they could bring them to him, he declined. It was as if he was blaming them for my failings. The poor children wondered aloud what had become of him. They asked if he had gone and when he would come back. I had to tell them he was sick, and that when he got better, he would come and see them again. It hurt me to have to tell them a lie. It made me angry.

Part of my anger was directed at Galla Placidia. She and Aetius had gone behind the Emperor's back to negotiate a treaty with the Vandals. I understood the urgency of the situation and realized what it would have meant had Placidius continued to delay, but at the same time I thought the way they had forced his hand was insensitive, cruel, and embarrassing.

In the end, Placidius approved the treaty. He had little choice. Carthago was formally recognized as Vandal territory, along with the rest of the province of Africa Proconsularis and large swaths of Numidia, Byzacena and Tripolitania. Rome retained Mauretania, and the Vandals withdrew from Sicilia. As part of the deal, the Vandals agreed to pay an annual surety in gold to the imperial treasury for the duration of Placidius's time on the throne. The agreement provided some much needed revenue and affirmed the Emperor's importance to the maintenance of the peace, a nice touch meant to mollify Placidius even though it shackled him to the deal. Yet the Emperor remained stubbornly resistant about the betrothal of Eudocia to Huneric. He wanted to send the message that he could not be coerced, but he only hurt himself by his re-fusal. The betrothal was the cement designed to hold the deal together. Without it, the Vandal threat remained, regardless of all the Emperor had surrendered.

I went to see Galla to express my dismay. She had been banished from court and retreated to the sprawling imperial villa outside Rome where she had grown up. Whether she would be permitted to remain there or would be exiled from the country altogether remained an open question. I was led through the atrium past the formal gardens to the bathhouse where I found Galla immersed in the caldarium, the hot water bath heated by a roaring furnace, the flames of which were vis-ible in the room beyond where slaves labored shoveling fuel into the fire. Steam rose from the surface of the water. She was leaning back with her arms outstretched against the edges of the pool. Her legs wagged slowly in the water. She was nude.

"Hello, Licinia," she said.

I asked for a stool. One was set on the mosaic tiles beside the water. I sat with my elbows on my knees.

"He's freezing me out again," I said. "He refuses to see me. It's worse than before. He even refuses to see the children."

"How petty," she said. "It's just like him. He pushes everyone away. Banishment, expulsion, exile. Those who have not been ejected have run away as if from a contagion. Aetius has gone north to fight the Burgundians more out of convenience than necessity. Placidius is now alone and without reliable council. It's not good."

She was immersed to the neck, her face flushed from the heat, her dark eyes unfocused.

"But you knew this would happen. You knew how he would react."

"The Empire was threatened. It was necessary."

"He could've been reasoned with."

"Do you think so? You tried to advise him. What happened?"

I had no response.

Galla shook her head. "He only wants to hear from those who agree with him. He must know he is right. It's the most important thing in the world to him, to be validated, to be stroked and cajoled. He's the most easily manipulated creature in the world."

"Oh, Galla," I said.

"It's always difficult to hear harsh things about the ones we love. Our natural instinct is to protect them. It's so much more difficult to accept the truth. Look, I've had to face some hard truths about my son just as you've had to face some hard truths about your aunt. But we do ourselves no favors by pretending ignorance."

Galla called for the servant to add some cold water to the bath. He poured the water from a silver pitcher. Steam rose and swirled, a temporary veil.

"I want you to know, I appreciate your attempt to reason with him. I know how hard it was for you, and I know what it cost you. It means a lot that you were willing to make the sacrifice."

"I tried to be as delicate as possible. His emotions are raw. He feels like he has been challenged and undermined at every turn. He believes nobody trusts him."

"He ingests a steady diet of fear and suspicion. Those books he reads by the African Fathers pervert the lessons of Christ and talk incessantly of heresies and conspiracies as if threats lurk around every corner—as if disagreement is the same thing as disloyalty and nuance is a trick designed by intellectuals to steal an advantage."

"I gave him those books."

"I know you did, and they were given to you by Pulcheria."

I had no answer.

"It would have been better if he had been introduced to the Gospel, to the example of Christ, which, if read openly without interference, is clearly a lesson of sacrifice, of surrendering oneself for the betterment of others. Sadly, Placidius is incapable of such a sacrifice. He has been taught to put the Empire first, but he has gotten it turned inside out. He wants what is good for the Empire, but only so far as it is good for him. If it costs him anything personally, he has no use for it. Unfortunately, he is not the first emperor to believe that what is best for him is best for the Empire, but if he is not careful, he may be the last."

She paused for a moment.

"We went around his back to make peace," she said. "We knew it might result in our banishment, or worst, but it was necessary. Time was running out. The Vandals would have struck. We were willing to make the sacrifice, to risk everything to avoid a terrible calamity. We knew what it would cost us, but we did it anyway, just as you knew what you were risking when you dared to advise him. So now we are all pushed away. But the Empire is safe, for the time being until another crisis confronts us, and we must decide again."

Steam wreathed her face. "It's a depressing state of affairs, always waiting to see what Placidius will do next, and then having to rush in to prevent disaster." She looked profoundly sad. "I never wanted this for Rome," she said. "I did everything I could do to prevent it. I knew what my son was like. I could see the danger. So, I wrote him a long letter. I wanted to get it just right. I tried to advise him, to give him the benefit of my experience. I believed he could overcome his shortcomings. But I was wrong. He is just the boy he has always been, stubborn and prickly, given to rash decisions. If this goes on much longer, I'm afraid we will lose everything."

Her eyes drilled into me, demanding a response, and the question they were asking me required my complicity. I wanted to shrink from her gaze. I looked at the opposite wall.

"A sacrifice is necessary," she said. "Something bitter and difficult. I would do it myself, but I'm too old. This requires a young person, someone resilient and strong, someone with courage and determination, a person unafraid to see things as they are."

A part of me wanted to know what she was asking, but another part of me was against it, for once I knew—once I knew it specifically—I would either have to report it to Placidius or become a party to it. I put my hands over my ears and shut my eyes.

"Don't say another word," I said.

I didn't have to see her face to know she was disappointed in me. I heard a long ragged sigh. Then the water stirred. She emerged from the pool and a servant came forward to dry her. Then I heard a voice that made me stiffen with anxiety. My eyes snapped open.

Justa was standing behind her, drying her with a towel. She smirked at my surprise. "Go ahead and put your hands back over your eyes," she said. "It suits you."

I glared at her. "You should not be here. You're supposed to be exiled."

Justa continued rubbing her mother with the towel. "As you're learning, Licinia, things are not always as they appear. Besides, my exile was relegatio, which means voluntary and temporary, like your mother's and your aunt's, not permanent like a common criminal's. I was free to come back any time I wanted."

"With the permission of the proper people," Galla said.

"Which you have graciously granted," Justa said. She spoke directly into her mother's ear. Galla brushed her away with the flip of her hand. Justa giggled.

"Bring me my robe," Galla demanded.

"As you wish, Excellency."

The robe was in an adjoining room and Justa went to get it.

I turned on Galla in anger. "You can't do this. This is madness."

"He has left me no choice. The Empire is at risk. We have to consider the alternatives."

"But her? You must be out of your mind."

"Great men have gone to desperate measures to keep our family in power. As the oldest living inheritor of that power, it falls to me to keep the Theodosian dynasty alive. With Placidius behaving the way he is, and no male heir on the horizon, my hand is forced. It's not ideal, but what choice do I have? You tell me, Licinia. What choice do I have?"

Justa was coming back with the robe.

I came up close to Galla and whispered in her ear. "I will have a son. I will give you an heir. Anything but this."

Galla gave me a resigned look. "Very well. I'll give you a little more time. But if we don't have an heir soon, we'll have to think of something else."

"Think of what else?" Justa asked draping the robe over her mother's shoulders.

"Think of a way of persuading Placidius to forgive Aetius."

Galla dissembled with ease.

"Ha! Good luck with that," Justa said.

I left the baths shaken, not only for the effortless way I had been drawn into their conspiracy, but also for the terrible thing that had been left unsaid. Once an heir was born, what would become of Placidius, my husband and Galla's son? What would become of the Emperor once his offspring made him expendable?

* * *

At first, I felt compelled to tell Placidius, not only because it was my duty as a wife, but also because the idea of Justa taking over was incomprehensible. She was glib, heartless, and without a conscience. She had conspired to prevent our marriage, made a mockery of me in front of the Pope, and poisoned me in an attempt to make me miscarry. Leaving aside what she might do to the Empire; she was a threat to my safety. This could not be allowed to happen.

On the other hand, I had to be cautious. I had to consider how Placidius would react if he learned they were plotting against him. Having banished them, his reaction this time would necessarily be more severe. They would have to be whipped or worse. He might even kill them. And if he did that, how would Aetius react?

No one had ever told me with certainty that Justa was Aetius's daughter. Certainly, Galla had never confessed it, but Placidius's behavior told me he took it as a fact. As brother and sister, they didn't look alike, and, while they were both thin-skinned and spiteful, Justa possessed a malevolent streak, which Placidius, for all his faults, lacked. It seemed plain to me they had been sired by different fathers. Justa's cynical, calculating nature seemed to have its antecedent in Aetius's devious ways. Were Placidius to hurt her, Aetius would likely hit back; and if an attack on his daughter were not enough to make him act, a threat to the life of Galla Placidia would spur him to action. I had to consider that the threat I was hoping to avert by betraying them might provoke the very crisis I was trying to prevent. It appeared the only way out was to do what was expected of me and provide an heir. But how? I had no reason not to take Galla at her word. I had no reason to believe she wouldn't give me another chance as she had said. But how long she would forbear was anyone's guess. If another crisis threatened, her patience might run out, so I had to get pregnant, and fast.

But Placidius would not see me. Repeated attempts to reconcile with him were rejected. Notes pleading for forgiveness and hinting at something special should he relent went unanswered. I was beginning to despair, so I went to the chapel to pray. The chapel on the palace grounds at Ravenna was approached through a ring of formal gardens and down a slope across a close-cropped lawn, bright green after a late spring shower. A stone path wound its way to the chapel's arched door. Sheep grazed on either side. A pair of egrets alighted farther on.

As I approached the building, the door swung open and Placidius emerged followed by his eunuchs. They started down the path toward me; I stood in place to greet them. Placidius saw me but swept past. It was a cruel snub. I had done nothing to deserve such treatment, and I fought the urge to object.

But then Placidius stopped and seemed to vacillate. Changing his mind, he turned back. "I have some news that might interest you," he said. "It seems your father has run into some trouble in Illyricum. The city of Naissus has been sacked. The citizenry fought gamely under siege, but the Huns scaled the walls, broke down the gates, and slaughtered them. Attila and Bleda have taken Hun warcraft to a whole new level. Now they've mastered siege technology. Walled cities can no longer resist them. I'm afraid it's a black day for your father.

What the Huns did at Naissus, they can do to other cities in Illyricum." He smiled and shook his head. "It's a good thing Illyricum is theirs and not ours. Otherwise, the Huns would be coming for us."

The news went through me like an arrow, and the sneering way he delivered it got under my skin. My country was being threatened. My people were at risk. How could he take satisfaction in my misfortune? I had to bite my tongue to keep from lashing out.

He went on in his smug way. "Nobody wanted me to do it. Oh, how they howled. 'Placidius is giving away Illyricum!' they cried. 'Placidius is such a fool!' But it turns out I was right. Illyricum has turned out to be a Trojan horse, a pastry full of poison, and now the East is suffering the consequences." He gave a little laugh. "Serves them right."

"Shut up!" I stamped my foot.

Startled, the egrets pranced along on their spindly legs and took off on long flapping wings. The sheep lifted their black faces and looked around.

Placidius gaped at me in astonishment.

I glared at him. "You're talking about my people, Placidius, not some enemy tribe. When you were in danger, they sent a fleet to help you. But now that they're in danger you laugh at their misfortune? What has become of you, Placidius?"

My outburst had caught him off guard. He was momentarily at a loss. I plunged ahead.

"You speak to me of my duty, but you have forgotten your own. You are responsible for the Empire, all of it, East and West. We were wed for the purpose of reuniting it, yet you shun my bed and evade your duty to make a son with me.

Then you turn around and speak as if you would be happy to see the East destroyed. Is that really what you want, Placidius, to see half of our birthright lost to the Huns?"

He struggled to recover his aplomb. He drew himself up. "Your father deprived me of the fleet. He took it away when I needed it. Where was his loyalty to me then? Where was his loyalty to the West?"

"He was under attack.

"So was I!"

"Placidius," I said, "someday the fleet will be ours. Don't you understand? You can send it wherever you want. But only if you don't ruin our prospects by alienating the East. Remember who you are. Remember your duty. Remember your purpose. Come to my bed. Give us an heir."

He watched my face, studying it, vaguely mystified, a hint of tenderness in his eyes. He took a step forward, and for a fleeting moment I thought he might take me in his arms. But then a long, bony hand insinuated itself and took hold of his shoulder. Heraclius whispered into his ear. When Placidius looked at me again, his expression had darkened.

"Beguile me not, woman. Your words are a trap to ensnare me. Like Eve to Adam, you would lead me to sin."

"Placidius, I am your wife."

"Augustine was ensnared by a life of licentiousness until God showed him the light. He writes

'But my sin was this, that I looked for pleasure, beauty, and truth not in Him but in myself and his other creatures, and the search led me instead to pain, confusion, and error.' He understood. I must follow his example and spurn temptation."

"But Placidius, you made a vow before God to be my husband!"

He shook his head. "Hear the words of Tertullian:

> Do you not know that you are Eve?
> God's sentence hangs over all your
> sex and His punishment weighs down
> upon you. You are the devil's gateway;
> you are she who first violated the for-
> bidden tree and broke the law of God.
> You must suffer in pain.

I clung to his arm. "I am not some whore. I'm your wife, the mother of your children! I'm trying to lay with you as a wife lays with her husband in order to bear you a son! What are you talking about, Placidius? This is madness!"

A quick glance at Heraclius, and then a placid smile at me. "I have read the words of St. Jerome, and they have enlightened me: 'Eve in paradise was a virgin. Virginity is natural and marriage comes after the Fall.'"

He lifted my hand from his arm like I had some infection of the skin. I was flabbergasted.

"Do not pretend you have not seduced me. Your womanly lies are like the slithering of a serpent's tongue. You have defiled me with sin."

"I have not!"

"When you took me into your mouth."

I fell back.

"I must wash your harlot's filth from me. I must find the strength to reject you."

Somehow I found the words to fight back. "Strength! You call that strength! The strength not to lay with me? The strength to deny us an heir? You call that strength! You call that holiness?"

He shook his head. "There is a virtue greater than the sowing of a man's seed. It is the virtue of cleanliness, the virtue of chastity."

"You are not chaste, Placidius. You have two daughters."

"No longer. You have taken them and given them to another."

"What are you talking about? Have you lost your mind?"

"My little Eudocia, I loved her so. I doted on her. But she is no longer mine. You gave her to the Vandals, to Huneric."

"Stop it!"

"When I was a child, I spoke as a child, I understood as a child, I thought as a child, but when I became a man, I put away childish things."

I grabbed my skull and screamed. "Stop quoting passages to me! I've heard enough! Speak to me as a human being! Speak to me as a man!"

Heraclius produced a Bible from his robes and handed it to Placidius who thumbed through the pages until he found the passage he was looking for. "Hear the words of St. Matthew and know me:

> For there are eunuchs, who were born
> so from their mother's womb: and
> there are eunuchs, who were made so
> by men: and there are eunuchs, who
> have made themselves eunuchs for

the kingdom of heaven. He that can
take it, let him take it.

I could hardly formulate a reaction.

He closed the book and addressed me evenly. "According to Tertullian there is no greater purity. 'Those who submit themselves to the knife for the glory of God are the most favored of all.' Father Origen was a eunuch. He removed the offending appendage to avoid temptation, demonstrating the highest degree of sanctity. It's something to aspire to. The holiest of men have made the sacrifice. Jesus was a eunuch. Did you know that? It's true."

I turned on Heraclius. "Did you do this to him? Did you put this insanity into his head?"

Heraclius shrugged. "Not me," he said. "You."

I gaped at his insolence.

"The Imperator is reading the books you gave him, studying them as you wished. You can hardly blame me. You're the one, not me."

"You devil!"

Placidius took a step toward me. "Watch your tongue, woman. You are growing too bold with my servant."

I clasped my hands before me and pleaded. "Please Placidius, listen to me. You don't know the harm you're doing. You don't know the danger you're in."

He scowled. "How dare you speak to me in that tone! You are a woman, and I am your husband. Such nerve. It is just as they say, 'You are the devil's gateway. You are the first deserter of the divine law. On account of you even the Son of God had to die!'" He raised his hand to strike me.

I sank to my knees and dropped my head. But the blow never came. He left me there, a miserable wretch, a beggar at the doorstep of power, my petition rejected, my appeal denied. He walked away, his eunuchs trailing after him, their silken robes flapping in the breeze.

A week later he returned the books I had given him, along with a note urging me to study them. "Read and understand," the note said. I crumpled it up and threw it away. Then I buried the books at the bottom of my chest so I would not have to think about them, so their presence would not reproach me, and I would not be reminded of the woman who had given them to me.

I had a sudden realization. It hit me like a bolt. I dashed off a letter to my father and sent it to him with the next courier heading east. I knew it would be weeks before he would receive it, but when he did, and when I had gotten his reply, I would know who my real enemy was, and the real reason I was being denigrated and ostracized. I could only hope the letter would reach him before the Huns overran the trade routes and cut off our lines of communication.

# Chapter 11
## The Year AD 443

Placidius appointed a new consul on the first of the year. According to custom, as Emperor of the Western Roman Empire, he was entitled to choose one consul, and my father, the Emperor of the East, would choose the other. The naming of consuls had once been an important political consideration in the long ago days of the Republic, but since the advent of the Imperium it had become a ceremonial appointment, a way to honor the most consequential men and curry their favor. The appointment went to men with substantial means, money that could be lent or donated to a favored emperor, to keep the Imperium solvent. This year was no exception.

Placidius appointed Petronius Maximus, a high ranking member of the aristocracy, as consul, a man whose wealth was so vast it was said he could fund the construction of an aqueduct without even feeling the pinch. The Empire could have used some of his riches, not only to shore up the military, which was still strapped after the humiliation with the Vandals, but also to bolster Placidius's standing in the eyes of the public. Of course, the Emperor could have extracted some of it through taxes, but that would have antagonized the very people he was trying to win over, the affluent members of the upper classes whose generosity could sustain him. Instead, he decided to flatter them by naming one of them as consul.

If Maximus was fooled by this transparent ruse, he never let on. He offered to pay for the celebrations out of his own pocket, something Placidius was certainly counting on as the government could hardly afford it. With Maximus financing the events, and his son Junius as the praetor,[11] the Emperor was free to relax and enjoy the impressive festivities.

The imperial guard marched through the city in full regalia ahead of a rank of colorfully attired musicians blowing horns and pounding drums. Behind them came a procession of exotic animals collected from the far reaches of the Empire: elephants, giraffes, and camels, followed by a single gray ostrich, the largest bird anyone had ever seen. The crowd gasped. Next came ranks of strange people: slant-eyed men with high cheek bones, each with a single shock of black hair that grew in a long tail from their otherwise bald heads, diminutive men in leopard skins herding miniature goats, burly white-haired Germans carrying war clubs, freckle-faced, red-haired Hiberians gamboling along in clunky shoes, dark-eyed Arabs, straight-backed and proud, astride white horses. The Pope celebrated an open air mass in the Forum where hundreds of doves were released into the sky above the basilica. But it was at the Hippodrome where the real excitement took place. Wild animal fights were followed by a succession of chariot races the likes of which were rarely seen; the blues and greens

---

11  Municipal official in charge of the games, chariot races, ceremonies, and public works

battled it out on the great oval, spinning around the turns in their two-wheeled chariots, lashing their horses to froths amidst the delirious cheers of the crowd.

Placidius grinned like a schoolboy. I had rarely seen him so elated. He loved nothing more than a good chariot race, and he loved to wager, but it was more than that. It was the way the crowd received him as he entered the arena. In recent weeks his popularity had risen. News had arrived of Aetius's triumph over the Burgundians. As part of the armistice, they had been settled in Sapaudia at the foot of the Alps and enlisted as allies to act as a buffer against the Bagaudae, thus relieving the government of the cost of patrolling the region. As a result, the public was freed from the threat of new taxation, something that pleased them more than parades or celebrations.

News of these achievements were broadcast on the alba, the public signboards placed throughout the city. Usually covered with the dry fare of legal decisions and political appointments, the alba had been pasted all over in recent weeks with handbills announcing Aetius's triumphs, news that accrued to the Emperor's benefit and, buoyed him in the public's opinion. This coincided with the announcement of the festivities to honor the new consul.

In a few days everything had seemed to swing in the Emperor's favor. Months of ineffectual efforts on the part of the clergy to bolster his reputation had been rendered unnecessary. Placidius couldn't have been more delighted. So rejuvenated were his spirits that even I benefited. Not wanting to appear callous or curmudgeonly, he ordered me by his side throughout the festivities, a tasteful adornment not unlike a handsome horse or sparkling raiment. But he barely looked at me.

His private scorn had not abated. He still spurned my every attempt at reconciliation and kept the children at arm's length. It was horribly frustrating given the threats against him from his sister and mother, but the situation was not yet beyond remedy for there had been no sign he had carried through on his threat to castrate himself, and his recent rise in popularity made it even less likely he would do so. Like so much Placidius did, the threat had been calculated to earn him admiration, and once he had gotten what he wanted, following through on it was no longer necessary. On the day of the races, his buoyant spirits were due in part to the relief he was feeling at being absolved of that requirement, and as we gathered in the imperial box to watch the competition, it soon became apparent he was still every bit a man.

We were seated next to the new consul and his wife, a lovely young woman named Lucina, who everyone called by her nickname Agnus, meaning "lamb" for her sweet and gentle nature. Her husband Maximus was 47-years-old, handsome, and graying. She was 21, the same age as I. They were newlyweds having been recently married after the death of Maximus's first wife by whom he had several grown children. The oldest was Junius, just two years older than his father's new wife. Junius had been named praetor for the events and appeared regularly to check on us during the festivities to make sure everything was to the Emperor's liking. He was a taciturn young man, not at all like his father who was animated and voluble.

The Emperor and his new consul wagered extravagantly, leaning over the edge of the box to watch the charioteers hurtling around the oval. Both men cheered and hollered as the horses came pounding down the stretch, only to sink back in mock disappointment or exult with pumping arms as the outcome dictated. They laughed and clapped each other on the back and had a grand time. Agnus and I smiled at each other, charmed by their antics. But Junius, who showed up during one such celebration, was not so exuberant. There was something dark and brooding about him. I watched him. He was good-looking with a heart-shaped face, large wide-set eyes, and a fine, delicate mouth that slackened into a frown far more often than it smiled.

After several races, Maximus suggested we go down to the track to get closer to the horses, and Placidius agreed. On the way down, Agnus touched my arm and said, "I love your brooch."

She was referring to the jewel-encrusted pin I had used to fasten my palla. I looked down at it. I had not taken much notice of it before.

"Why, thank you," I said. I was flattered, unaccustomed to compliments.

"My cousin has something similar," she said, "but not nearly as nice. It has a way of bringing out your eyes."

I thanked her again, and we continued down to the track-side. Once there, Agnus pointed out a horse to me. "You see him? He's my favorite. He belongs on Maurus's team. He used to belong to Ursus, but the trainer mistreated him. It broke my heart, so I asked Maximus to buy him. Now he's ours. Isn't he magnificent?"

He was a beautiful animal and I said so.

Maximus is so good to me," she said. She looked at her husband with loving eyes.

I looked away, slightly embarrassed.

She touched my arm. "Are you all right?"

"Of course," I said with a forced smile.

"What are you ladies talking about?" the consul asked. "Is it a secret? Can I get in on it?"

"Don't be silly," Agnus said with a bashful smile. She slapped him playfully on the arm.

Placidius stuck his head in. "They are probably plotting against us," he said, and everyone laughed.

"Look," Maximus said, "the race is starting."

We all pressed up to the rail.

The horses surged forward. The wheels of the chariots spun furiously and churned up the dirt. As the charioteers entered the first turn, the praetor joined us at the rail, as quiet and aloof as before. Even though the others grew more animated, he remained distant and apart.

"Look!" Agnus squealed. "Our team is winning!"

She jumped up and down on her toes. Maximus hooked his arm around her and drew her close, as much a declaration of ownership as of affection.

The horses came tearing down the stretch. The charioteers laid the whip to them with fierce determination. The crowd rose as one. The chariots drew nearer, hooves thundering, wheels churning, turf exploding. As they swept past, they showered us with dirt and grit. Everyone winced and turned away. But I was too late. A piece of grit got caught in my eye and made it water. I bent over and tried to pick it out.

Agnus noticed my plight and offered to help. She told me to blink rapidly. She told me to shut my eye and rub it with the heel of my hand. Nothing worked. If anything, her suggestions made it worse. By now tears were rolling down my cheek. The men were still watching the race and didn't notice. Then the praetor Junius came over. He was as quiet and subdued as ever. He spoke just two words to me. "Look up."

I did as he instructed.

He scrutinized my eye. He came closer. He was just inches away. I could feel his breath on my face, and when the breeze tossed his hair, a strand of it touched my cheek. He touched the corner of my eye, and I flinched. He held up his finger, as if testing the breeze, as if pointing to the heavens, and waited until I had absorbed his purpose. He said nothing. Then he leaned in again and plucked the speck from my eye. He looked at it on the tip of his finger, showed it to me, and with a faint smile, wiped it on his trousers, and was gone. "Did he get it?" Agnus asked.

"Yes," I said. My heart was beating faster.

"What happened?" Maximus asked.

"Licinia got something stuck in her eye and Junius took it out."

The consul looked after his son who was walking away down the rail. "Well, you never know when someone will surprise you."

My husband hovered in the background, only partly interested in my predicament, still distracted by the races. "Is something wrong?" he asked.

Agnus repeated the story.

"Isn't that nice?" Placidius said. He was speaking to Agnus. "Is she all right?" he asked her, even though I was just a few feet away. He flicked a glance at me.

"Oh, yes. She's fine. Isn't that right, Licinia?"

"Yes. I'm all right."

"You see? She's fine."

Placidius was still looking at Agnus, and it wasn't hard to see why. She was stunning. She had large, soft, liquid eyes, curved eyebrows, angular cheekbones, and a beautifully shaped mouth.

"You have to be careful when you're standing by the rail," he told her. "The chariots throw up so much dirt. A lady could get soiled." He smiled at her. "Maybe you should stand farther back"—another glance at me — "both of you."

"Yes," Maximus said. "That would be a good idea."

"Perhaps we should do that," Agnus said, a little discomfited by Placidius's attention. She took me by the arm, and we moved away. Placidius stood looking after her for a long time. Then he turned to Maximus and the two men moved back to the rail.

"Are you all right?" she asked me.

"I'm afraid I'll make you miss the next race. Don't worry about me. I'm all right," I said.

"Nonsense," she said. "There are always more races." She smiled.

I was grateful.

"Did your team win?" I asked.

"Probably. Maximus doesn't like to lose. He demands the best of everything. We are extraordinarily blessed. To tell you the truth, it's almost too much sometimes. It's almost embarrassing." She gave me a guilty look and ducked her head. It was charming because it was so completely guileless.

"Wealth and status can be a burden sometimes," I said.

She looked relieved. "Oh, Licinia. You cannot imagine—or maybe you can—how isolated it can make you feel. The grievances you have in your heart but which you cannot say. How selfish you feel to even have such thoughts. The way you reproach yourself for thinking them. Yet there they are. You cannot escape them, and you cannot mention them to anyone else, lest you be thought ungrateful."

"I know how you feel," I told her.

"You are sweet," she said. "I'm glad we met."

"So am I."

And so, our friendship began. I had come upon it unexpectedly like a drowning person comes upon a branch, and it buoyed me at a time when I was sinking. But it was not without its price. And it did nothing to relieve the threat that was hanging over my head, a threat that grew deeper with each passing day.

★ ★ ★

In the spring news arrived of the Eastern Empire's painful sellout to the Huns. My father, unable to muster a force large enough to expel them from Illyricum, had agreed to pay Attila and his brother an annual gratuity of 700 pounds of gold to leave the province and withdraw beyond the Danube. The ransom extorted by the Huns was almost double what had been agreed to under the previous treaty. In addition, my father consented to return any Hun deserters who had fled into the Empire. The Huns, for their part, left a wake of destruction in retreat. The whole thing was a shameful embarrassment to Constantinople.

Placidius had nothing but contempt for the agreement and spoke of it with disdain in my presence until I could no longer stand it and had to leave the room to avoid losing my temper. Which was just fine with him. He didn't want me around anyway. He considered it my due to suffer the grinding sequestration of a woman scorned, unloved, and kept apart, subject to an internal exile not unlike incarceration. I longed to get away from Ravenna…and from him.

Toward the end of the spring, I received a letter. I assumed it was from my father, a reply to the communication I had sent some weeks earlier. But it was not from him at all. It was from my mother. I had not heard from her since my wedding, a period of more than five years. She must have been feeling guilty because from the beginning she tried to explain everything away by saying my aunt had planted spies in her entourage who had intercepted her letters and destroyed them. With my aunt in exile, my mother could finally write freely and express how much she loved and missed me. I was dubious.

She wrote about the happy reconciliation between my father and her and how the misfortunes of the past had been put behind them. She spoke of righting the wrongs perpetrated by my aunt and of repairing the damage. She told me about Heraclius, about how had been placed in our household, not as part of my dowry, as I had been given to believe, but at my aunt's insistence, and against my mother's wishes. "I suspected he might have been put there to disrupt your marriage," my mother wrote.

This made me angry. If my mother knew Heraclius posed a threat to my marriage, why hadn't she informed me earlier? Unless, of course, she had known no such thing until she read my letter to my father, understood that I was concerned about Heraclius, and then used it to claim sympathy for my plight while vilifying Pulcheria. I wouldn't have put it past her. I decided I wanted to hear the truth from my father, and the only way I was going to be able to do that was to see him face to face. I wrote a note to Placidius asking his permission to visit Constantinople. He turned me down flat.

The war was over. The Eastern Empire was at peace. Even their altercation with the Persians, which had occasioned so much anxiety, had been put to rest. There was no reason to refuse my request other than petty spite. I wrote to him again. I reminded him that I had not seen my parents for more than five years. He refused me again.

At this juncture, I received a note from my mother-in-law asking me to meet her at her villa outside of Rome. I considered it. I knew I could arrange permission to go there and see her, but I didn't want to. I feared what she might say to me, more threats about what might happen if I didn't get Placidius to give us an heir. It was the last thing I wanted to hear, so I politely declined.

Instead, I agreed to an invitation to visit Agnus in Rome. It was easily enough arranged. All it took was a letter from Petronius Maximus asking for my presence on behalf of his wife. Placidius, eager to curry favor with his wealthy patron, approved. And so, in the summer of that year, I made the first of many trips to Rome to visit my new friend.

Rome was liberating and exciting, and Agnus lifted my spirits. She was keen about fashion and taught me all about makeup and the sculpting of hair into fetching styles. We shopped for clothes. We purchased jewelry. We strolled the streets arm in arm, turning heads and making men stop and stare. She, the comely young beauty, and me, the Augusta. We dined regularly at the public garden of a fashionable cauponae[12] frequented by members of the senatorial class. We frequented the baths where we were fussed over and pampered. We attended the theatre to watch the pantomime and went to the Forum to watch the street performers. It was wonderful, a welcome respite from the endless grind of my existence at Ravenna. But behind it all lurked the shadows of nemesis. It could not last.

One day, as Agnus and I were strolling through the city, we came upon an alba. We saw reports of Aetius's recent achievements in Hispania. He had put down a revolt of the Bagaudae, those peasant revolutionaries who seemed to be popping up all over the Empire. They killed Roman tax collectors, defied governmental authority, and deprived the state of much needed revenue. Aetius had forced them back into obedience at the point of a sword and started collecting taxes again. For this he was praised lavishly in the text of the flyer, so much so it seemed almost gratuitous. As I stood reading it, Agnus drifted away to the shop of a nearby goldsmith. I read more closely. Behind the words I could see Galla's handiwork. She was raising Aetius's public image in preparation for what would come next should I fail to produce an heir. Agnus came up beside me.

---

12  An inn and restaurant

"Have you heard this?" I asked. "This news about Aetius?"

"Oh, yes," she said. "Maximus was speaking of it. He was quite keen about it."

"Keen about it?" I asked, surprised he should be in favor of it given the aristocracy's longstanding contempt for Aetius.

"The Senate is all atwitter," she said. "Symmachus, Olybrius, Albinus, all of them. They are praising his exploits in Hispania. They think it's wonderful."

That struck me as odd. The Senate thrilled with Aetius? I couldn't get it out of my head. Later, as we were having lunch in the public garden of the cauponae, I brought it up again. Agnus was unconcerned.

"I don't give it much thought," she said. "It's not my place. That's the business of men."

Her careless indifference came across as naïve, although I couldn't blame her. She was behaving the way people expected me to behave, and maybe I should have been more like her, but this was too strange. The aristocracy's sudden change in attitude toward Aetius was worrisome in light of the threat hanging over our heads. If they were shifting their allegiances, it could spell trouble for Placidius.

Agnus saw the disquiet in my eyes.

"Oh, poor Licinia," she said. She reached across the table and squeezed my hand. "This is bothering you, isn't it? Let me see if I can find an answer."

She looked around the cauponae and picked out Junius who was lunching with a deputy financial officer on the other side of the garden. Before I could stop her, she called him over. He approached our table. He was aloof as always. He stood beside the table and looked away, before looking directly at me and forcing a smile. "I'm sorry. I didn't mean to disturb you," he said.

"Not at all," I said.

"Go ahead," Agnus said. "Ask him. Junius knows all about such things. As praetor he is one of the best informed officials in Rome."

I thought I saw him blush. I went ahead. "Well, it's just this thing with Aetius—"

"What thing with Aetius?"

"Well, his sudden popularity among the senatorial class. It seems peculiar to me. I don't understand it."

He swallowed hard and looked away to gather his thoughts. Then he said, "It's the money."

"The money?" I asked.

"The taxes. Aetius is restoring tax revenues, putting down the insurrectionists. It means more money for the treasury, which means the senatorial class will not have to part with any of their own. They like that, so they applaud him."

I thought this over. "But isn't Aetius forcing the Bagaudae back into tax compliance at the point of a sword?".

"I suppose so," he said.

"So that means government revenues are dependent on the imposition of taxes on a people who have rebelled before and are likely to rebel again."

He looked at me like he was considering a strange creature he had never seen before.

Agnus laughed. "Licinia is as curious as a cat. It's a spirited quality in a woman, wouldn't you say, Junius?"

Junius looked at her. There was a softness in his gaze that wasn't there before, a sudden shift from the standoffishness of his former demeanor. "She is certainly perceptive," he said.

She gave him a sweet smile. Again, the slight blush. He looked back at me. "I have to go now. I'm afraid I'm being rude to my guest. Have I answered your question, Augusta?" He was gentle now, accommodating.

I told him I was satisfied, and he withdrew. He cast an embarrassed glance back at us as he made his way across the garden.

"You have thrown him off balance," Agnus said. She returned to her meal.

"Me?"

"Yes," she said. She took a bite of bread. "He's not used to women who speak their minds."

"Well, I didn't mean to make him uncomfortable," I said. But it was obvious what was troubling him. Junius was in love with Agnus. Junius was in love with his father's wife.

* * *

During the summer I received two more requests from Galla to meet with her, and I spurned them both. With nothing positive to report about my progress in producing an heir I couldn't see the point. I trusted the providential events of recent months had made her less determined to replace the Emperor. On the other hand, it seemed just as likely she would perceive the aristocracy's change of heart regarding Aetius as the perfect opportunity to present him as a viable alternative to her son. She might even have been planning on it. I didn't know. I didn't want to think about it. The idea of Justa rising to a position of influence, even one where she was merely the visible representative of her father's power, turned my stomach.

Then something unexpected happened. Justa was caught cavorting with a mid-level administrator in a taberna in Ostia. By all reports she was drunk and lewd. The man she was with was married. The story stirred up a scandal, and Placidius ordered her arrested. For reasons not altogether clear to me, Placidius wanted me by his side when his sister was hauled before him to answer for her outrageous behavior.

Rain lashed the windows and thunder rumbled in the distance as we took our seats in an audience chamber dimly lit by oil lamps and braziers. Placidius was surrounded by his eunuchs, Heraclius at his side. Galla was absent. When Justa came in, she was draped in chains. I had seen prisoners in chains before and they were usually downcast and frightened. Justa wore hers like a gown. She was as upright and as defiant as ever. She even had her dogs with her.

"Who let those curs in here!" Placidius leapt to his feet. "Remove them at once!"

The dogs were dragged away amid yelps and squeals. Justa looked after them and shrugged. "Go ahead, mistreat them all you want," she said. "They'll remain loyal no matter how badly you treat them, not unlike some women we know." She looked at me and smiled.

"Shut your mouth!" Placidius snapped. "If you speak again, I'll have you flogged!"

Justa gave him a weary look and rolled her eyes.

"Do you understand the concept of relegatio?" he asked. "It means voluntary exile, a consideration to members of a privileged class so they are not unduly humiliated. In exchange for this act of leniency, they comply. They leave the place where they are no longer wanted, and they do not come back without permission. If they do, they are subject to more severe measures."

She smirked.

"I'll tell you what they do not do, sister of mine. They do not return unannounced and end up drunk and cavorting in some sleazy waterside taverna with a married man." He affected great disappointment. "It is just as Origen writes: 'Women are worse than animals because they are continuously full of lust.'"

Justa refused to dignify that with a response.

"Ah, but you think you're clever, don't you? You think you can pursue your depravity like a bitch in heat and nothing will happen to you. You think you can avoid the sting of my wrath because you are Aetius's daughter. And you may be right—for now. But don't think I lack the means to make you suffer, dear sister." He turned to the guards. "Bring those dogs back."

Justa glanced up. "You wouldn't."

The dogs were jerked in by their leashes. They scrabbled at the floor with their claws.

Placidius looked at Heraclius and nodded. The eunuch descended the steps and removed a long knife from his robes.

"Don't!"

The first dog shrank back and growled. Heraclius grabbed it around the neck and with a jerk of his arm slit its throat. Blood gushed out onto the floor. Justa blanched.

Heraclius walked over to the second dog and plunged the knife deep into its skull. The dog yelped, clipped off in mid-cry and splayed down on all fours. Its muzzle struck the floor.

I screamed and pressed my hands to my mouth.

Justa fell to her knees, her face gone pale.

Placidius waved his hand. "Throw her in the dungeon. If she makes another sound, kill her."

"You can't do that," I said. "If Aetius hears about it—"

"Silence!" His face was contorted in rage. "It's not your place to counsel me. Keep your mouth shut!"

"But I'm telling you, Placidius. You're more vulnerable than you think. The city is plastered all over with handbills lauding Aetius's achievements. The aristocracy speaks favorably of him—even Petronius Maximus. He is popular now, and he has the army behind him. Now is not the time to make an enemy of him."

He opened his mouth to rebuke me, but then faltered and turned to Heraclius who was standing over the dead animals with the dripping knife in his hand.

"Is this so?"

Heraclius looked at me, a long, baleful look, and nodded.

Placidius pressed his hands to his head. "Oh, no. Not this. They despise Aetius. They always have. They wouldn't celebrate him. Say it isn't so."

"By suppressing the Bagaudae and making peace with the Burgundians, he has begun restoring tax revenues," I said. "He is filling up the treasury again, which means they won't have to pay anything out of their own pockets. So, they celebrate him."

Placidius looked as if he was about to cry. "But I was the one who made peace with the Vandals," he said. "I was the one who demanded the annual payments in gold. That is what is filling up the treasury, not tax revenues from the provinces. They should celebrate me."

I didn't bother to point out that he had resisted the treaty with the Vandals at every step, and had still not agreed to the final condition, the betrothal of Eudocia and Huneric.

He looked glumly at his hands.

There was a time when my heart would have gone out to him, but all my sympathy was gone. He had squandered it with his brutality. "You should make sure they don't harm Justa," I said. "You should give them an order."

He called a member of the guard to his side and spoke softly into his ear. The man hastened away. Placidius turned his back to me and put his head in his hands.

Heraclius watched me with his dark inscrutable gaze. The knife dangled from his long white fingers. Crimson blood streamed down the blade and dripped on the floor. I refused to avert my eyes. I stared at him with all the loathing I felt in my heart. If I could have killed him with a look, I would have.

The blood puddled around his feet and stained his silken slippers.

* * *

I first heard about the persecution of the Manicheans from one of the servants who looked after my children. It was a cold day in late autumn, and little Placidia had splashed herself playing at the watering trough. I thought she would be uncomfortable being wet, but in the way of little children she seemed oblivious. I commented on this to one of the servants who surprised me with her reaction. Her eyes filled with tears, she ducked her head in embarrassment, and she excused herself. I asked another servant standing nearby what was wrong and learned that the poor girl's beloved brother had been deliberately drowned in a river.

"Drowned?" I asked. "Deliberately? By whom?"

"The Pope."

I couldn't believe my ears. I asked her to repeat what she had said, and that's when I learned the facts. The Manicheans were an obscure religious sect numbering no more than a few hundred, the tattered remnants of a once mighty rival to the Early Christian Church. Previous persecutions had all but wiped them out, and what remained could hardly be characterized as a threat, but the Pope had commenced a vicious campaign to annihilate all heretics, the Manicheans among them. The woman's brother had been a follower. He had been drowned in the river after refusing to renounce his faith.

He was not alone. Others had been beaten, whipped, and burned alive. It was exactly what Galla had warned about when Leo first came to us seeking power. She knew he would divide the public over matters of faith and set the people against each other, and now his purpose was revealed. He was seeking to strengthen his own hand at the expense of civic harmony.

He could not have done it without the Emperor's approval, or at least without his willful disregard, and it troubled me deeply. It seemed too important to brush aside; a man who claimed to represent Jesus Christ, the Prince of Peace, was putting innocent people to death. I had to know why Placidius was permitting it to happen, but I dared not confront him directly.

I thought maybe Agnus could help. She attended services at the Lateran Basilica where the Pope led the mass. I wanted to know if she had witnessed the Pope calling for the persecution of the Manicheans and whether he had mentioned the Emperor's position regarding it. Agnus could recall nothing of the sort. The only thing she could remember was that the Pope, who had been singing Aetius's praises from the pulpit, had suddenly stopped. That's when I understood.

Placidius had traded his tacit endorsement of the Pope's persecutions for silence about Aetius's success. The Emperor was fighting the campaign to lionize his rival by doing the one thing his mother feared most, letting the Church grab more power. But perhaps I was assuming too much. Agnus's casual observations about the contents of the mass were hardly enough to confirm the scope of such a devious arrangement. My attempts to draw her out further on the subject failed; Agnus didn't like to discuss politics. It made her uncomfortable. She suggested I speak to Junius instead.

"He knows everything about everything," she said.

She told me where to find him. He was organizing the importation of wild beasts for the venationes, the wild animal hunts, that were to take place in the Colosseum during the celebration for the new consul. They would occur after the first of the year when Petronius Maximus would step down after his one-year tenure and a new consul would be named.

I found Junius in a long, low building on the Esquiline Hill overlooking the Colosseum. The building housed animal cages and was reputedly constructed of stones salvaged from the destruction of Nero's palace. It was dingy and stank of animal urine. The roars and shrieks of caged beasts echoed down the corridors.

Junius was standing before a cage in which a spotted leopard prowled. He was talking to a man with a whip. Behind him, on the other side of the bars, the cat paced. It slunk through its turns at either end of the confinement. Junius greeted me with a smile. Then, as if he had suddenly remembered his manners, he grew serious.

"Greetings, Augusta," he said with a bow. The man he was talking with backed away.

"Please," I said. "Finish your business. Don't let me interrupt." But Junius insisted they were done. The man bowed and walked away.

"How can I be of service to you, Augusta?" Junius asked with a formality that seemed disproportionate to our surroundings.

I told him he needn't be so formal, that I considered him a friend, and he could relax. He seemed momentarily discomfited. He would not meet my eyes.

"I wanted to ask your opinion about something," I said. "I wanted to ask about the Pope and his persecution of the Manicheans." He looked up. "The Pope is doing this with the Emperor's permission, I presume."

I waited for some indication from him that I was correct. He hesitated. The cat unleashed a low growl but never quit moving.

"Agnus tells me the Pope has been uncharacteristically complimentary of Aetius of late, but now he has stopped. I was wondering if you think there's any connection between the Pope's sudden change of heart and his license to conduct these persecutions."

Junius looked down at the leopard. "It's not my place to say."

"Of course not," I said. I felt badly for putting him on the spot. "It's just that you're so knowledgeable, and you perceive more than you let on. Forgive me. I'm curious, and you seem to have the insight I desire. I'm rather like a treasurer fumbling with a lock. I have the right key, but I'm too clumsy to unlock it."

"You're not clumsy," he said with a heartfelt earnestness that caught me off guard.

I felt something lurch inside me, something unsettling, yet at the same time exciting. I put my hand to my chest. The cat turned in its cage and I saw its black, slotted eyes, its strange inhuman gaze. I moved to go.

He caught me by the hand, and I stopped. "You're not wrong, Augusta. You see things the way they are." He looked at me with a forlorn wistfulness, a barely suppressed longing.

I felt the heat rising to my cheeks. I had been wrong about him. It was not Agnus he was in love with. It was me.

# Chapter 12
## The Years 444-445

I was tempted. I could not deny it. But it was precisely the sort of thing the Church Fathers had warned about, the weakness of our sex, our tendency toward wantonness. It was Eve in the garden. It was why we were sinful. It was why we bled. So, I had to fight my urges; I had to resist.

I stopped going to Rome. I remained in Ravenna and went to the chapel four times a day to pray, but it was useless. I couldn't stop thinking about him. In the eyes of others, it might have been accounted a small thing, a look between two people, a casual glance, but I knew what it was, and it scared me.

The mood around the palace didn't make things any easier. Placidius was constantly on edge, irritated by the news of Aetius's achievements in Hispania and Gaul. What might have brightened the spirits of another emperor, reports of his master of soldier's successes, made Placidius sour. He worried, correctly I suppose, that Aetius was becoming ever more popular, even though the Church had stopped lauding him from the pulpit. He was snappish to the girls and mean to me.

He barked at us during the rare times he agreed to see us at all. It made my heart break to see the girls hurt by him.

One day, after he had lashed out at them, I smelled wine on his breath. It was unusual. Up to this point Placidius had never been a heavy drinker. This was something new and a bit concerning. But I could do nothing about it. I was alone and impotent and fighting the temptation to take the girls and return to Rome where friendship and companionship awaited.

I wasn't the only one sulking around the palace that winter. Justa was there too, and she dogged me relentlessly, appearing like a wraith on a battlement overlooking the courtyard or stepping out from behind a row of columns to try to catch my eye. I avoided her, but she persisted. She sent notes. She enlisted servants to waylay me. When I learned she had tried to visit the children, I ordered them kept away from her. She should have been in prison or exiled, but instead she lingered in the shadows like a ghost.

At the first of the year Placidius named the new consul. It was to be Albinus, the selfsame Albinus who had conspired with Leo to undermine the Emperor's attempt to provide Aetius the funding he needed to fight the Goths. It was the clearest indication yet of the lengths Placidius was willing to go to curry favor with the aristocracy and the Church. It struck me as unwise. He was allying himself with those who had already proven their willingness to betray him. But, of course, I could say nothing.

Placidius ordered me to accompany him to Rome to preside over the ceremonies. Although I had my misgivings, I was greatly relieved to be getting out of Ravenna. Seeing Agnus again after so many weeks was a breath of fresh air.

Thankfully, Junius was not there. He was busy organizing the festivities. He was to be named praetor again for the coming year, something out of the ordinary. The incoming consul usually chose his own man, but Maximus pulled some strings and arranged it. He was off somewhere in the lower warrens of the Colosseum preparing for the venationes.

My time with Agnus was brief. I was required to accompany the Emperor and the new consul in the imperial box. Agnus was to be seated with Maximus in the box of honor farther down. Placidius was standing in our box, searching the crowd. When his eyes lighted on Agnus, he homed in on her like a hawk. He excused himself on the pretense of having a few words with Maximus, but Maximus had stepped away. Placidius went down and spoke to Agnus. He was down there for so long I had to send a servant to remind him the show was about to begin.

Even after he had returned to our box and was seated next to Albinus and his wife, Placidius kept stealing looks at Agnus. She had that effect on men. But Placidius had sworn himself to a life of celibacy and had rejected his wife. He had openly contemplated making himself a eunuch and had been willing to imperil the future of the Empire in pursuit of his desire to be chaste. Yet here he was lusting after Agnus.

The show began. A trap door opened in the center of the arena and a bewildered bear stepped out into the light. It was immediately set upon by two bare-chested gladiators with tridents and whips who harried it around the arena until it reared up on its haunches and roared, delighting the crowd. At this juncture, a gate slid back, and an elephant lumbered forth, prodded by three men with long poles. The elephant, confused and distressed, curled its trunk and trumpeted.

The whole spectacle was difficult for me to watch. I didn't like wild animal hunts. Albinus saw my discomfort and asked if I was all right. I told him I wasn't feeling well and excused myself. Placidius watched me go.

Down below in the concourse I tried to compose myself. I wanted to go home. But I knew I had to return to the box or risk Placidius's wrath. Then I heard a voice behind me.

"Are you all right?" Junius was watching me with a concerned expression. He took a step closer. "You look pale."

"Oh," I said, "it's just the animal hunt. It's so—so cruel."

He searched my face with compassion. "I'm sorry," he said, as if it were his fault. "It's what they hunger for, the violence."

"I understand," I said. "I'll pull myself together. I just need a moment."

He reached up and touched my cheek. "I wish I could make it better for you," he said.

I smiled at him.

"What's this?" The voice of Petronius Maximus.

Junius dropped his hand like it had been burned. A moment later his father was by my side. "Is something wrong, Augusta?"

"She's upset by the hunt," Junius said

"Isn't that sweet?" Maximus said with a condescending grin. "Another tender womanly heart to grace us. Come along with me and sit with Agnus. You can console each other. If the hunt becomes too gruesome, you can bury your faces in each other's breasts." He laughed and took me by the hand. I thought I detected a slight grimace on Junius's lips.

I resisted as Maximus tugged on my hand. "I have to get back to the Emperor," I said.

"Nonsense," Maximus said. "I'll send a man up to let him know you're sitting with us."

"But the consul Albinus will be insulted."

"Don't worry about the consul. He answers to me."

I looked helplessly at Junius who averted his eyes.

Maximus turned to Junius. "Return to your duties," he said. "You're still the praetor. You have a lot of work to do."

Junius did as he was told.

Back in the arena things had turned ugly. The bear lay in a pool of its own blood, its head half-decapitated. The elephant pounded frantically around the ring pursued by the hunters who were prodding and stabbing it. It mounted with its feet upon the wall and trumpeted in distress as if it was pleading for mercy from the crowd. They jeered and threw things at it. The hunters fell upon it with swords and axes. Blood and viscera flew everywhere. After an interminably long time, the poor animal collapsed and rolled over with a final pitiable groan.

Agnus buried her face in her hands and wept. Maximus laughed.

"Oh, my poor dear," he said. "Don't take it so hard. Look, I have brought Licinia to comfort you."

Agnus practically flung herself into my arms. "Oh, it's horrible! Horrible!"

I stroked her head and soothed her.

Now a pair of leopards appeared. They were immediately set upon by a pack of snarling dogs. The big cats had been lacerated before being set loose so that they left trails of blood in the dirt. The dogs, driven mad by hunger, lunged and snapped. The leopards sent them tumbling with swipes of their mighty claws. Once the dogs were sufficiently stunned, the leopards pounced, tearing them apart with their claws and teeth. It all took a horribly long time, and when it was done, the eviscerated bodies of the dogs were strewn across the arena. But the cats were not the victors, after all. Panting and slobbering with exhaustion, they were set upon by the hunters who tormented them with whips and axes until they struck back. Then they hacked them to death.

When it was over the crowd leapt to its feet and roared. Maximus was the most enthusiastic of all. He reminded everyone around him that his son Junius had orchestrated the whole thing. Poor Agnus was in pieces. I led her away from the crush of spectators to console her. The crowd had dispersed and was filing out of the stadium by the time she got control of her tears. In the course of things, we had become separated from Maximus. We couldn't find him anywhere. Agnus suggested we look for him in the director's offices, which were below in the warren of rooms beneath the Colosseum's floor.

We descended the steps to the lower level. It was dark and cramped with long narrow corridors. Shadowy chambers lined either side. As we were passing one, we heard Maximus's voice, low and intense, as if he were arguing with someone. Agnus wanted to keep going, but I was curious. Agnus went ahead, and I drifted back.

From my place in the shadows, I could see through an open doorway. Maximus was involved in a heated discussion with someone whose identity was unclear. Whoever it was stood with his back to me and seemed to cower beneath Maximus's accusatory glare. Then I heard him speak. It was Junius. His voice was strained.

"There's nothing between us!" he cried. "She's just a friend!"

"Men are not friends with women. You're either trying to seduce her or you're conspiring with her. Which is it?"

Junius groaned. "Why do you always think everyone is conspiring against you? Just because you're not made privy to a private conversation doesn't mean you're being plotted against. As hard as it may be to believe, it doesn't involve you. It's none of your business."

"You've been tolerating her impertinence," Maximus said. "Tell me why."

"It's not impertinence. She's inquisitive. That's all. She sees things and wants to know. I feel sorry for her, the way he treats her. He ignores her and pushes her away. It's like he's trying to divorce her. She has no friends. She's all alone, except for Agnus and me."

"It's not your problem. Stay away from her. People will get the wrong idea."

Junius scoffed. "I'm not going to complicate things for you, father. Don't worry."

"I'm warning you. This constant prying of hers will be her undoing. The Emperor doesn't like it, and she will be made to answer for it. Keep your distance from her."

"And what about Agnus? Should Agnus avoid her too?"

"Agnus is a woman. Women can gossip all they want. It's what they do. But when a man engages in it, it raises eyebrows, if you know what I mean."

"I'm afraid I don't. What are you getting at?"

"Let's just say I would have preferred to believe you were trying to seduce her. It would have made more sense to me. Sometimes when I look at you Junius I wonder if my blood actually runs in your veins."

There was a long pause in the conversation. Then I heard Maximus say, "Stop that. Take hold of your emotions. For God's sake, be a man."

And with that their conversation was over. Maximus stalked out. I shrank back into the shadows. He swept past without seeing me. Junius remained behind, staring at the floor with slumped shoulders. I longed to go to him, but I dared not. I had gotten him into enough trouble already. I went out into the street.

My mind was made up. I would not impose myself on them again. I was the Augusta, and as such I could only complicate their lives, so I had to stay away. Like an exotic animal in a cage, it was my lot to remain confined, let out from time to time to impress the public before being shut away again until the next time when I could be made an example of in the most brutal and heartless way.

* * *

From the vantage point of my confinement, I watched as Placidius made decision after decision that weakened his grip on power and led him into deeper trouble. In the spring news arrived that Aetius had installed the barbarian king Gondioc along the Loire River in central Gaul where the king and his sturdy people had bottled up the Bagaudae in Armorica. The announcement was met with applause in Rome where it was recognized as an extension of Aetius's shrewd policy of using friendly barbarian tribes to suppress peasant uprisings and restore civil order. Tax revenues long considered lost were restored.

But in Ravenna the Emperor was furious at the presumption of Aetius in making these decisions without his sanction. Yet instead of rebuking him, he moved to upstage him by using the opportunity to proclaim a general lowering of taxes throughout Italia. He insisted the lost revenues would be more than offset by the restored tax revenues from the provinces. It was a transparent ruse to win the public's affection, but it was ill advised. Placidius was giving away revenues just as fast as Aetius was restoring them.

More accolades were heaped on Aetius when it was reported in the summer that his settlement of the Burgundians in Sapaudia had paid off with the subjugation of insurgents in that region. Envious of his master of soldier's growing popularity, Placidius countered with an announcement that he had at last betrothed Eudocia to Huneric thus solidifying the peace treaty with the Vandals, albeit a couple of years delayed, and ensuring the continued annual payments in gold. He got the public accolades he wanted, but to my way of thinking he should have been paying closer attention to what was happening.

It never seemed to have occurred to him that Aetius's settlement of barbarian tribes in various regions throughout the Empire amounted to the establishment of new client states in what had once been Roman provinces. Those tribes, well-armed and encouraged to militarism, were unlikely to be uprooted ever again. Placidius saw only the restoration of tax revenues and the popularity it generated. He overlooked the fact that the continued flow of those revenues was now reliant on the enforcement of Roman law by barbarians who could decide to withhold the taxes and keep the revenue for themselves whenever it suited them.

The culmination of this policy and the clearest indication of where things were headed came the following spring when Aetius, acting on his own, utilized the services of Avitus, the former praetorian prefect of Gaul, to make peace with King Theodoric by permitting the Goths to annex the port at Narbo, the very same port Rome had fought so hard to expel them from years earlier. For all intents and purposes, this amounted to official recognition of Gothic sovereignty in Aquitaine, something the Emperor had long opposed, but which Aetius had granted in a stroke.

Just like that, decades of hostility between Rome and the Goths was finally put to rest. The reaction among the public was one of great relief. They saw only the end of a decades long conflict that had depleted the treasury and increased their tax burden. They conveniently ignored the slow dismemberment of the Empire, the gradual division of it into vassal states, which, while each state still owed its allegiance to Rome, were now objectively independent nations.

Undoubtedly, they still believed that if any of these states rose up our army would put them down. But they overlooked the fact that our army was now largely composed of barbarians, and not Romans, most of whom disdained military service as beneath them. They had forgotten—although the histories still existed to remind them—that Rome had grown powerful on the service provided by each citizen on behalf of the nation, and that, in the long ago days of its founding, Rome fielded an army of citizens who considered it an honor to serve.

Our present day citizens wanted no part of that. All they cared about was their comfort and privilege, so when they heard news of Aetius's arrangement with the Goths, they celebrated it in the streets, much to the chagrin of Placidius, who resented Aetius for receiving all the credit. Casting around for a way to one-up him, Placidius found it in the Pope's request for a decree asserting the supremacy of the Roman Church over other bishoprics in the West. Knowing the public favored anything that affirmed the authority of Rome over the provinces, Placidius issued the decree without giving it much thought. He completely overlooked the fact that it concentrated even more power in the hands of the Pontiff.

For my part, I kept quiet. I observed it all from afar and grew ever more worried and anxious. Months had gone by. I wanted to go home to Constantinople. I wanted Placidius to make it official and divorce me, so I could take the children and go.

I sent him another note requesting permission to visit my parents. This time he did not even dignify it with a response.

* * *

All through that time Justa kept after me. She sent notes. She tried to intercept me as I passed. She insisted she had something to tell me. By then it had come forcefully to my mind that the scandalous behavior she had been arrested for might well have been orchestrated to bring her into closer contact with me. It was beginning to appear that, whatever she and Galla were up to, they were holding back until they could make one last attempt to recruit me. But they didn't understand. Even if I had been inclined to help, I was useless. Placidius was not going to give me another child.

One day, after months of Justa's interference, I'd had enough. She was waiting for me after mass. When I passed through the door of the church into the chill of the autumn air, she stepped into my path. I demanded to know what she wanted.

She seemed taken aback. She watched my guards warily as if worried they would try to chase her off, but I dismissed them. She waited until they were gone, and then said, "At last your highness deigns to speak to me."

I refused to be baited. "Get to your point."

"I know how you feel," she said. "I know what it feels like to be scorned and rejected. I know your pain."

"No, you don't. You deserve everything that's happened to you."

"Fine. Okay. On that much we agree. I deserve it because I provoked it. I'm not innocent. I would never claim otherwise. But I'm not as bad as you seem to think."

I didn't answer.

She smiled. "You realize it's no accident I'm here, don't you?"

"I figured as much."

"That's because you're clever, Licinia. But what about Placidius? Do you think he's clever? Do you think he's figured out the same things you have."

"I don't care whether he has or not. It's not my concern."

She gaped at me. "Not your concern? You can't be serious."

"Leave me alone, Justa. I can't help you."

"You're smarter than you act," she said. "And you're smarter than him—a lot smarter."

I turned back to her. "Listen. I have no control over him. He's the Emperor. He does what he wants. I'm merely his wife, and a poor one at that. Justa, he's not going to give me a son. He won't even talk to me, much less sleep with me, so whatever you and Galla think you're going to get from me, you're mistaken. I can't help you." I walked away.

She came after me. "But you *can* make him talk to you. You *can* make him take you back."

I raised my hand to fend her off. "I'm not interested in your conspiracies. Leave me alone."

"It wasn't me," she said. "I know what you think, but you're wrong. It wasn't me."

I squinted at her. "What are you talking about?"

"It was Heraclius," she said. "He was the one who gave you the pennyroyal. He was the one who tried to poison you."

"What?"

"It was Heraclius. He was the one who tried to make you lose your baby. Not me."

I was speechless.

"Your aunt was behind it. She planted him in your household. He was put there to prevent you from having a child. You don't know your aunt. She would do anything to prevent you from producing an heir. It's true. I know it for a fact. I know it because she tried to involve me. I had done similar things for her in the past, so she thought I would help her with this. But I refused."

I could not find the means to utter a response.

"Don't look so shocked," she said. "It's not as if you just arrived here yesterday. You know how things work. If you bear an heir, the two halves of the Empire will be united under one ruler. Pulcheria's hopes of ruling the East will be dashed. She's not going to stand for that. In fact, she tried to stop it before it started. She hired me, and together we conspired to prevent your marriage. Placidius was correct. For once he actually figured something out. We hired agents to plant heretical documents on him, so the Church would object to the union. It didn't work, but we tried."

I stared at her open-mouthed.

"It was your aunt's idea," she said. "She masterminded the whole thing."

I felt dizzy. There was a low stone wall nearby, and I sank down on it.

"I'm not innocent," Justa said. "I was jealous, and I acted out of spite. I was wrong to do what I did, and I'm sorry. But that doesn't change the way things are. There are people who want to hurt you, Licinia. You mustn't let them. You must show them you're on to them. You must fight back."

"And how do you propose I do that?"

"By disappointing them. By giving us an heir."

I groaned and threw up my hands. "I already told you. He won't sleep with me. He barely even speaks to me. I'm powerless to do anything about it."

She gave me a skeptical look. "Don't say that. Never say that. You are a woman. You have more power than you think. If Placidius won't sleep with you, there's still another way."

"What way?"

"Sleep with someone else."

I drew back in disgust. "What are you saying?"

"Get pregnant. It doesn't matter by whom. If you bear a son, Placidius will have no choice but to acknowledge him. To do otherwise would cast him as a laughingstock in the eyes of the public. He'll never allow that to happen."

I was appalled. "Just what kind of a person do you take me for?"

Justa rolled her eyes. "Stopping pretending to be so naïve, Licinia. You're smarter than you act. The Empire needs an heir. It does not need Placidius."

I lurched to my feet intending to leave. She grabbed my arm.

"Listen to me," she said. "You're in danger. He's trying to put you aside. He's trying to make you expendable."

The tears squeezed out of my eyes. "Leave me alone!" I jerked away from her.

"There are others," she said.

"Others?"

"Other women," she said. "There has been for months. Everyone knows it. He's trying to replace you. You mustn't let him."

Her words struck me like a blow. My flesh went cold.

She watched my reaction. "Don't tell me you believed he was celibate. If you did, you were the only one in the Empire.

Even the public howls at that. It's a joke in every taberna from here to Alexandria."

I bent over and steadied myself against the wall. She must have thought I was about to collapse because she reached out to steady me. And that's when I saw it. It had fallen out of the neck of her tunic: a circular amulet cast in lead with a picture of Christ entering Jerusalem and a three-line inscription reading, "God be with you."

I tried to grab it.

She drew back. "What are you doing?"

"Give me that," I said.

She held it in the palm of her hand. "What? This?"

"Give it to me."

She laughed. "Why should I?"

"I want it."

She drew back a few steps. "If you want it, you can have it. But you have to do as I ask. Give us an heir."

I glared at her.

She dangled it in front of my face. "It's really not so much to ask."

* * *

All during that time Agnus wrote to me asking if something was wrong and wondering why I didn't come to Rome to visit her. I assured her I was well and not upset with her but that I was taking some time for myself, to "reevaluate things," as I put it. On several occasions Petronius Maximus visited Ravenna to consult with the Placidius. They had become fast friends, and Placidius was relying more and more on the wealthy patrician for advice and guidance. Yet only twice did Maximus bring Agnus with him to Ravenna, and both times we were confined to our ceremonial roles and kept apart.

More often, Placidius made the journey to Rome. He liked the excitement the city offered: the chariot races, the theatre, and the spectacles. If he was committed to remaining chaste, his frequent trips to Rome told a different story. Certainly, his decision to become a eunuch had been forgotten, and he was seen less and less often at prayer. All the evidence lent credence to Justa's accusations. But I had heard nothing to confirm he was actually cheating on me.

On several occasions Junius came to Ravenna to discuss matters pertaining to his duties. During the summer he visited to discuss the construction of a road between Patavium and Venetia. In the fall, the conversation was about the festivities surrounding the announcement of the new consul, which that year was to be the Emperor himself. After the first of the year, having retained his position as praetor for a third term, Junius came to talk about the erection of a monument honoring the Emperor and the dredging of the port at Aquileia. On each of these occasions he sought me out. He sent notes by way of a messenger and requested that I meet with him privately. In every case, I declined. He could only have assumed I was spurning him, which was not my intention at all. I contemplated writing him a short message to explain things, to confess I had overheard his conversation with his father and saw the trouble I was causing him, but I worried he might regard it as a plea for sympathy on my part, and I didn't want that. Things were complicated enough.

After my conversation with Justa, Junius came to Ravenna one more time to discuss the celebrations surrounding the naming of his father as patrician. To grant Maximus that title was a direct jab at Aetius, who was the last person so honored. The title of patrician was rarely granted, and then only to generals and military leaders, so to give it to a mere aristocrat had the effect of diminishing the previous honoree's status, which was intended I suppose.

This time Junius did not send a note to request a meeting, which, if I am to be honest, wounded me more than I would have liked, but I swallowed my tears. Later in the day, to occupy my mind, I went to visit the children and was withdrawing from their company when I turned a corner and ran smack into him. He looked around to see if we were alone. Then he gathered my hands in his and looked into my eyes.

"What have I done? Please tell me. Whatever it was I apologize."

"It— it's not your fault," I said. "It's just complicated."

"It's not Agnus. Tell me it's not Agnus. She thinks she's the one to blame."

"Perish the thought. She's the sweetest creature in the world."

"Then what can it be?"

I twisted away from him. He pulled me back.

"You must tell me," he said. "I miss you. We both do. What have we done wrong?"

"Nothing," I said. I looked down at my hands. "I'm sorry. I'm afraid I've made things difficult for you. I never intended to."

"What are you talking about?"

I looked up. "I am the Augusta. I am the Emperor's wife. That carries with it certain…challenges."

His expression clouded. "Is this about my father?"

"We cannot do this."

"Do what? We're friends. That's all. I care about you."

"Others might see it differently."

"Someone has told you to stay away from me. Is that it? Someone's threatening to report falsehoods about us if you don't cooperate."

"It's nothing like that. You're wrong."

He looked past me, his eyes gleaming with anger. "I should have known. It's so like my father. He thinks by keeping you in the dark he can gain an advantage. He wants to keep us apart because he's worried I'll tell you the truth."

"The truth?"

He turned back to me with a pained expression. "The Emperor has a mistress. Several actually. It's all over Rome."

There it was. Justa had been telling the truth. My heart sank. I could not contain my tears.

He gathered me to him. "I'm sorry," he said. "You would have heard it from someone eventually anyway. It's better coming from me."

I sobbed. It was another blow. The final insult.

"Oh, poor Licinia. It's so cruel. You deserve better."

Our eyes locked. Then he kissed me.

The feeling I had was unlike anything I had ever experienced before. It made me lightheaded and giddy. A wave of pleasure washed over me. He kissed me again and I surrendered to him.

Somewhere down the corridor a door swung open. We heard footsteps approaching. We sprang apart, our hair and clothing disheveled.

Heraclius rounded the corner and stopped to look at us. He gave us a knowing smile.

"Shocking," he said in his high-pitched voice. He bowed and hurried off snickering under his breath.

The next day I received a note from Placidius granting me permission to visit my parents in Constantinople. I was to leave within a fortnight and stay away until I received permission to return. I was not to take the children. I was to go alone. It was obvious what he was doing. He was sending me into exile.

# Chapter 13
The Years AD 446 – AD 448

My journey to Constantinople was an ordeal. It started with a painful parting from my children. On the morning of my departure, Eudocia and Placidia were upset. Placidia who had just turned five went so far as to accuse me of abandoning her.

"You don't love me anymore! You hate me!"

I tried to comfort her, but she was having none of it. When I went to the door, she started shrieking. Eudocia stood silently against the wall, her bottom lip quivering, tears rolling down her cheeks. When I turned to say goodbye, she flung herself into my arms.

"I want to go with you. Don't leave me."

Placidia joined her. Both of them clung to me and wailed. I had to tear myself away from them. Their cries followed me down the corridor.

Separating from my daughters was hard enough but leaving Ravenna knowing that my absence would only encourage Placidius's infidelities grated on me.

It was all my fault. I should have shown him an example of unerring piety, and instead I had introduced him to perversion. I had given him a taste of wickedness, and then, when he had developed an appetite for it, I refused him. I was a sinner, and I had corrupted him.

Added to my self-loathing was an abiding sense of dread. Threats were closing in on all sides, not only Galla and Justa and Aetius, but also the Pope, and now the aristocracy as well.

I had lost the love of my husband, offended God, and been cruelly separated from my children. I had failed in every conceivable way. And now I was returning home to my father. I could only pray I would not disappoint him as well.

I traveled with a full retinue and a score of mounted soldiers. Our journey took us through a country laid waste by the Huns. Appalling raids had left whole villages reduced to ashes, the occupants murdered or sent fleeing to the nearest walled cities. The peace agreement had brought the depredations to an end, yet there remained a palpable sense of unease, an apprehension born of experience that the Huns might go back on the offensive, provoked by some perceived slight, and destroy even more.

The feeling had been intensified in recent weeks by news that Bleda, one of the two Hun brothers who had ruled for years, had been killed under mysterious circumstances. It was rumored that his brother, Attila, had murdered him, an ominous development because, of the two, Bleda had been regarded as the more restrained and rational. Attila, on the other hand, was capable of anything.

Anxiety gripped the members of my entourage as we traveled through the Nisava Gorge beside the tumbling waters of a raging river. We made camp beside a stream, and, although my tent was heavily guarded, I lay awake, unable to sleep. In the morning my mind was a jumble of worries and apprehensions. All day long I was jumpy and on edge and could not order my thoughts. My nervousness lasted the remainder of the journey and was accompanied by upwellings of emotions, sudden bouts of weeping, and long stretches of brooding self-contempt. By the time we got to Constantinople I was an emotional wreck and practically threw myself into my father's arms.

He gathered me to him and spoke soothing words as he petted my head. By degrees, my anxiety waned, and I took a bath and went to bed. I slept far into the next day. When I awoke my father was sitting at my bedside. He held my hand and told me everything would be all right.

It was good to be home.

*  *  *

My first few months in Constantinople were a reprieve. The cares and woes that had clouded my life in Ravenna began to dissipate and permit in a few rays of sunlight. My father's presence lifted my spirits, and my mother was there as well. Still, something was off. I couldn't quite put my finger on it. The atmosphere around the palace was strained. My father, who had always impressed me as relaxed and confident, seemed ill at ease now. I wondered if it had anything to do with my aunt, so I asked him the question that had been gnawing at me for weeks. Had she really tried to sabotage my marriage?

The vague and non-committal answer I got did little to ease my burden.

"It's possible," he said, "given what we know about her now. On the other hand, there were those who stood to benefit from her misfortune."

I didn't bother to ask him if he was referring to my mother.

He went on. "It would be wrong to disparage Pulcheria without acknowledging her good points. I have felt her absence more than I would like to admit."

Still, the possibility remained that she was guilty of the awful things she had been accused of, and it bothered me more than I wanted to admit. As for my mother, she wasn't gloating over her triumph. On the contrary, she seemed anxious and guarded, and when I asked her about Pulcheria's treachery, she declined to discuss it and told me to put it out of my mind.

I suppose I should have been charitable and accepted her reticence as concern for my wellbeing, but I couldn't help but recall that this was the same woman who had embarrassed us all by bringing scandal and disgrace on our household. She was no stranger to selfishness and duplicity, and her reluctance to speak now about a topic she had been more than happy to discuss in her letter struck me as hypocritical. The impression was only magnified by what happened next.

My father held a banquet in my honor. I didn't really want it. I was still working through the trauma of what had happened and preferred to remain out of the public eye, but my father insisted. I was the Empress of the West, he said, and as such, I had to be formally welcomed to the Eastern court.

I went along with it.

In the end it was pleasant enough. I met some important people in my father's administration, some of whom I had known as a child, but whose functions had meant little to me. Now I could appreciate the contributions they were making and could evaluate their merits. I found them impressive—or at least some of them. Others I found shallow and mercenary.

One among them stood out for his poise and intellect, the Praetorian Prefect of the East, Flavius Constantinus. Constantinus had demonstrated remarkable skill in engineering by erecting a complex system of watermills consisting of sixteen water wheels in descending rows fed by two aqueducts. The system was capable of grinding wheat or sawing timber in great numbers. All who saw it marveled at its design, but Flavius Constantinus downplayed his accomplishment with disarming modesty.

I was introduced to this remarkable individual by another person of distinction, General Aspar, a former consul who had played a vital role in returning Galla Placidia to power when she and Placidius, who had been six-years-old at the time, were usurped by the pretender Joannes. Aspar struck me as a canny and capable man with a deep knowledge of military affairs and a passionate commitment to the Empire.

At his side was his captain of the guards, Flavius Marcian, an affable, well-spoken figure, quick with a joke, but with the reputation of being a tiger in battle. They all seemed to know my mother and were comfortable with her, but my mother seemed awkward with them as if they might say or do something inadvertently to embarrass her. So, she made her formalities and excused herself with due haste.

Among those who struck me as ill-mannered and untrustworthy was the eunuch Chrysaphius. A mere cubicularius, a keeper of the imperial bedchamber, when I was a girl, this frivolous person had risen to the post of chamberlain, making him one of my father's chief deputies. He swaggered about in embroidered robes and gold earrings, face powdered, eyes lined in kohl, displaying a feminine arrogance I found impertinent. He had a retinue of his own, which he ordered about with an imperiousness that bordered on cruelty. Most disturbing, he seemed not at all constrained about intruding on any conversation in which my father was engaged as if he were entitled to hear every word.

I was within earshot of one such conversation between my father and the new archbishop of Constantinople, a man named Flavian. They were talking about a gift the churchman had given my father in appreciation for his endorsement. The archbishop had given the Emperor three loaves of consecrated bread, and my father had thanked him for it. But Chrysaphius insinuated himself into the conversation. He claimed the gift fell short of what was appropriate. The archbishop looked from Chrysaphius to my father, hoping for some clarification, but seeing my father would not rescue him, asked the eunuch what he would consider adequate.

"Gold," Chrysaphius said.

The archbishop promised he would deliver it. My father said nothing.

I found the whole episode disconcerting and asked my father about it later.

"It's nothing," he said. "You needn't worry about it. This is business between men. Let the men take care of it."

His response felt a little demeaning as if he thought me incapable of comprehending the complexity of our court politics, as if I was some sort of child…

…or an idiot.

* * *

I had occasion to meet General Aspar and Captain Marcian again several months later when they came to the palace to discuss a matter of grave concern. Attila had sent a letter to my father reminding him of his obligations under the Treaty of Margus to return asylum seekers who had crossed the Danube to seek refuge in the Empire. The letter was alarming because the Huns had used the same pretense the last time they had violated the peace and invaded the East.

Aspar and Marcian tried to reassure my father that, unlike the last time, should the Huns strike now, they would be ready for them. The legions protecting the Danube had been restored to full strength and the frontier defenses were solid. This time if the Huns attacked, they would not be caught off guard as they had been before, an oblique reference to the fact that the last time the Huns had invaded most of the army had been away defending the West.

But my father wasn't sure. The Huns had evolved under Attila. They were no longer the fractious, impulsive brigands they had been in earlier times. They were highly organized and strategic. They seemed able to look beyond their immediate needs to longer term objectives. Most worrisome, they appeared to have mastered the art of siege warfare.

For decades walled cities had been the Huns' Achille's heel. Frightened townspeople ravaged by their raids had only to flee to the nearest walled cities for protection. When it came to heavy fortifications, the Huns had been like flies against glass. However, in their most recent raids they had shown a new aptitude. They had overcome at least three walled defenses. It was beyond imagining that they might surmount the walls of Constantinople, but my father didn't want to take any chances. He ordered the asylum seekers rounded up and returned to Attila. After they were all sent back, Father ordered a few dozen random people sent to the Huns as an added precaution. Then he authorized the payment of the tribute.

The generals were appalled. After the meeting, they sought out my mother. They pleaded with her to reason with my father, to impress on him the folly of trying to appease the Huns. The annual tribute of 700 pounds of gold the government was obliged to pay under the terms of the treaty would not prevent Attila from attacking again should the spirit move him. What's more, the burden placed on the treasury was draining the military of the resources it needed for defense. In their view the policy was suicidal. Better to refuse to pay the tribute and use the money to attack the Huns. But my mother was no help. Her nervous equivocation left them dissatisfied. After they left, I asked my mother why she had declined to advocate on their behalf.

"My dear girl," she said. "Why do you insist on prying into things that will only upset you. Put them out of your mind. Go find something to do. Isn't there some weaving you can occupy yourself with?"

I felt my temper rising. "I'm not a child any longer, Mother. I've been the Augusta of the West for ten years. In spite of what you may think, I have not kept my head in the sand. I've seen a few things."

She reached out and placed her hand on my cheek. "And I have seen how it affects you. Please leave it alone. It's none of your business."

"Tell me!"

She looked at me for a long time. Then without speaking another word, she walked away and left me looking after her in frustration. Once again, she was keeping secrets, secrets that threatened the stability of our family. I wondered if she were up to her old tricks again, involved in some shameful indecency that would force my father to send her away, to deprive me of my mother just when I needed her most. It was so selfish and stupid of her, so inconsiderate. She made me so mad.

* * *

My mother was not altogether wrong about the fragility of my emotions. The pain she detected in me was authentic; the wounds inflicted by the collapse of my marriage were real. For six months after arriving in Constantinople, I awaited word that my banishment was repealed and I could go home to my children, but the word never came. My longing for them was a physical thing, a tangible ache. They were six and seven-years-old now, ages at which young girls needed their mother, and to think they were growing up without me filled me with sorrow.

Yet, for all that, I was glad to be in Constantinople, back in the bosom of my family, and away from the isolation that had weighed so heavily upon me in Ravenna, but it didn't mean I was content. Often, I would sit by myself gazing out at the Bosporus and let my eyes drift off across the gently rolling waters to the sea and the world beyond. I reflected on my failings, the terrible things I had done to cause the dissolution of my marriage. Sometimes I thought about Placidius and the cruel way he had treated me, and I became angry. But then I reminded myself that I was at least partially to blame. He was my husband and I owed him deference and obedience, areas where I had failed.

Occasionally I recalled the words of the African Fathers and how they laid the blame for so many of the world's problems at the feet of women. I thought of how I had pressed those books on Placidius and how he had taken them to heart. No wonder he had come to see me as the source of all his troubles. Those hateful screeds had told him so. But then I thought it was wrong of me to feel that way.

The words of the African Fathers were divinely inspired. To think of them in derogatory terms was but a weak attempt by a proud and sinful woman to blame the failings of her gender on others. It was immoral to have such thoughts, and so I banished them from my mind. But they never went away. Like mischievous imps caught peeking in at the door, they crooked their fingers at me and invited me to ponder them anew. Sometimes I did, before I chased them away again.

I didn't flagellate myself. Not this time. I had suffered enough. And, while two wrongs don't make a right, it did occur to me that Placidius had not only failed to do penance for his iniquity but had also compounded it by engaging in adultery. Why should a woman suffer twice as much as man for the same sins? I had desired Junius; it was true. But I had not acted on it the way Placidius had. Why should I punish myself for contemplating the same sin he had indulged in with impunity? Why should I add to the suffering I had already endured—exile and separation from my children—with even more pain?

Even Pulcheria had suffered a greater punishment for a lesser crime, albeit a similar one, for it had come to my knowledge through gossip and innuendo that my father had exiled her for the crime of fornication. She had broken her vow of celibacy and lain with a man. For that she had been expelled, not for plotting against my father, not for intriguing against me, but for having had sex. It was a charge she vehemently denied, yet one that carried greater opprobrium in the public eye than anything else she had been suspected of. Pulcheria was renowned for her piety and purity, so to have failed in it so spectacularly was a cause for disgrace and scorn. As a result, she was driven from the palace and now resided at Antioch, some 350 miles away.

Before long it came to my attention that the eunuch Chrysaphius had had a hand in her undoing. He had brought witnesses against her and pressed for her exile. My mother played a role as well, although her involvement was unclear. She certainly benefited from my aunt's removal. Within days of Pulcheria's expulsion, Mother had been recalled from banishment and restored to my father's side. Her crime expunged.

I learned all of this as time went by even though my father and mother never discussed it. I heard it in dribs and drabs from courtiers and servants. Whenever I tried to broach the subject with my parents directly, they were evasive and refused to discuss it. Their excuse was always the same: they didn't want to upset me; these were matters best put behind us. But something was off, and I eventually figured out what it was.

My mother and father were both under the thumb of Chrysaphius. That strutting eunuch was working them like puppets, and his policies were leading the Eastern Roman Empire toward ruin.

* * *

How my father had fallen under the sway of Chrysaphius was a mystery as were so many things about my parents, but the effects were beyond dispute. Chrysaphius had been the author of my father's misguided policy of appeasing the Huns. It was he who had insisted on paying them off, and it was he who had fought against every attempt to rescind the policy and redeploy the money to strengthen the army. It was rumored that Chrysaphius was getting kickbacks from Attila and had grown fabulously rich by it. Certainly, Aspar and Marcian believed that, which is why they had been trying to get my mother to persuade my father to ditch the policy and beat Attila to the punch by going on the attack. My mother was unwilling to become involved, which was why they turned to me in desperation.

They approached me at the feast of Brumalia, the fall harvest festival, nine months after I had returned. The first vintages of the year were unsealed on the occasion and were the cause of much drinking, impromptu parades, and boisterous masquerades. My father insisted I participate, thinking it might lift my spirits. I went along. I donned a leering comedy mask and an ornate robe and passed through the streets of the city unrecognized. I got caught up in the revelry and was danced about and given too much to drink and carried along in a rowdy procession. I found the whole thing great fun and enjoyed myself immensely.

Marcian came upon me while I was cavorting. I don't know whether he identified me and then approached me or the other way around. But we danced in the street and then sat on the curb to catch our breath and pass an amphora between us. He was twenty years my senior and handsome, but on that night, he was wearing a mask of Bacchus and acting the part. His capacity for drink was considerable. Mine, not so much. Perhaps it was my inebriated state—or perhaps his—that emboldened him to air his grievances.

He spoke of his frustration with my father. He complained bitterly of Chrysaphius and his interference. He warned about the volatility of the Huns and the likelihood they would strike again without warning. He spoke of the urgency of hitting them first and putting them on the defensive.

"When the Huns are on the offensive, they are an irresistible force," he said.

While we were sitting there, Aspar came up behind us and clapped Marcian on the shoulder.

"There you are," he said. "I've been looking all over for you." Aspar was not wearing a mask.

Marcian explained. "I was enticed by this antic figure and drawn into the revelry," Marcian said. "Do you recognize her?"

Aspar squinted. "Give me a hint."

"Well, let us say she is very close to the Emperor."

A look of surprise came over Aspar's face. "Is that you, Augusta?"

I tipped up my mask and grinned. He let out a whoop of laughter.

"We've been dancing in the street," Marcian said. "Our young princess here is more spirited than she lets on. When she puts on a happy face, she positively inhabits the part."

"The mask becomes me, I guess."

"Or the mask *is* you," Marcian said. "Sometimes we have to don a mask to show the world who we really are."

"Which means that the person I've been showing the world all along is someone else."

"We have to allow for the possibility," Marcian said.

Aspar sat down on the curb beside us. "Well, this is very interesting." He gestured for the amphora. "We've been looking for someone with the right spirit, someone willing to confront the Emperor and persuade him to act." He took a drink. "Listen Empress, the situation is dire. There has been another message from the Huns. They continue to accuse us of harboring asylum seekers. Your father's attempt to appease them isn't working."

"Attila is a monster," Marcian said.

"And now they've added another accusation," Aspar said. "They accuse us of withholding payment owed to them under the original treaty signed more than twenty years ago."

"The same treaty *they* violated when they invaded Illyricum," Marcian said.

"It's a pretense to attack," Aspar said. "They're sending us a clear warning. We must act. We cannot sit on our hands."

"How can I help?" I asked.

"You must speak to your father. You must tell him to ignore Chrysaphius. Chrysaphius is in the pay of the Huns. The policy of appeasement he endorses is designed to drain our coffers while it fills theirs. If we don't act, before long our armies will be too weak to withstand them."

I looked at them through my mask. "But why don't you tell him that yourselves?"

"Chrysaphius has his ear. If we press him too hard, he may sack us. We need someone close to him, someone he trusts, someone he can't spurn."

"How about my mother?"

They exchanged a dismal glance. "We tried to speak with her, but it got us nowhere. It's as if she has fallen under the sway of the eunuch as well."

"We need Pulcheria back," Marcian said. "She would know how to handle this." He took another drink and passed the amphora to me. I lifted my mask, took a drink, and passed it to Aspar.

"Pulcheria was falsely charged," Aspar said. "She's not guilty of the crimes she's accused of. She remains chaste. She has never lain with any man."

I turned to him in astonishment. "How do you know that?"

"Because I know your aunt."

"Was it my mother?" I asked.

They looked at each other. "No. It was not her. It was Chrysaphius."

"I will talk to my parents," I said. "I will demand answers."

"Be careful. It could be dangerous."

"Dangerous? How?"

They looked at each other in consternation.

I took off my mask and set it aside. As I twisted around, I accidentally knocked over the amphora. The contents spilled, leaving a blood red stain on the pavement. We all looked down at it with gloomy expressions.

Marcian picked it up and peered down the neck. "All gone," he said.

"There's always more where that came from," Aspar said, trying to make light of it.

We went to get more wine, but the fun had gone out of the night. I excused myself and went home.

I lay awake that night as drunk as I'd ever been. I was sick to my stomach. In the morning I felt wretched. I swore to myself I would never drink again. Yet two days later, after the poison was out of my system, I had still not fully recovered. Obviously, something more than wine was afflicting me. My mood had soured, and I wanted to be left alone.

* * *

Weeks went by, and the Huns did not attack. It seemed the generals' dire warnings had been exaggerated. In a feeble attempt to assuage my guilt for having failed to act, I told my-self their fears had been unfounded. I had failed to speak to my parents as I had promised. Maybe my fragile state would not permit it, or maybe it was because I had seen the conse-quences of interfering in the affairs of others and learned my lesson. But increasingly I knew it was neither of those things.

To be honest, I feared what might happen should my par-ents perceive me as taking a position against them. As a result,

I betrayed my promise to Aspar and Marcian to assist them. My wavering commitment had regrettable consequences.

Early in the new year the Huns dropped all pretense of negotiating and went on the attack. They poured across the border at Aquae. They overran a series of forts along the Danube, culminating in the conquest of Ratiaria, the home of the Danube fleet. The speed and totality of their attack were stunning. It looked very much like our army had overestimated their ability to withstand them, an impression that only deepened when the Huns spread south and east to take Philippopolis and Arcadiopolis and approach within 100 miles of Constantinople.

By late January the city was in a panic. Then, things got worse. A powerful earthquake struck. The city's massive walls crumbled. Constantinople was exposed and vulnerable, and the Huns were fast approaching. My father was beside himself with fear and anxiety. He rushed around in a frenzy. He begged his advisors for answers; he received only blank stares and ashen faces. Even Chrysaphius wept in terror.

But then I remembered something I had heard months earlier, something about an engineering marvel performed by the Praetorian Prefect of the East, a dignified, unflappable man name Flavius Constantinus. I urged my father to call on him.

Constantinus arrived and assessed the situation. The walls could be repaired. There were enough materials on hand, but the problem was labor. With so many men away fighting the Huns, there wasn't enough manpower to get the job done. He applied his formidable intellect to the problem and came up with a solution. There were a great many sports fans in

Constantinople, avid followers of the two chariot racing factions: the blues and the greens. These men were mostly older members of the patrician class who could not be bothered to send their sons off to war but were fanatical supporters of the chariot races and fiercely competitive with each other.

Constantinus hit upon the idea of setting up a competition between them to rebuild the walls as rapidly as possible. First, he recruited the charioteers. When the fans saw their heroes throwing themselves into the task, they gathered to cheer them. And when the charioteers called for volunteers to assist, the fans rushed forward with a will. The walls went up incredibly fast.

Meanwhile, Aspar and Marcian had succeeded in blunting the Huns' attack and diverting them south and east where they fell on Sestus and Callipolis before advancing north along the coast to Athyras, a mere twenty miles from the city. They were within a day's ride when the last stone was set in place and the walls completed. Constantinus's brilliant idea had rebuilt the walls of Constantinople in an astonishing sixty days.

The Huns were caught by surprise. They had not expected the walls to be repaired so quickly. Although they had mastered the art of siege warfare and overcome the walls of smaller cities, overwhelming the walls of Constantinople was another matter. What's more, sickness had broken out in their camp.

In the end Attila opted not to attack and marched his army west to consolidate earlier gains and dig in. Aspar, seeing his chance, went on the attack and pursued the retreating Huns. On the banks of the Utus River west of Marcianople, fresh Roman troops led by General Arnegisclus blocked the Huns' path and caught them in a vise. The Huns fought back.

At first it looked like our armies had the advantage, but the Huns would not give up. The fighting raged for three bloody days until we began to fall short of supplies. Chrysaphius's misguided policy of redirecting resources to buy the Huns' restraint hit us hard. Our soldiers were forced to withdraw. The Huns fell on Marcianople and razed it. After it was over, both armies retreated, beaten down and exhausted. The Huns limped back across the Danube, battered and much reduced.

A message arrived at the capital a few weeks later offering a truce. Everyone breathed a sigh of relief. My father sent an envoy to negotiate, but the resulting agreement was a travesty. Attila resumed his demands that Hun asylum seekers be returned. What's more, the annual tribute in gold was to be tripled. Now it was to be 2,100 pounds plus any amounts in arrears, a staggering amount that threatened to bankrupt us.

My father agreed to it anyway. When Aspar and Marcian objected, they were summarily sacked. The near disaster, so magnificently thwarted by Flavius Constantinus, went to waste. The self-defeating policy of buying the Huns' forbearance was resumed, and the benefits to Chrysaphius in the form of kickbacks grew larger.

The whole situation made me mad. What might have been celebrated as a mighty victory became ashes in our hands. I could not understand my father's cowardice or his deference to Chrysaphius. Things had gone from bad to worse, and large portions of the Empire lay in ruins. It was shameful.

And judging by my mother's reaction I wasn't the only one who thought so.

# Chapter 14
## Summer-Fall AD 448

I came upon my mother weeping in the chapel, an image of Christ rendered in mosaic on the wall above her. When I asked her what was wrong, she crumbled and admitted her guilt over the sad state of affairs.

"Why, what have you done?" I asked.

She hung her head, tears streaming down her face. I felt a twinge of sympathy for her.

"I really don't want to involve you in this," she said. "I should be protecting you, not putting you at risk. Please understand."

When I thought about it, I had to admit if I were in the same situation, I would do everything I could to protect my daughters. I would not want to involve them in something that could hurt them.

My mother rubbed the tears from her eyes. "When you first came back, you were so hurt by what happened in Ravenna. My heart went out to you. I wanted to shield you from any more pain, so when you asked to know the truth, I tried to put you off. Maybe I was wrong to do that, and I'm sorry. God knows since then things have only gotten worse. I'm at my wits' ends, and I don't know where to turn. I need help, Licinia. I'm desperate."

"Why, what's wrong, Mother? What's going on?"

"You're smarter than most people give you credit for. You deserve to be told the truth, and I'm prepared to tell you, but I want you to know that it goes against all of my motherly instincts. Are you sure you want to hear this?"

Suddenly I wasn't so sure. Did I really want to look the truth in the face? All my girlish fantasies would be destroyed, and I would have to deal with the facts. As Galla Placidia had said, "Ignorance and obedience have their benefits." Once I stepped through the door there would be no turning back. I could never again pretend to be oblivious to what was going on around me. At twenty-seven I understood myself sufficiently to know what I wanted, and what I wanted was the truth.

But was I strong enough to take it?

My mother could see my hesitation. She reached out and touched my hand. "What you did in the face of danger was amazing. When everyone else was losing their heads, you focused on the problem and came up with a solution. Bringing Flavius Constantinus in to repair the walls was brilliant. We would have been lost without you."

I blushed and was diffident.

"It's never easy to see things as they are," she said. "Looking the truth in the face is difficult. Accepting the facts can be hard. It's not for the faint of heart, Licinia. But you are strong. You make me proud."

Tears leapt to my eyes. "But I'm afraid, Mother."

She put my head against her bosom and stroked my hair. "Your grandfather, my father, was a philosopher," she said. "When I was a girl, he taught me to seek wisdom. He taught me to seek truth. Your aunt never liked that about me; it was not what she had bargained for. She was looking for something else. I don't know if I ever told you this, but your aunt was the one who selected me to be your father's wife. Out of hundreds of candidates I was chosen. She picked me for my beauty and charm. She never dreamed I would have a mind of my own.

"I came from a pagan family, so she insisted I convert to Christianity. I told her I would, but I didn't know how difficult it would be. Once you know something you cannot unknow it. All you can do is pretend. Your aunt understood that. She had chosen the truth. She was able to see it better than most. But she also knew how to pretend. She pretended to be pure and decent. She pretended to be pious and obedient. But she was not."

I felt the urge to come to my aunt's defense, but I held back.

"She was both stronger and smarter than your father," she said. "She controlled him. She told him what to do, and he went along. But with me it was a different story. She couldn't control me, and it drove her mad. That's when she decided to get rid of me."

"By making up lies?"

My mother brushed aside the question. "Galla was staying with us then. She had been exiled from Ravenna, driven out of town by a false scandal. She was accused of incest. Do you know what incest is?"

I did, although the idea of it turned my stomach.

"There was no truth to it, but Pulcheria seized on it. Galla was a bright, intelligent young woman, a potential rival, and Pulcheria felt threatened by her, so she used the scandal to keep Galla in her place. But Galla was no easy target. She fought back and turned to me. She enlisted me as her ally, and we worked together to weaken Pulcheria's grip on power."

"How did you do that?"

"We betrothed you to Placidius. At the ages of five and two, you were promised to each other. Which meant, in the course of time, the two halves of the Empire would be reunited under one ruler, your son. It meant Pulcheria's grip on power would one day be broken. Naturally, she fought back with all the weapons she had.

"When, after a time, Galla returned to Ravenna to take up her role as regent, Pulcheria got her revenge. She accused me of perversion, roused public opinion against me, and urged your father to divorce me. He would not agree to a divorce, but he sent me away. I was cruelly separated from you, my only child, and driven into exile. But it was only the start. Having gotten rid of me, she moved to replace me in your affections. She raised you and tried to mold you into the kind of meek, submissive young woman who would give her what she wanted. She tried to persuade you to take on celibacy, which would have solved all her problems. But you foiled her. You proved more intelligent and independent than she had hoped, so she tried to attack the problem a different way. She tried to undermine your marriage. First, she tried to get the Church to oppose it. When that didn't work and the marriage went ahead anyway, she planted Heraclius in your household to turn your husband against you."

I pulled back from her. "If you knew all this, why didn't you tell me?"

"I didn't know how you would react. If you were the kind of woman who preferred to be kept in the dark, knowing all this would traumatize you. But if you were strong enough to take it —well…"

I shook my head in disbelief.

She continued. "I asked Galla to help me. I asked her to reveal the truth to you slowly, to see how you would respond. The results were not promising. You seemed unwilling to accept what she was telling you, so I told her to quit. You didn't seem like the kind of woman who wanted the burden of the facts."

That stung, but she was not wrong.

"Believe me, your safety and wellbeing were my only concern," she said. "I wanted to remove Heraclius, knowing the threat he posed to you, but it wouldn't have done much good as long as Pulcheria was in power. She would simply have replaced him with someone else. To remove the threat, I had to remove Pulcheria. So, when Chrysaphius approached me with a plot to discredit her, I went along."

"So, you are in league with Chrysaphius after all."

"Yes. Or at least I was. In the end, the eunuch proved even more duplicitous than your aunt, but at first he seemed quite reasonable. Pulcheria was adamantly against sending the fleet to help you fight the Vandals. Chrysaphius took your part, persuading your father that he owed it to the future of the Empire to defend you. He reminded him, in your aunt's presence, that you would bear us an heir. We would be reunited, but only if the West survived. Few words could be more calculated to antagonize your aunt, and she used all her persuasive powers to try to change your father's mind. On the face of it, however, her argument was weak. There was no rational reason not to send the fleet. We were facing no imminent threat, and her own beloved niece's life was at risk. Her attitude only served to reinforce what Chrysaphius had been telling your father, that Pulcheria was working against you, trying to prevent you from bearing an heir so she could come to power upon his demise."

She paused to study my expression, to see how I was taking this. She went on. "The next step came when the Huns took advantage of our weakened defenses and invaded. Pulcheria pointed to this as evidence she had been right. But Chrysaphius convinced your father that the problem was easily solved by buying the Huns off. The Eastern Empire was rich then, and buying the Huns' forbearance was not unprecedented. In any case, it was better than trying to fight them while most of our army was away in the West."

"Makes sense," I said.

Mother nodded. "Pulcheria was against it and argued—correctly, as it turned out—that paying the Huns now would only invite more demands from them later. But your father sided with the eunuch, which incurred your aunt's wrath and caused her to speak out against your father in public. That did not sit well with your father. And when it began to be whispered about that she was hatching a scheme to usurp him, he took notice. That's when Chrysaphius reached out to me. He convinced me that your father had become so disillusioned with his sister he was reconsidering decisions he had made earlier at her urging, including his decision to exile me. Chrysaphius thought it would be an easy matter to get your father to recall me, particularly if he, Chrysaphius, championed the idea. But there were strings attached. If I wanted his assistance, I would have to do something in exchange." Here she hesitated and grew pensive.

"What did he want you to do?"

"He wanted me to bear false testimony against Pulcheria. He wanted me to testify that I had seen her coupling with a married man, carrying on the affair under the nose of the Emperor for years. I wouldn't have to bear the weight of the lie alone, he assured me. There were others who would corroborate my testimony. The combined weight would be enough to sway the Emperor. He was sure of it. Well, it didn't take me long to make up my mind. If I ever wanted to rescue you from the threat your aunt posed to you, this was my chance."

The openness of her confession stunned me, but I was not about to interrupt her. "Go ahead," I said.

"In private session I leveled the charge, along with Chrysaphius and the others," she said. "The charges stuck. The accusations were made public, and the people turned against Pulcheria. It's an odd quirk of human nature that the carnal misdeeds of others provoke greater moral outrage than treachery or corruption. If you want to assassinate someone's character, it's always better to charge them with depravity than with deceit. Pulcheria was guilty of all sorts of terrible things, much of it based on duplicity, and all of it designed to advance her own interests at the expense of others, but it took accusations of sexual impropriety to bring her down. She was driven from the capital in disgrace. A week later, I was welcomed back with great fanfare.

"I couldn't have been more relieved, for now I was in a position to save you at last. As soon as I got home, I made arrangements to have Heraclius removed. I sent the orders and waited. I expected confirmation any day. No word came. Then Chrysaphius informed me that he had revoked my order. He was in charge now, and only he would decide the fate of the agents in his employ. What's more, should I ever issue an order without his permission again, he would have me taken out and horsewhipped. I was stunned. How dare he speak to me like that. I was the Empress, and he was a servant. But when I threatened to go to Theodosius, he laughed in my face. 'Your husband does as I tell him,' he informed me flatly. 'He is my creature. I own him.'"

I couldn't believe what I was hearing. "But how could that be? How could a mere servant have more influence with Father than his own wife?"

My mother turned reflective. The moment stretched itself out. "I'm sorry," she said at length. "This is the part I didn't want to have to tell you."

"Go ahead," I said. "I want to know."

She took a deep breath. "Your father is in love with him," she said. "He's infatuated with Chrysaphius. He will do anything to remain in his affections, even going so far as to banish his own sister—and, if necessary, his wife."

I could hardly speak. I struggled for words. She folded me in her arms. When the initial shock receded, the tears came. I sobbed against her shoulder. She led me to a seat. We sat down beneath the image of Christ.

"I made a mistake," she said. "As bad as your aunt was, she always cared deeply, passionately about the Empire. She may have thought she was the only one who could lead it, but she really cared. Not Chrysaphius. He cares only for himself, for his jewelry and silks and perfumes, for the power he has over others, and for gold—especially gold. His policies are designed to make him rich. The gold we pay the Huns drains our resources even as it fills his purse. This last debacle has made things even worse. 2,100 pounds of gold annually is unsustainable. Yet if we miss even one payment, the Huns will invade again, and it is an open question whether we can repel them now with Aspar and Marcian gone. I'm afraid we may have missed the opportunity to get rid of our enemies off once and for all. What makes it all the more demoralizing is that we were so close. After the battle at the Utus River, the Huns were badly beaten, crippled by disease and loss. Had we pursued them then, we could have destroyed them and been rid of them once and for all. Instead, we stood back and let them lay waste to Marcianople, and then sued for peace after they arrived safely back at their camps. That was Chrysaphius's doing. Now we owe them tribute three times the size of what we owed them before." She shook her head. "It's a disaster, and I don't know what to do about it."

I gathered her hands in mine. "Don't worry, Mother. I'll talk to Father. He'll listen to me."

"You must not. Anything you say will get back to Chrysaphius."

"So, what if it does? I'm innocent. Chrysaphius can't do anything to me."

My mother gave me a sad, sorry look. "Are you sure about that?

"What do you mean?"

"I have heard rumors about a certain young man, the praetor Junius. An affection existed between you. Is that right?"

My eyes grew large. "How do you know about that?"

"The eunuchs are in league with each other, even if the two Emperors are not. Heraclius works for Chrysaphius now. Together they are using their access to control our families. If you try to oppose them, they will turn the public against you, and you can exercise no influence if the public dislikes you. Believe me. I know."

"But it's not true. I never had an affair with Junius. We were friends."

"It's not the impropriety that matters. It's the appearance of an impropriety. They can use it to destroy you."

"As was done to you?"

"As was done to Pulcheria. Listen, Pulcheria is guilty of many wrongdoings, some of them far worse than sleeping with a man, but she did not commit the crime she is condemned for. As far as I know, she is still a virgin. I, on the other, am guilty of duplicity." She hung her head. "The charges against me were true."

"What do you mean?"

"The scandal that drove me from power was not fabricated. All your life you've been told I did something reprehensible to alienate your father's affections, but you never really knew what it was. Now I will tell you."

"Go ahead," I said warily, the tears staining my cheeks.

"They accused me of loving a person who was forbidden to me. That was my sin, the thing that got me exiled."

"Who was it? A general? A senator? A Pleb?"

"No, Licinia. It was none of those. In fact, it was not a man at all. It was a woman." She looked down at her hands.

My mouth fell open.

She reached out and touched me. "It was Galla. I fell in love with Galla Placidia."

* * *

The truth can be a terrible thing. It can turn your world upside down and force you to see things from a different perspective. It can separate you from all that is familiar to you and make you a stranger in your own existence. Having been forced to acknowledge my parents' wickedness, I now had to decide how to regard them. I could condemn them, as the Church would have me do, but above all things they were still my parents and I loved them. I could accept them without question, but that would be a tacit endorsement, which would be offensive to God.

Finally, I decided to weigh one sin against another in light of the crisis before us.

The immediate problem was Chrysaphius and the corrosive arrangement he had made with the Huns, a sin of malicious deceit buttressed by the sin of greed. Those sins were threatening to bring down the Eastern Empire and most of civilization along with it. If the Huns conquered the East, the Church would be eradicated too, its piety and godliness ripped apart by a tempest of malicious brutality. Surely God would not look unfavorably on me for trying to prevent that, even if it meant prioritizing the sins of Chrysaphius over those of my parents.

Once I began this process of weighing up one sin against another, the world was no longer a place inhabited by those who were good or bad, but by all those who fell short of godliness by differing degrees and particularities. I remembered Paul's epistle to the Romans: "For all have sinned and fall short of the glory of God." And I was strengthened by it. No longer was the purpose of the priests and theologians to define good and evil, but to evaluate the sins of disparate people and rank them according to the dangers they represented. It was a new way of thinking about things, and once I understood it, I grasped something even more unsettling. The priests and theologians had their own agenda.

My object was to save the Empire, to end the crippling policy that was weakening us while it gave strength and encouragement to our enemies. But the clergy seemed more interested in protecting their own interests. They were out to destroy anyone who threatened their authority, namely pagans, heretics, and anyone else who disagreed with their definition of orthodoxy—and along with them, women. The Church was a patriarchal institution. Women were at best an inconvenience, at worse a threat. The idea of women claiming any degree of authority was unacceptable to the Church leaders. Only someone like Pulcheria who pretended submissiveness while using her wits to play one off against another, was acceptable to them as they competed for her favor. I didn't have time to play that game. What I had to do I had to do quickly, so I made no attempt to square things with the

Church. Instead, with my mother's blessing, I boarded a ship and set sail for Antioch to speak with my aunt.

I arrived at her domicile after wending my way through a maze of narrow, dusty streets mostly empty on a Sabbath morning. Sunlight slanted down and cut oblong shapes into the cobbled corridors. The light flashed bright and hot on my face as I passed between the buildings. I expected her to be away at mass and to be admitted by a servant and ushered into the peristylum to wait among the flowers. But she answered the door.

If she was surprised by my unannounced appearance, she didn't show it. She looked me up and down as if inspecting my attire. Then she opened the door wider and stood aside with no word of greeting. Her manner was stiff and haughty. She was wearing a snow white gown and a black wimple pulled tight around her face, so her features stood out like those of a prisoner peering through bars. She had aged more than her years. She did not offer me a seat or refreshments. We stood in the forecourt of her atrium. Bright sunlight poured in through the opening in the ceiling and glittered on the water of the impluvium. The air was dead, and the heat slowly gathered, auguring the sweltering day to come.

"It's good to see you," I said. "It's been many years."

She said nothing; she just looked at me.

"I wrote you a letter. You never replied."

She shifted her eyes away from me and then brought them back. "You were sent here by your mother," she said. "It's Chrysaphius. She can't control him."

"He's receiving payments from the Huns to keep his policies in place. The Huns are demanding a ransom to continue the peace. The amount has more than tripled. The government is being slowly bled to death."

Pulcheria gave a hint of a smile. "Entirely predictable," she said. "I should have squashed him like a cockroach when I had the chance."

"We need you to stop him now."

"He's your mother's creature. Let her stop him."

"She can't. She's out of her depth. She doesn't know how."

Pulcheria laughed. "You mean she doesn't know how without risking her reputation. If she tries to persuade your father, the eunuch will accuse her of some wrongdoing and scandalize her again. Poor Eustacia. And she had just gotten back."

I tried not to let my distaste for her pettiness show. "Mother doesn't have the ability to influence him, not the way you did. That's why we need your help. Only you can get through to Father and make him see the error of his ways."

"And what about you, Licinia? Can't you persuade him? After all, you're his daughter, the eventual bearer of his much belated heir." There was a hint of mockery in her tone.

"If I try, my enemies will come after me."

"Your enemies?" Her smile was cruel. "How could a dear, sweet girl like you have enemies?"

"By failing to be the person they wanted me to be."

Her eyes narrowed.

"Our military resources are dwindling," I said. "Aspar and Marcian are worried we won't have the strength to withstand another attack. Something must be done."

She gave a snort of contempt. "Isn't it obvious? You must stop paying the Huns their extortion. You must put your foot down. You must defy them. It's as simple as that."

"But Father won't do that. Chrysaphius has his ear. Somehow, we must break the eunuch's hold on him. It's our only chance."

This seemed to puncture her arrogance. "Go on."

"Look, Mother is willing to confess that she furnished false testimony against you. She's willing to accept the public backlash."

"How big of her."

"She's willing to restore you as Augusta."

"Is she willing to step aside?"

"She's willing to share the title with you as she did before."

Pulcheria scoffed.

I gave her a hard smile. "Tell me, aunt, why are you incapable of sharing power? Why does it always have to be you and you alone?"

Her eyes bored into me, black and icy. "For the very reason you are standing before me now begging for assistance. Some people are better suited to rule than others."

"You've threatened my marriage. You've threatened my children."

"Look at you. You think you're entitled. You think that gives you the right to govern. But you're wrong. Good governance has nothing to do with entitlement. The line of succession is an arbitrary selector of princes. More often than not it gives us weak, ineffectual men unsuited to the job. If we are fortunate, those men have someone capable beside them to guide them, to keep them from wrecking everything with their incompetence. But if not, the Empire is at risk. I have ruled the East effectively as your father's surrogate for more than thirty years. Until Chrysaphius came along, we were rich and at peace even as the West was mired in chaos. And now that I've been pushed aside everything has fallen apart. Coincidence? It's not. Your presence here acknowledges as much, so don't act offended if I tell you frankly, I'm willing to do whatever it takes to hold on to power. Your male offspring, should you ever have one, may be another Caesar, but more likely than not he will be like his father, ill-tempered and rash. I'm not willing to be replaced by such a man. That's why I did what I did. I love you, Licinia. But I love the Empire more."

I studied her face, the pallid skin, the drawn lips, the cold eyes. I saw something I had never seen before.

"Tell me, aunt, I gave birth to two daughters before you were able to slow me down. I wonder. What would you have done if I had borne a son?"

She held my gaze. Perspiration gleamed on her brow. The day had grown hot. She said, "You knew what I wanted from you. You should have married yourself to Christ. If you had, we would not be having this conversation. But you wanted to be a mother. You wanted to see what it would be like to lie with a man and bear his children. You wanted to be like your mother and swim in the polluted waters of sin."

"It is not a sin to love a man and bear his children."

Her eyes flashed with anger. "Don't tell me what a sin is! I've carried the weight of a terrible sin in order to make things right for you, in order to save the Empire! But you had to complicate things, you and your mother, and that vile reprobate, Galla Placidia! You forced my hand. I didn't want to do it—Heraclius is a hideous creature; the sight of him makes me sick, but you left me no choice. You chose marriage and motherhood. You turned your back on God. You turned your back on me. Do you think God wants the Empire to be destroyed? Do you, Licinia? Do you!"

"You would have tried to kill my child."

She gave me a disgusted look and snarled. "What do you want, Licinia? Why are you here?"

"I told you. I want Chrysaphius stopped."

"Shall I murder him? Go ahead and say it. It's all right. You ought to at least speak the name of the thing you want me to do on your behalf, the sin you would condemn me for. You want to save the Empire. You want to remove the person who is threatening it. You want him dead."

"Well, I—"

"Don't judge me, not when you're begging me to commit the crime you're too cowardly to carry out yourself."

She was as cold and heartless as Galla said she was.

"Yes," I said. "I want Chrysaphius removed. I want the Huns stopped. And I don't care how you do it."

She gave me a tepid smile. "There. Now at least you're not being a hypocrite." She wiped the perspiration from her brow. "Very well, I can remove Chrysaphius. I can regain your father's good opinion and steer him toward a policy that's more palatable, but my assistance comes with a price. I want your mother to pay for her betrayal of me."

I scowled. How petty she was.

"Oh, come now, Licinia. It isn't all that bad. This will give her the chance to prove herself. Tell her to go to your father and try to convince him to dismiss Chrysaphius. If she succeeds, you will have no need of me. I will remain here in Antioch, and she will be the sole reigning Augusta. But if she fails, she must pay the price. She must go back into exile and never return to Constantinople. I will not rule by her side. There is room for only one Augusta."

I glared at her. "You are as cruel as Attila."

"Your mother is a hypocrite and a sinner. She presumes to sit in judgment of me, but she's guilty of the most the shocking perversion. Before you take her part, you should know the horrible thing she's done."

"She fell in love with Galla Placidia. She slept with another woman."

She was momentarily caught off guard, her composure shaken. "How do you know about that?"

"She told me, and I forgive her."

"Forgive her? How can you forgive her?"

"Who am I to judge? Who am I to cast the first stone?"

She stiffened in indignation. "It emasculated your father. It unmanned him. She's responsible for his degeneracy. She drove him into Chrysaphius's arms with her depravity."

I shook my head. "Hasn't that always been the way with you, Aunt. You're always quick to blame other women for the failings of men. No wonder the Church admires you. You're a traitor to your sex."

"How dare you criticize the Church!"

"Spare me the sanctimony. I know who you are. You're no saint. I reject your terms. My mother will not step aside to make way for you. If you cannot help us when we need you, if you cannot help your own family for the good of the Empire, then I have no further use for you. I reject you."

"Don't be a fool!" she cried as I turned my back on her. "You need me! The Empire needs me! Without me the Empire will fall!"

I whipped around. "Whatever happens, you will live in the knowledge that you could have saved it— if you hadn't been so small." I walked out into the heat of the day.

She stood in the doorway and called after me. "It's her fault! She tried to have me banished! There has to be a price!"

I turned the corner and made my way to the wharf, but I could still hear her shouting in the distance, her shrieks reverberating through the sultry sabbath streets of Antioch.

* * *

When my mother heard Pulcheria's answer she gave a hoarse, raw-throated sob and buried her face in her hands. My heart went out to her. She had made a terrible mistake, and now the Empire was at risk. It was a heavy burden. I put my arms around her. I told her I would make the case to Father no matter what it cost.

"I've been driven from home," I said. "My husband scorns me. My children are lost to me. What more can I lose?"

She urged me to reconsider. I was still young, she said. Circumstances would change. I must not endanger my future by allowing Chrysaphius to slander me. At the very least we should do this together. We should present a united front. It would be harder for Father to reject us both.

I agreed. Allowing her to be a part of the solution might lighten her burden, so we resolved to do it together, mother and daughter. But she asked me to wait. She had to think through what she wanted to say and how she wanted to say it. She needed time to make plans in case she got exiled again. She asked for a fortnight, and I gave it to her.

During that time, I received two letters, one from Agnus, and one from—of all people—Justa. Agnus's letter was puzzling. It spoke in vague terms about some sort of difficulty Junius was in. He had fallen out with his father over something having to do with the Emperor's unseemly behavior, and had been stripped of his praetorship and relegated to an inferior status. Olybrius, his father's newly adopted son, had been given the position.

Olybrius was the eighteen-year-old scion of the Anicia clan, the son of a powerful aristocrat whose recent death had left him fatherless. Maximus's adoption of him was a naked attempt to associate his gens with the lofty Anicia pedigree and to elevate his prestige. Agnus did not specify what Junius had done to get himself subordinated to Olybrius in his father's esteem, but, whatever it was, it had upset her. She pleaded with me to come home and set things right by appealing to the Emperor. She seemed to have forgotten it was just that sort of intrusion into my husband's affairs that had gotten me exiled in the first place.

Justa's letter was more disturbing. It decried her brother's misrule and expressed the desperation she and her mother felt about the disaster to come if someone was not found to replace him. At first, I assumed this was yet another veiled threat to give Aetius the throne, but as the letter went on it became clear she was almost as frustrated with Aetius as she was with Placidius. It seemed the Master of Soldiers had run into some difficulties in Hispania. His success at suppressing the Bagaudae had been short-lived. Those intractable insurgents had risen again, killed the Roman tax collectors, and overthrown the civil government. In doing so, they had peeled away large swaths of Roman territory much to the Emperor's chagrin. But that wasn't the worst of it.

Since I had been away, Rechila, the King of the Suebi, had died, and his son Rechiar had risen to power. The new king was more bellicose than his father and had no love for Rome. His first act was to seal an alliance with the Goths. Then, with the power of the Goths behind him, he exploited Roman weakness by attacking Tarraconensis, the Empire's last stronghold in the province of Hispania. Aetius was up to his neck in calamities as he struggled to hold Hispania together. The last thing on his mind was overthrowing Placidius.

But Justa wanted her brother gone and was prepared to do anything to make it happen. She was especially motivated by Placidius's decision to force her into a marriage with a feckless aristocrat of his acquaintance, a bland, oafish fellow with the incongruous name of Bassus Herculanus. Proud Justa was not about to let that happen. Her letter sounded like a final, desperate plea.

> If he tries to make me marry that lout,
> I will make him regret it. This is the
> last time I will write to you, Licinia.
> You must return to Ravenna and
> conceive a son. If you do not, you will
> have only yourself to blame for what
> will happen.

Naturally we prefer that the throne remain in our house, but Placidius is totally unsuitable, so if you cannot provide an heir, we may be forced to look elsewhere. What the Empire needs now is strong leadership to repair the damage he has done.

Then she surprised me.

As a measure of my earnestness, permit me to compensate you in advance for your cooperation. I have sent you a gift, something you have always wanted. But I withheld it from you, hoping to entice you. Seeing I have failed in that, I am giving it to you. Perhaps it will soften your resistance and make you see the light. Placidius must go. You will either be a part of that, or you will suffer the consequences. Please help!

The servant who brought me the letter had remained standing in the doorway. When I finished, he came forward and handed me a package. I opened it and fairly lost my breath. Inside was the amulet. I picked it up. My heart quickened as I slipped it around my neck. Suddenly I knew what I must do.

* * *

My mother didn't wait for me as agreed. She went to Father on her own. She tried to make her case. She said Chrysaphius had lured her into his plot and misled her. She confessed that the charges against Pulcheria were false. Chrysaphius had tried to use them to benefit himself. Father heard her out and then called for Chrysaphius. He made her stand there while Chrysaphius answered the charges.

The eunuch responded with a weary smile. He dismissed Mother's accusations as the last desperate play of a blameworthy sinner. Mother had been caught in an act of betrayal and was trying to head off the consequences. He then produced several witnesses who told lurid tales of my mother's longstanding infidelities with a servant girl. My father listened with growing irritation as my mother protested her innocence. The girl in question was hauled before them and confessed her crimes under intense examination. She was arrested and condemned. My mother was ordered back into exile and told never to show her face in Constantinople again.

At no time during the entire ordeal did my mother bring up my name. It was plain what she had done. She had sacrificed herself so I could carry on. It was as clear as day, although she never got the chance to say so herself. She was gone by the time I heard the news, having set sail for the Holy Land where she would live out the rest of her days in penance for sins both real and imagined.

As for me, I refused to diminish her sacrifice by inviting the damage she had sought to avert. I would not pit myself against the power of Chrysaphius. Instead, I would return to

Ravenna. The time had come. My mother would have wanted it that way. I would go and make a difference where I could. Above all, I would return to my children and prevent them from being raised without a mother as I had been. Then, with both of us out of the way, the one person capable of taking down Chrysaphius would have a clear path should she choose to take it.

My mother's sacrifice had another positive effect. It jarred my father from his complacency and caused him to modify his policy toward the Huns in spite of Chrysaphius's objections. In a surprising show of regal authority, Father refused the Huns' most recent demands and sent an envoy to negotiate. His sudden show of resolve produced an unexpected result. Attila did not attack but appeared to vacillate. He removed the bulk of his forces from the Danube and withdrew into Pannonia. The crisis seemed over. But so unexpected and inscrutable was the Huns' reaction that it raised alarms 1,500 miles away in Hispania where Aetius smelled a rat. He wrote Placidius and urged him to take precautions in case the Huns turned in our direction.

Unfortunately, he used the same letter to bemoan his plight. Things were going badly in Hispania. It was not out of the question that Rome might lose the territory altogether. This news had the force of a threat. The mineral resources of Hispania had furnished the Empire's mints for centuries. To lose them meant doing without a major source of revenue at a time when tax proceeds from the provinces were drying up once again after the resurgence of the Bagaudae and the Emperor's frivolous tax cuts. Placidius's public approval began to slide. He was so shaken that he began to cast around for ways to restore the public's good opinion. In his haste he overlooked Aetius's warning about the Huns and instituted a policy destined to throw fuel on the fire and bring the conflagration home to the West.

# Chapter 15
## Autumn, The Year AD 448

I left Constantinople before winter set in. I was intent on sailing to Ravenna. I traveled discreetly—one might say clandestinely—with no ceremony and little in the way of a retinue. I was returning to the West without having been formally recalled, an act of defiance so egregious it practically invited reprisal. It was best to avoid attention.

I traveled on a merchant ship carrying a cargo of incense, spices, and perfume and spent every hour immersed in a cloying aroma that clashed inharmoniously with the sweat and stink of the sailors. The passage was rough, the weather was bitter, and the ship pitched and rolled. I was sick during most of the voyage. I wondered how the sailors were able to endure it.

Nine days out off the coast of Messina we were waylaid by pirates. We tried our best to outrun them, but the pirates had a shallower draft and overtook us. They were Vandals, a rough looking bunch, scarred all over by previous fracases, wearing top knots, hoop earrings, and long unkempt beards. They shoved the sailors aside and went through our cargo in search of valuable things. When they discovered me cowering in the cabin, they laughed heartily and dragged me on deck. I was terrified.

In an effort to save me, the sailors told them the truth, that I was Licinia Eudocia, the Augusta of the West on my way back to Ravenna. The pirates didn't believe them. Why would a woman of such elevated status be traveling on a grubby merchant ship? They grabbed me as if to take me right there on the deck, but then they caught sight of the amulet hanging around my neck. They looked at each other in surprise. One of them bent down and, peered at it intently. He reached out to touch it.

"What is it?" came the booming voice of a barrel-chested man with long, golden hair spilling over his shoulders.

"We found this woman," explained the curious one. His response was so intimidated and servile, I presumed the long-haired man was their leader. "The sailors say she's an Empress, but she's dressed like a commoner and has no jewelry other than this peculiar necklace."

The longhaired man bent down and examined it. He scoffed. "It's a common metal, most likely lead. It doesn't sparkle or shine. Forget it. Here, grab these amphorae and take those sacks of grain."

The man who had taken such a keen interest in the amulet looked disappointed. "So, what should we do with her?"

The longhaired man appraised me as if evaluating a slave. "An Empress, eh? Tell us again who you are?"

"I am Licinia Eudocia, Augusta of the Western Roman Empire."

The longhaired man chuckled. "Nonsense. This ship is bound for Ravenna. The Augusta of Rome was banished from

Ravenna two years ago. If you were her, you would not be going there unless you were recalled, and I've heard no such news."

"You seem well informed about the goings-on at Ravenna," I said.

"I serve my master the prince, and he has an interest in such things. His future wife resides there, and he expects one day to occupy the throne."

"I believe I may know your master. Do you speak of Huneric?"

"I do," he said. He stood erect as if proud of the association.

"Huneric is my friend," I said. "He would be disappointed to hear you've been threatening me. Most disappointed."

The longhaired man considered me. "I don't believe you. You're playing a chance. You're trying to deceive me."

"If I am, you should kill me right now," I said. "It's your best bet. That way there will be no witnesses to report what you did here, because if Huneric finds out you injured or molested the Augusta of the West, he will surely have you executed."

He narrowed his eyes. "You think you're pretty clever, don't you? But I'm afraid you have overplayed your hand, woman. It just so happens we are returning to Ogylos where Prince Huneric is encamped. I'll take you there, and if it turns out you're lying, I'll ravage you like a whore before I choke the life out of you."

I was careful not to show him fear.

"Take me to him," I said, "but I'm warning you, if you so much as brush against me, I'll take it as an unwelcome liberty and report it to the prince."

He glowered.

The Vandal ship came alongside, and the pirates passed over their plunder. Then they laid down a plank and shepherded me aboard.

The journey to Ogylos took the better part of two days. I spent an anxious night huddled among the amphoras. I held a shard of broken pottery in my hand so tightly I cut my palm and bled.

At Ogylos I was taken off the ship and led up a rugged path to a crude timber structure on a hill overlooking the sea. The building was surrounded by tents made of goat hides. Cook fires licked and twisted in the wind. A group of men had just finished their midday repast. They were a coarse looking bunch. I was left in their company as my escorts went inside. Filthy and unkempt, the men crept up to me like half-starved dogs. One of them was just reaching out to touch me when a dark figure emerged from the building.

"Stop, fool!"

It was Huneric.

He had grown broad-shouldered since I had seen him last. He was wearing a leather tunic and a heavy belt. He had a long mustache and a bushy beard. His hair cascaded down his back. He approached us with his fists clenched and anger in his eyes. When the man stole a cringing look up at him, Huneric sent him sprawling with the back of his hand.

"Are you all right, Augusta?"

"I don't suppose they've seen a woman in a while."

"The lack of something doesn't excuse the theft of it," he said.

I thought this a peculiar sentiment from someone who was running a pirate fleet, but he was sincere. The quiet earnestness he had shown as a boy was still with him.

"Come," he said. "Let's talk."

We passed a row of men standing before a tent. Among them was the longhaired man. He gave me an apologetic look and bowed his head. I nodded solemnly in his direction and kept walking.

Huneric led me up a rocky path past a stand of cypress trees to a cliff overlooking the sea. A raw wind knifed over the precipice. A large fire had been prepared. The flames whipped and sawed in the wind and the smoke spiraled away. It was cold. Huneric sent a man to fetch me a robe. We sat down beside the fire and looked out to sea.

"You are well, I trust," he said. "The news has not been altogether good as regards you."

"You're speaking of my banishment?"

"Your husband has not been good to you. A good leader recognizes his assets."

"Placidius is a slave to his temperament."

"It's not a good quality. It makes him vulnerable."

I looked down at my hands.

"How are you, Huneric? You seem strong. Your men are loyal to you."

"I give them a reason to be. But I do not take their loyalty for granted. I must earn it anew every day."

"They owe you as much. You are their prince."

He turned to look at me. "Owe? How would they owe me anything if I didn't earn it? Men who are loyal because they are in debt are not men to be trusted."

I regarded him evenly. He sat with his arms wrapped around his knees. His hair streamed out behind him. The sea was a vast, glittering plain stretching out to the horizon.

"You are returning home," he said. "But I have heard no news of your being recalled. Do you go in defiance?"

"I do."

He paused a moment. "You're a brave woman, Licinia Eudocia. But what is your purpose?"

"To fix what I can."

"You're acting above your station. Does not your religion instruct you to be submissive?"

"You know it does. You're well acquainted with the differences in our faiths. They were drummed into you while you were living among us."

He smiled at the recollection. "Yes, while I was in Ravenna the inadequacies of my faith were pounded into me daily, as was the faultlessness of yours. I swear you Nicenes never tire of self-aggrandizement. We Arians are humbler."

"Humility can be a weakness. It's better to have confidence, I think."

"Perhaps, but confidence doesn't require discrediting those who disagree with you. It's better to be humble and firm than boastful and prickly. A man who's secure in his beliefs doesn't have to disparage others."

"I've learned a few things about disparagement," I said.

He gave me a small smile.

I watched a ship working its way out to sea. Crewmen worked the sails to catch the wind.

"All my life I've been put down, told I was unworthy, told I was wrong. I was instructed to remain silent and obedient. To do otherwise was against the will of God—or so they said."

"Do you still believe that?"

"It's a fiction put forward to suppress my sex."

"And to concentrate power in the hands of men," he added, "the men to whom you owe allegiance."

"Yes, to them." I watched the wind fill the sails, bellying them outward. The ship plunged ahead, great sheets of spray bursting from its bow.

"So, you're going home in defiance of your exile," he said. "What will you do when you get there?"

"I'm not sure."

"You'll figure it out."

I nodded.

He pointed to the amulet. "That's very strong. It speaks to your piety."

"My faith remains firm despite how my religion disdains me."

A sudden shift in the wind sent the smoke from the fire tumbling over our shoulders. We sat in silence for a long moment.

Huneric's voice was heartfelt and sincere. "Should you ever need me, you need only ask, and I'll be there. You know that, don't you?"

"I do."

We stood up and embraced. I took his shoulders in either hand and held him at arm's length. "I'm glad you're promised to Eudocia," I said. "We couldn't have found a better man."

He laughed. "You seem to forget; you're my captive. We have taken you against your will. Our ships are preying on your commerce. This is hardly grounds for praise."

I smiled warmly. "I would rather have Eudocia in the hands of an honorable Arian brigand like you than under the thumb of the noblest Nicene in Rome."

"Ha! You *are* defiant, aren't you?" Firelight reflected from this smile.

Huneric arranged to have me taken aboard a ship and delivered to a merchant vessel. The merchants must have been surprised to find the pirates had no interest in seizing their cargo, but only wanted to deliver a passenger into their hands, a strange women in plain clothing who claimed to be the Augusta of Rome. A week later I disembarked at Ostia, twenty miles from the city and made my way to the domicile of the one person in Rome that I knew could help me.

* * *

I found Galla at her villa. It had been almost five years since I had seen her. She had deep wrinkles around her eyes, and the skin at her throat had gone slack. Her hair had turned gray. When she rose to greet me, her hands trembled. She seemed happy to see me. Her eyes went straight to the amulet. She seemed startled. "Did Justa give you that?"

"She sent it as an inducement to bring me home."

Her eyes, sharp and perceptive as always, scrutinized me. "It looks good on you. It's not for everyone, you know. It doesn't always complement. Sometimes it clashes."

"Do you want it back?"

She smiled without mirth. "As much as I cherished it once, it no longer does me justice. You keep it."

We went into the tablinum, her private study. It was late autumn, and the morning was cold, but the relative compactness of the space concentrated the heat from the under-floor heating system and made the room cozy. She sat down across the desk from me and picked up a paperweight. It was in the shape of a centurion's helmet. She turned it in her hands.

"I'm glad to see you, Licinia, but I'm a little concerned. You're here without permission. Are you not?"

"That's true."

"You're taking a risk."

"I lived with Justa at the palace. I saw how she endured her confinement. It was no more nor less than I was subjected to as his wife."

"Maybe so, but Placidius has been restrained in his desire to punish her by the threat of how Aetius might react. You may not be granted the same leniency."

"My father should provide a good enough indemnity against violence."

She examined the weight in her hands. Her hands trembled slightly. She ran her finger along the leaden plume.

"Your father is pinned down in Constantinople. I wouldn't rely on his intervention to save you."

"Aetius is bogged down in Hispania with the Suebi and the Bagaudae. He's in no better position to intervene on Justa's behalf."

"True, but he'll return to Ravenna one day," Galla said, "and when he does, Placidius prefers it not be at the head of a hostile army."

She set the paperweight down.

"You realize of course there's a point beyond which even the threat of Aetius's intervention will save her," I said. "I don't know what she's contemplating, but I'm worried; her letter hinted of treason."

Galla dismissed the idea with a contemptuous sniff, but the reflexive way she did it spoke of deeper misgivings.

"Look," I said, "if Justa does something that provokes Placidius and causes Aetius to intervene, the situation could deteriorate rapidly. Any attempt to usurp the Emperor will be resisted. As much as the aristocracy may dislike Placidius, they want someone they can control, which means they definitely do not want Aetius. A civil war would divide us at precisely the moment the barbarians are looking to gain an advantage. I shudder to think of the consequences."

Galla tugged her bottom lip. "You're not wrong, Licinia, and the situation may be even worse than you imagine. After Aetius broke the resistance of the Bagaudae in Armorica, their leadership fled to Attila for protection. The Huns enlisted them as vassals, which gave Attila a new and terrifying idea: vassal states in the West, a coalition of disillusioned barbarian tribes willing to pledge their allegiance to the Huns as a way of severing their ties to Rome. Aetius was so shaken by the possibility he wrote to Placidius urging him to make a gesture of conciliation to Attila. Aetius obviously meant a gift of gold, but in the same letter he complained about the dwindling resources of his army, which only served to remind the Emperor of our precarious financial state. So, he offered the Hun king something else. Placidius gave him a title."

"A title?"

"He made him the magister militum of the East, a rank just below that of Aetius."

I was dumbfounded.

"I know. I know," Galla said. "The stupidity of it is breathtaking. But the West doesn't have the gold reserves the East does. Placidius thought he was being clever by giving Attila something of apparent value with no real cost. When Aetius heard, he was furious. Few Romans understand the Huns better than Aetius, and he knows Placidius's ill-advised gambit will be interpreted as an invitation to make claims upon the government for support, the refusal of which will be grounds for war. Placidius, in his bungling way, gave the Huns the justification they need to attack. Attila will hold it in reserve until he's ready, like a man with a knife in his boot."

I felt the blood drain from my face. "The crisis may be closer than you think. My father is digging in. He refuses to pay any more extortion to the Huns. In the East they're girding themselves for an attack, but this changes the equation from Attila's perspective. Why attack the East again when the East has already proven its willingness to resist? I'm afraid the Huns may react differently now. I'm afraid they may attack the West."

Galla looked past me to a spot on the wall. She closed her eyes and shook her head. "What a mess."

"Things are coming to a head," I said. "We mustn't sit on our hands. We must act."

Galla opened her eyes and considered me as if seeing me for the first time. "What do you propose?"

I folded my hands on the desk. "Placidius had been following the advice of Heraclius."

"Yes."

"Heraclius is in league with Chrysaphius, my father's cubicularius. Chrysaphius has my father under his thumb. Those two villains have been enriching themselves at our expense. They are selling us out to the Huns."

"So, what do you propose to do about it?"

"I don't know."

Galla examined my expression. "Are you not constrained by moral considerations, Licinia?"

"Only the moral consideration of not letting the Empire be overrun by a horde of godless beasts who will destroy every vestige of our civilization and the Church as well if given the chance."

Galla pursed her lips. "We're going to need allies if we're going to pull this off. I suggest Justa."

I balked.

Galla sounded like a patient mother explaining something to an overexcited child. "Look, we need someone inside the palace, and Justa is well positioned to help. I understand your hesitation, but if Justa is the danger you imagine her to be, you can win her cooperation by the simple expediency of showing her your willingness to act."

"I don't trust her," I said.

"And for good reason," Galla said, "but if you don't rely on her, you'll have to have to find someone else, someone with the ability to get close to the eunuch while keeping Placidius at bay."

"I know someone," I said.

"Who?"

"Petronius Maximus. He'll help us, if for no other reason than to keep Placidius in power and Aetius at arm's length."

Galla was leery. "Petronius Maximus is not to be trusted. His political ambitions are transparent, and he has the resources to arrange things in his favor. If you misjudge him, you'll find him difficult to control. Are you sure you want to get involved with a man like that?"

"I'm close with his wife. He dotes on her. I believe I can reach him through her. He'll do anything she asks of him."

"Be careful, Licinia. Men like Petronius Maximus never do anything out of the kindness of their hearts. If he is to serve us, he'll want to be compensated, and merely maintaining the status quo won't be enough. He can't be purchased with gold; he has plenty of that, and Placidius has already lavished him with titles and honors. But there's something else that motivates him, his contempt for Aetius. Offer him an opportunity to become our new Master of Soldiers and you'll win his support. Promise him Aetius's title and position in exchange for his assistance and you'll be trading in a coin he accepts."

"Then what becomes of Aetius?" I asked, surprised to find her turning against her longtime ally.

"Never trouble yourself about Aetius," she said.

I didn't understand.

She explained. "Maximus has the arrogance of men who inherit great wealth. They believe themselves exceptional. In their eyes everything seems easy. Maximus is sure he can replace Aetius. All you have to do is make him the offer, and he'll jump at it. But there's something Maximus doesn't understand. You may give him Aetius's title, but that doesn't mean he can command the loyalty of Aetius's men. He may pay them handsomely, but there's more to a soldier's loyalty than a full belly and a freshly shoed horse. If it comes down to a fight between them, Aetius will win, and the problem of what to do with Maximus when this is all over will be solved."

I foresaw another problem. "I'm in no position to offer Maximus Aetius's title."

"That's right. You're not," she said. "But I am. Tell him I've grown disillusioned with our Master of Soldiers. Tell him the recent setbacks in Gaul and Hispania have soured me. Tell him I'm ready to admit I've been wrong about Aetius. Tell him I'll champion the Emperor's decision to replace him, but that I must have my daughter-in-law back in the Emperor's bed. Tell him I want an heir as the price for his advancement."

I reflected for a moment. "Assuming it works, assuming Placidius takes me back, assuming I bear him a son, what then? What becomes of the Emperor?"

Galla was blunt. "Placidius is my son. I could never do anything to harm him, but he's a poor ruler. His gambling is out of control. His drunkenness and depravity are being gossiped about all over Rome. Only the love of a good woman, perhaps the mother of his children, can bring him back to his senses. Failing that, he will almost certainly destroy himself. If that happens, the line of succession must be made clear. Otherwise, a bloody power struggle will ensue. For that reason alone, it's imperative that you give us an heir."

"And, if he refuses to lay with me?"

"His narcissism and gullibility are the levers by which others turn him to their purposes. Are we to reject those same levers in an effort to turn him to ours?"

She gave me a sympathetic look. "Look, I once believed I could shape him into a decent ruler. I spent years writing out the story of my life in an attempt to give him the benefit of my experience. But as soon as he took the throne, he forgot everything and fell under the sway of sycophants and flatterers.

He has governed for one purpose and one purpose alone, to burnish his own reputation. As a result, the Empire is on the brink of ruin. I'm afraid he must be removed."

"To be replaced by his heir," I said. "But the boy may be a mere infant when he ascends to the purple. In the meantime, who will act as his regent?"

She gave me a warm smile and placed her hand on mine. "Go to Maximus and see if you can enlist him. Remove the malignant influence that has turned Placidius against us. And when it's done, you will have another chance to win your way back into your husband's good graces. If it fails, we may have to look at the other option, the one Justa suggested."

I winced at the thought.

"Never mind for now," Galla said. "We'll cross that bridge when we come to it. For now, let's deal with the eunuch. It's overdue."

I nodded silently and stared down at the floor. What was I getting myself into?

* * *

"What's wrong?" Galla asked.

It seemed unkind to say, but she should have seen it. "It's Justa," I said.

We were still sitting in the tablinum in Galla's private study in her villa outside Rome. The conversation went on.

Galla was behind the desk. She picked up the paperweight, the little centurion's helmet, and began fiddling with it again. "Don't worry, Justa wants the same things we do, and she's remarkably cooperative when she gets what she wants."

"But will it be enough? Once the power is in the hands of a regent, will it be enough to appease her or will she continue plotting?"

"Justa is jealous and vindictive. I don't deny that. But above all she's angry about the rules of succession, about how they deny the ascension of a woman even when the male is incompetent. Justa has always felt she's better qualified to rule than her brother, and she regards it as a great injustice that she'll never get the chance. But she's not against every alternative, only those she considers beneath her."

"How will she consider me?"

"I think you've already seen. She went to a great deal of trouble to make her case to you, even so far as to have confined herself in the palace to be near you. She wouldn't have done that if you weren't acceptable to her."

"You know if you're wrong, she'll wreck everything. Hadn't we better separate her from all this? Perhaps we should send her some place where Placidius can't get his hands on her? We could present it to her in the guise of helping her avoid the marriage he's trying to force her into."

Galla set the paperweight down. She sat looking at it. She nudged it with her finger.

I went on. "She's not going to marry Bassus Herculanus. The idea of it repulses her. She'll stop at nothing to avoid it—nothing. In her letter to me she made some cryptic threats."

Galla raised her eyebrows. "What do you mean cryptic threats?"

"She's not above turning to our enemies if it comes to that."

Galla dismissed this. "That's typical of her. She's trying to get your attention."

"Maybe, but we underestimate her at our peril. The last time we made that mistake, she tried to sabotage my wedding."

"Oh, that's just Placidius talking."

"Justa admits it. More importantly Pulcheria confirms it. Justa was in on the plot. She conspired with Pulcheria to prevent the wedding."

"You spoke to Pulcheria?"

"I went to her in Antioch. I was trying to get her to come back to Constantinople to deal with Chrysaphius, but she refused."

"I'm not surprised."

"She rejected a perfectly reasonable offer to share the title of Augusta with my mother. When I returned to Constantinople, my mother took it upon herself to set things right. She was exiled for a second time and now she lives in the Holy Land."

Galla shook her head. "Poor, dear Eustacia."

"Before she went, she told me everything. But don't worry. Christ admonished us, 'Judge not, lest you be judged.' I consider His words divine. I intend to abide by them."

"Too bad others do not."

"Yes. Too bad."

She regarded me with a kind of admiration.

"I should go," I said.

"Wait," she said. "I have something for you."

She got up and left the room. When she came back, she was carrying a codex made of parchment leaves. She pressed it into my hands. "This is the letter I wrote to Placidius. It's the story of my life."

I recalled that Placidius had told her he had given it away. I wondered aloud how she had gotten back.

"I have my ways" she said.

I thanked her for entrusting me with it and promised I would read it. We said our goodbyes.

At the door she had some parting words for me. "Allegiance is not everything, Licinia. Remember that. Sometimes it's necessary to sacrifice allegiance for duty, and when the time comes, you should do what's right."

I wasn't exactly sure what she meant by that, but later when I thought about it, it became clear. What she was saying was that sometimes it becomes necessary to sacrifice allegiance to a person for duty to country.

I did not see Galla again alive.

* * *

I sought out Agnus at the public garden of the fashionable cauponae where we used to meet for lunch. The proprietor said she had just left and pointed me to the shops beneath the covered colonnade along Via Patricius.

I made my way through the bustling afternoon streets of Rome. They were crowded with people of all kinds: tall slender men with olive-colored skin wearing robes and sandals, short, wiry men with unkempt beards and leather trousers, haughty, square-jawed men with their hair combed forward on their foreheads in the manner of Julius Caesar. There were women of all types as well, some in rich, swirling silks, others barefoot and slatternly. Bands of little children ran in and out of the crowd. I was hoping the sheer number and variety of people would keep me anonymous. Few people had ever laid eyes on the Augusta of Rome, and those who had would probably not recognize me dressed as I was.

I passed through a succession of smells. I passed from the exotic fragrance of spices and herbs to the acrid, penetrating odors of urine and defecation. I passed from the greasy odors of oily cooking to the delicious aroma of fresh baked bread. I entered a public square crowded with spectators and entertainers: jugglers, acrobats, and dwarves. One man was making a monkey do tricks. Another was tormenting an idiot with a stick. I passed an open-air shrine to the Virgin Mother before which a number of people were genuflecting. A town crier was standing on a wall and shouting out news of Aetius's troubles in Hispania.

I passed a large marble statue of the Emperor Augustus. Three slaves were cleaning the bird dropping from it wetted towels. I turned south onto the Via Patricius lined on either side with covered walkways beneath stone arches. The storefronts below the arcades opened onto the sidewalks and the merchant's wares were stacked before them so that one had to pick their way through a maze of crates and amphorae. I passed a bronzesmith and a cloth merchant and greengrocer. I looked in at the shoemaker and the florist. I found Agnus at the margaritarius, the pearl merchant where she was bent over a glass bowl that contained exquisite pearls.

Four other women, the wives and daughters of men of distinction, flanked her, oohing and aahing over the iridescent gems. They traded comments and laughed. She smiled around at them. For a moment I was envious of their comradery, but it lasted only a moment.

Agnus caught sight of me. She brightened and began to wave, but I gave her a look that demanded discretion, and she dropped her hand. A moment later, her friends departed.

"Licinia, you're back!" She rushed to embrace me.

"Illicitly," I whispered. I took her by the arm and steered her into the back of the shop where we could speak in private. "The Emperor doesn't know I'm here. I'm taking a big risk by coming. I need your help."

Her enthusiasm evaporated. "It's not my place," she said. "Maximus wouldn't like it."

"This involves Maximus directly. I have an offer for him. Will you convey it to him for me?"

"What kind of offer?"

I looked around circumspectly. "I've spoken to Galla Placidia. She's lost faith in Aetius. His setbacks in Hispania are the final straw. She's ready to replace him. She favors Maximus."

Agnus drew back in surprise.

"That's right. She's prepared to recommend Maximus as the new Master of Soldiers. But she's going to need something from him in return."

"Something in return?" Agnus asked.

"She needs his help in restoring me to the Emperor's favor."

"I don't want to get involved," she said curtly.

"Wait," I said. "Don't you see? It's absolutely vital we provide the Empire with an heir. Without a clear line of succession, we risk civil war. But Placidius has frozen me out. He's been taking the advice of the eunuch Heraclius, which is leading us down a dangerous path. We have to break the eunuch's hold on him. Placidius trusts Maximus. He looks up to him. If Maximus advises him to take me back, he will."

"That's between you and the Emperor," she said.

I blinked in disbelief. "But Agnus you wrote to me. You urged me to come home. You practically begged me. I'm here now. But I can't stay if Placidius won't accept me."

"It's not my place," she said. "Don't keep asking me. It's not fair."

"What's come over you?"

She bristled. "Nothing's come over me. You're the one who's changed. You've grown too bold. You shouldn't have come here without your husband's permission. It's wrong. Go back to Constantinople and wait for him to recall you."

My mouth fell open. "But the Empire is at risk."

"That's not for you to decide. Let the men handle it. That's what they do."

She forced a smile and gave me a reassuring pat on the arm. Then she went to the front of the shop where she continued shopping for pearls.

I hung back for a moment, at a loss. Then I collected myself and went after her. When I came up beside her, she held up a pearl.

"Look," she said. "See how it catches the light? Isn't it beautiful?"

"You wrote to me about Junius," I said. "You claimed he was in trouble; you said he had been stripped of his praetorship. Tell me more about that."

She sighed. "Oh, Licinia. Leave it alone, will you?" She went back to sorting through the pearls.

I refused to budge. After a moment she said, "All right. If you must know, Junius can tell you. But leave me out of it. It's none of my business."

"Where can I find him?"

"He's at the cattle market."

That seemed an odd place for an official with the lofty rank of praetor.

Agnus explained. "He's been demoted to purchasing agent for the family estate."

"But why?"

She held up another pearl. "What about this one? Such brilliance and luster. You can see your reflection in it."

"Agnus," I said, "there will come a time when you won't be able to avoid the truth, when you'll have to face up to it no matter how uncomfortable it makes you."

She continued sorting through the pearls, pretending to be indifferent, but I saw the color rise to her cheeks.

"I'm shopping now," she said. "Please leave me alone. You're upsetting me."

I left her there in her room full of pearls. But she was right about one thing. She had not changed.

I had.

# Chapter 16
### Winter, The Year AD 449 – Summer, The Year AD 450

The cattle market was raucous and visceral. I had never experienced anything like it, a large piazza bordered by colonnades and crammed full of shacks, tents, and corrals stretching into the distance. A kinetic swirl of humanity streaming past or standing in knots, surging and flowing like a tide, massing before bottlenecks, growing anxious and impatient. A sea of voices roiled around me: shouts and laughter and whoops, and, behind them, the bawl of cattle or the agonized screech of some poor creature being put to the knife. And the smell—oh, the smell: a pungent mix of dung and blood and rot.

I moved into the crowd hoping to find Junius. I was bumped, jostled, and pressed. Faces loomed up before me, peered past, searched for a way through, and ducked around me. A man brushed his hand across my breast. Another pinched my rear. I was elbowed and pushed.

I stumbled and nearly fell before being roughly ejected into an open space before a butcher's stall. On the counter were assembled a row of goats' heads, their eyes glazed, their tongues hanging out. I was repulsed and turned away only to be confronted by the stomach-churning sight of a pig being hoisted up by the hooves and squealing as its belly was ripped open and its guts splashed on the ground. I backed away, my hand to my mouth and bumped into someone who spun me around and shoved me. I nearly tripped over a tangle of deer antlers piled up before a stall. I caught myself just before pitching headlong to the ground.

Junius saw me before I saw him. He hurried over. Mercifully, he reached me before I swooned. He took me by the arm and led me through the crowd. He pushed aside anyone who got in our way. Once we were outside the crowd, he sat me down and knelt before me, holding my hands.

"My God!" he said. "What are you doing here? This is no place for a woman."

"I came to find you. I need your help."

He searched my face with a look of anguished perplexity.

"But you shouldn't be here. You should be in Constantinople. If the Emperor finds out…" His voice trailed off. Suddenly he was alert again. "Come with me," he said.

He led me down a series of narrow streets and up some squalid back alleys to the hospitia of a friend, a kind, well-to-do man who he believed could be trusted. He brought me to a comfortably furnished room that opened onto a private garden. In the corner of the garden was a knee-high temple to the goddess Minerva that had been repurposed as shrine to Saint Marciana who had been martyred by the pagans for destroying a statue of the goddess Diana. Saint Marciana had been gored to death by a bull, hers the fate of many an early Christian woman who dared defy the Roman authorities.

Junius brought me a cup of wine and asked me what I was doing there.

"The Emperor is in danger. He's being manipulated by the chamberlain Heraclius. If this is not corrected soon, the situation could go from bad to worse. Heraclius has to be eliminated."

Junius looked like he had been slapped. "Augusta!"

"I have the backing of Galla Placidia in this," I said. "But we need the cooperation of someone who the Emperor trusts, so I came here with the intention of reaching out to Maximus to make him an offer in exchange for his assistance."

Junius shook his head.

"Before seeking you out, I tracked down Agnus and asked for her help, but she refused. I don't understand. She wrote to me. She said something had happened to you. But when I asked for more details, she clammed up. Something is upsetting her. But I can't figure out what it is. Something's happened between you and your father, didn't it?"

"We quarreled. About you."

"About me? Why?"

He looked at me with a soft expression. "It's the Emperor," he said. "He's been behaving in the most disturbing manner, and I believe my father is to blame. I confronted him, and we quarreled."

"What's going on with the Emperor?"

"I'm sorry to have to tell you this, Augusta, but what started out as a few random infidelities has degenerated into a gross indulgence in drinking, gambling, and whoring. I think my father is behind it. That's why we quarreled. I don't like it. It's hurting people, innocent people. You, for one. You're the innocent victim in this…this—sinfulness, and you don't deserve it. I confronted him, we argued, and in the end, he stripped me of my title and threatened to disinherit me."

"Oh, Junius."

"That wasn't the end of it. As it happened, several months back my father adopted Olybrius in order to associate us with the noble House of Ancii and increase our social standing. But the adoption also gave him a route by which to punish me once I stood up to him. Olybrius is my equal in age and education, you know. He's a good man, but he will do anything my father asks. My father made Olybrius the praetor. I was relegated to the post of purchasing agent for the estate. I was demoted. That's what happened."

"I'm sorry, Junius."

"Listen to me, Augusta. You should understand something. My father will not help you, not in the way you think. He's not your friend. He has his own agenda."

"What agenda?"

Junius took a deep breath. "He means to become Emperor himself. "

I was stunned.

"He's too smart to attempt an actual overthrow," Junius said. "He knows Aetius wouldn't stand for it. But if he can get the Emperor to destroy himself, his eventual demise will be a foregone conclusion. In the meantime, my father can position himself to take over."

I broke into a cold sweat. I had to steady myself by holding onto his arm.

"I'm sorry I didn't recognize it sooner, Augusta," Junius said. "It started out innocently enough, the companionable days at the races, the dinners at each other's villas, the lending of money. I dare say even the development of a warm relationship between you and Agnus was part of it. But soon there was favorable talk about Aetius, praise for his exploits, a general approbation among the moneyed classes. It was all calculated to make the Emperor insecure and envious, the better to win his confidence."

"So, it was Maximus who orchestrated the aristocracy's sudden change of heart about Aetius."

"That's right. Fliers announcing the general's successes appeared on the city's albas. Public criers spoke in favor of him. Everything was designed to make the Emperor insecure. That way, when Maximus offered his sympathy and support, it was welcomed. Once the Emperor had been drawn in, my father began to prey on his weaknesses, his fondness for gambling and drink, which led in time to drunkenness and infidelity. Believe me, Augusta, whatever influence Heraclius had over your husband, a far more powerful influence has come to replace it. The danger is no longer the chamberlain. It's my father. We have to get you out of Rome. If Maximus discovers you're here, your life is at risk."

I was shaken. I would cooperate with whatever Junius wanted. I was in no position to engage an enemy I knew so little about. But there was something I had to say before we parted.

"I know what you did for me, Junius. You risked everything for me, and I'm grateful."

He took me by the hands. "I care for you, Augusta. Don't you see? I care for you a great deal."

Then it happened. He took me in his arms. I didn't resist. I put my arms around him and gazed up into his eyes.

"Licinia," he said as if testing the shape of my name on his tongue. He moved closer and kissed me. It was sudden and unbidden, and I was glad of it. Our lips lingered. Something stirred within me, something new and exhilarating. I wanted more. But he pulled away.

"I have to make plans. Every moment you remain here increases the risk. Are you certain no one has recognized you?"

I thought for a fleeting moment of the proprietor at the cauponae who had directed me to find Agnus. He knew me, but he was a man who understood the importance of discretion. It was part of his job.

"No one," I said.

"Good," he said. "I will come for you in the morning. Be ready."

I assured him I would.

He started away but thought better of it. He strode up to me and we kissed again, deeply and passionately. Then he was gone.

I went inside and lay down on the bed. I had never felt like this before. I hoped he would come back again tonight. I hoped he would come back before morning, and we could continue what we started.

★ ★ ★

It was deep in the night, that time of the evening when the dogs stop barking and the city goes silent. I awoke to the sound of footsteps outside my door. My pulse quickened as I sat up.

"Licinia?" came the voice, but it was not his.

"Maximus!" I cried. "What are you doing here?"

A moment later he was at my bedside holding my hand. "I heard you had a proposition for me. I came at once."

I tried to pull away, but he held me fast. "Don't be afraid," he said.

It was dark in the room, so I could barely make out his features, but I could see the contours of his figure as he loomed before me.

"So, you want to be restored to your husband's good graces? Of course, you do. But he's upset with you. Surely, you understand that. You've angered him with your rebelliousness. And now this—this defiance of your exile. You are too bold, Licinia, like a naughty child." I couldn't actually see the grin on his face, but I could hear it in his voice. "Some men find such behavior exciting"—he leaned closer—"but others, like the poor Emperor, only find it aggravating."

I pulled free of him. He reached for my hand again. I snatched it to my chest. "Thank you, Maximus. It was good of you to come. But I no longer need your help. You may go now."

"Oh, but I was informed otherwise, something about gaining the Emperor's trust and returning you to his favor."

"Who told you that?"

"Why, Agnus, of course. You sought her out and informed her of your plans. You don't deny it, do you?"

"I went to her, but she told me she didn't want to get involved. I didn't think she would pass it on to you."

"Ah, my sweet Agnus, such a good girl. She knows she shouldn't involve herself in things that are none of her business, so she tries to keep out of it. But when her lord commands it of her, she obeys. She's a dutiful wife. But she lacks your spunk. You're something special, Licinia. Yes, you are."

He brushed his fingers against my cheek. I recoiled.

"You're mistaken," I said. "She misunderstood what I meant."

"Really?" he asked. He knelt at the side of the bed. "What a shame. I should have liked to become the Master of Soldiers. I would have been prepared to reconcile you to your husband in exchange for such a plum, and to bring Galla Placidia back into the Emperor's good graces as well. But, alas, it was a mistake. The offer never actually existed. And yet here you are in violation of the Emperor's order, a lawbreaker, and if you are found out, it will go hard on you. It seems you need some help after all. Fortunately, I am willing to be generous—for a price."

He reached out and touched me. I knocked his hand away and scrambled to my feet. He lunged at me. I dodged him and ran for the door. I pulled it open. He slammed it shut. He pinned my face against the wood and pressed his body against mine. An arm slithered around my waist and pulled me against him. His lips brushed my ear. He spoke in a tight whisper.

"Let's stop playing games. You came here with an offer, and I accept it. Now all you have to do is go back and tell Galla. When that's done, I'll begin the process of restoring you to the Emperor's good graces, a necessary requirement if we are to be partners." He pinned my wrists against the door and pressed himself against my buttocks. "For the good of the Empire."

I grimaced and struggled to break free.

"Don't defy me," he said. "I'm not your husband, and I won't stand for it." He kissed my neck.

I writhed and twisted, but he held me fast. "Such a curious girl. Always so keen to know everything that's going on. Well, aren't you curious to know how I found you? Of course, you are. I have agents all over the city. I heard of your return the moment you came through the Esquiline gate. Nothing escapes me—nothing, least of all the actions of my son. He's really quite ridiculous, you know. He casts himself as your protector. His heart bleeds for you. But if you think he's going to be your lover, you're mistaken. He's not that sort of a man."

"Let go of me."

"You aren't the first woman I've had to rescue from him," he said. "He lacks what it takes to keep a woman engaged. Ask Agnus. She can tell you."

He touched me. My breath caught in my throat.

"A woman needs more than a soft, sympathetic ear," he said. "She needs a man. You more than most." He spun me around and tore at my dress.

Suddenly there was a pounding at the door.

"Licinia!" It was Junius. "Open up! Hurry! My father's coming! You're in danger!"

"He's here now! Help me!"

With a roar, Maximus swept me aside and jerked open the door.

"Father! Stop!"

Maximus struck him, knocking him back. Junius stumbled to his knees and put up his arm. Maximus pushed it aside and struck him again, coming down over the top with a balled-up fist. He hit him again and again like an angry man beats a dog.

I looked around. My eyes fell on the shrine to Saint Marciana. I wrapped my arms around the statue. It was made of heavy stone. I lifted it with great effort. Somehow I got it up over my head. I brought it crashing down on Petronius Maximus.

He let out a grunt and dropped unconscious to the ground.

I stood above him, waves of guilt washing over me.

Junius put an arm around me. "Are you all right?"

"Is he dead?"

Junius bent over him. "No," he said. "But it would be better for us if he was. He'll stop at nothing to make us pay for this. We have to get out of here. It's not safe for us in Rome. Quick, get dressed."

I threw on my clothes, and we fled. In the blink of an eye all my plans had gone awry, and my future was uncertain. We were headed for a faraway place neither of us had ever been before. We were headed for the ends of the earth.

* * *

Junius insisted we get out of the country. Maximus's reach extended to every town and city on the peninsula. There was no safe place in Italia. Junius suggested we go to Gaul, specifically the city of Aurelianum on the northern bend of the Loire River, the farthest city on the Roman frontier. It was like a remote island in a sea of barbarians.

North of Aurelianum the Salian Franks had formed a client state under their warlord King Merovich. To the east the Burgundians of Sapudia had been subjugated by Aetius and were acting as federates. South, in Aquitaine, the Goths under King Theodoric had reached a peace settlement with Aetius after seizing the port at Narbo and were pressing no more territorial gains. As a result, even though we would be surrounded by barbarians on all sides, we would be under no imminent threat. And Aurelianum would be the last place on earth anyone would think to look for us.

But I could not leave Italia without seeing my children first. It had been three years and not a day had passed when my heart did not ache for them. Junius tried to talk me out of it. He thought it would be too dangerous; surely Maximus would have eyes on them. But I insisted. It was pointless to save my own life if I could never see my daughters. Somewhere deep down I was confident we would be reunited someday, but in the meantime I needed to contact them, if only briefly, to prove to them I was still alive and would return for them when the time was right.

Junius devised an elaborate plan involving a pair of renowned dressmakers from Mediolanum who were traveling to Ravenna for the purpose of consulting with Eudocia and Placidia about Eudocia's upcoming wedding, which Placidius had scheduled for two years in the future when Eudocia would turn twelve. I would go with them, concealed in the back of a wagon beneath a stack of fabrics. Once inside the city, I would slip out and take cover in a gem shop. The girls would be brought to the shop to select the jewels to be sewn into their gowns. I would meet them in the shop owner's private quarters above the back of the shop.

The plan went off without a hitch. When my daughters saw me, they threw themselves into my arms with shrieks of joy. They had grown so much since I had seen them last. They had lost all their baby fat and were like little women now. They had been well schooled in the manners of princesses and spoke with a grace and dignity befitting young ladies of their status.

I told them what had happened. I had broken my exile and returned to them, but I had to leave again to avoid arrest. I would come back soon, and we would be reunited. I cautioned them not to speak of our meeting to anyone. They assured me they understood. It was nothing new to them. They lived in a world of secrets. They had witnessed their father's drunkenness and debauchery but were under the strictest orders never to breathe a word about what they saw. They confirmed what I heard about Placidius. He had been corrupted by Maximus who had assumed many of the Emperor's duties. It frightened and dismayed them. They wondered what they could do, but now that they had seen me, they would take heart and await my return.

Before I left, nine-year-old Placidia approached me, her eyes fastened on the amulet. "Mother where did you get that?" She was very taken with it.

I smiled affectionately and placed my palm against her face. "It used to belong to your grandmother," I said. "Maybe someday I will give it to you."

A look came into her eyes that I can only describe as rapturous. She bounced on her toes with excitement. I wrapped my arms around her and kissed the top of her head.

"Patience, dear. All things will come right with time."

I left Ravenna the way I had come, hidden in the back of the dressmaker's wagon. Junius picked me up in a forest beyond the marshes and spirited me away on horseback. Later we learned the authorities had been alerted to my presence and ransacked the dressmaker's shop for any sign of me, but to no avail. Two weeks later we passed over the border into Gaul. By late spring we were peacefully ensconced in Aurelianum. We lived together there under assumed names as husband and wife. Time marched on.

Although our love was chaste, it was filled with the most endearing affection. Junius showed me ways a man might love a woman that I had not known before, and yet we did not share our bodies. Our abstention owed less to my probity than to his restraint, for he wanted nothing to come between us that might cause regret.

At first, he was worried about how I had suffered from his father's assault. He did not want me to associate intimacy with the ugliness of the attack on me by Maximus and carefully avoided pressing his desires. As time went on, we found we could be close without being sexual. He knew my reputation for piety and worried that the violation of my wedding vows—even considering the depravity of my spouse and the obligatory nature of our marriage—would weigh too heavily on me and drive a wedge between us. Perhaps he was right. I don't know. I know I wanted him. I could feel the warm tingle on my skin when he touched me, or the moistness between my legs when he held me in his arms. But although I was prepared to surrender to him, I lacked the shamelessness to seduce him, so we lived together in platonic bliss as God would have it. And we were content.

During that time I read Galla's the letter, the one she had written to Placidius before he set out to marry me. I was astonished at its frankness. In many ways she was far more ruthless and hardhearted than I imagined. Her piety, while not insincere, was always a means to an end. Every decision she made, save one, was aimed at protecting the Empire. Her one big mistake—the one she would come to regret—was the belief that her son could evolve, overcome his irascible and impulsive nature, and become a responsible and diligent human being. In fact, she had a weakness for both her children, which clouded her ability to see their flaws. It was an oversight destined to cause her sorrow.

Junius and I lived in Aurelianum for more than a year. I wished it could have gone on that way forever, but it was not to be. Galla's error of judgment when it came to her children sparked consequences that spread throughout the Empire and impacted all of us.

In the spring news arrived of something Justa had done, something so mind-bogglingly reckless, so beyond even her appalling standards, that it beggared the imagination. Once again, our serenity was shattered, and we found ourselves facing a danger far worse than we could have imagined.

* * *

Ever alert to the double standard that prevailed between Placidius and herself, Justa never missed an opportunity to make him pay for his hypocritical arrogance. The very behavior that had gotten her confined to the palace and sentenced to a life of grinding tedium had become commonplace for him. While she was being forced into marriage with an odious man as a punishment for her sins, Placidius was making a mockery of his professed piety by sleeping with whores and drinking himself stupid. It was inevitable there would come a reckoning.

Who knows what put the idea into her head? Justa was a shrewd observer of politics. Perhaps it was a measure of her faith that she would come to power someday through a combination of her brother's ineptitude and her father's influence. She watched and reflected. She took note of the political decisions being made and drew lessons from them. She had seen Aetius maneuver former adversaries into arrangements that obligated them to fight on the Empire's behalf, and she had watched as he had settled former enemies near our borders as a way to quell internal revolt. She knew the value of calling on the fearsome reputation of barbarian warlords to force compliance with a desired course of action. She understood how an individual capable of orchestrating such arrangements could be formidable indeed. Perhaps she aspired to be such a person. God knew she felt herself superior to most men. Not a few had been seduced and dominated by her. She had made others do her bidding by the power of her purse; and she had never hesitated to use her position to get what she wanted. But with Attila she went too far.

The idea probably first occurred to her when she saw Placidius clumsily trying to buy the Hun's forbearance with a title. No doubt Placidius thought he was getting something for nothing and counted himself clever for doing so. Of course,

Aetius was of a different mindset. He warned Placidius that he would soon regret the heavy cost of giving away what he thought was of little value. But from Justa's perspective, it was a situation ripe for revenge. If it was a simple matter of making empty gestures to a gullible warlord, she could go her brother one better. She wrote Atilla with a proposal.

She sent her servant, the eunuch Hyacinthus, to deliver it. It was a message shocking in its duplicity. It detailed the abuse she had been suffering at the hands of her brother. It complained of the way he was forcing her against her will to marry a man she despised. It pleaded with Atilla to come and rescue her, and, as a token of her sincerity and to prove she was truly she who she said she was, she sent along her signet ring.

That was all Attila needed. Having recently reached an impasse with the ambassadors of the East regarding the payment of any more ransom in exchange for his forbearance, the Hun king was left with a decision: to invade the East for a third time and risk a revitalized Roman army financed by the money it withheld or look for a new victim to extort.

Attila was playing host to the Bagaudae leader who had slipped through Aetius's grasp and fled to the Huns after the failed uprising in Armorica. The man had offered to make Armorica a Hun vassal state if Attila would help him recover his lost possessions. Until now Attila had only paid him lip service, but the arrival of Justa's letter changed everything. Now, using the Bagaudae leader's claim, Attila could justifiably claim portions of the Western Empire as a dowry for his new bride, including Armorica. The ring Justa had sent as a guarantee of the letter's legitimacy was interpreted as a wedding proposal, and Attila wasted no time in accepting it. He sent along his reply and with it a demand for half of the Western Roman Empire, which he regarded as his due as the future husband of the Emperor's sister, who wore the title of Augusta. Any hesitation on the part of the Emperor to surrender it would be considered an insult worthy of reprisal.

Placidius was blindsided. It had all come out of nowhere. Now he was being threatened by the most fearsome warlord in the world. He called his advisors into emergency session and told them about the letter. To a man they were appalled and as much at a loss about what to do as he was. Comprised largely of sycophants and flatterers, there was not an experienced military man among them, and none of them had ever dealt with a foreign policy crisis of such magnitude.

In a panic, and in spite of all his former proclamations to the contrary, Placidius reached out to his mother who hurried to Ravenna to help. What unfolded next was related to me in a letter from Galla who wrote to me afterwards.

Galla had cautioned her son to show restraint. The Emperor must not be seen to be resisting the Huns. He must pretend to go along with them to buy time until Aetius could determine the best course of action. Placidius listened morosely, anxiously biting the edge of his thumb. At the mention of Aetius's name, he flew into a rage and demanded that Justa be brought before him.

She arrived, slumped between two guards, head bowed, exhibiting none of her usual insolence. She seemed to understand she had gone too far. Galla strode up to her and slapped her across the face. The smack reverberated through the hall, stunning the onlookers. It was the first time her mother had struck her, and Justa gaped in shock. The red mark from her mother's hand burned on her cheek; tears welled in her eyes. The silence was broken by a strange sound, a deep, guttural roar rising to a shriek. In the next instant Placidius got his hands around his sister's throat and was strangling her. With some effort the guards pulled him off.

Red-faced and disheveled, Placidius demanded Justa be put to death. His clemency had been exhausted. If she were allowed to go on living, she would doom them all. As always Galla tried to talk him out of it, not because Justa deserved any better—she didn't—but because Attila would not sit idly by if his betrothed was killed. They had to hold back, at least until Aetius got there and could assess the situation.

In the meantime, they could marry Justa to Bassus Herculanus as originally planned and send a message to Attila informing him that Justa had never intended her ring as a proposal, but only as proof of her identity. Since she had married another, she could not marry the Hun.

Justa started to object, but Galla froze her with a look.

Placidius mulled it over. "Will it work?" he asked. His voice barely registered.

"The Huns will not attack without first replying to the message, even if it's their intention to reject it. That will give Aetius time to get here."

Exhausted and demoralized, Placidius gave in.

Justa was hauled away in chains. For a few days it was hit or miss whether she would truly escape Placidius's wrath, but by the end of the week she was remanded to her mother's custody and taken away to Rome where she was forced to marry the man she loathed.

The eunuch Hycanthus who had delivered the letter to Attila bore the brunt of the Emperor's wrath. That innocent servant was torn limb from limb, his body parts fed to the pigs. All of this was done against the strenuous objections of the chamberlain Heraclius, whose once formidable influence was suddenly on the decline.

Placidius had not been well served by those around him, something that was only beginning to dawn on him. To cope with the ugliness of that reality, he went off by himself and drank himself into oblivion.

*   *   *

Alerted to the debacle brought on by Justa's letter, Aetius rode to Rome to consult with Galla. He did not go to Ravenna first. His departure from Tarraconensis made the situation in Hispania even more precarious than earlier and were it not for the valiant efforts of a young cavalry officer named Majorian, and his able colleague Ricimer, the territory might have been lost in his absence.

Once in Rome, Aetius set to work raising troops for the army on the assumption that the Huns would invade Italia. He sent orders mobilizing the Burgundians in Sapudia in fulfillment of their treaty obligations and sought a bill in the Senate introducing conscription with the object of raising troops from among the Roman people. The Burgundians came at once. The conscription effort failed. Well acquainted with the reluctance of Roman citizens to sully themselves with their own defense, Aetius sought an alliance with King Theodoric of the Goths but was rejected. The Goths were allied with the

Suebi in an effort to discourage Roman claims on Hispania, so they could hardly be expected to join Aetius in his defense of Italia. As usual, Aetius was shorthanded and desperate for resources.

His restoration of tax revenues in recent years had enriched the aristocracy and lightened the tax burden on the middle class, but it had not filtered down to the military in the form of increased defense spending. While in the provinces he had been able to skim what he needed from the treasury before the money was sent to Rome (a precedent set years before by his rifling of the mint at Arelate), but once in Rome, he found it increasingly difficult to get the contributions he needed. The senatorial class, led by Petronius Maximus, preferred to keep their wealth, and no amount of dire warnings about the existential threat posed by the Huns could loosen their purse strings. Aetius was advised to seek his funding elsewhere. He began to fret openly that he might not be able to patch together an army strong enough to resist the coming attack.

Fortunately for Rome, an incident occurred that delayed the impending crisis. In the heat of a mid-summer afternoon, my father went out riding and was thrown from his horse. His head struck a rock and he died. Just like that, the East was back in play. It had no ruler except for the conniving eunuch Chrysaphius whose willingness to barter the Empire for personal gain was well established.

In the time it took for the news to travel to Attila, General Aspar had already dispatched a courier to Antioch bearing an offer to Pulcheria. He begged her to come back and save them. In the meantime, a third courier was streaking toward Ravenna to inform Placidius that the time had come to assert his claim to the East. The race was on, and for the next few weeks who or what would become the power in the East was an open question.

# Chapter 17
Autumn, The Year AD 450 – Summer, The Year AD 451

Even before the events of mid-summer—before my father fell from his horse, and before Justa wrote the letter to Attila—I had been secretly corresponding with my mother-in-law Galla Placidia. I first wrote to her after reading the letter she had written for Placidius. So impressed was I by the lengths she had gone to advise him, I wanted to tell her. I didn't worry she would betray me to Placidius. We were kindred spirits. What Galla had been willing to do, increasingly, was the kind of thing I thought I would be willing to do in similar circumstances.

She wrote back and informed me about the turmoil in Ravenna, Justa's letter and Placidius's reaction to it, the threat from Attila, and Aetius's dire predicament. She also informed me of my father's death and the subsequent jockeying for position in Constantinople. It seemed Pulcheria had replied to Aspar's summons and sailed for the capital. Aspar was waiting with a proposition. She could be returned to power and enjoy the kind of influence she had known before, but she could not reign alone, not as a woman. The Church and the public would not permit it, not even with a woman whose reputation for strong leadership was as universally recognized as hers. Pulcheria understood and agreed to be married. But she wanted it understood that she would never surrender her virginity. Whoever she wed would have to agree to a sexless marriage.

The candidate Aspar had in mind was not himself. Aspar was of Alanic-Gothic descent and would never be acceptable to the public. Instead, he suggested Marcian.

Pulcheria was forty-nine-years-old and Marcian was fifty-six. Their days of youthful lust were behind them. Yet they shared, along with Aspar, a burning desire to excise the cancer that was Chrysaphius and put an end to the debilitating policy of appeasing the Huns. Celibacy was no impediment. Pulcheria's conditions were readily agreed to, and within a fortnight she and Marcian were married.

At the wedding ceremony Pulcheria broke with tradition by presenting her new husband with the royal diadem and purple robe. For the first time in Roman history the imperial insignia were conferred by a woman on a man. The crowd cheered, and it was done. The Eastern Empire had a new emperor, and it was Marcian.

About this time, Placidius was feverishly trying to reach me in Constantinople. He thought I was still there. He was urging me to assert our claim to the throne. According to the laws of succession, I was the next in line—along with my husband. I could only imagine the bravado with which he proclaimed our birthright and declared the Eastern Empire his. Little did he realize that, even as he wrote, Marcian was ascending to the purple. Placidius's thirteen years of ignoring and rejecting me had finally produced their bitter harvest. We would never fulfill the promise of our marriage. We would never reunite the Empire because we had no heir.

Six weeks later he received the sobering news that his letter had not reached its intended target. I was not in Constantinople. I had been gone for more than a year. My whereabouts were unknown.

He erupted. Not only had he been thwarted in his ambitions, but he also had been defied by his wife—again. To make matters worse, the current situation with the Huns precluded his taking any action against Marcian and Pulcheria. His hands were tied. Angry and spiteful, he called for my immediate apprehension and arrest. He wanted me brought before him to answer for my crime.

Suddenly I was a hunted woman.

Fortunately, the only one who knew of my whereabouts was Galla, and it was unlikely she would betray me. As her letters expressed, she still considered me the last best hope for the survival of the House of Theodosius. She was still hoping and praying I would produce an heir—any male child with the blood of our ancestors in its veins—that could lay claim to the Western throne when Placidius passed. For my part, I was coming around to her point of view. I must produce a son, if not by Placidius then by someone else.

One morning after months of living together in chastity I went to Junius where he lay in bed, drew back the covers and crawled in beside him. I had taken my clothes off.

He turned to me in surprise. "What are you doing?"

"You're my husband in every way but one. Let's change that."

He was staring at me open-mouthed. He began to splutter out an answer. "But we're not married in the eyes of God. You're married to another."

I put my finger to his lips. "Shh," I said. "I need your help. I need you to give me a son. If Placidius were to die without an heir, the struggle for the throne will tear the Empire apart. Placidius will not lay with me. You must."

He started to protest again, but I shook my head.

"I love you Junius. In any other circumstances I would lay with you as your wife. Up until now we've been restrained by our morals, but things have changed; the situation is bigger than us. If we don't do this, I fear we may not live long."

He looked at me in alarm. "What do you mean?"

"The Emperor has no further use for me. I haven't given him what he wants, and I have become an impediment to him. The only thing keeping me alive is the promise of the Eastern throne. With that possibility taken from him, he doesn't need me anymore. If he catches me, he'll kill me. The only thing that can stay his hand is a child in my womb." I lay back on my pillow and smiled. "Lay with me now and give me a son. Save me—and save the Empire. Don't worry. God will forgive you."

As his anxious gaze began to soften, I put my hand behind his neck and pulled him to me. When he entered me, it was the first time I had ever felt such love and tenderness. There was no violent urgency, no hunger or madness. I gave myself up to him, and it was glorious.

His father had been wrong. He was not incapable of making love to a woman. He was only incapable of taking a woman as some men do, like a wild beast feeding on prey. With Junius

I didn't require jewels or titles or promises as compensation for his cruelty.

With Junius, all I needed was him.

* * *

If Attila had any hesitation about attacking the East before now, the ascension of Marcian discouraged him further. Within days of his coming to power, Marcian dealt with Attila's most influential puppet in a way that left no doubt as to his opinion about the Empire's policy of appeasing the Huns. Practically the moment Marcian settled into the throne notices began appearing on signposts throughout the city announcing the imposition of new taxes. These levies were necessary to replenish the treasury, they said, which had been depleted by the ongoing and unnecessary payment of tribute to the Huns, a policy implemented and promoted by the eunuch Chrysaphius.

Among the populace not a few had lost loved ones to the depredations of the Huns. The idea that they had sacrificed blood and treasure to enrich some preening eunuch roused them to anger. A mob gathered before the palace and demanded Chrysaphius's head. Chrysaphius begged to see Marcian to make his case and to seek his protection. Marcian ignored him.

Terrified, Chrysaphius tried to slip away but was spotted. The mob beat him senseless. They gouged out his eyes, stabbed him repeatedly, and dragged his body through the streets. His corpse was hanged upside down from the city gates for the crows to pick at. Anyone who had supported and enabled him soon met a similar fate.

Attila was put on notice. The paying of tribute was over. What's more, the treasury of the Eastern Roman Empire was being replenished, which meant the military would henceforth be getting the resources it needed to wage all-out war. Attila sent an envoy to Constantinople. This person made demands and issued threats. He was expelled. Attila fell silent. No one was quite sure what was going to happen next.

Galla wrote to me and shared the news. She also told me what she had learned about the Franks, interesting new developments destined to have a profound effect on future events.

For years the Huns had been expanding their reach west of the Danube. They had been subordinating smaller tribes. The Rugians, Gepids, Sciri, Ostrogoths, and, most importantly, the Thuringians had fallen under their control. The Thuringians resided in the Hartz Mountains of Germania four hundred miles to the east of the Frankish stronghold of Camaracum.

During the year I was in Aurelianum, the Frankish king Chlodio died. He left two sons, both of whom coveted their father's throne. By rights, the eldest son, Childeric, should have succeeded his father, but Aetius preferred the younger son, Merovech and sent troops to support him. Merovech seized the throne and turned the Frankish kingdom into a Roman client state. Childeric fled east and sought help from the Thuringians who sent him on to Attila.

So, when Marcian dug in and refused to pay Attila's tribute, Attila had two disaffected leaders from Gaul in his camp who were seeking assistance in restoring them to power, the leader of the Bagaudae from Armorica, and the rightful heir to the Frankish throne, Childeric. The restoration of these two leaders would allow Attila to establish vassal states in Gaul, which would break Roman control of the region, and isolate Roman power in Italia. What's more, by attacking Gaul, the Huns would be striking the Roman military where it was weakest.

In Aurelianum, Junius and I were in the dark. We presumed ourselves safe, well out of the way of any danger. Galla's letter told us otherwise, and more.

In the autumn, Attila's envoy had arrived in Ravenna with his reply to Placidius's letter. Attila rejected the contention that Justa had intended anything other than an offer of marriage when she sent her ring to him, and he dismissed the assertion that she was already married to someone else. He wanted half the Western Empire as his dowry, and now, because the Emperor had proven resistant, the Hun king wanted more. He expected to be named co-emperor. Failure to meet his demands at once would be considered a provocation.

Placidius was dumbfounded. He asked for time to consult with his counsel, but the envoy had been instructed to demand an immediate answer. There could be no further delay. Would the emperor agree to Attila's demands?

Placidius's eyes filled with tears. His counselors looked at each other in consternation. The moment drew itself out. Then Petronius Maximus stepped forward, and, with a show of bitter defiance, rejected Attila's demands. Attila's envoy regarded him with a narrow, piercing gaze, then packed his things and left.

The ensuing silence was ominous, broken only by the Emperor's piteous sobbing.

* * *

In the final weeks of that year, I wrote to Galla to thank her for her informative correspondence. I also wanted to report some happy news. I was pregnant. At last, her fondest wish was coming true. The Theodosian bloodline might well continue after all. If I bore a son, the succession would be clear. To my dismay, however, my letter went unanswered.

Weeks went by and then months. News kept coming. For the second year in a row, the Emperor would appoint himself consul. Pope Leo had issued a statement repudiating his rivals and threatening them with expulsion. Word arrived of a new statue to be erected in the forum, a statue of Sextus Claudius Probus, Maximus's father, financed from the public coffers. But it took until the snow melted to receive news of Galla's death.

I had no idea whether she had died in the happy knowledge that I had fulfilled her ambitions or whether she had gone to her grave wondering if anything would ever come of her efforts to persuade me to have a child. I was heartbroken at the loss.

In March, the Huns went on the offensive. They had assembled a formidable coalition of Rugians, Gepids, Sciri, Ostrogoths, and Thuringians as well as those Franks loyal to Childeric, and men of the Bagaudae most hostile to Rome. They advanced across Germania and into Gaul bypassing Italia altogether and taking Aetius by surprise.

The Master of Soldiers, more alarmed than anyone had ever seen him, gathered his army, and, to the strenuous objections of Placidius and the Senate, hastened to Gaul. In so doing he left the Italian peninsula almost entirely undefended. Along the way, he sent riders to Tolosa to repeat his request for an alliance with King Theodoric of the Goths. The Huns were coming. It was now or never. They had to present a united front or Gaul would be overrun. Theodoric didn't answer.

Attila crossed the Rhine and smashed into the city of Divodorum. He razed the city and slaughtered the inhabitants. One of the few structures left standing was the chapel of St. Peter, in all likelihood saved by its hearty stone structure. Pope Leo, however, who never missed an opportunity to claim credit, attributed the chapel's survival to the intervention of God, and suggested his own prayers might have been the cause. He downplayed the fact that all of the priests and most of the parishioners had been butchered.

The Huns rolled on. They destroyed a score of town and villages, raping and pillaging as they went. They overwhelmed both hastily assembled militias and fortified garrisons. They approached the town of Reims like a mighty storm. The carnage was staggering. By mid-afternoon the streets were piled high with corpses, and the cries of the wounded and dying rent the air.

At the Cathedral of Reims, the bishop's head was lopped off as he knelt beneath the portico reading Psalm 119. As legend would have it, his head tumbled down the stairs still reciting the verse as if the holocaust of the Huns could not conquer the devotion of a priest in the middle of liturgy. The Church was silent about the suffering of the untold thousands who had not been spared by the miracle of the rolling head except to suggest they had probably fallen short of their devotions.

From Reims the Huns surged westward and bypassed the small, backwater city of Lutetia altogether. Situated on an island in the middle of the Seine River, it might have made a worthy outpost had the Huns elected to turn to it, but they didn't. Nevertheless, that didn't stop the Church from crafting another legend designed to advertise the piety of the people there. In the Church's accounting, a devout virgin named Genevieve begged the populace not to run away. She insisted they could divert the Huns by fasting and prayer. They did, and the town was saved even though the Huns were ninety miles to the south, not interested in Lutetia at all, and on a direct line to Aurelianum where Junius and I were hiding.

I was six months pregnant and frightened out of my wits. Nevertheless, I had to find the courage to face the situation, the kind of courage imputed to the fictional Genevieve. But my weapons would not be prayers and fasting alone. I was a Christian, but I was also a Roman, and I would call on additional resources. I remembered well the lesson Galla Placidia had taught me. Use everything at your disposal. Then stand and resist.

* * *

It wasn't as if I hadn't experienced a similar situation before. I had been inside the walls of Constantinople when we had turned back the Huns, and I knew two things for certain: the Huns were rowdy and impatient, and although they might have mastered the skills of siege warfare, they were no match for determined engineers. If we could hold them off long enough, they would give up and withdraw. But to get my message across to the town's leaders I would have to reveal who I was, a risky proposition.

Junius was dead set against it. If the bounty hunters seeking the reward for my capture should hear of it, my life and that of my unborn child's would be at risk.

"We should leave," he said. "Get away while we can."

"You can't run from the Huns," I said. "They excel at slaughtering those who try to run away. Besides, it would be sending the wrong message. No. We are better off trying to resist."

He plowed his fingers through his hair. "Very well then, I'll go to the magistrates and reveal my true identity. I'm the former praetor of Rome; that will carry some weight. They'll listen to me."

"Think about it, Junius. Your father is looking for you. He knows I'm with you. If you're found, then so am I. If one of us steps forward, we both do, and my influence is greater than yours. I should be the one."

He looked at the ground and sighed. "We can't stay here—when this is over, we'll have to run again."

"One crisis at a time," I said. "Be strong."

We went to the magistrates and told them who we were. In a curious echo of the appalling deed that had initiated the whole debacle, I showed them my signet ring as proof. They were astonished and unsettled by that fact that I was obviously pregnant. I had been in Aurelianum the entire time, so it was easy to deduce the child could not possibly be the Emperor's. It must have occurred to them that cooperating with me might make them complicit in my transgression, but they pretended deference.

"You must tell no one," I said. They agreed with a false show of humility.

I urged them to stand firm against the Huns, but they were not convinced. Some objected. Others thought they could still negotiate. They cited similar situations where they had negotiated with the Franks and the Saxons.

"The Huns are not the Franks or Saxons," I said. "You cannot negotiate with them. They will bleed you dry until you are weak and vulnerable, and then they will kill you anyway."

Some suggested they could surrender and be treated mercifully.

"The Huns know no mercy. If you surrender, you will be enslaved, your women will be violated, and your children murdered."

Others wanted to abandon the city and flee. I shook my head.

"Running away is the greatest folly of all. They will hunt you down and destroy you." I fixed them with a stern, unwavering gaze. "There's only one option. You must fight."

Equally inspired and bewildered by such bravado from a woman, they went along.

I instructed them to round up the best engineers in the city. I told them to dig trenches and erect ramparts. I told them to repair any weaknesses in the walls. Every available hand had to be put to the task. They did as I told them.

Arrows were fashioned, oil set to boiling. Women and children were sent out into the countryside to gather up food in anticipation of a long siege. Farmers in the vicinity were instructed to hand over all their cattle and livestock. Anyone who resisted was arrested. Gradually, our defenses grew stronger, and our reserves of food and water mounted up.

At the end of two weeks a small contingent of Roman soldiers arrived under the command of a general named Avitus. He had been instrumental in negotiating the peace that had ended the hostilities with the Goths several years earlier. During the course of those discussions, he had developed a close personal relationship with Theodoric. Having failed to move Theodoric himself, Aetius had called Avitus out of retirement to make Rome's appeal to the Gothic king.

Avitus was a tall, slender, white-haired man with an affable nature and a quick smile. Seeing the preparations being made to defend Aurelianum, he was impressed and asked to meet the officer in charge.

I was standing beside the portcullis discussing the reinforcements of the gates with a couple of engineers when we met.

"Who are you?" he asked.

"An interested woman of the city, the daughter of a magistrate."

"Which magistrate?"

"The chief magistrate of another city."

"A city in the East judging by your accent."

"Yes."

"Are you a holy woman?"

"Pious, but not holy."

"Then why do these men follow you? A mere interested woman of the city could not move them. You must possess some authority to command them, some authority you wish to conceal." He regarded me and stroked his chin.

"The Augusta of Rome is missing," he said. "The Emperor is offering a rich reward for her return." He gave me a weighty look. "I must tell you I do not think it a wise use of the public purse to expend resources looking for her, I mean, with war approaching and so many others needing funding. Besides, the Augusta is far too bright to be lost. If she is missing, I suspect it's because she wants it that way."

He looked down at my swollen belly and sighed. "Well, wherever she is, I'm sure she's contributing in some important way. Wouldn't you agree, interested woman of the city?"

I smiled faintly. He gave me a curt nod and moved away. Later I got word he had left a handful of soldiers behind to aid us and continued on to Tolosa unguarded.

"Is that wise?" I asked one of the soldiers.

"General Avitus is a survivor," he said. "He'll get to where he wants to go, with or without a guard."

Six days later as the finishing touches were being put on our defenses, a large cloud of dust appeared on the horizon. The soldiers on the battlements looked at each other in consternation. They had been working hard for three weeks to prepare, but the sight of the cloud portended a force many times larger than they had expected.

"Take heart," I said. "They want you to lose your nerve. They're counting on it. They feed on your weakness. They thrive on your fear. Deny them. Stand up and face them, and they will bend."

They looked at me with uncertainty, this strange pregnant woman trying to whip up their courage. When they looked again at the horizon, trepidation painted their faces. Whether they would have the courage to do what was required was hard to say. If they wavered, they were doomed, as was I—both me and my child. And if my baby died, all hope for the survival of the Western Roman Empire would die with him. We were fighting for everything.

* * *

They came in their thousands, a great rolling horde that stretched out on the plain before us like a slow-moving tide. They came on foot and horseback, tromping through the dust amidst the sounds of creaking leather, clacking greaves, and rattling swords. They came in curious wagons topped with sheepskin tents and peaked roofs from which rippled long pennants. They came driving their livestock, swarming herds of sheep and pigs and goats. They shepherded them forward with whips and staffs, more like refugees than an advancing army. They came with their families, squealing children, beckoning mothers, and shouting men. They came with their slaves, the squalid, dejected remnants of defeated tribes, once proud men and women who had made the mistake of falling on their mercy. They came with their plunder, wagons piled high with the treasures they had stripped from the towns and cities they had demolished, riches they had torn from the hands of weeping victims and picked from the bodies of the dead as they stood ankle-deep in blood.

They came with their siege engines, the mighty machines of war: the fearsome onager, so called because of the sound it made when it flung its combustible 200-pound ball from its long, swooping arm, a braying shout like a jackass; and the musculus, a turtle-shaped shelter on wheels, open at both ends, that could be rolled over obstacles and trenches and pushed up against walls so that those inside could set to work undermining the structure even while they were shielded from the arrows and stones raining down from above; and the siege towers, rectangular wooden structures thirty feet tall, swaying and jolting along on wooden wheels, covered with animal skins and containing crude scaffolding designed to permit the occupants to climb to the height of the walls and throw down planks to cross over and fight the defenders on the battlements; and the great, triangular A-frame of the battering ram, twenty feet tall at its peak and equipped with an oaken crossbeam from which a massive log hung by chains that, when set to swinging, could smash the tall wooden gates of a city like the fist of a Titan.

They came with their cavalry, a mounted host like nothing ever seen before in the green rolling hills of central Gaul, an unnerving assemblage of Asiatic men in conical caps and embroidered boots riding stout ponies with black manes and bulging eyes. Each man came armed with a composite bow constructed of horn, wood, and sinew laminated together for increased force and accuracy as well as a quiver of arrows, like a basket of reeds, from which a skilled archer could snatch, notch, and shoot with the rapidity of raindrops driven by a storm.

They came with their grievances. Ever the sufferers, disdained, insulted, cheated, making use of that favored contrivance of bullies and scoundrels, the resort to victimhood that robs their victims of sympathy and appropriates it to justify evil. Poor Attila – mistreated and abused. He could not stand by while he was cruelly denied his just deserts—a ruse as transparent as it was disingenuous. He had been robbed of his tribute, deprived of his subjects, and pushed from his land. What could he do? He must attack, if for no other reason than to salvage his dignity in the face of such contumely. He was a man, after all.

More like a beast. He would take and take and take, and when opposed, he would cry foul, and go on the attack. He and his horde had to be stopped.

They numbered something on the order of 60,000, while we, their presumed oppressors, were a little under 4,000, half of us women and children.

At first sight, some in the town wanted to sue for peace. A group of more than thirty went to the magistrates and argued that to oppose such a force was nothing short of madness. We must send an emissary to ask for terms. But the magistrates refused. Upon hearing this, some of the malcontents tried to run away, but were caught and brought before me for justice. I ordered them detained, although it pained me to do so. If I had learned anything from Galla, it was that there were times when one could not afford to be soft. Still, detaining them depleted our numbers, which were already strained.

Some were atrophied by fear. I came upon one such cowering in the corner of his hut. He was a complete wreck. To put a sword in his hand would've been worse than useless. Others had gathered in the church to pray, hundreds of them filling the sanctuary to overflowing. They spilled out into the street, surrounded the building several rows deep, and prayed up at the structure as if it were a god. They sought rescue in the divine rather than in doing the hard work of defending themselves. They poured money into the collection plates, which delighted the priests who grinned as they waved blessings over the crowd. They were weak and deluded and ill prepared for what was to come.

I prayed as well. I prayed for them to find courage. I prayed God would help us find the strength to withstand the impending storm. I prayed and prayed until the men on the parapet began to stir, their black forms silhouetted against the late afternoon sky, taking up their positions, testing the resiliency of their bows. I thanked God for the arrival of Avitus's men, the only experienced soldiers among us. Without them our defenders would not have had the discipline to hold their fire and might have wasted our precious ammunition. Time dragged on.

The Huns had not fired a shot. They were organizing behind our trenches, two hundred yards out, going about it in a workmanlike manner as if they were erecting an aqueduct. They positioned their siege engines, divided into regiments, and established command posts. Before they were finished, darkness fell over the land. Little by little, their campfires came to life. It was a daunting sight, a thousand rippling beacons illuminating the night like stars in a constellation.

Within the walls, the inhabitants of the city could not rest. Some were so anxious they could not eat. Others wept and cried out to God for mercy. Others could be heard vomiting in fear.

At dawn the first balls were slung and catapulted against the walls amid the braying honk of the onagers. Six landed in rapid succession, and then… stunned silence. Six more. The last two described long arcs across the morning sky and smashed through the roofs of houses set well back within our walls. The opening shots were a warning. There had been no formal request for parlay, no demand for surrender. It was clear what they wanted. Twelve shots. Surrender now.

Then, after another prolonged silence, it began.

* * *

It started with volley upon volley of arrows, thousands of them. They sprayed the battlements like waves bursting upon a rock. The defenders took cover to no avail. The arrows fell in an unrelenting shower. Anyone foolish enough to stick their heads out were skewered instantly. Only the protection of the arrow slits in the bastion permitted us to observe. One of Avitus's soldiers invited me to take a look. I saw the Huns moving their musculi forward, those oddly shaped shelters on wheels commonly referred to as "tortoises" because of their rounded shells and sluggish progress. There were three of them and they inched forward as if in a slow-motion race. Inside each were a dozen men with shovels. They advanced to the first line of trenches and began to fill them in. From above I could see bundles of wood being lobbed out, followed by shovelfuls of dirt.

This activity was met with almost no resistance. Our men had fired barely a single shot and could not have if they wanted to, pinned down as they were. It seemed inconceivable that the deluge of arrows could keep on showering down, but it did, launched by rank upon rank of standing archers strung out in long rows who fired and restrung with the smooth rapidity of the spokes of a wheel.

By mid-morning the first line of trenches was full, and the musculi trundled forward to the next. As the men inside went about their business, the siege towers and battering rams approached. The onagers remained well back. The second line of trenches began to fill in. At this rate it looked like the enemy would reach the wall and undermine it before we could mount a defense. I went to find the commander in charge, the chief officer assigned to us by Avitus, a man named Quirinus. I asked him what we were doing to slow the advance.

"We're taking what they give us," he said. He pointed to the courtyard below where thousands of enemy arrows had fallen. A line of men was moving through it, holding up rounded shields to fend of the falling projectiles and picking up the arrows off the ground. "They have the advantage of us at the moment, but if they keep contributing in such numbers, we may soon match them."

"But are the arrows any good once they've been shot? Will they fly true?"

"They won't have to. By the time we use them, the targets will be so numerous, even the errant darts will find a mark."

This wasn't exactly encouraging. Quirinus saw my frightened expression and asked me to come with him. He brought me to a place along the parapet where a cauldron of pitch was on the boil. All around it were smaller pots into which the pitch would be ladled when the time was right. He hurried me to another location where a large bellows, the kind used by blacksmiths for smelting iron, was being mounted on a wheeled device with a large bowl for holding the fire. He showed me a ballista, a bolt-throwing device with a grooved shaft for propelling a single large arrow with great force. A town the size of Aurelianum should have been defended with more than a dozen of these, but we had only one. Quirinus directed my attention to where a man was carefully fitting the bolt with a grappling hook.

He smiled. "Circumstances require us to be inventive."

"Tell me the truth," I said. "Do we have a chance?"

He held his tongue for a moment. "There is always a chance, Augusta. But the people must be roused to action. At the moment we have more arrows than defenders willing to shoot them."

I understood.

Back on the parapet, I peered through the slit. The enemy had filled in the next line of trenches and was advancing toward the wall. The siege towers had been brought nearer, permitting the archers to shoot down on the parapet from above. I pressed closer to the wall to reduce the angle of sight. The shower of arrows from the archers in the rear began to abate. What had been an indiscriminate torrent of arrows against a largely unseen adversary now became a surgical targeting of individual defenders.

Junius came up behind me. "What do you think?"

"I'm afraid we don't have the resources to withstand this."

He frowned. "Then it's in God's hands."

I felt a swell of indignation. "Is it really? Before we've fired a single arrow, before we've even tried to fight back, we're going to lay down our arms and pray to God?"

I didn't know where this was coming from, but I couldn't hold back. "You know that won't happen, Junius. If we sit around and wait for God to reach down and strike the enemy dead, we will be massacred. God may aid us, but first we have to do everything in our power to stop them. The people have to understand that. If they think the priests are going to save them, they'll be on their knees when the Huns chop their heads off. They must be reminded of who they are and what they're capable of. They must be reminded they are Romans."

Junius was taken aback at my outburst and began to say something in response, but I cut him off. "Come with me," I said. "Let's go to the church."

At the church we waded through the crowd of supplicants. They were hunched over, mouthing their prayers. They were weeping and wailing and throwing their arms in the air. We mounted the steps and confronted the bishop.

"Give me access to the tower," I said.

"Why?" he said.

"I must speak to the people."

"But you are a woman."

"I am the Augusta."

"It is highly irregular. I'm afraid it cannot be done."

"Move aside," Junius said, elbowing him out of the way.

We climbed the tower and Junius stood behind me as I stepped out onto the balcony.

I spoke with all the power I could muster. "People of Aurelianum hear me. I am the Augusta of Rome."

A ripple of astonishment went through the crowd. Every face turned up to see me. I showed them a brave countenance.

"I have watched you pray, and your prayers do you honor. God is listening to you, and He marks your piety. But He may require more from you. Listen. I have faced the Huns before. I was at Constantinople when they besieged the city. We withstood them, and they withdrew. We can achieve the same here. But every person must do his or her part. Prayer is not enough. We must act."

I could see the disapproving look of the bishop. He glared up at me. I let my eyes rest firmly on his for a moment before carrying on.

"There is a time for prayer, which is before the battle when you are mustering your courage and girding yourself for the struggle to come. But when the enemy attacks, you must engage. To sit idly by hoping God will save you is arrogant for it rejects the idea that you have any agency and clings to the selfish belief that something more can be solicited from God, a supernatural intervention, a miracle of some kind. You may believe yourself worthy, but how can you expect such generosity from God if you are not willing to lift a hand in your own defense?"

They were still listening – it was something at least.

"I can tell you this. Such was not the case at Constantinople. There we found ourselves in a hopeless situation. An earthquake had caused the walls of the city to collapse, large sections had fallen to the ground. There were huge gaps, enormous vulnerabilities. We could have huddled in the basilica and offered up prayers. We could have fallen to our knees and begged God to save us. But there was no time for that. We had to act. The Huns were getting nearer. So, we organized every able-bodied man and rebuilt those walls. Ultimately, the Huns were thwarted and turned back."

They were listening…rapt attention…a good sign. I kept going.

"Such a miracle can happen here, but not without your commitment. If you do not act, you cannot expect to survive.

Even now the Huns are rolling their siege towers up to your walls. If they are not opposed, they will drop gangplanks onto the battlements and cross over. If they are not opposed, they will be marauding through your streets before nightfall, and they will bring a blackness upon you like nothing you've ever experienced before. Then what will your prayers avail you? You are Romans. You must gird yourself for the battle and trust that God will defend you. You must stand and fight. Will you do that?"

There was a moment's silence, and then one man rose up and offered the imperial salute, fist to chest, arm outstretched. Another followed suit, and then another and another. Before long, every person in the crowd had risen and expressed their allegiance to Rome. Only the bishop hung back.

On our way down the steps he blocked our path. "You will regret this," he said.

We swept past him without a second look and went out among the people. We rounded up scores of volunteers and led them to Quirinus who organized them into fighting units, and none too soon for the Huns had already advanced their first siege tower to within a few dozen feet of our walls.

# Chapter 18
June, The Year AD 451

As the gangplank of the first siege tower ratcheted down, the assailants in the second tower, which stood a hundred feet back, showered arrows down on our defenders, keeping them at bay. If our fighters could not get to the gangplank, the enemy would cross over unchecked. We had to stop the covering fire from the second siege tower if we were to have a chance.

Our archers could hit the target, but their arrows could not penetrate the fresh animal hides that covered the wooden framework of the tower.

As the gangplank ratcheted down, the raiders became visible: filthy, wild-eyed men with drooping mustaches and howling mouths. Swords raised, they fidgeted in anticipation of the attack.

Then came a new sound, a sudden scrape and a twang, and our ballista loosed its first bolt. It zoomed out of the confines of the town with tremendous force and struck the face of the second tower tearing through the animal skin wall and knocking over several men within. The bolt trailed a rope. The moment it penetrated the wall, our defenders began to reel it back in. At the end of the bolt was a grappling hook which caught on the animal skins and ripped them apart, exposing a large breach. At a signal, a column of archers dipped the heads of their arrows in pitch, ignited them and fired. The flaming arrows penetrated the breach and set the tower ablaze. The men inside were enveloped in flames and flailed about screaming in agony. With the covering fire from the second tower suppressed, our fighters rushed up to the battlements to engage the invaders.

The marauders came pounding across howling with rage. They were met with an enfilading fire from both ends of the battlements. Half of them fell at once; several of them toppled from the gangplank and plummeted to the earth below. The rest made it onto the parapet where they engaged in hand-to-hand combat. Some were pushed back. Others fought their way onto the walkway where they were overcome by slashing swords. The Hun's initial assault ended in defeat.

But it was not over. New raiders scrambled up the interior scaffolding of the siege tower intending to cross over to the parapet. As they ascended, the second tower burst into flame and collapsed in an explosion of swirling embers. Flaming debris scattered over a wide area and ignited the wooden apron of one of the musculi. The men inside rushed out and were cut down by arrows fired from the battlements.

The raiders clambering up the siege tower stopped to observe the fate of their luckless fellows and were riddled by a volley of flaming arrows. They fell screaming through the scaffolding. A moment later the tower was ablaze.

The grappling hook was reeled back in. It came clanking up the stone wall. In the courtyard below Quirinus ordered the repositioning of the ballista. He situated it in the far corner where it could fire its bolt at an angle to the newly ignited tower. The grappling hook was reloaded.

In the meantime, the attackers had managed to get their remaining two musculi tucked up against the base of the wall. The men inside began digging feverishly with the intention of tunneling beneath. At the same time, the great A-frame containing the battering ram rumbled up to the gates.

In the courtyard the artillerymen adjusted the positioning of the ballista. Quirinus gave the signal, and the bolt flew out trailing the rope. It struck the flaming tower, penetrating it at an angle. When the rope was retracted, the grappling hook caught within the scaffolding and tugged the tower to one side. It fell sidelong against the wall and landed on top of one of the musculi. The men inside could be heard screaming as they were roasted alive.

Undeterred by the fate of their fellows, the men in the remaining musculus kept digging. Close by, the great A-frame that housed the battering ram reached the gates. Our defenders fired down on it, riddling its thick oaken roof with dozens of arrows, to no avail. Then the pitch pots were brought up. Our defenders dipped their arrows and ignited them. The arrows spread fire upon impact. The A-frame began to burn, prompting lusty cheers from the defenders. But then they heard something that made their cries freeze in their throats: the croak and bray of the onagers.

The first ball struck the wall just below the parapet with a concussion so powerful it caused the top of the wall to explode, vomiting rubble down its face. Several men lost their footing and toppled to their deaths. A moment later another ball struck farther down with similar results. The defenders fled in a panic as more balls zoomed over their heads and struck buildings within the town, smashing them to splinters.

With the defensive fire temporarily suppressed, the Huns rushed forward with buckets of water and doused the burning A-frame. Once the fire was out, the battering ram was anchored into position.

I ran down the steps with my hands under my pregnant belly. Our defenders had gathered in the courtyard and were rushing around in a panic.

"Take heart!" I cried. "Don't stop now! They're preparing to batter down the gates!"

They looked at me in despair.

I was roused to a fury. "If you want to save your lives—if you want to save the lives of your wives and children, you must trust in God and take the battle to them!"

They hung back.

"Listen to me. You've come too far to quit now."

When even this did not move them, I drew myself up and strode across the courtyard to where a cauldron of boiling oil was seething and bubbling. I picked up a wooden bucket and filled it. Then I went back across the courtyard and climbed the steps to the wall. Oil sloshed and spilled over the rim of the bucket. Some of it got on my dress. Some of it splashed my feet and ankles. It caused me great pain, but I kept going. I climbed the steps to the wall and passed along the ramparts in full view of both the attackers and the defenders.

I went to the barbican[13] and looked down on the men anchoring the battering ram. I emptied my bucket on them. Two of them fell screaming to the ground, desperately trying to wipe the burning oil from their flesh. But I didn't wait to watch. I stalked back along the ramparts and down the steps. Junius rushed up to stop me.

"You can't do this! You're putting yourself in danger! Remember, you're carrying our child!"

I brushed past him and went back to the cauldron where I refilled my bucket.

Junius followed. "Think of the baby," he said.

I turned to him. "If Aurelianum falls, the baby will die. If Aurelianum falls, we will all die. If you want to save the baby, save the town." I pushed a bucket into his hands.

He filled two buckets and followed me. We climbed the steps and passed down the parapet to the barbican where we dumped the oil on the enemy. Again, there were screams and cries of agony. We ducked as several arrows went whizzing by so close that we could feel the breeze as they passed. But our performance had the desired effect.

A couple of men rushed forward to help. They filled their buckets and climbed the steps and emptied them on the enemy. Soon others followed. But the Huns were not deterred. Inside the A-frame they had set the gigantic log to swinging; once it built up enough momentum it would smash the gates to pieces.

The moment was critical. Conscious that the men in the courtyard were watching, I turned to face our attackers. I raised my arms to present an easy target. I don't know if the

---

13  Tower situated over a gate.

sight of a pregnant woman so astonished them they misfired, but for whatever reason, they missed me. I turned around and shouted down to the men in the courtyard.

"God protects us! God protects the people of Aurelianum!"

A mighty shout went up from the men. They rushed forward and filled their buckets. I turned to Junius and smiled. I could feel the amulet resting against my breastbone.

The men hastened up the steps and poured the burning pitch onto the roof of the A-frame. Before the swinging log had reached its full momentum, the A-frame was ablaze. When the log struck the door, it did so amid belching smoke and showering sparks. The concussion was so intense the men atop the barbican were knocked off their feet. Yet the gates held.

The A-frame didn't fare as well. The consuming fire and the force of the blow caused it to collapse. A dozen Huns were killed as the log broke free of its chains and crushed them.

The mood inside the town shifted. Suddenly everyone was cheering and eager for the fight. But the jubilation was short-lived. Again, came the croak of the onagers. Two huge round stones came arcing over the walls one after the other. The first smashed through the roof of a stable and killed a horse. The second went hurtling down a street, bouncing and spinning before crashing through a blacksmith's shop. People fled helter-skelter.

Two more stones descended. But these were different. Made of hard-packed clay and burning with a furious intensity, they shattered on impact and sent fiery fragments in every direction. A hay wagon caught fire and the roofs of several buildings ignited. The townspeople rushed about trying to extinguish the flames, but they couldn't keep pace with the fusillade. Dozens of people were wounded. The urgency of the fires drew a number of defenders away from the wall, weakening our defenses. Then the tunnelers broke through.

They emerged from beneath the wall like feral moles, blinking in the sunlight. As yet the tunnel was narrow, admitting only a single file, but they were coming up unchecked. At least a half dozen Huns had emerged by the time anyone noticed them.

Quirinus rushed forward with his soldiers and cut them to pieces. Then he called for the curious bellows on wheels he had shown me earlier to be brought forward. Its bowl had been loaded with dampened sticks that smoldered and steamed on the red-hot coals beneath. The contraption was rolled up to the mouth of the tunnel and the nozzle of the bellows placed in the opening. When the bellows were compressed, a steady stream of smoke flooded into the passage. The Huns inside were choked and blinded. A few made it through. They staggered out squinting and coughing only to be fallen upon by slashing swords. Quirinus's men stuffed the bodies back into the hole to obstruct the passage.

The battle of the tunnel was the last major engagement. After that, the onslaught slackened. Several more fireballs fell into the town, but the worst had passed. By nightfall the enemy's offensive ceased altogether.

The next morning, we braced for another assault, but it didn't happen. Two of the Huns' three siege engines had been reduced to smoldering wreckage. The battering ram had been completely destroyed. The tunnel was plugged with the bodies of their dead. They sent a message demanding our surrender. We ignored it. Then we waited.

This was exactly what I had hoped for. The Huns were too edgy and impatient to maintain a siege for long. They were not really interested in Aurelianum as a prize—they had too many other, easier targets that would yield as much—and the town gave them no strategic advantage. They had only targeted it because it lay in their path of advance as they made their way to the sea for the purpose of cutting Gaul in half. Had the town fallen easily, it would have replenished their stores, but having proven problematic, it cost them more than they had gained and was not worth the effort. We had only to hold out a week or more and they would withdraw. I was sure of it, and I told the people as much. I spoke to them from the tower of the church and encouraged them to stay strong. The bishop scowled at me from the shadows.

A mere two days later the Huns packed up and left. Even faster than I thought, the nightmare had ended.

The people fell to their knees and wept tears of gratitude. They sung my praises and spoke of erecting a statue in my honor. I begged for their discretion. I urged them to remain silent about who had led them, to speak of it to no one. If they loved me, I asked only their circumspection. And they gave it to me—for the most part.

A day or two later it became clear why the Huns had left so abruptly. Reports reached us that a large Gothic army under King Theodoric was moving north to cut off the Hun's line of retreat to the east. It seemed Avitus had won the Goth's commitment to our cause. At last, our allies were moving to engage the enemy and thwart their advance. But while we now had some idea of the Goth's disposition, one question remained. Where were Aetius and the bulk of the Roman army?

★ ★ ★

The next day a body of Roman troops arrived at the battered gates of Aurelianum. At first, we were relieved, but no sooner were the troops inside the gates than they demanded to see the Augusta. I knew we had been betrayed. I turned to Junius. My eyes spoke volumes. Should we try to slip away? Should we run? And if we did, would the people of Aurelianum protect us? But before Junius could respond, Quirinus put a hand on my shoulder.

"Here she is." My heart sank.

Without a word they took us into custody. We were herded into the back of a wagon and told to remain silent and obedient. As the wagon bore us away, the energy that had sustained me during the fight drained away leaving me dispirited and exhausted. My eyelids began to droop, and I fell asleep.

I slept for a time stretched out in the bed of the wagon, and awoke sore, achy, and desperately thirsty. Junius called for water and our captors delivered it without hesitation, indicating, perhaps, they were not as hostile as their manner had initially suggested. They were aloof to be sure, and tight-lipped when questioned about our destination, but they were not unkind. I began to entertain the possibility that they might not be delivering us to the Emperor.

It was a glimmer of hope in a gathering gloom because my spirit grew increasingly dejected. We made our way through the green hills of central Gaul beneath a bright blue sky. The skylarks chirped their happy songs, and the fields danced with flitting butterflies and buzzing insects. I was afraid, yes, and dismayed that everything we had done had earned us nothing but betrayal and mistrust, but it was more than that. I was also overcome by an unaccountable melancholy prompted by a growing tightness in my belly that augured darkly. By degrees it resolved itself into cramps.

I hunched and moaned. Alarmed, Junius called for the driver to stop. Together they carried me out of the wagon and lowered me onto the grass. Our captors wanted to know how they could help. When they learned I was about to give birth, they dispatched a soldier to the nearest village to inquire after a midwife.

The cramps came in waves. When they struck, I stiffened and clenched. Perspiration coursed down my brow. When they passed, I fell back in the grass, exhausted. I had no illusions about what it meant.

The midwife was too late. Her services were not required. Before she showed up, I gave birth to a half-developed fetus in a torrent of blood that turned the grass a ghastly hue of brownish red. Most of the men turned away, sickened. Only Junius remained. He held my hand, his face drained of color.

We made camp and I was permitted to rest for two days before resuming the journey. I felt hollowed out, emptied, a shell of my former self. Junius's awkward attempts at conversation were met with dull stares and one-word answers. I could fairly say I didn't care whether I lived or died. When we resumed, I remained distant and uncommunicative, and when we arrived at our destination, a sprawling Roman army camp along a bend of the Marne and given comfortable quarters in a command tent outfitted to accommodate us, I felt no particular relief at the knowledge that we were safe and would not be handed over to Placidius's bounty hunters.

I went to bed and asked to be left alone. When everyone had withdrawn, I stared up at the calfskin ceiling of the tent. Then I turned over and groaned, a single unbidden note of misery that broke from me like a wave. I sobbed and wept until the sun went down and the tent was immersed in darkness.

The next morning a visitor asked permission to see me.

"Who is it?" I asked.

"The Magister Militum Flavius Aetius."

"Let him in," I said. I straightened my clothes and rubbed the sleep from my eyes.

Aetius ducked into the tent. I was surprised by how much he had aged. It had been nearly a decade since he had stood before the Emperor and told him the only good way to keep the Vandals at bay was to marry Eudocia to Huneric. He was still lean and muscular with an upright bearing, but the skin had gone slack at his throat, and he had deep wrinkles at the corners of his eyes. He knelt on one knee and bowed his head.

"Augusta," he said.

"Aetius, it's good to see you. Please stand."

He got to his feet.

"I assume Avitus informed you of my presence at Aurelianum."

"That's correct. He was worried about your safety. I understand you've been through quite an ordeal."

"We were hard pressed, but the people of the town were strong and courageous. They were good Romans. The very best."

"Rumor has it they were bravely led, an interested woman of the city as I've heard it… someone who wishes to remain anonymous."

"Yes. Someone who wishes to remain anonymous," I said.

"Whoever she is, we owe her a debt of gratitude," Aetius said. "She accomplished more than she knows. The siege at Aurelianum bought us the time we needed to prepare our response to the invasion. The Goths are with us now, as are the Franks and the Burgundians. We're prepared to take the fight to the enemy. We couldn't have done it without her."

Suddenly I burst into tears. Perhaps I had saved Aurelianum and turned the tide of war, but not without paying an awful price. I put my head in my hands and wept.

I expected Aetius to withdraw, but he sat down beside me and put a comforting hand on my shoulder.

"I heard," he said. "I'm sorry."

I was incoherent.

Aetius went on. "You did what you could. You put the Empire first. Galla would've been proud, such courage and nobility. She always believed in you, Licinia. She always considered you the most promising of her children. Unfortunately, she had to give precedence to her own blood as any parent would do. Such a tragedy. She realized her mistake too late and regretted it. I won't repeat her error."

I looked up at him and swallowed back my tears. "What do you mean?"

He regarded me with something akin to affection. "Don't worry, Licinia. I'll protect you. I won't let the Emperor hurt you. When this is over, we'll return to Ravenna, and you'll be restored. You'll resume your position at his side, and if he tries to oppose me, he'll rue the day."

I didn't particularly like the idea of becoming an object of contention between the Emperor and Aetius, but I didn't have much choice. I couldn't continue to run and hide, and I would need a strong protector if I wanted to survive the wrath of Placidius and Maximus when I got back to Ravenna.

"But what will become of Junius?" I asked.

"My patronage extends to him as well. If his anyone tries to harm him, they'll answer to me. I stand by those who stand by me. I always have."

I thanked him. Tears streamed down my cheeks.

He held me by the shoulders and looked me in the eyes. "Much as I would like to send you back now, it's too risky. I wouldn't want you to find yourself dealing with the Huns again. I think it's safer if you remain with us until we have met the enemy and driven him down in defeat. Don't worry. You'll remain far in the rear well away from any engagement. If, perchance, we are thrown back, you'll be at the head of the retreat."

I told him I understood and would do whatever he asked of me.

And so I found myself traveling with the Roman army when it came into contact with the Huns at a place called the Catalaunian Plains. A thousand years of Roman history was suddenly, irrevocably on the line.

* * *

Long before the Huns had mastered the art of siege warfare, they were renowned for their superior horsemanship. For more than a generation, tales of Hun warriors slashing and shooting and throwing nets and lassos while riding nimble ponies with acrobatic skill had been reported by survivors. A wide-open plain was the ideal setting for such warfare, which is why, upon coming into contact with King Theodoric's Gothic army, the Huns turned and fled, and, as expected, the Goths pursued. By this ruse, the Huns led the Goths away from the rugged woodlands where the Goths might have enjoyed an advantage to the plains of Catalaunia where the Huns could best perform.

But before the Huns reached the Catalaunian Plains they suffered a setback. A large body of troops consisting of their Gepid allies had been placed in their rear to cover their retreat from Aurelianum. Aetius received news of this and sent a large force to destroy them. The Gepids, unaccustomed to fighting the Romans on such a large scale, were overwhelmed, and defeated. But the victory was not without a cost for it meant the Roman army was at less than full strength when it met the Huns. As Aetius waited for his force to come back he received a dispatch from King Theodoric informing him that the Huns had checked their retreat and were assembling on the Catalaunian Plains.

The plains themselves sloped gradually from the base of a ridge in the center to lower ground farther out. The Huns chose the ground because it was scattered with rock outcroppings and traversed by a deeply recessed brook, which would give them cover. When the Goths arrived, they seized the ridge. When the Romans arrived later, they were not tempted by the Huns' feigned vulnerability, and did not attack at once, but circled around and came up beside their Gothic allies. They took a position to King Theodoric's left where they could look down on the enemy from the ridge.

Aetius rode over to greet King Theodoric. From a vantage point of some distance, I watched this reunion of old rivals. There was warmth between them as they smiled and embraced; they exchanged witticisms and laughter. It became clear to me that if Aetius had been permitted to assemble a policy toward the Goths without interference from Placidius, Rome would have done well by it. Instead, distrust and animosity had been allowed to fester, which had nearly prevented their coming together at this crucial moment. I watched King Theodoric introduce Aetius to his son, Prince Thorismund. Aetius bowed to him, displaying deference that was both unexpected and warmly appreciated. Monarch and general parted and returned to their respective stations where they waited.

They waited and waited, expecting the Huns to attack first. In the interim Aetius straightened his lines and arranged his troops. In addition to Theodoric's Goths on his right, he placed the Burgundians to his left next to the Franks under their client king, Merovech. Facing them across the field were the allies of the Huns, the Rugians, Sciiri, and Thuringians as well as those Franks who were loyal to Childeric. Everyone was restless. Horses blew and snorted; armor rattled. But no one moved. It was as if each side was daring the other to go first.

Finally, late in the day the Huns arrayed their archers and let loose a shower of arrows much as they had in Aurelianum. So thick was the deluge it nearly blotted it out the sky. The soldiers on the ground raised their shields. In seconds their protective disks bristled with quills like the backs of porcupines. Then the Huns changed tactics. While half of their archers continued to rain down arrows on our soldiers' heads, the other half dropped to their knees and shot directly at them. Unable to hold their shields in two places at once, hundreds of our soldiers were cut down.

Aetius called for our fighters to fall back and shelter behind the ridge. The Huns took the opportunity to charge. A vanguard of warriors pounded up the hill on foot, whooping and hollering, brandishing swords and spears. As they ran, they spread out right and left. They intended to attack with a long front to prevent being outflanked. Seeing the fan-shaped attack, Prince Thorismund split off with a large body of mounted troops and raced down the ridge to the right and circled around behind the attackers. The Huns in that quadrant had no choice but to turn and engage them, which peeled off a large portion of their forces from the frontal attack.

In the meantime, on the crest of the ridge the Huns and Romans clashed. They fought furiously at close quarters with swords and spears. Steel flashed and dust swirled. Then, without warning, the Hun horsemen charged. Rising and falling in their saddles, they stretched arrows onto their bows and let loose, shooting with lethal precision. They impaled their adversaries, then trampled them under the hooves of their stout ponies.

On the right the situation was also going poorly. King Theodoric was facing the Huns on his front and left. Seeing their plight, the Gothic troops panicked and began to withdraw. King Theodoric checked them, not with words, but with action. He pulled his horse around and charged into the midst of the fight.

Seeing their leader react with such fearless courage, his troops gave an enthusiastic whoop and rushed in after him. They hacked and stabbed, lopped off the limbs of their foes, and cleaved their skulls like melons. Blood splattered everywhere. The storied Hun horsemen, so deadly in open combat, were less effective in close contact. At close quarters they could not use their bows and arrows; they could not throw their nets or their lassos. They were reduced to swords and spears, which were not their greatest assets. Gradually, they were driven back.

Somewhere in the midst of the tumult King Theodoric was unhorsed. Some of his fellows saw him fall but in the heavy fighting they could not reach him. His body was found later with the skull caved in. His hand was still holding the sword he had used to rally his men. Word spread among his troops, igniting an irrepressible fury, which they poured out on the Huns like molten lava.

The Huns were pushed back to the crest of the ridge where they were confronted by a body of soldiers from the Roman left, who had swung around and come up behind them. The Huns turned to engage them, which freed up the Goths to wheel and strike them on their flank. Caught in a vise, the Huns fought desperately, but they were doomed, slaughtered like pigs in a pen.

With the collapse of their left, the Huns in the center were in danger of being overwhelmed as well. Attila ordered a retreat. They withdrew down the long slope, fighting a rearguard action as the Goths pursued them. When they reached level ground at the base of the ridge, the Huns received covering fire from behind the rock outcroppings and retreated the rest of the way to their camp.

Daylight was beginning to fade, so Aetius ordered a halt to the fighting. He gathered his commanders, and they reviewed the day's action. The general consensus was that the enemy appeared beat. Aetius took a small squadron to reconnoiter the Hun perimeter and probe for weak spots. As he left, darkness set in. A long stretch of time passed before he came back. He and his men had gotten confused in the dark and almost stumbled into the Hun's camp. Still, the general impression was confirmed; the Huns appeared badly beaten. The night was filled with the cries of their wounded and dying. He thought it unlikely they would resume the attack in the morning.

As dawn spread a gray glow across the eastern sky, a scene of horrific carnage came to light. The slope leading up to the ridge was blanketed with the bodies of the dead and dying. Blood ran down the hill in meandering streams and gathered in crimson puddles. Flies swirled in furious, buzzing clouds. A putrid stench filled the air.

Leaving a strong defensive force to keep watch, Aetius and Thorismund withdrew to eat and sleep. Later in the day they reconvened to discuss what to do next. I was present at that meeting.

Thorismund was a vigorous young man, strong and broad-shouldered with a mane of blonde hair that fell past his shoulders. He bore himself with the dignity of a sovereign. He was in every way the antithesis of Placidius. Thorismund was confident and poised, sensitive and quick of mind. He began by suggesting they should surround and besiege the Hun camp, entrap Attila, and kill him.

Aetius agreed but was concerned about the state of affairs in Tolosa.

Thorismund looked bewildered.

Aetius explained. "With your father dead, the Gothic throne is vacant. You are the rightful heir. Everyone knows that. But you are not in Tolosa. You are here." He paused to let his words sink in. "You have brothers, don't you?"

It was true. Thorismund had two brothers, as Aetius well knew.

Thorismund tried to dismiss the possibility as beneath his consideration, but the seed was planted. As Thorismund continued to press his case for a siege of the Hun camp, he grew confused and distracted. He stopped several times to gather his thoughts.

Finally Aetius said, "Go. Return to Tolosa. Take your army with you. Don't worry. We have enough men here to keep the Huns in check. They won't attack now. It would be suicide if they did."

"But we could destroy them," Thorismund said, "and be done with them once and for all."

"Not without heavy losses," Aetius said, "which would delay our departure and invite temptation from your rivals back home. Listen, we are saddened by the loss of your father, the noble king Theodoric, but you are the rightful heir. Even if you were not entitled to your throne by birthright, you have earned it on the field of battle. We would not want to see anyone else claim it. Go. Secure what is yours and know that we support you."

Thorismund dropped to his knee and kissed Aetius's hand. Then he stood up and ordered his men to withdraw. We watched them go.

I looked at Aetius in alarm. "Are you sure?"

"I know what I'm doing."

He was right. After the Goths left, the Huns did not attack. They hunkered down, panting and dazed like a wounded animal. Aetius didn't even surround their camp. He waited one more day to see if they would withdraw, and when they didn't, he ordered our soldiers to break camp. This order might have been met with resistance under normal circumstances—it was unheard of for a victorious army to withdraw before finishing off a defeated enemy—but our soldiers had seen enough killing. They didn't object.

Two days later as we were making our way south toward Ravenna, a scout rode up and reported the welcome news that the Huns were retreating to the east. It was over. The Huns invasion of the West had been met with fierce resistance, and they had paid a heavy price. Never again would a Hun army set foot in Gaul.

Aetius turned to me. "You see," he said. "The situation is well in hand."

Then he smiled the smile of a gambler who had won a risky throw.

# Chapter 19
Summer, The Year AD 451 – Summer, The Year AD 452

Three weeks later we stood before the Emperor in Ravenna. As usual Placidius was incensed.

"What do you mean, they got away?" he shouted, pounding his fist on the arm of his throne.

"They withdrew," Aetius said. "They gave up their offensive and abandoned Gaul."

Placidius seemed to be having a hard time wrapping his mind around this. He looked older now. He was fleshier around the cheeks. His hair was thinning. His eyes had shrunk. It had been six years since I had seen him, but he barely acknowledged my presence. He was speaking to Aetius, and he was angry.

"What do you mean they withdrew? Why didn't you destroy them?"

"They left Gaul. We should be grateful."

Placidius's mouth fell open. "Grateful? We should be grateful? A bloodthirsty horde of uncivilized savages runs amok through our country, killing thousands of people, and we should be grateful?"

Behind him on the dais were Heraclius and a half dozen other advisors, including Maximus. The sight of that man made my skin crawl. Even two years after he attacked me, his presence made me uncomfortable. He stepped forward and spoke to Aetius in a high-handed manner.

"Where are they now? Why are you not chasing them?"

Aetius ignored Maximus and addressed himself to the Emperor. "The Huns are retreating to the east, returning home to lick their wounds and reconsider their folly. There will be no more demands for wealth or territory. You are in a stronger position now, Imperator, due to our efforts."

"But they got away," Placidius said. "I wanted them crushed, and you let them get away."

"They were forced to withdraw," Aetius said. "They gave up their offensive. Gaul is no longer under threat."

Maximus stepped between Aetius and the Emperor. "You must think you're very clever, Flavius Aetius, but we're not stupid. By letting them go, you think you can make yourself indispensable to us. When next they come at us, who else can we turn to but the man who knows them so well, the man who once lived among them. Only you, Flavius Aetius."

"Don't be ridiculous," Aetius said.

"You should be careful," Maximus said. "Your support here is on the wane. If you provoke the wrong people, you may regret it."

Aetius's reply was so quiet and restrained Maximus didn't hear him. He leaned forward and demanded he say it again. Aetius lifted his chin and spoke clearly, "You're in my way."

Maximus reared back as if he'd been slapped.

"I'm speaking with the Emperor, and you're in my way." He stepped to one side, never letting let his gaze waver from the Emperor. "I advise you to seek peace with the Huns," he said. "Send an emissary to work out the terms. It'll be best in the long run."

Placidius drew himself up in indignation. "Are you implying we cannot defeat them?"

Aetius sighed. "I'm advising you to avoid any more bloodshed."

"Don't listen to him," Maximus said. "He's planning to use them against you."

"Look," Aetius said. "We don't have the resources to wage a long war. If you want to keep fighting, you'll have to raise more financing, which means you'll have to tax the aristocracy."

Maximus scoffed. "Nonsense. The army has plenty of money."

Aetius shook his head. "Do what you want, Imperator. But if you want to keep fighting the Huns with inadequate resources, I cannot be responsible for what happens."

Placidius looked from one to the other of them, flustered. Finally, he turned to me. "What is *she* doing here?"

"She's the Augusta," Aetius said.

Placidius began to splutter. "You dare bring her before me like a cat dragging in a half-spoiled fish. I will not countenance this. She offends me. Take her out of my sight and throw her on the trash heap where she belongs."

I remained calm. I was determined not to give him the satisfaction of seeing me upset.

"She's your wife," Aetius said. "She's the Augusta of Rome. Whatever grievance you have against her is misguided. She's done nothing to earn your scorn, nothing to merit your anger."

Placidius laughed. "Oh, I see. You mean to defend her. You consider her a thing of value."

"You should not disparage her until you know what happened to her."

"I know all I need to know. She was ordered into exile. She came back without permission. She defied me, and her insolence has cost me my claim to the Eastern throne. She should be punished."

Aetius regarded him evenly. "Then you are meaner and more vindictive than I imagined."

Placidius gaped in astonishment. "How dare you speak to me like that!" He appealed to Maximus. "He cannot speak to me like that!"

"He certainly cannot," Maximus said. "Arrest him. Strip him of his title."

Heraclius stood back, arms folded, a smirk playing around the corners of his lips.

Aetius was unemotional. "She was forced to flee Constantinople," he explained. "She had no choice. When her father died, the eunuch Chrysaphius put a bounty on her head. She went underground and escaped into the countryside. For a long time, she dared not breathe a word of her true identity for fear that Chrysaphius would find her. Had he succeeded, any hope you had of a future heir would have died with her. By the time it was safe for her to emerge, you had already turned against her."

The narrative was almost entirely fictional, but Aetius delivered it with convincing sincerity. "You forced her to become a fugitive," he said. "Your vendetta against her made her into an outlaw. She had no choice but to seek asylum with someone who could protect her."

"Like you?"

"That's right. The Augusta appealed to me, so I took her in. She's a brave woman. You should be honored by her loyalty, her determination to safeguard your claim to the Eastern throne in spite of all that was working against her."

Placidius made a surly remark under his breath.

"She could have given in," Aetius said. "She could have run away and hidden. Instead, she survived and figured out a way to come back to you. Together you still have a claim. All you have to do is wait for the right moment to assert it."

"And when might that be?" Placidius asked. "Since you're the man with all the answers."

"When the Huns have been placated."

"Placated? I want them eradicated!"

"You would be wiser to work with them. Pulcheria and Marcian are going to be formidable adversaries. You will need all the help you can get to oppose them. The Huns can be recruited."

"Are you mad?" Placidius asked. "I'm not going to make common cause with the Huns!"

"Then I don't know how you're going to assert your claim to the Eastern throne. You're not strong enough to fight Pulcheria and Marcian without allies, and if you insist on making enemies of the Huns, you'll have to contend with them as well. It's not feasible unless you're willing to raise a great deal more money, and it looks like no one has any stomach for that." He shot a glance at Maximus. "My advice to you, Imperator, is that you start recognizing who's on your side and who's not. I'm trying to advise you in a way that will help. You may not want to hear it, but the Augusta gives you the best chance to make a legitimate claim. If you insist on ignoring my advice and spurning her, I can only conclude that you have no interest in the Eastern throne, in which case I am of no further use to you, and I will resign."

There was an audible gasp from the onlookers. Placidius shot them a dark look.

"Excellent!" Maximus said. He clapped his hands. "Resign and make us all happy. Go ahead. Save us the trouble of removing you."

Aetius put his fists on his hips. "Is that what you desire, Imperator?"

"He's trying to coerce you," Maximus said. "Don't let him. Stand up to him, for once."

Placidius whipped around and glared at Maximus. "Silence! I'm thinking."

Maximus scowled but said nothing more.

Placidius squinted at Aetius. "If I were to take her back, would you help me regain what was lost when the Empire was split in half? Will you help me reunite the Empire under a single ruler?"

"If you take her back, I will remain your Master of Soldiers. Then, when conditions are right, we can press your claim."

"With the help of the Huns."

"Yes."

Maximus groaned.

"Silence!" the Emperor snapped at him. He regarded Aetius for a long while. He angled forward. "Tell me more."

"If you want my help, the Augusta must be permitted to resume her former role. She must be allowed to see her children and carry out her duties. She must not be hurt or humiliated, and her exile must be revoked. The legitimacy of your claim is rooted in the honor due to the daughter of the late Emperor of the East. If you don't honor his daughter, how can you expect anyone else to? If you don't honor her, how can you assert your right to the throne?"

Placidius sat back in thought.

"If you want to reunite the Empire," Aetius said, "you must first be reunited yourselves."

Placidius said nothing.

The silence dragged on. A few minutes later Aetius asked permission to withdraw.

Placidius made a half-hearted gesture.

"Follow me," Aetius whispered as he went past.

Out in the corridor, he took me aside where no one could hear us. "Wait a few minutes," he said. "Then go to your apartments. No one will try to stop you."

"Thank you," I said.

He squeezed my shoulder. "Don't worry," he said. "He'll see the light. You'll see."

I gave him a weak smile.

Without ever intending to, I had cast my lot with Aetius. For the moment at least I felt safe under his protection, but should anything happen to him, I would be vulnerable. It occurred to me I was just like Justa. We were both dependent on Aetius for our survival, and we were both surrounded by enemies.

* * *

My reunion with Eudocia and Placida was pure joy. All three of us broke down and wept. We clung to each other as if we would never let go. They were twelve and thirteen now, practically marrying age. In fact, Eudocia, whose September wedding to Huneric had been postponed for a third time, was looking forward to being wed in the new year. For her part, Placidia had been betrothed to a young cavalry officer of good reputation by the name of Majorian, although she complained about it bitterly.

"What if I don't like him?" she said. "What if he beats me? You know if he tries to beat me, I won't stand for it. I'll rise up and kill him. I promise."

"I'm sure your father wouldn't pick a vicious brute for you."

She studied my expression. "What makes you so sure?"

I couldn't answer. Instead, I told her I would speak to her father about it, but that was easier said than done. Placidius rebuffed every attempt I made to meet with him, even when I explained I only wanted to discuss our daughters. I found out later, however, that the betrothal was not an innocent attempt to reward a highly valued cavalry officer. Far from it. Placidius had a more personal reason for choosing Majorian.

Since the Emperor and I had failed to produce an heir, the men chosen to marry our daughters would become first in the line of succession. With Eudocia betrothed to the Vandal prince, it was unlikely she or her offspring would have a legitimate claim to the throne, unless of course the Vandals conquered Rome, which seemed unlikely now. Therefore, Placidia's husband would be the most likely successor. By betrothing her to Majorian, the Emperor was effectively naming his successor, a move with significant ramifications, not only for the man he named, but also for the man he didn't.

Aetius might have approved of the Emperor's choice under different circumstances because Majorian was a trusted subordinate who had performed well in the fight to keep Hispania from falling into barbarian hands, but Aetius had plans of his own for the succession. He had long planned to marry his oldest son, Gaudentius, to Placidia. Gaudentius was a friendly and well-mannered young man, and Placidia knew him well having shared the same tutors with him growing up. In recent months she had developed a girlish crush on him, and had been looking forward with giddy eagerness to marrying him. But her father had other ideas.

Having fought every attempt by Aetius to upstage him over the years, the Emperor was not about to be usurped by him through marriage. Simply put, Aetius's son was never going to be permitted to marry the Emperor's daughter, but with Aetius's star on the rise again after his defeat of the Huns on the Catalaunian Plains, pressure was mounting for the Emperor to do something to honor him, and a betrothal was whispered as a possibility. Placidius meant to put a stop to such talk, so he plucked Majorian from obscurity and made him the heir apparent.

Upon learning of the betrothal, Aetius showed what he thought of it by stripping Majorian of his rank and sending him to work on a country estate as a lowly stable master. The demotion was meant to send a clear message about the danger of conspiring against him while at the same time reducing Majorian to a status unacceptable as a marriage partner for the Emperor's daughter. When the Emperor learned of it, he was furious, but powerless to do anything about it.

For her part, Placidia was grateful to Aetius for saving her from marriage to a man she didn't even know. But Maximus, who had suggested Majorian in the first place, was beside himself. A letter from Agnus to Junius painted a grim picture of a man in a frenzy, shouting at everyone around him, over-turning furniture, and even raising his hand to his wife. Junius was so concerned he wrote to me suggesting I intervene on her behalf. I thought this a bad idea.

Upon our return to Rome, Junius had been given a discreet position as an assistant to the armicustos[14] in a garrison on the coast at Rhegium, a position that allowed him to keep out of his father's way. It was doubtful Maximus even knew he was there, so to discover Junius had been corresponding with Agnus struck me as not only reckless, but also as a rejection of everything Aetius had done to protect him. To take this further and begin actively interfering in his father's affairs was madness. When I wrote back, I rejected his suggestion in the strongest possible terms and warned him not to get involved.

His silence told me all I needed to know. He didn't write back. It appeared our relationship had ended.

* * *

---

14  The keeper of arms.

In the new year Aetius sent an envoy to the Huns without the Emperor's permission. Incensed, the Emperor ordered the Master of Soldiers to appear before him to answer for his insubordination. As before, Maximus and Heraclius were there with seven or eight others, as was I. The audience began with Placidius asking Aetius if he was guilty of what he was accused of. Aetius admitted it without hesitation. Flabbergasted, Placidius demanded to know what had made him think he could act without the Emperor's permission.

"I'm trying to save the Empire," Aetius said.

Indignant, Maximus called for Aetius's immediate execution. Aetius ignored him and directed his comments to the Emperor.

"If nothing is done to open a channel of communication with the Huns, they'll assume we're preparing to attack them. If they believe that, they won't wait; they'll seize the initiative and go on the offensive. I'm trying to preclude that possibility."

Placidius muttered under his breath. Maximus shook a finger in Aetius's face. "If our army is so weak, why aren't you doing something about it? Don't tell me you don't have enough money. You have plenty of money. All that tax revenue from the provinces, where did it go? Up your sleeve is my guess. You've been doing quite well for yourself, haven't you, Flavius Aetius."

Aetius watched him, unmoved. "The provincial taxes you're referring to were spent a long time ago," he said. "They were spent to defend Gaul. At the moment our coffers are empty. Defending the Empire costs money, Maximus, more money than it costs to defend a single country, but that's what we'll be reduced to if you have your way."

Maximus seethed.

Placidius spoke up. "Assuming we need more money, where are we supposed to get it?"

Aetius shrugged. "We could press the commons again, but they've already given too much. To lean on them any further would incite more uprisings, which would demand more military resources to put them down. We would be spread even thinner. We're going to have to look elsewhere."

"Then call on the Goths," Maximus said. "Bring them in. Command them to fight. They were magnificent in Gaul. They could save Italia as well."

"That would be ill advised," Aetius said. "The Goths have grown strong. If we invite them here to fight our battles because we're too weak to fight them ourselves, they'll never leave. No. We'd better not do that. The best way forward is to buy time through diplomacy until we can raise enough money to build a strong domestic army, Roman soldiers recruited from the Roman populace and supported by Roman resources. That's what we need. Without it, your dreams of defeating the Huns and asserting your claim to Constantinople cannot be realized."

"I ask you again," Placidius said. "How do you propose we do that?"

"Tax the aristocracy," Aetius said. "Time is running out and you've waited long enough for them to be charitable. Compel them to pay. They have a duty to the country that enriched them. If they refuse to comply, have them arrested and imprisoned."

Spittle flew from Maximus's lips. "Seize this man! Arrest him at once! He's a traitor!"

The Emperor sank down in his throne.

Maximus worked himself into a tirade. "He's already confessed his disloyalty. He let the Huns go when he could've destroyed them! Now he's using them to blackmail you! If that's not treason, I don't know what is!"

Aetius looked askance at Maximus and shook his head. He turned to the Emperor. "It's obvious Maximus cares more about his purse than he does about Rome. He doesn't understand that if Rome is lost, his fortune will disappear along with it."

Maximus was shouting now. "First he prevents them from being wiped out and then he counsels collusion with them! His motives are clear. Remember, this is the same man who enlisted the Huns to force your mother into naming him the Master of Soldiers. They are his instrument!"

Sadly, this was true. Galla's letter had not tried to downplay it. Many years ago, when Galla was regent, Aetius had employed the Huns to force her hand, and while she had resented his tactics at the time, she eventually forgave him. It was better to have him on her side than not. Having gotten what he wanted, Aetius sent the Huns away, but not without buying them off first with a strip of land along the Danube, which they subsequently used to stage raids into the Illyricum. The raids enriched the Huns, made them a formidable force, and emboldened them in their ambitions. When his detractors claimed that everything was Aetius's fault, they were not far wrong. But now Aetius was trying to right those wrongs by rescuing the Empire from itself, and he was being undermined by his past. There wasn't much he could say to refute the accusations, so he said nothing, which only encouraged

Maximus to go on. He banged away in a damning harangue until the Emperor grew tired of it.

"That will be enough, Petronius Maximus. We've heard what you had to say. Be quiet now."

The rebuke chafed Maximus who glared at Placidius with the same insolence he had shown Aetius, but when the Emperor glared back, Maximus remembered his place and concealed his outrage behind a guilty smile.

The Emperor waved Heraclius forward and consulted with him in whispers. Heraclius stepped back, and Placidius announced his decision: Aetius had overstepped his bounds and must pay a fine.

On hearing this, Maximus lost his temper again. He shook his fists and fulminated. Fed up, the Emperor ordered him from his presence. Eyes burning with contempt, Maximus was led out. Aetius watched, arms folded.

On his way out, Maximus whipped around and glared at me. His eyes bore into mine as if they were sharpened to pikes to stab me with. That he should blame me for his predicament seemed incredible, but Maximus was a man who preyed on the vulnerable. Having failed to best Aetius, he was looking to strike out at someone weaker. I would not give him the satisfaction. I glared back until he flounced from the room in a huff.

I was not naïve enough to consider it a victory. It would not be so easy to go toe to toe with him again. He was a ruthless antagonist willing to stoop to anything, and he frightened me. I would probably never get another the chance to sneak up on him again when he wasn't looking.

* * *

If Aetius thought he had won the Emperor's cooperation in dealing with the Huns, he couldn't have been more wrong. Two days after the meeting in the audience chamber, Placidius reversed himself and cut off all communication with the Huns. He disavowed the embassy sent by Aetius and declared that the Empire would not negotiate. As a result, by summer the Huns, who had been beaten and were in retreat, were on the move again and headed in our direction. The Emperor's decision was epic in its stupidity.

The news hit Ravenna like a thunderbolt. Half the populace packed up and fled. Soon a mighty tide of refugees was streaming south toward Rome, leaving a vacuum in Ravenna that was quickly filled by refugees from villages to the north who were rushing south to stay ahead of the Hun's advance. In a panic, the city's urban prefect appeared before the Emperor and begged for help. Placidius refused him. Civic order fell apart. Fights broke out between the incoming refugees and the few residents who had remained. The city descended into turmoil.

The Pope declared it the long awaited apocalypse as prophesied in the *Book of the Revelation*. He encouraged people to give up their worldly goods and prepare for the Second Coming. As a result, castoff items were scattered along the roadsides. The Church wasted no time in picking them up, sifting through them, identifying those of value and removing the rest for safekeeping.

Panic stricken, Placidius summoned Aetius and ordered him to stop the Hun advance. As before, Aetius cited a lack of resources. He advised the Emperor to leave for Rome while he still had the chance. Placidius didn't need to be told twice. He left Ravenna in a hurry, never once inquiring after the well-being of his wife and daughters. Fortunately for us, Aetius had arranged for our evacuation, and we were delivered to Rome safely. We took up residence in the old imperial palace overlooking the Forum where were provided regular updates as the situation unfolded.

The Huns swept down from Pannonia, pillaging towns and villages as they came. What few troops opposed them were quickly overwhelmed. Aetius guessed they were headed to Aquilea and sent troops to reinforce that city. A week later the Huns stood before the gates. For the next three days, they tried repeatedly to breach its defenses, but failed. It was beginning to look like Aetius's decision had been correct. But, unlike the situation at Aurelianum, there were no allied troops angling to cut off the Hun's retreat, so the Huns had no reason to lift their siege.

The siege dragged on for weeks. People inside the gates began to starve. Attempts to reinforce the city by sea were thwarted by Vandal pirates, who appeared to be working in concert with the Huns. Placidius was frantic with fear. If Aquilea fell, the way lay open to Ravenna, and even though the palace and treasury were surrounded by marshes, the city lay virtually undefended since almost everyone had fled, including the troops.

The situation had far-reaching implications. The looting of Ravenna would deal a huge blow to the Empire's finances. The Emperor would have little choice but to tax the aristocracy, an expediency that would almost certainly cost him the support of one of the two remaining constituencies who didn't despise him already. The rest of country certainly did. The Plebes hated him for the way he had leaned on them for taxes, ostensibly to defend them from outsiders, only to find they were being repeatedly attacked by barbarians. The Equites, the mid-level administrators, hated him for trimming their wages while demanding more from them, all the while threatening to replace them with immigrant labor—Goths and Burgundians—if they didn't comply. The military hated him because he was always putting them in impossible situations without providing the financial support they needed. And the Comites, the provincial governors, hated him because they recognized him for the doomed, feckless leader he was.

Only the Church and the aristocracy still backed him, and only because he kept buying them off with favors. If Aquilea fell, those indulgences were endangered.

And then it did.

# Chapter 20
June-July, The Year AD 452

Aquilea couldn't hold out. After a month-long siege, a small contingent of city officials made the fatal error so many had made before. They sought terms with the Huns. They offered to surrender the city in exchange for mercy. Of course, the Huns said yes. Then they proceeded to slaughter everyone in sight. Men, women, and children were put to the sword. The old and infirm were trampled beneath hooves. Priests and prelates were decapitated while at prayer. Young women were violated. Infants were snatched from their mothers' arms and slung against walls. For those who had been expecting an apocalypse, their expectations were fulfilled. This was a horror beyond imagining, but it didn't stop there. Having littered the street with bodies, the Huns set about destroying the city. For five long days they went about the task, burning and toppling and pounding and flattening until there was nothing left of the once great seaport but a vast expanse of smoking rubble.

The unhinged ferocity of Attila's vengeance had all the earmarks of a man giving vent to his frustrations. Whether his failure to conquer Gaul was the provocation, Aquilea lay in ruins, and those few who survived fled not to Ravenna, but to a cluster of small, marshy islands along the coast where they hunkered down in their stress and trauma and lived out their days, a place called Venitia.

Attila had other plans. He did not make for Ravenna as expected but headed west across the Po Valley toward Mediolanum leveling Concordia, Altinum and Patavium along the way. The counselors that surrounded Placidius were baffled by the move and suggested perhaps Attila was heading west with the objective of invading Gaul from the south to finish what he had started. Maximus seized on this theory. It was unlikely the Huns were headed for Rome, he said. They had already demonstrated their disinterest in Ravenna by bypassing it on their journey westward. The worst had passed, he declared, so it was no longer necessary to waste money shoring up the city's defenses. I disagreed and would not be silenced.

I had not been invited to sit in on the council, but the counselors had left the door open, and when I heard what Maximus was saying, I burst in and interrupted. I had some experience with the Huns, I reminded them. I had been in Aurelianum during the siege. I had been on the Catalaunian Plains during the battle. I was well acquainted with their tactics. They were not above making a feint to the west, and then turning south and attacking Rome when our guard was down. To underestimate them would be a grave error. It was absolutely crucial to fortify our defenses and recruit more fighters. Now was not the time to relax.

Maximus started to rebuke me, but Placidius cut him off. "Did you say you were in Aurelianum?"

"Yes. And on the Catalaunian Plains."

Placidius reached for a pitcher of wine and began to refill his goblet. "Interesting," he said. "That's the first time I've heard of it."

I shook my head in disbelief. How he could not have known was a mystery to me. Maximus knew. Eudocia and Placidia knew. It wasn't as if I had been trying to keep it a secret. Even the most casual inquiry about my whereabouts during the years I was away would have brought it to light, but somehow, he was ignorant of it.

He turned to his counselors. "Is this true?"

They confirmed my story.

Placidius took a long drink and wiped his mouth on the back of his sleeve. "So, are the Huns really as horrible as they say?"

"The most treacherous demons you can imagine. You can't try to outsmart them. All you can do is confront them, and then you must never, never back down."

Maximus spoke up. "Are we really doing this, Imperator? Are we really listening to this woman? What does she know?"

"She was there!"

Maximus lowered his eyes and muttered something under his breath.

Placidius was annoyed. "Speak up, Maximus. What are you trying to say?"

"She's a liar. She can't be trusted. Okay, maybe she was in Aurelianum, but she fled at the first sign of the Huns. I have it on good authority that she ran away and never saw them. As for the Catalaunian Plains, that's a story Aetius made up to explain how she came to be in his company. It's not to be believed."

I began to object, but Placidius ordered me to be silent. He spoke to Maximus. "How do you know this?"

Maximus gave me a smug look. Then he turned to the Emperor. "I was told by the man she was with."

Maximus was playing a dangerous game. By bringing up my relationship with Junius he was risking bringing to light the reason we had fled Rome in the first place, but he plunged ahead. "The man she was with owes me a duty and would not deceive me."

"What man?" Placidius asked.

I could see Maximus calculating in his head. He was weighing the ramifications of exposing his son. To do so would mean a death sentence for Junius, but that's not what held him back. The truth was Maximus had not yet worked out what would happen if the Emperor found out he had tried to rape me.

"General Avitus," he said. "He stopped in Aurelianum on his way to negotiate with the Goths. She left the city with him and took refuge in Tolosa. She was not in Aurelianum when the Huns attacked."

"That's a lie," I said. "You can ask Aetius. He will tell you."

"Oh, sure," Maximus said. "Aetius is trustworthy."

"Then ask Avitus. He was with me in Aurelianum. He gave us troops to help in our defense. He can confirm I was there and didn't leave before the fight."

"Where is Avitus now?" Placidius asked. "Summon him here. He'll settle this."

"He's in his villa at Augustonementum," one of the counselors said. "It'll take a week for him to get here."

"We don't have time for that," I said. "You can either believe me or not, but ask yourself, why would I lie?"

Placidius chewed on the inside of his lip. He spoke over his shoulder to Heraclius. "What do you think?"

The eunuch leaned down and whispered. As he did so, his eyes shifted to Maximus. A look of mutual distrust passed between them. Heraclius finished speaking and stood back. Placidius took a long drink and addressed himself to me.

"Very well," he said. "Explain something to me. Why did the Huns bypass Ravenna? They could easily have attacked it and still made their feint to the west. The city is full of treasure. The impact on Roman morale would have been worth it all by itself. It doesn't make any sense."

"On the contrary, it makes perfect sense," I said. "The Huns are heavily reliant on their supply lines when mounting a siege. Without a steady flow of materials coming up from their rear, they are as much under siege as the cities they are besieging. The marshes around Ravenna would divide their supply lines into narrow conduits that could be easily ambushed. They probably assumed the city was well defended and feared getting bogged down. And then there is the matter of disease."

"Disease?"

"Yes. The Huns are a cold weather people. They are originally from Sarmatia where the winters are frigid, and the days are short. They are susceptible to warm weather infections, especially those in low marshy areas. Diseases that are merely inconvenient to us can be fatal to them. They feared getting caught in a place like Ravenna. That's why they bypassed it."

Placidius drank off his wine and poured some more. "And the only reason they are heading west is to trick us. Is that your theory?"

"Not the only reason. They also have to feed their army. As marauders they must live off the land. They probably thought there would be plenty of crops to loot. They didn't reckon on the extent of the famine here last summer, so they turned west into the Po Valley because it's more fertile. They're trying to bolster their strength before turning south to attack Rome."

Maximus waved off the theory. "Nonsense. What makes her such an expert on the Huns?"

I leaned forward. "I learned from the best," I said. "Aetius taught me. He lived with them as a youth. He knows the Huns better than any man in the Empire. I listened to him. Something you should try some time. It might help you."

Maximus turned red. He was boiling with anger, but he bit his tongue.

Placidius looked around at the others. "What Licinia is saying makes sense to me."

They all nodded, even Heraclius.

"We must prepare to withstand them," Placidius said. "We must prepare for a siege."

Maximus turned to Placidius with a weary, embittered look. "And where do you expect to get the money for that?"

Placidius sighed. "The time has come, Maximus."

"The aristocracy will resist you," Maximus said.

Placidius took another drink. He swung his gaze to me. "Where is Aetius now? What is he doing?"

The fact he didn't know amazed me, but I did my best to reply. "He's in the Po Valley," I said. "He's harassing the Huns, keeping them off balance, trying to make it hard for them to stay in one place and replenish their stores."

"Then why doesn't he engage them and be done with it?" Maximus asked.

"Because he doesn't have enough men," I replied.

Placidius slapped his hands on his knees and stood up. "Let's get ready for a siege," he said. "Let's show the Huns what we're made of."

Everyone began to stir. Placidius turned to me. "Licinia, remain behind. I want to speak with you. Everyone else, you may go."

His counselors trailed out of the room. Once they had closed the door, Placidius spoke to me in a far gentler tone. "You've changed, Licinia," he said. "Perhaps it's time we get reacquainted."

* * *

The council chamber was brightly lit. Sun poured in at the windows. But nothing could hide the telltale decay of the crumbling old palace. It had been built in the reign of Domitian more than three hundred years before. The marble walls, thirty feet high, supported a coffered ceiling that was broken in places. The floor had fissures running through it, and the statues were yellow with age. There was an unpleasant smell of damp stone and rotting vegetation.

The Emperor took my hand.

"Your counsel is sound, Augusta. Forgive me if I've been too hard on you. I've been under a lot of pressure."

I said nothing.

He stroked my cheek with the backs of his fingers. "Is it true what they say, that Chrysaphius tried to kill you? Is that why you left Constantinople?" His eyes were bloodshot. His breath stank of wine.

"When my father died, Chrysaphius seized power," I said. "I was the heir. Naturally he would see me as a threat."

He looked at my hair, at the way the light shone in it. His mind seemed to drift. His eyelids grew heavy, and for a moment I thought he was going to nod off. Then he snapped awake and remembered his train of thought. "It's not too late for us," he said. "We can still claim what is ours."

"We have more pressing matters before us now."

He seemed a little bewildered.

"The Huns," I said. "Rome. We have to get ready."

He frowned and shook his head. "Listen to me. I'm sorry for the way I treated you. There was no excuse. I'm a horrible man. Forgive me?" He cocked his head and made a pouty face. He drew me toward him. "Let's get comfortable."

He pulled me onto his lap. He wrapped his arms around me. He began to nuzzle my neck. I didn't fight him, but neither did I give in.

He detected my resistance and drew back. "Are you refusing me?"

"Never, Excellency, but we should not be distracted. There's much to be done."

He dropped his chin on his chest. For a moment I thought he had passed out, but then he looked up with bleary eyes. "Pass me that wine."

I reached across the table and handed him the pitcher. He filled his cup. That's when he saw the amulet hanging around my neck. His eyes grew large. "Where did you get that?"

"Your mother gave it to me."

"When?"

"A few years back. She said it complemented me."

He nudged me off his lap. "Who were you with at Aurelianum? Don't lie to me. I know you were with someone. Maximus told me."

"I was with a friend. He brought me there."

"He was helping you get away from me."

"I was buying time until I could get back to you and explain things."

"What happened to him? Where is he now?"

"He died in the siege trying to defend me."

"Was he your lover? Did you share your bed with him?"

I considered my answer carefully, but the words were out before I could restrain them. "I was fond of him. He treated me kindly."

He seemed confused by the idea. "Did he love you?"

"Yes. I think so."

"Did you love him in return?"

"I did."

He didn't know what to say. His eyes clouded over and for a moment I thought he was going to break down in tears or lose consciousness, but then he took another drink, crossed his legs at the ankles, and stared off into space. After a spell, he spoke again. His voice was low and hard.

"Did you make love to him?"

"I couldn't."

"You couldn't?"

"I couldn't bring myself to do it."

"Because you didn't want to betray me?"

"Not that. No."

"Not that?"

"That was not the reason."

"Ah, so you were afraid of offending God. That was it. Wasn't it?"

"It was not that either."

He seemed perplexed.

"Someone tried to rape me," I said. "It was traumatizing. After that, the thought of laying with another man repulsed me, so I couldn't."

His eyes opened wide. "Someone tried to rape you?"

"Yes."

He squinted down at his cup of wine. He shook his head as if trying to clear it of cobwebs. "I don't understand. Are you telling me you would have made love to this man if someone had not tried to rape you? What about your duty to me? What about your duty to God?"

"I don't know. I don't know what I would have done if I had not been attacked. But I was. And that's why I didn't have sex with him."

He sat in sullen silence for a moment, and then slammed his fist down on the table. "Who did it!" His voice bounced off the stone walls. "Who raped you!"

"Does it matter?"

"Yes, it matters! I'll have him arrested. I'll have him torn limb from limb and thrown to the dogs!"

I sighed. "Never mind. It happened. It's in the past. Let's concentrate on what's happening now. We must prepare for the siege."

He took another drink. "Right. A siege. We need to strengthen our defenses."

"And store up provisions."

"That's right. Store up provisions. There's no time to spare."

"You're going to have to get the aristocracy to fund it."

The thought of this made him uncomfortable. "They won't like it. They'll resist. Maybe there's some other way."

"There's no other way, Placidius. Rome made them rich. Rome gave them privileges others could only dream of. If they refuse to defend her now, they must be compelled."

"You're very bold," he said. "I don't like it. I sense Aetius behind this. You're his puppet, aren't you?"

I gave him a sharp look. "I work for no man. I'm my own person. I work for myself, and I work for Rome."

He dismissed my bravado with a contemptuous snort. "Go now. I'm finished with you. You offend me. I don't take advice from a woman." He grabbed the pitcher and poured himself another drink.

I left the room, head held high, but as I rounded the corner a figure stepped into my path. It was Heraclius. He was wearing his high conical cap and silk robes.

"You owe me," he said. "He would've thrown you out if I hadn't stopped him."

I slapped him across the face so hard it knocked his cap sideways revealing a bald pate beneath a few sickly strands of hair. His grin fell away.

"Pennyroyal," I said. "You tried to poison me with pennyroyal. Do you have any idea what would happen to you if the Emperor found out you tried to make me miscarry his child?"

He began to splutter out an answer, but I struck him again. He ducked and cringed; a whimper escaped him.

"You work for me now," I said. "You'll do as I tell you, and if you betray me, I'll destroy you. Do you understand me?"

Suddenly he was fawning, practically groveling at my feet. "Get up," I said.

He got to his feet and cowered.

"Listen to me. The Emperor needs to start raising revenue fast. We need to start preparing our defenses. Push him in the right direction. Don't let Maximus stand in your way."

"Yes, Your Highness," he said.

He didn't fool me. I knew it was just an act. He was trying to buy time until he could figure out his next move. The truth was he was experienced at this sort of thing, and I wasn't. I was the one who was out of my depth, and in due time I would pay the price.

* * *

The occupants of villas and estates in the surrounding countryside had come into the city to take refuge behind its growing defenses. Among them was Junius, who had taken up residence at the domus of a senior military officer upon the recommendation of Aetius. I went to see him and explained what happened during my meeting with the Emperor. He was not pleased. He had warned me about interfering with his father, just as I had warned him.

"He's not going to take this lying down," he said. "He's already taken steps to undermine you."

I demanded an explanation, and I got it.

Maximus was putting together an envoy to the Huns and preparing to send it north with an attractive offer in exchange for an end to the conflict. He was doing this without the Emperor's permission.

"What's the offer?" I asked.

"Justa," he said. "He's offering them Justa in exchange for peace."

It was a resurrection of the debacle that had brought about the crisis in the first place, and it was breathtakingly short-sighted and stupid. Attila would seize the opportunity to wed Justa as a way to claim the Empire through marriage. It might deter the current crisis, but it would lay the groundwork for worse things to come.

"They're going to abduct her," Junius explained. "Bassus Herculanus is on it. He's eager to be rid of her. She rides him relentlessly, criticizes him without ceasing, and refuses to grant him the privileges due a husband. Remember he only agreed to marry her so he could get closer to the Emperor. He's as mercenary as the rest, and now that he sees a way out of his predicament, he's happy to cooperate. They're going to abduct her and deliver her to Attila."

"How do you know all this?" I asked.

"Don't ask."

"I assume it's Agnus."

He put his finger to my lips. "Shh," he said. "Don't say that name."

"Ah, I see. She's decided to share her misgivings with you. That's a new wrinkle. I was under the impression her devotion to her husband precluded such intimacy."

"She doesn't like what she's seeing. It scares her, so she shared it with me in the strictest confidence. If she knew I was telling you, she would be upset."

"And yet you have. I guess I should feel privileged."

"Leave it alone, Licinia. My father is a dangerous man. You should count yourself lucky he didn't come for you after what you did to him in the garden of the hospitia."

"What I did to him!"

Junius grabbed me by the wrists and shook me. "Listen to me. You're not going to outwit him. If you insist on fighting him, he'll destroy you. And Aetius won't be able to protect you."

I pulled my hands free. "I thank you for your concern," I said, "but I have other considerations besides Agnus's tender feelings."

I stalked off.

Now the question was whether I should tell Aetius what I had learned. If he found out they were planning to abduct Justa, he might try to stop them, which would open a wider rift between the army and the aristocracy at the precise moment when they needed to be coming together to defend the Empire.

On the other hand, if Justa was not available to be abducted, Maximus's plan could not be implemented. I knew what I had to do.

I had to warn Justa.

* * *

Like others who resided in sprawling estates outside the city, Justa had come inside for protection. Unlike them, she had arrived in disguise, her face concealed beneath a shawl. She could not be recognized by the public who despised her for her role in bringing about the crisis. If she had been discovered, she would have been killed. The people of Rome were notoriously prickly toward anyone who upset their comfortable lifestyles. To someone who had invited a barbarian invasion of their city they would have shown no mercy.

Justa had taken refuge in the domus of her husband's second cousin, an ordinary merchant whose modest dwelling provided barely tolerable conditions for a woman who, in spite of her wrongdoings, still held the title of Augusta. After some discreet inquiries, I found her. She looked much depleted.

I was directed by a servant to a room in the back, a cramped cubicle off a narrow corridor stacked high with wooden crates and amphorae. A rat scurried away as I turned the corner. I discovered Justa gazing out the window, her arm draped along the sill, her long, bony fingers dangling. The room was hot and close. The odor of a nearby latrine wafted in. She appeared lost in thought and didn't look up when I entered. I cleared my throat. Her body tensed visibly, but when she saw who it was, she relaxed.

"Hello Licinia," she said. "Fancy meeting you here."

It had been two years since I had seen her last. At that time, she was being dragged off in chains, her face scratched and bleeding from Placidius's attack on her. She was young and healthy then, if anxious and distraught. Now she looked old and wasted like she had aged twenty years and not two. Her time with Bassus Herculanus had taken its toll. She had fresh cuts on her face and hands, wounds the old Justa would never have permitted any man to inflict on her. She was not bruised, but she had developed a nervous tick, a twitch at the corner of her mouth like an aborted smile.

"What brings you here?" she asked. "Did you come to gloat at the disgrace of your old enemy?"

"You're not my enemy," I said,

"Am I not? But I'm the one who tried to poison you and deprive you of your child. Or haven't you heard?"

"You are guilty of many crimes, Justa, but you are not guilty of that. Why take credit for something you didn't do?"

"I have a reputation to uphold."

"You have no obligation to be reviled."

"And yet I am. It seems to be my only talent."

"Stop it, Justa. Self-pity doesn't suit you."

Her face twitched. She shrugged. She went back to looking out the window. Outside, beneath the window frame, flies were swarming, feeding on something. From time to time, they rose in a swirling cloud; a few zipped away, and some lingered swaying in the air as they descended again.

"I knew you were coming," she said. "I had a dream about you. We were at a banquet, the two of us. We were there with some dignitaries, senators and aristocrats and the like. We were trying to impress them. Then a bird flew in the window, a most marvelous creature with yellow and black plumage and a crest of bright red. It flew around the room. The men were annoyed by it. They scowled and reproved us for not chasing it out. I looked at you, and our eyes locked. We were thinking the same thing. If we wanted to catch that marvelous bird, we were going to have to kill it. We chased it around the room, but we could not capture it. The dignitaries were becoming impatient. They demanded it be gotten rid of at once. Again, I looked at you, and your eyes looked back their answer. To hell with the dignitaries, the bird would not be harmed. The dignitaries stormed out. We were left alone in the room with the bird. It flitted around. We sat watching it with our chins on our fists. It skimmed and darted over the dinner fare: roast hare and guinea fowl, oysters and dormice, half-finished goblets of wine. At last, it lighted on the windowsill and stood looking at us. Then it spread its wings and flew off."

"And this dream told you I was coming?"

"You came to warn me," she said. "But I already know. My husband has no talent for secrets, nor for anything else for that matter. The fact they have named him consul is an indication how far we have fallen. A man like him. If that's the best we can come up with, maybe it's best the Empire is lost."

"Don't say that."

"You're very concerned about the Empire these days. What's come over you?"

"I need you to go away. Don't let them take you."

She looked out the window with her back to me. A pair of flies defined a spiral in the air and zoomed off. After a while, she turned and looked at me. "You're wearing the amulet," she said.

I looked down at it, lifted the round leaden disk and considered the crude image of Christ entering Jerusalem and the three-line inscription of hope and encouragement. I let it fall against my breast. "You gave it to me."

"Mother always wanted you to have it. She never said so in so many words, but I knew. She certainly didn't want me to have it. That was clear."

"It's not for everyone."

"Mother always believed a person could change. Against all evidence she wanted to believe that. She thought Placidius could change, but she was wrong. In the end she realized her error."

"I can arrange a ship for you at Rhegina. You can go to Egypt and from there to Judea."

She looked at her hands. "When she asked me to advocate on her behalf, to act as her proxy in persuading you to bear a child, I went along. It was not something I would normally have done. After all, what was in it for me? I wanted the throne for myself. I wanted to rule like she had, in my own right with Aetius to support me and no one to interfere. But after having worn the amulet for a while, I understood. That was never going to happen. I didn't have the public's support. They never liked me. I'm not complaining. That's just the way it is—the way it always has been. When I was younger, it used to tear me up. I used cry about it in private, burning with resentment, vowing to get even. In the end, I decided to embrace it, to wear it like a badge, to wave it in people's faces, to flaunt it. If they thought I was such a horrible person, I would not disappoint them. But that was no good. It didn't make me any happier, and it led me to do things I later regretted. Then I put on the amulet, and it helped me. It took away the raw edge. It made me see there was more to life than my own grievances.

It made me realize that working for something bigger than myself could give me purpose and take away the pain. That's when I took up my mother's cause. I got myself arrested and confined to the palace so I could be near you. It wasn't easy. It went against everything I stood for. Nevertheless, I did it. Even when you scorned me and pushed me away, I persisted. I was determined to persuade you to have a child, to give us the heir we so desperately needed. But I failed. You didn't trust me, and for good reason. What had I been I thinking? Why would you ever have listened to me? Then, after you were sent away to Constantinople, I realized something. The amulet wasn't for me. It was for you. So, I took it off and sent it to you. It was the right thing to do, and it's what Mother would have wanted."

"I need you to go away," I said. "I need you to leave here as soon as possible. If you don't, and if you end up being abducted, I'm worried Aetius might do something reckless. If he goes after Maximus, it may end in civil war, which is the last thing we need now. If we end up fighting each other, it will make us weak and distracted, easy prey for the Huns."

She looked genuinely perplexed. "Why would Aetius do that?"

"Surely he would not want his daughter to be abducted and traded to the Huns."

She threw back her head and let out a high, braying laugh. So sudden and unexpected was her response it took me by surprise.

"You're as crazy as the rest of them," she said. "What makes you think Aetius would risk losing the Empire to save me? I'll let you in on a little secret. He cares nothing for me.

Never has. If he actually *is* my father, which is debatable, he's never shown the first sign of it. He might as well be a stranger. Believe me, Licinia, your anxiety in that regard is misguided."

"But Galla Placidia said—"

"I don't care what she said. Even if it's true, it doesn't matter. My well-being doesn't motivate Flavius Aetius. He's a cold, calculating man, not given to feelings of affection. In fact, as a strategic consideration, he might welcome my abduction. It would buy him time to think up another avenue for negotiation and forestall an immediate attack. If you want to know the truth, I was rather thinking of going along with it."

"They're talking about handing you over to Attila."

She responded with a defeated shrug. "If I stay here, it's just a matter of time before I'm found out. Then the public will come for me. It won't be pretty."

"Then don't stay here. Go away. Leave. I'm offering you a way out."

A fly swooped and dodged around her head. She didn't flinch. It was then I noticed a number of dead flies on the windowsill, pushed off into the corner like she had been collecting them.

"I'm the problem, not the solution," she said. "Always have been."

"This crisis is partly your doing," I said. "You've lost the right to lie around wringing your hands in self-pity over it. For God's sake, think about someone other than yourself for a change. Do the right thing. Go away. Disappear."

She sighed. "Maybe I should go to Attila. He couldn't possibly treat me any worse than this."

I gave a little grunt of disgust. "You're so full of your-self. Can't you think of anyone else? Can't you think of the Empire?"

She regarded me with icy contempt. "I was thinking of the Empire when I tried to stop Placidius from becoming Em-peror. I was thinking of the Empire when I tried to persuade you to have another baby. I was thinking of the Empire when I tried to sabotage your wedding."

I narrowed my eyes. "So, you admit it."

"Yes. I admit it. Placidius had to be married to be fully in-vested. By preventing your wedding, we would have stopped him from coming to power. Had we succeeded the regency would have remained intact. Mother would have stayed the head of government, and everything would have been better, at least better than what we have now."

"And this thing with Attila, your ill-considered appeal for help, am I to believe this was for the good of the Empire as well?"

"Desperate times require desperate measures."

I glowered at her. "You're no hero, Justa. Don't flatter yourself."

She put both hands on the windowsill and pressed down on it as if preparing to stand up, but she remained in place.

She said, "Let me ask you something. When Placidius is gone, who will be next in line for the throne?"

"My daughter's husband."

"But not Eudocia. Eudocia is betrothed to the Vandal prince, and a Vandal cannot rule Rome."

"That's right. Most likely it will be Placidia's husband."

"Which is why it was so important to marry her to a low ranking cavalry officer who could be easily controlled."

"That was the plan, but it didn't work. Aetius saw to that."

She turned and looked at me. "You are correct, Licinia. But suppose Aetius hadn't intervened. Suppose Maximus had actually succeeded in betrothing Placidia to Majorian. What would you have done?"

My answer surprised me. "I would have supported Aetius in whatever he thought necessary."

"Even if it meant overthrowing your husband?"

I declined to answer.

Justa smiled. "We are more alike than you would like to think. We would rather keep the pretty bird and put out the dignitaries, no matter the cost."

"Will you go?" I asked.

"I will," she said. "But only because I know we are of one accord now. Duty before allegiance. That's what Mother would have wanted."

"Shall I send a servant with instructions?"

"Sure," she said with that peculiar twitch playing at the corner of her mouth. "Whatever you want."

I should have recognized her agreement as a sign.

Later that evening I got the news. She had taken her own life. A lethal dose of pennyroyal, the same herb she had been accused of poisoning me with. There was poetry in that—poetry of a sly, vindictive nature, Justa's stock in trade. In the end, she had done what she had promised, but she had done it her own way, defying me at the same time as she was capitulating. She was nothing if not contrary.

She would not be missed.

* * *

Without Justa to dangle before Attila, I expected the envoy to be called back, but to my horror it was not. It had left Rome the previous afternoon while I had been speaking to Justa, and no move had been made to send a courier once news of her death reached the palace. I went to Placidius and demanded he recall it, but he was unconcerned.

"They'll be all right," he said. "They have the Pope with them."

I was taken aback. The Pope! What's he doing with them?

"He's a man of God," he said. "He'll know how to talk to the Huns. They'll listen to him."

I went around the table and shook him. He looked up at me in woozy surprise. "Don't be so naïve," I said. "That envoy must be stopped. They must not reach Attila."

He vacillated. He inspected his hands. He looked around the room, and seeing no one there, shouted for his eunuch.

Heraclius appeared in the doorway.

"Yes, Excellency."

"Licinia says we should recall the envoy. What do you think?"

He shifted uncomfortably.

Placidius banged his goblet down on the table. "Speak up! I asked you a question."

In the end it was a simple matter of proximity. I was in the room and Maximus was not. If Heraclius betrayed me now, justice would be swift. He would be dead before Maximus could help him, and he knew it.

"The Augusta is right," he said. "They should be recalled."

Placidius gave the order, and I assumed that was the end of it. I left the room feeling vindicated. But I was mistaken. No sooner had I stepped out than Heraclius slunk back in and urged the Emperor to do as Maximus wished and let the envoy continue on its way.

The next morning when I learned of his duplicity, it was too late to call the eunuch to account. Time was running out; there was not a moment to spare. The envoy had to be stopped. If it reached Attila and made him an offer it could not fulfill, the consequences would be swift and terrible. I ordered the servants to ready my livery. If Placidius would not stop the delegation, I would. Somebody had to save the Empire, and I was the only one who had enough sense to do it.

# Chapter 21
August, The Year AD 452

We rode through the night, me with a small retinue, a three-man guard, my servants, my secretary, and my hostler, ten of us in all. We traveled at breakneck speed. I took the lead; the others raced to keep up. They must have been wondering if I had been possessed by some demon unwilling to listen to reason. They knew what I was trying to do, but they warned me against being rash. I was the Augusta, after all, and it was their responsibility to protect me, but I ignored them and plunged ahead determined to overtake the envoy and stop it with weapons drawn, if necessary.

The envoy we were pursuing consisted of two seasoned emissaries, Avienus and Trigetius, learned diplomats who had done service in Hispania. With them was Pope Leo and his retinue, which numbered a half dozen as well as three clerks and a recording secretary who had been called away from penning a hagiography of Pope Celestine to chronicle the Pope's efforts. Also in their number were nine soldiers, triple the number I had at my command, so that should they try to resist, I had only my authority as Augusta to make them back down.

Still, I rode. I saw nothing before me but the consequences of failure, the horrors of Aquilea ten-fold, a holocaust like nothing Rome had ever dreamed of. Throwing caution to the wind, disregarding the warning signs, growing weary and disoriented, I spurred my horse through the night. Twice I lost the path. Then the road seemed to peter out. By dawn we were hopelessly lost.

We were surrounded by deep forest, tall stands of fir trees, and rocky outcroppings amidst sharply rising hillsides. My guards speculated that we had ridden some distance in the wrong direction and must turn back. I started to pull my horse around when one of the guards grabbed my reins and told me to stop. The horses were blown; they were foaming at the mouths. They had to rest, or we would kill them. Deflated, I gave in.

I sat with my back against a tree. I declined the offer of food and blankets. I tilted my face up to the high forest canopy and studied the intricate interlacing of the branches. After a while, I drifted off to sleep.

I awoke sometime later to the sounds of panic, dark figures rushing to and fro, arrows whizzing past. One of my guards staggered up, an arrow protruded from his chest. He dropped to his knees.

"Run." His voice was a croak. He pitched forward onto his face.

A quick look around revealed three of my servants lying dead. The horses were rearing and whinnying. An ax flashed through the trees, turning end over end, before burying itself in the skull of the hostler. He toppled over dead. I bolted to my feet and ran, tearing blindly into the forest, tripping over my stola, getting snagged and tangled. Branches tore at me like claws. I fell headlong onto the ground and lay trembling in fear. I waited for the blow that would end my life.

It didn't come. Instead, I heard footsteps, the snap and crunch of leaves, and then someone was standing over me. He crouched down and took my hand. His fingers were short and stubby, the skin rough and calloused. He inspected my rings, the onyx and the emerald, and especially the blood red carnelian surrounded in gold and debossed with a cameo. He tried pull them off. Under the circumstances, it was difficult to keep up the pretense of being dead. I opened my eyes.

I thought I knew the Huns, thought I had witnessed them at Aurelianum, but the creature before me was unlike any I had ever seen. He was Asiatic in appearance with high cheek-bones and eyes that slanted. The flesh of his face was horribly disfigured with long ragged scars. His skull was misshapen, the forehead sloping back from the brow, the cranium large and bulbous. He wore a drooping mustache and a pointed beard. His teeth were yellow, and his breath was vile. He was intent on the business at hand and didn't notice me looking at him. He kept tugging at my rings until finally he became frustrated and reached behind him for an ax. He pinned my hand to the ground and raised the weapon. Something caught his eye. He leaned in closer. Then he stood up, staggered back, and ran.

I got to my knees and looked around. The only sound came from the rustle of the hot summer wind in the trees. Behind me was a scene of carnage. Most of my company had been slaughtered. Only the remaining guard and two of the servants had escaped. Fortunately, several of the horses were still alive. But no sooner did I reach up to take hold of a halter than an arrow snatched it from my hand as neatly as if it had been jerked away by a fist. I froze. They were out there somewhere, watching me. What's more, they possessed such accuracy in marksmanship they could cut me down in an instant if they wanted to. But for some reason they didn't.

I heard footsteps. My heart hammered in my chest. I dared not move. To run would mean death. Someone shouted at me in a strange language. I turned and raised my hands. I was shivering with terror. My throat had gone dry. I could not control my bladder; hot urine spilled down my thighs.

Three men walked up to me and pulled down my arms. They inspected my hands. They scrutinized the rings and discussed them with great intensity. One ring attracted the most attention. I suddenly realized what was happening.

They had identified my signet ring, the symbol of the Augusta of Rome. They had snared a great prize.

They put me on the back of a pony. They took me to their camp, where, if they hoped to survive, they would be obligated to deliver me to their leader intact. Stupid me. If Attila had thought that laying claim to Justa could provide him the leverage he needed to force the Emperor's hand, I had just provided him with something far better. The Augusta of Rome was now a prisoner of the Huns, and they could do with her as they wanted.

* * *

The Hun camp occupied and spilled over the borders of the town of Mantua on the banks of the river Mincio. Although the town had been sacked—doors kicked in, chattel thrown into the street, livestock slaughtered—it had been spared the torch, and most of the inhabitants had fled well ahead of the attack. The streets were not littered with corpses as might have been expected.

I rode into the town on the back of a pony led by my captors. Warriors on either side of the road rose to catch a glimpse of me. All up and down the streets they stood in rows like spectators at a parade. It was not unlike the scene depicted on my amulet of Christ entering Jerusalem, but in this case, no one was strewing palms to smooth my path. Instead, they stood as if stunned, having never seen a woman of such obvious distinction in their midst.

They were a diverse lot, some of them ritually disfigured and scarred like the men who had captured me. Others were unexceptional save for their long drooping moustaches, pointy beards, and fur-rimmed conical caps. Some were severely Asiatic in their features, while others were blonde-haired and red-faced with top-knots and bushy beards. Still others were olive-skinned with bulbous-noses and deep-set eyes. They represented the various tribes that comprised the Huns' vassal states, the multitude of nations that had been subjugated by them and forced into servitude, warriors by coercion, forced to fight on their conquerors' behalf.

It was clear they were not well. In addition to obvious signs of fatigue—pale, exhausted faces and bloodshot, hooded eyes—many were ill. They clutched themselves and shivered; perspiration glistened on their brows. Some coughed. Others were groaning in misery. A disease had broken out among them, that much was clear, the sort of warm weather illness of which Aetius had warned, an affliction that was merely distressing to us, but which was lethal to tribesmen from colder climates. They hardly looked like an army on the verge of conquest.

I was led to a domus in the wealthier part of town where I was ordered to dismount. Presently a man of Asiatic origins came out to greet me. He spoke a labored and weirdly inflected Greek that was difficult to understand, but which, by patient effort, I was able to grasp. He said his name was Onegesius, a figure of some importance to the Huns. He asked me who I was.

It was no use trying to lie; my signet ring had given me away. I told him I was Licinia Eudocia the Imperial Augusta of Rome. I said it proudly with a hint of disdain to keep him at his distance, to make him respect me.

He observed that I was a long way from home.

I told him I had come to recall an envoy that was approaching with a peace offer for their king. I had been trying to stop them because the terms were no longer feasible. He remarked that it seemed peculiar to dispatch a woman of such distinction to deliver such a message. I told him the envoy was comprised of determined men of forthright character who would not have been constrained by some lesser person. He seemed unconvinced but said nothing more and led me into the domus. It had been the home of some wealthy personage. Save for some chipped tiles and broken statuary, it was largely intact. He brought me into the peristylum where he invited me to make myself comfortable and ordered the servants to bring me something to eat. Then he disappeared.

As I awaited his return, I noted a number of older women moving in and out of an adjoining room. Judging by their dress and manner, these were not slaves or servants but relatives of Onegesius. I was ravenously hungry and wolfed down the food I was given. When I was finished, I looked around. Seeing no one watching, I looked into the room where they had gone. Seven of the women were seated in a circle bent over their work. They were embroidering gems and appliques onto items of clothing: trousers, boots, and tunics. They chatted as they worked. Quite unexpectedly, one of them looked up and saw me. I shrank back, but she smiled and waved me forward in a kindly manner.

I stepped tentatively into the room. With a broad smile the woman came forward and took me by the hand. She led me to a seat among them and bid me sit. I did.

The women twittered and giggled as they worked. I could not understand what they were saying, but they were friendly. They presumed a keen interest on my part in what they were doing and held forth their embroidery, explaining it in detail, even going so far as to furnish me with a needle and yarn and encouraging me to join in, which I did. I was thus engaged when Onegesius returned. He did a double take and laughed. Grinning, he explained to the women who I was. When they heard, their eyes grew large and they fell about in unrestrained mirth, slapping their knees and stamping their feet to emphasize their amusement. I smiled helplessly.

When their laughter subsided, Onegesius explained that these were his wives, all of them. They were inordinately proud of their craft, he said, and would seize any opportunity to crow about it. While he was telling me this, one of them interrupted. I thought he would reprimand her for her insolence. Instead, he engaged her, drawing her out, asking her to explain herself so he could better understand her, a hint of irony in his tone. They fell into good-natured bickering, and before long the others had joined in, taking her side against him. They were all laughing, shaking their fingers, and scolding him; one even going so far as to pinch his bottom. I looked on in astonishment. I had never seen such easygoing familiarity between men and women.

Later I was to learn that Onegesius had nine wives—two were absent—and seventeen children. All of them lived with him and traveled with him on his campaigns. This was common among the Huns. Most warriors brought their families with them, which explained why maintaining their supply lines was so important. Should they be cut off from their base, not just they, but their entire families were at risk. It also explained their insatiable appetite for plunder. Like roving birds delivering much needed sustenance to their nests, there was never enough to insure them against future deprivation. On this score, Onegesius was boastful, ticking off their most recent victories with barely concealed glee. Aside from the towns and cities I already knew about, they had surrounded and sacked Mediolanum, the former capital of the Western Empire and carried away cartloads of riches, but not before flushing out the citizenry in a howling storm of terror.

"Did you pursue them and slaughter them?" I asked. I tried to keep the disapproval out of my voice.

Onegesius was not fooled. "It would have been worthless to pursue cowards," he said.

"You despise cowardice only a little less than you abhor resistance," I said.

He affected a dignified air. "Both are disagreeable," he said. "But resistance whets the appetite."

"As does deceit, I presume."

He studied my expression.

"I have come to warn Attila of an offer that cannot be fulfilled, an offer that must be withdrawn before it is submitted. I should not want us to be perceived as duplicitous."

"Yes," he said. He scratched at his beard. "It would go badly for you."

"May I have an audience with your king before the envoy arrives?"

He thought it over. "I will arrange it," he said. "Tomorrow. He will receive you at a feast being held in his honor."

"Tomorrow," I said. "I'm grateful for your help. I'll look forward to it."

But, as grateful as I was, I was not really looking forward to it. Truth to be told, I was terrified.

* * *

The next morning, I received a curious guest. He was announced by one of Onegesius's wives who seemed quite intimate with him, as if they had been friends a long time. They laughed and teased each another in the Hun language. So quick and fluid was their banter I felt sure I would need a translator to understand him, but when he turned to address me, he spoke perfect Latin.

His name was Orestes, and he was the king's secretary. He was not a Hun. He was originally from Pannonia Prima and was descended from Roman nobility. He was the son-in-law of Romulus who had once served as comes[15] of that province until Aetius decided to cede it to the Huns. At twenty-five, he was six years younger than I, but he had been working for the Huns for almost ten years, the last five of them for Attila.

He was relaxed and easygoing and discussed the Huns' situation in strictly political terms as if they had not been engaged in the wholesale slaughter of innocents and the complete eradication of towns and cities. The Huns looked upon Rome with admiration, he informed me. They wanted to emulate us.

I guessed I was supposed to be flattered by this—he was watching me expectantly—but I declined to give him the pleasure.

He went on in more detail, thinking perhaps that I had not appreciated what he was saying. Yes, Attila was illiterate, he allowed, but the king liked to have the histories read to him. He was particularly fond of Livy. Attila was better acquainted with Roman history than most Romans, Orestes declared, and had come to the conclusion that Rome had reached its zenith during the reign of Julius Caesar.

"The Empire was aggressively expanding its borders then," he said. "If you're not going forward, you're going backwards."

"Is that right?" I asked.

---

15  Title granted to a trusted official.

"That's what Attila believes," he answered, "and the histories support it." He told me all this with a good-natured smile as if we were discussing some benign amusement like fishing or throwing quoits and not the massacre of thousands of people.

"The Huns of today are like the Romans at their peak," he said. He offered me a handful of the figs he had brought with him. When I demurred, he shrugged and popped one into his mouth. "Victory after victory. Keeping your enemies on the run. That's how the Romans used to do it."

"But don't you think it's exhausting to be on the offensive all the time?" I asked.

"No less exhausting than being constantly on the run," he said.

"You don't think much of us Romans these days, do you, Orestes?"

He smiled to himself and shook his head. "Rome has become a sniveling coward," he said. "It's a shame. But then I don't suppose I'm telling you something you don't already know." He talked around the fig in his mouth, gnawing the meat and then sucking on the pit.

I forced a polite smile.

He spit the pit into his hand and looked at it. "Fortunately, Attila is prepared to be reasonable. He doesn't want the Empire destroyed. He wants it restored it to its former glory. You should consider yourself lucky. I mean when you consider the alternative." He turned his hand over and the pit fell to the ground. He popped another fig into his mouth. "Are you sure you don't want one?" He held out his hand again. I declined. "The offer of marriage from the princess Justa couldn't have come at a better time," he said. "It's the one thing he needs to ensure his legitimacy as Emperor." He smiled, and then affected concern. "Don't worry," he said. "No harm will come to you or your daughters. Attila has no quarrel with you. Your husband on the other hand…"

"The princess is dead," I said.

He stopped chewing and looked at me.

"That's right," I said. "Princess Justa committed suicide. I've come here to warn you not to accept the assurances of anyone claiming otherwise. I don't want your king to be misled. I fear the consequences of such a misunderstanding."

My interlocutor didn't know how to digest what I had just told him. He spit a pit into his hand, studied it with a furrowed brow, and then he cast it aside. He shook his head. "This is not good," he said. "Not good at all." A pall had fallen over him. "Are you sure?" he asked. "Are you absolutely certain?"

"She's dead," I said.

He bit his lip and looked around anxiously.

"Don't worry," I said. "You needn't deliver the bad news. I've been granted an audience with your king this evening. I'll tell him."

Relief flooded his expression.

"You can act like you never heard it from me," I said. "I won't tell anyone I shared it with you first."

He caught up my hands and squeezed them. "Oh, thank you, Augusta. You have no idea what that means to me."

"Oh, but you're wrong," I said. "I do know what it means to you. It means your life will be spared. It means you won't be made to answer for being the bearer of bad news."

He gave me a look of mingled surprise and apprehension.

"I'm going to give you something you could never get from Attila. I'm going to give you something only a weak, cowardly Roman can give you."

"What's that?" he asked.

"Mercy."

* * *

Attila did not preside in a confiscated Roman domus but in a large circular tent with a peaked roof from which a long pennant flew, a yurt as the Huns called it. Attila's yurt stood close to the city's public baths and was adjoined to them by a covered walk. It seemed even this most barbaric of barbarian kings enjoyed a few civilized comforts. But if Attila was pampered, his warriors were anything but. On the way to my reception, I was once again witness to the hunger and deprivation of his warriors. It seemed they were far from ready to mount a major offensive on a fortified city like Rome. For many of them, considering their physical conditions, it would be tantamount to suicide.

Onegesius stationed a guard to watch over me and went into the yurt. I waited on the other side of the plaza for instructions. It was growing dark.

A young woman approached. She introduced herself as Idilico and said she was honored to make my acquaintance. She spoke fluent Greek and went on for some time citing things she had learned about me, holding forth in the giddy, apologetic manner of a starstruck admirer. She was originally from Thessalonika, the birthplace of my mother. Her father was a Goth. When she was a little girl, her family moved to the Danube frontier where her father worked as a river patrolman. They were there less than a month when the Huns attacked, burned their town, and killed most of its inhabitants including both of her parents. She was taken captive and sold into slavery.

Her first owner was a kindly old man who treated her well. When he died, she was claimed by his nephew who raped her and forced her into all sorts of disgusting perversions. Fortunately, this brute soon met a fatal end, and she was sold on to Onegesius, who recognized her facility with Greek and put her to work translating documents for his secretary. It was there she acquired the name of Idilico, which meant "warrior," a tongue-in-cheek reference to her fiery temperament. It was there too she learned about me through the documents she translated. The Huns kept a cache of intelligence on everyone in the imperial family. They were not as mindless as they appeared.

Idilico was going on in her bubbly, effusive way when I was called to make my entrance. She stood aside to let me pass. Then, as if remembering something, she rushed alongside me and tugged on my sleeve. I stopped. She whispered, "He's afraid. The shaman has read the cracks in the bones and seen a vision. He will die soon, and he's terrified."

The guard yelled at her to get back and she did. I continued on across the plaza toward the yurt and wondered what she was talking about.

I ducked under the flap and into a large circular room outfitted with a wooden floor and illuminated by pine torches. The walls were decorated with tapestries and lined with couches. Seated on the couches were dozens of men and women attired in silk robes and wearing glittering jewelry, a marked contrast to the miserable wretches who lined the roads outside.

No sooner had I stepped across the threshold than a goblet was pressed into my hands and a toast proposed. Everyone stood in unison and raised their goblets. I did the same. We were toasting a thickset man who presided on a center sofa. He was half-reclining with his legs splayed open and his feet turned out, his arms spread wide on the backrest. He was short in stature with a broad chest and large head. He had a swarthy complexion and Asiatic eyes that squinted out from beneath heavy lids. His teeth were small; his lips were thin. His beard was unkempt and sprinkled with gray. He was not richly attired like the others but wore a coat of plain ibex fur, embroidered trousers, sheepskin boots, and a fur-brimmed conical cap. This was Attila, king of the Huns.

We drank off the toast whereupon I was directed to sit opposite him, the circular floor between us. Though my heart was beating in my chest, something told me it would be a mistake to look down or avert my gaze, so I kept my eyes fastened on him. He was speaking over his shoulder to the person on his left, a person of prominence whose youth and proximity suggested he might be his son. Farther away on his left were two other young men, probably his other sons. Onegesius was on his right. Orestes was not present.

A servant came forward and filled my goblet. Other servants went around the room doing the same, and when all the goblets were refilled, another toast was proposed. Everyone stood and drank. I wanted to keep my wits about me, so I didn't down the entire contents of the vessel, leaving it half full, but when the servant came around again and noticed there was still some in it, he frowned and indicated I should drink it all. His manner suggested that failure to do so might be considered an insult by the king. I drank.

Attila himself had not yet imbibed, but a servant came forward and, bowing low, filled his vessel, which was not a goblet, but a plain wooden cup. Attila took a sip and handed it to Onegesius who did the same, whereupon the cup was handed around the room, passing from one hand to another until all had taken a sip from it before it was returned to Attila. I was glad I had not been required to participate in this unsanitary ritual, but no sooner was the cup back in Attila's hands and refilled than another toast was proposed. We stood and drank for the third time.

I was not accustomed to such heavy drinking. Having gulped my wine too fast, a belch was out before I could restrain it. The room exploded with laughter. In my half-drunken state, I was mortified and blushed, which elicited another round of laughter. When it had subsided, Attila raised his cup and toasted me. I gave him a wan smile.

As I was the object of the toast, I was not required to drink for which I was thankful. Attila spoke. Onegesius translated. The king welcomed me and thanked the gods for bringing me to him in such a timely manner. He considered it a gift. This wasn't exactly reassuring. Being considered a gift implied I had become a possession, which I had no intention of becoming, but I did my best to appear gracious. We all sat down.

Now long tables were carried in and a feast was laid before us. Wild boar, horse meat, root vegetables, pigeons, dormice, and lamb, as sumptuous a feast as any seen in a nobleman's villa in Rome. The guests set in without preamble, pulling the meat from the bones with their hands, swabbing it in the grease, and stuffing it into their mouths so that the juice ran down their chins and glistened in their beards. They laughed and spoke with their mouths full. They belched and farted to show their appreciation. The whole spectacle made me a little nauseated, but I put on a brave face and pretended to enjoy myself.

When the platters had been emptied, the company lay about bloated and content like a passel of hogs. Onegesius rose to offer another toast. By now the drinking was becoming oppressive, and I tried to decline, but I was scolded with a look and grudgingly gave in. It became apparent that I wasn't the only one who was reaching her limit. The man next to me suddenly lurched forward and vomited, splattering me with the violence of his expulsion. It was too much. The putrid smell combined with the instability of my own stomach brought forth a torrent I was powerless to resist.

When it was over, I sat upright and sheepishly wiped the spew from my lips. I tried to focus on the room through glassy eyes and was surprised to find Attila regarding me with a grin as if I had just paid him an unexpected compliment. He began to applaud; the others joined in. In my drunken state, I was unable to determine whether they were joking or truly valued my contribution.

A pair of servants rushed in with damp rags and wiped off my clothing while others cleared away the platters and removed the tables. A figure appeared beside me with water. I took it gratefully and sipped slowly, testing the steadiness of my stomach. I was relieved to find the storm had passed. I handed the cup back and was surprised to find my benefactor was Idilico. She bent down and whispered. "Continue to persist. You are doing well." Then she was gone.

When the tables were cleared away, the party joined together in song. It was a strange discordant song with a rhythm and melody foreign to me. Judging by the way the company turned to Attila as they crooned, it seemed the song was about him, likely in honor of his exploits, which was partly confirmed by the self-satisfied expression on his face.

When the song was over, a strange person was brought in and left in the center of the room. He was a wretched creature, filthy and emaciated. He cowered and clutched his hands before him while he babbled incoherently much to the delight of the company who jeered and taunted. To enhance the sport, Attila spoke to the poor creature as if he were addressing an entirely rational being, even going so far as to call him Onegesius, which caused the company to fall about in gales of laughter. Onegesius lowered his head and snickered self-consciously.

When the amusement had run its course, the man was led away, and a dwarf was led in by a collar and leash like a dog. Unlike the lunatic, the dwarf bore himself with an air of dignity, which was not easy to do in the face of all the heckling. The dwarf attempted to address Attila in a sensible manner, and Attila pretended to listen. I could not understand what was being said. Seeing my confusion, Onegesius called for an interpreter lest I miss the fun. Idilico was assigned to assist me.

"That's Zercon," Idilico explained. She pointed toward the dwarf. "He used to belong to Attila's brother, Bleda. Attila doesn't like dwarves; they make him uneasy, so when Bleda died, he sent Zercon to Aetius as a present. The dwarf should have stayed where he was, but he has come back for his wife who's still being held by the Huns. He's making his case to Attila. He's arguing—quite logically, as you can see—that the Huns ought to let her go as a gesture of courtesy to Aetius. He's saying that since it was his intention to gratify Aetius with the gift of a servant—meaning himself—the effect has been only partially achieved because the servant has been sullen and distracted on account of the absence of his wife. If Attila will be good enough to release his wife, he will be the happiest and best of all servants, which will please Aetius and demonstrate the generosity of Attila's gift."

Attila listened with exaggerated deliberation, prompting sniggers and snorts from the onlookers. When the dwarf was finished, Attila stroked his chin and pretended to think it over. More laughter. He asked the dwarf to repeat some of his arguments. Zercon, seeing he was being made fun of, grimaced and revisited what he had said. Attila mused, and then he said, "I'm sorry. I cannot think clearly. I need some tricks. Something to clear my mind. Surely you understand."

"Tricks?"

"Yes, perhaps some cartwheels and back handsprings. I especially like somersaults. If you will perform some somersaults and stand on your head, I'm sure it will help me to concentrate."

The company roared with laughter.

The dwarf looked vexed, but he did as he was asked. He turned cartwheels and somersaults in a mechanical manner and with a surly expression. His chains rattled and banged. The company laughed and laughed. I felt sorry for the dwarf, to be made to suffer such humiliation for no other purpose than to amuse these cruel people. When he was finished, he stood expectantly in front of the king and awaited his answer.

Attila leaned forward and shouted into his face. "No!"

The dwarf looked stricken. For a moment it appeared he would cry, which caused the company to fall about with whoops of laughter. Then the dwarf's expression hardened.

"I will return to Aetius and report your answer," he said. "He will not be pleased. He sent me here with the hope that some tiny bit of clemency might be granted, some nobility to leaven the great power you wield, some sign that you are a man of reason. The countryside lies in ruin. You have exacted a terrible price for the way you were treated in Gaul. Perhaps you were justified. But now you have taken your due and the balance of power has shifted. It is up to you to demonstrate mercy and restraint. Clemency in a small, inconsequential matter such as mine would say much to Aetius about the kind of king you are."

Attila snorted and waved him off. "Aetius will know soon enough what kind of king I am."

The company laughed and jeered.

But the dwarf wasn't finished. "The famine here has taken a toll on your army. Your warriors are sick and starving. Your supply lines are stretched thin. Even now, Marcian, the Emperor of the East, is moving to strike your base in Pannonia. Reason dictates that you withdraw if for no other reason than to protect your rear. But perhaps you are not motivated by reason. Perhaps the only thing that motivates you is cruelty and spite. If so, Aetius understands what he must do, although he is loath to do it. Having the Goths in Rome creates all kinds of problems for him. Once they are there he doesn't know if he can remove them. Yet they are on their way, an army six thousand strong under King Thorismund, intent on finishing what they started on the Catalaunian Plains."

Attila's eyes went cold. Somewhere behind them feared flickered. Then he swung his gaze on me. "Is this true?" he asked.

Until that moment I had felt woozy and off kilter, but now, unaccountably, my senses sharpened. I knew the dwarf was lying. I had received no news of any alliance with the Goths. Indeed, I knew it was the last thing in the world Aetius would want. But Attila was unsettled by what he had heard. He was back on his heels. And, as I had learned only too well from the Huns, when your enemy is at his weakest, that's when you strike.

"Yes," I said. "It's true."

Attila looked daggers at me. Then he began to smile, a sinister, leering grin full of malevolence. "You wouldn't be trying to trick me, would you?"

I denied it.

"Zercon has nothing to lose," he said. "He knows he's a dead man, so he will say anything. But your fate is not yet determined. There are many ways I could make use of you that might spare your life… unless you offend me, that is. Tell the truth. Has Aetius enlisted the Goths?"

"You asked me what I heard, and I told you."

"Heard?" he said. "I didn't ask you what you heard. I asked you what you knew. Don't play word games with me."

"I cannot report the presence of the Goths as a fact. I have not seen them with my own eyes. I can only tell you what I heard."

He shook his head. "And the assault on our base at Pannonia, what have you heard about that?"

"Nothing," I said.

He studied me. "I don't believe you. I think you're telling me what you want me to hear. You're trying to play me for a fool. You're making the same mistake as all the others." He waited a moment as Idilico caught up with the translation. "You consider yourself better than me," he continued. "You think you're more cultured and refined, and therefore destined to prevail. But you're wrong. Your civilization earns you nothing. Those refinements you hold dear are like jewelry on a corpse. Your world is in decline, your essence is drained, and anyone bold enough to take advantage of the situation can claim your adornments at will."

He turned on the dwarf. "You no longer amuse me. But before I kill you, I have a little treat for you. You see, you were right when you said your wife is of no consequence to me. Which is why I won't regret having her torn apart by dogs— while you watch."

The company gasped.

The dwarf fell to his knees and begged. Attila laughed in his face. The dwarf was dragged away, clutching his hands, and pleading. His chains rattled across the floor. For once, the crowd saw no humor in his plight.

Attila turned to me. "You consider me a monster," he said. "But you are no better. What you call your civilization is a cynical plot to deprive the many and enrich the few. You impose a system of justice that punishes the poor for the same crimes the wealthy commit with impunity. Your wars are fought to profit your aristocracy at the expense of your people, and you don't even have the courage to fight them yourselves. I pity your citizens. They are untrained in the use of weapons and misled by their leaders whose job it is to defend them. If this is your idea of civilization, it's rotten to the core and must end. Call me cruel, call me barbarous, call me a monster, but I'm doing a job that needs to be done. I'm taking out the trash. It's time for a new order."

When Idilico had finished translating, I was at a loss for words. It had never occurred to me that a vicious warlord like Attila had worked out a rationalization for his actions. But on reflection it made sense. Wanton destruction can only motivate men so far. At some point they have to feel they are in pursuit of some higher calling. Attila had set his nation on a path to sanitize the West by ridding it of the corruption that Rome had become. I didn't know what to say.

Then it came to me. The words flowed across my lips as if they came from some inner voice. My drunken state vanished, and I was clear and lucid. I showed no fear.

"You perceive rightly, great king," I said. "We Romans are weak and selfish. We have lost the ability to work together for the greater good. We are jealous for entitlements and fearful of sacrifice. We spurn compromise, delight in division, and revel in wickedness. And yet, we are protected by God. Look around. Even now as we lay prostate before you, our cities in ashes, our people slaughtered, you cannot win. Your warriors are sapped by sickness and hunger. Your supply lines are overextended. And in spite of the bounty you have plundered, you lack the resources to maintain your offensive. Marcian will destroy your base at Pannonia if you do not return at once to defend it. To make matters worse, Aetius is gaining strength. He will fight for us as he did in Gaul, enlisting the Goths to finish what he started. But how can this be? By any measure you should be on the verge of victory. Yet you are not. You have taken on a power greater than you know, and if you don't desist, you will suffer the consequences."

Attila looked surprised. He folded his arms. "You want me to fear your god?"

I sighed and shook my head. "Fear? You think fear is what I ask of you? Fear is an ambush. Fear is a wall. Fear is temporary and unconvincing. Fear does not move things forward but holds things in place to decay and rot. No, I seek understanding. I seek reason." I took a step toward him. "No one can win this war. Not you. Not us. All that can be gained is death and destruction. You must stop this waste. You must take the first step toward reconciliation, and in so doing ensure your own survival."

He looked at me under lowering brows. "Are you threatening me?"

"Quite the opposite. I'm offering you a way to save yourself—not from me, not from Rome, but from the wrath of God."

He laughed. "Don't be absurd."

I took another step forward. I was deadly serious. "Very well, if you refuse to fear our God, then fear your own. Your shaman has read the cracks in the bones. Your fate is sealed." Idilico shot me a worried look. I went on. "The prophecy is irreversible. You are doomed."

For a fleeting moment a look of childish vulnerability came into his eyes. Then he collected himself. His voice boomed throughout the tent. "Where did you hear that?"

"It's common knowledge. Everyone knows it. But there's a way you can save yourself. There's a power greater than the shaman's bones, a gift greater than survival, the gift of grace."

"Grace?"

"The opposite of fear. Fear is a wolf that hunts and devours. Fear takes and takes. When fear is your driver, you must keep going, you must keep attacking, for the moment you let up the fear you have inspired in others turns against you. Then the hunter becomes the hunted. You will be tracked down and destroyed. Fear gains only temporary victories and earns its own destruction. But grace is the gift of God. Grace is getting what you *don't* deserve, instead of what you do. Grace is how the doomed are saved. Grace is your way out."

He scoffed, but there was a hint of uncertainty in his disdain.

"Listen," I said, "as we speak, an envoy is approaching with an offer, something they cannot deliver, the hand of Justa Grata Honoria in marriage. She cannot marry you for she is dead. She has taken her own life."

"You lie."

"I speak the truth. This is what I came to tell you. The offer they make cannot be fulfilled. They are hastening here prematurely, driven by fear, hoping to appease you. But they don't know it's not possible. They don't know she's dead, which is why I rode ahead, to explain. I don't want you to misunderstand. When they fail to deliver on their promise, I don't want you to see it as bad faith and take revenge."

He glowered at me. "Is there no one else in Rome who can deliver such a message? Only the Augusta herself?"

"No one whose credibility is higher."

He examined me through narrowing eyes. "You are either incredibly brave or stupid."

"Make no mistake," I said, "I fear you. We all do. The very name Attila strikes terror into the hearts of every Roman. Panic makes us blunder, and so we compound the crisis with errors. Fear has made a mess of things, and no one stands to gain. But grace can rescue the situation."

"What are you talking about?"

"The one thing you want, the thing you have set your heart on, you cannot have. No amount of blood and terror can change that, but if you desist, if you give your enemies that which they have not earned and do not deserve, you set things moving in a new direction and give us all the opportunity to recover and heal, your people and mine."

"My death is foretold," he said. "What do I care about what comes after?"

"That which we find it in our hearts to give to others in this life may be granted to us in heaven."

He dismissed my comments with a sneer.

I said nothing more.

He picked up his cup and took a drink. He looked around at the assembled company. He went from face to face seeking confirmation or repudiation but got only trepidation. With an air of annoyance, he ordered the entertainment to resume.

A band of musicians struck up a tune, and a dozen dancing girls entered the floor. They spun around and clapped their hands. As they danced, Attila drank. He imbibed more than his fellows until he was drunk. He bellowed for more and sang with all the skill of a wounded elephant. Presently he sent a servant to bring me to him, but no sooner did the servant take hold of my arm than Attila changed his mind and called for Idilico instead. She was tugged across the floor and forced to sit on his lap. The pained look on her face as he groped and molested her was pitiable.

When the dancing was over, a pair of oiled wrestlers grappled and strained, but Attila lost interest and turned all of his attention to Idilico. He kissed her and caressed her in full view of the others. Before long, his carnal urges demanded greater satisfaction and he dragged her out of the tent by the wrist as she fought and cried.

With the king departed, the party broke up. Onegesius escorted me back to the domus where his wives stood to greet us. They were eager to hear news of the festivities. He recounted what had happened as they listened in rapt atten-tion. They chuckled at the funny parts and chattered among themselves at the news of my defiance. They all turned to me in astonishment.

"Oooh," they said, and "Aah." Apparently, they approved of my daring.

I went to bed.

* * *

In the morning I was surprised to discover the Hun camp abuzz with activity. I was informed they were preparing to break camp and return to Pannonia.

"Is this true?" I asked Onegesius.

"Yes. The offensive is at an end."

"Why?"

He gave me a ponderous look. "It may interest you to know that your envoy has arrived. Their appearance bearing the selfsame offer you spoke of yesterday has been taken as a measure of your sincerity. It seems you have won the king's trust. He wishes all his counselors were as persuasive as you."

I could hardly believe my ears. I tried not to let my pleasure show.

"You are free to go," Onegesius said. "The king has no further use of you. You may return to Rome."

I could not resist a smile.

Onegesius was not nearly so sanguine. "It might interest you to know that I tried to talk him out of it. I tried to convince him that you would make an excellent hostage, but he refused. He reasoned if you were with us, we would be pursued. He prefers not to fight a rearguard action against the Goths as he withdraws. We have lost too many men already. He would rather return home with as many warriors as possible so we can fight another day. I guess you would call that grace, something you did not deserve but received anyway."

I tried not to react to the bitterness in his tone. "Tell the king I'm grateful for his mercy."

Onegesius bid me farewell and moved away more resigned than disillusioned. He had no doubt dealt with Attila's caprices before.

I went to find the envoy. On the way I came across Idilico. She was frantic.

"I heard you're leaving," she said. "Please take me with you."

"I can't do that," I said. "It would be regarded as theft."

"Oh, but you must," she said. Her eyes brimmed with tears. "Please."

I knew better than to ask the reason for her anguish, but my captors had granted me a reprieve. To incite them now by stealing one of their slaves would be senseless.

"Look," I said, "if I try to take you away, it will not go well for either of us. If I try to buy you from them, they will refuse. I'm sure they feel they've given me enough already."

"You don't understand," she said. "It's too awful to bear. I won't go through that again. I won't. If he tries to make me, I don't know what I'll do."

I thought it over. "Give me a little time," I said. "Wait for me by the water trough, and I'll see what I can arrange."

She moved away wiping her tears with the back of her hand.

I went to look for the envoy and came upon the king's secretary Orestes.

He bowed. "Augusta," he said. "I'm glad to see you out and about this morning. I was afraid I might not see you again."

"It turns out your king is not without mercy after all."

Orestes had nothing to say to that.

"I'm looking for the envoy," I said. "I understand they've arrived."

"Yes," he said. "I had the pleasure of meeting the Pope. What a great man. He exudes warmth and compassion. I'm excited by the possibilities. His meeting with Attila is sure to yield great benefits."

"Undoubtedly," I said. "Where may I find him?"

He directed me to a place just ahead, a domus even more spacious and comfortable than the one Onegesius had appropriated. Inside, standing beside the impluvium talking with his entourage was Pope Leo. He acted surprised to see me.

"Augusta!" he said. "What are you doing here?"

"I was trying to intercept you," I said. "I have bad news. Justa is dead. Suicide."

"Yes, I know," he said. "Attila informed us before we had a chance to make the offer. You averted a disaster by your actions. We are grateful."

"Fortunately, the king was willing to listen to reason. But I could not have done it without the help of a friend, a young woman, a slave. She was essential to our success, and now she needs our assistance."

"Surely. Surely. But Augusta you should not have taken such a risk. You could have been killed or, worse, taken hostage."

"I felt it was my duty. There was no time to enlist anyone's aid. Now about that slave girl. Her name is Idilico—"

"Kneel with me. Let's give thanks and praise to the Lord who protected and sustained you."

"Fine. Yes. But about the girl—"

The Pope pressed me down on my knees. Then he stood above me, arms spread, eyes lifted to heaven. He pronounced an invocation that went on for some time. I shifted uncomfortably. When he was finished, he helped me to my feet.

"There now. We have placed the honor where it is due."

"I need you to purchase her from the Huns," I said. "I need you to buy her from Attila."

He held my eyes for a moment, then shook his head. "I'm sorry. I can't do that. The Church is on a very strict budget."

"Don't worry. I'll give you the money. I'll reimburse you."

He regarded me with suspicion. "But that will require the approval of the Emperor."

"I'll get his approval."

He stroked his chin. "As you know, the Huns are notorious for commanding a high price."

"Whatever it costs," I said.

He smiled warmly. "I'm a man of God. Of course, I'll help. I'll do whatever I can to protect the poor child."

I thanked him and went to find Idilico and tell her what I had arranged. She was standing beside the water trough. "The Pope is going to purchase you from the Huns," I said. "Everything is going to be all right."

She fell sobbing into my arms.

In hindsight, I should have made certain. I should have watched to see her delivered into the Pope's hands. But after appropriating a part of the Pope's retinue to accompany me, I left as soon as possible. I thought it best to get away from that place before Attila changed his mind.

It was a mistake. The Pope didn't buy Idilico. He left her behind. Later he claimed the Huns had reneged on their promise to sell her.

"I paid them," he said, "but they refused to hand her over. It just goes to show you, you can't trust the Huns." Still, he demanded to be reimbursed. "The Church cannot be burdened by the expense of a political gambit gone wrong," he said. "That must be the responsibility of the State."

I urged Placidius not to pay him, but he did anyway, all the while berating me for being so stupid. As a punishment he even took away one of my servants. Later I found out he had had sex with her against her will.

# Chapter 22
Autumn, The Year AD 452 – Spring, The Year 454

I cannot say I was surprised to find Pope Leo boasting about his great victory over the Huns. He proclaimed it from the pulpit every Sunday to the captivated attention of his parishioners. Needless to say, he made no mention of his failed attempt to buy off Attila by abducting the Emperor's sister, nor anything about my role in averting the crisis. Certainly, Aetius received no credit, nor did Marcian. Only God, and by extension Leo, God's representative on earth. He was applauded and celebrated. Petronius Maximus called him a shining example of piety and virtue and suggested he be canonized.

In all the hubbub over Leo, the Emperor was nowhere to be found. It appeared he had contributed nothing to Leo's embassy other than to permit it. The Emperor, who might have expected to profit from the retreat of the Huns, got nothing from it. He was still held up to public scorn, blamed for letting it happen, and reviled as an impairment whose continued reign could only result in more such disasters. Rather than fight back in the court of public opinion as he had in the past, he turned silent and morose.

I tried to draw him out. I told him the truth about what had happened, that Leo had done nothing. I relayed how, with the help of a slave girl and a dwarf, I had saved Rome from being attacked. But Placidius was having none of it. He was drunk and irritable and told me to shut up.

We were in the triclinium. He had just finished his breakfast. His plates had been pushed to one side. He was reclining on the couch and cradling a cup of wine. Heraclius was standing nearby with a simpering look on his face. The sight of him made me angry, and I told him to get out.

At first, he defied me, but when I advanced on him, he shrank back. I got to within inches of his face and shouted.

"Out!"

I pointed to the door.

Before leaving he turned to the Emperor and reminded him about something they had discussed. Foggy though he was, the Emperor seemed to remember and nodded his head in assent. Heraclius went out.

"What was that?" I asked.

"You're trying to usurp me," he said apathetically. He took a drink of wine.

I had not forgotten the eunuch's betrayal. I fully intended to pay him out for his treachery, and the account was mounting. But Placidius seemed not to care.

"As I understand it, you're working with Aetius. You're plotting against me. You're just like my mother and sister. You're planning to usurp me."

"That's not true," I said.

He shrugged and took another drink. "Women are all the same."

I rolled my eyes. "It's pointless to argue with you with you when you're drunk."

He muttered something under his breath.

I leaned in closer. I had not understood him. He launched his goblet at my head, showering me with wine.

"Tell the truth!"

I looked at him in disgust and stormed out. I could hear him railing against me as I went down the hall. Presently, however, his ranting faded and all that remained was the swish of my silks and the rattle of my jewelry as I hastened to my room.

* * *

I should have been more worried. I should have been more cautious. It was not Placidius who presented the biggest threat to me. Yet at some level I still believed his power as Emperor made him my most formidable adversary, and since he was neutralized by drink and despair, I let my guard down.

I went to see Junius, to bounce things off of him as I had in the past. By that time, he had left Aetius's villa and taken up residence in the seaside port of Ostia where had taken a job overseeing the importation of goods, a position arranged for him by his adoptive brother Olybrius who was now the praetor. For Junius it was a sharp come down from his previous post. That he had agreed to it at all was a little disconcerting, and when I asked him about it, he refused to discuss it. On the whole, his attitude toward me was frosty, and when I asked him what I had done wrong, he told me he was busy and couldn't talk. I asked him when he might find the time, and he was noncommittal. Finally, I demanded to know what was going on.

He stopped what he was doing. We were standing among the stacks of crates and bundles that crowded the dock. He pulled me aside.

"We have to stop meeting like this," he said. "It's too risky."

"It's your father. Isn't it?"

He gave me a hard look. "I can't do this anymore," he said. "It's time to move on."

"What are you talking about?"

He plowed his fingers through his hair. "Look, Licinia. It's been more than a year since we were together at Aurelianum. It's been more than a year since… since the baby. All this time I've been living at the villa waiting for you to come back. But eventually I realized it was never going to happen. The truth is you were never going to come back. You are the Augusta of Rome. You are not my wife. You never were. Our life together was a fiction, and now it's over."

"But you can't be working here. Not for these people."

"Listen, Olybrius is a good man. He offered me a job. There's nothing wrong with that."

"But Olybrius works for your father. He was adopted to replace you, to demean you."

"It's something to keep me busy, to keep my mind off things. Anyway, it was none of Olybrius's doing. He saw that I needed something, so he helped me."

"You could have come to me. I could have arranged something."

"And that would have been less demeaning?" He gave me a sad, apologetic look and went back to inventorying the freight on the dock.

I turned things over in my mind, and, as I did so, he disappeared among the stacks of cargo. But I wasn't finished with him, so I went looking for him. I found him engaged in a conversation with a tall, slender person, Olybrius. I knew him on sight. He was young and handsome, the heir of the powerful Anicia clan whose father's demise had vaulted him into a position of prominence in the Senate and made him available for adoption by someone of elevated status. Maximus had seized the opportunity and made the eighteen-year-old his son. Still, Olybrius displayed none of the smug attitude of other young men of his station. He was informal and relaxed and seemed to get along with everyone.

He was chatting amiably with Junius. He even made a joke. They laughed together. I could see how Junius had been seduced into thinking he had nothing to fear from him. But the fact remained. Olybrius worked for Maximus, and Maximus was our enemy.

So, it had come to this. Maximus had turned my best friend against me. I went home and wrote a letter to the only person I knew who could help. I wrote to Aetius.

* * *

My letter passed Aetius in transit having been carried to his headquarters while he was enroute to Ravenna with shocking news. When I heard it, I had to sit down. Attila had been killed. The Hun king had been murdered in his wedding bed by his most recent bride, a comely young maiden known among the Huns for her pluck and spirit, a slave girl by the name of Idilico.

It was a poisoning—or so it seemed. After the wedding, Attila had celebrated late into the night, holding his new bride on his lap, and taking gross liberties with her in full view of the others. When he tried to drag her off to bed, she resisted. He beat her, and dragged her, kicking and screaming, into his tent.

The next morning the guard outside found it curious when the king did not appear. He called out, but the king did not answer. Then the sound of a woman weeping came to the guard's ears. He looked into the tent and saw Idilico bent over the king's body. The king was drenched in blood. It appeared he had suffered some kind of hemorrhage. Blood was congealed in his beard. His flesh had turned a ghastly gray. Flies were crawling on his eyes.

Idilico was arrested on the spot. She did not live out the morning. She was tortured and mutilated; her entrails were pulled out while she was still breathing.

Attila was given a lavish funeral. The Roman spies who had gathered the intelligence reported a three-day ceremony during which the king had lain in state covered in silks and precious gems. His warriors came forward to express their grief. They howled in misery, slashed their cheeks, yanked out clumps of their hair, and struck their heads on the ground. The women stood in long ranks singing funeral songs and making lamentations. Children came forward and placed flowers on the body.

The next day there were games, races, and feats of strength. Stories were shared of his many victories. There were sumptuous feasts. On the final day he was interred. The tomb was filled with the weapons of his vanquished enemies; precious jewels were scattered over his body. The slaves tasked with his burial were put to death so they could not reveal the grave's location. A great bonfire burned through the night and sent showers of cinders high into the air. The next morning there was nothing left but a circle of black ash. Attila was gone.

Aetius could barely contain his joy. I had never seen him so jubilant; he was practically giddy. Naturally the Pope claimed credit and declared that the hand of God had reached out to smite the evildoer in answer to his prayers. Leo's triumph over Attila was proclaimed from every pulpit. Yet not a single word of praise was offered for the lowly slave girl whose selfless courage had been Rome's deliverance.

Leo was not alone in claiming divine intervention. In Constantinople Marcian declared he had experienced a vision. An angel had appeared at the foot of his bed and shown him a broken bow. The meaning was clear once the pious Pulcheria had interpreted it. Attila was dead, his power broken. The Emperor and Empress of the East had saved the Empire through their incomparable piety.

Not to be outdone, Aetius also claimed credit. He put it about that he had bribed the commander of Attila's guard to kill him; the slave girl had nothing to do with it. Those inclined to support the Master of Soldiers clung to his explanation. Others chose different narratives. In the end, all parties who stood to gain from Attila's death had a story to tell—all except one.

Placidius was silent on the subject. His failure to capitalize on the situation might have been ascribed to some clever stratagem he had cooked up, perhaps at the behest of his deputies, but it was not the case. He simply didn't care. He had given himself over to drink and was on a path to self-destruction that took little note of what was going on around him. Attila's death had gone over his head. It was up to others to take political advantage of it.

It was exactly as Maximus had planned; the dissipated Emperor had become putty in his hands. The only things standing between Maximus and complete control of the Empire now were Aetius and me. No doubt he would be coming for us next.

*　*　*

My attempts to contact Aetius were thwarted by informers. My personal bodyguards had been instructed not to let me out of their site. Every movement I made was reported to Maximus. Should I attempt to meet with Aetius in person, it would be exposed and used as an excuse to accuse us both of treason, so I had to tread lightly.

Fortunately, the Emperor had squandered the loyalty of his staff. Among them were several men of sincere religious conviction whose morals had been offended by the Emperor's behavior. They could be approached with an invitation to work on my behalf, but it was a delicate business. Like picking out a thread to follow through the warp, it required careful scrutiny…and time. Weeks went by. Then months.

As I was working to build support behind the palace walls, Aetius was making things more difficult for me. He demanded that Placidia and Gaudentius be married before he returned to his headquarters in August. Of course, Placidius balked. He had opposed the marriage from the start and was not about to be coerced, especially with Maximus whispering in his ear and reminding him that the future of the Empire was at stake. So, Placidius told Aetius it was never going to happen. But Aetius had a tried and true method of getting what he wanted, and he was not averse to using it.

The situation with the Huns was in flux. It had taken less than two months after Attila's death for things to start falling apart. His three sons began quarreling among themselves and the coalition split into factions each backed by a handful of those vassal states that had previously owed allegiance to Attila. In turn, a few of those vassal states moved to assert their independence. One of the first to peel away was the Gepids under their king Ardaric. Attila's oldest son, Ellac, appealed to his brothers for help in trying to force the Gepids back into subservience, but they refused to assist him. In response Ellac reached out to Aetius.

Ellac offered to marry his eleven-year-old daughter to Aetius's fourteen-year-old son, Gaudentius, as a way of cementing an alliance with Rome and building a powerful coalition to oppose his rivals. At first, Aetius was inclined to say it couldn't happen, given that Gaudentius was to marry Placidia. But when the Emperor declared the wedding off, Aetius let it be known he might consider Ellac's offer. The threat was implicit. If Placidius and Maximus refused to endorse the marriage of Gaudentius and Placidia, Aeitus would become related through marriage to the Huns and seal a new alliance with Rome's most daunting enemy.

Placidius didn't even put up a fight. He told Aetius to do whatever he wanted and not to bother him about it anymore. Maximus objected. He warned the Emperor that Aetius's threat was a naked attempt to install Gaudentius in the line of succession.

"Once Gaudentius is married to your daughter, you're as good as dead," he told Placidius. "Are you going to hand Aetius the sword to slay you with?"

Thirteen-year-old Placidia was present at this discussion of her future spouse and bristled at Maximus's presumption.

"Who are you to tell my father what to think about Gaudentius's intentions? Does it not occur to you that Gaudentius may have another reason for wanting to marry me, like affection? You don't know him. He wouldn't risk alienating my love for him by hurting my father. What kind of cold blooded creature are you to think that every act is motivated by a lust for power? Shame on you, Petronius Maximus."

Maximus was unaccustomed to receiving a tongue lashing from a thirteen-year-old girl. He spluttered for an answer. Not a few of those present hid guilty smiles behind their hands. Even Placidius roused himself from his half-drunken state to grin.

Maximus reddened but held his temper.

Placidia glared, chin raised, arms folded.

"I'm sorry, Princess" Maximus said. "I had not meant to offend. I was just saying—"

Placidia cut him off. "I will marry Gaudentius," she said. "That's my choice. My father has endorsed it. Aetius has given his consent. Gaudentius is willing. That's all there is to it. There will be no further discussion."

Maximus looked helplessly at the Emperor who looked away.

Placidia drew herself up and looked down her nose at Maximus. It was all I could do to keep from applauding. I had a new ally in the palace, and it was my adolescent daughter.

The date was set for autumn. But before the wedding could happen other events interceded. In mid-summer Pulcheria died. Aetius was dispatched to Constantinople to attend the funeral. With the Augusta's passing, Marcian ruled the east singlehandedly, and the link to the House of Theodosius was broken and would never be restored. As a result, family ties no longer bound us to Constantinople, which meant the opportunity to reunite the Empire had passed. Like a mirage, our fondest dream vanished. The world we had known would continue on into the future, a world with two separate Romes, one in the east and one in the west, each following two different and often irreconcilable paths.

* * *

The death of my aunt left me cold. Pulcheria, a woman I had once honored and admired, had dwindled in my estimation until she had winked out like a wick collapsed in a lamp. From that fateful day in Antioch when she had revealed her true colors not a single word of correspondence had passed between us even though we held the same position in two different halves of the empire. We were two separate Augustas, cold and distant.

Her resentment toward me for rejecting celibacy and taking my mother's part was bottomless. She was a woman who knew how to hold a grudge. She also knew how to buy influence and had instructed that upon her death all her wealth be given to the Church. As a consequence, the Eastern Church thrived. Structural additions were commissioned; lavish new ornamentation added. The high clergy traveled around in litters trimmed with gold and dressed in richly embroidered silks dripping with jewelry. Shortly after her death Pulcheria was declared a saint. She had used her fortune to purchase her reputation in perpetuity. Even in death she was conniving.

In Constantinople Aetius stood in for the rest of us at her funeral. By all accounts, his meeting with Marcian had been stiff but cordial. Although both were military men, Aetius and Marcian served in different halves of the empire with vastly different military ranks. Before Marcian became Emperor, he was a little known officer of the Domesticus[16] whose highest accomplishment was as General Aspar's most trusted deputy. Aetius, on the other hand, had been the West's most senior general for years. Clearly, Aetius felt himself superior, notwithstanding the fact that Marcian was Emperor. Perhaps it was the opportunity to underscore his supremacy in a showcase setting like Constantinople that led him to accept the offer from Maximus to represent us at the funeral.

Certainly, it was an inopportune time for Aetius to be away. He had just pressed the Emperor into consenting to a marriage he didn't want, and he was leaving before the wedding had taken place. It struck me as reckless for a man who, time and again, had demonstrated his flawless political acuity.

---

16  A servant in a noble house or a high ranking military position. After service to the Emperor, the Domestici often became leaders themselves, sometimes commanding their own regiment of legionaries in the military.

Not surprisingly as soon as he was gone the wedding was postponed. The reason given was that the Emperor had fallen ill, a blatant lie. Its only relation to the truth was the Emperor's continuing downward spiral into drunkenness and infidelity. Rumors abounded of multiple assignations with women of all sorts, some consensual, some coerced. I did my best to protect my daughters from the chatter, but they were in their teens now and could not be shielded from the gossip.

Eudocia seemed resigned to her father's behavior. He had disappointed her so many times over the years, she had become hardened to it. Her wedding to Huneric, which was to have taken place the previous autumn, had been postponed twice. But she didn't complain. It was a part of her nature to endure. She had always been a calm, even-tempered, and thoughtful person, not unlike her great-grandfather who had been a philosopher.

Placidia, on the other hand, was fiery and temperamental. When she heard her own wedding was postponed, she threw a fit. She berated her father and those who counseled him, especially Maximus. When she was finished and sat exhausted by her tirade, breathing heavily through flaring nostrils, and clutching her fists, I saw a sudden change come over her. Her eyes took on a different cast. She was thinking—hard. Her mental wheels were turning as she considered her options. I had seen that look before in Galla's eyes and it frightened me.

I tried to remain rational. With Aetius away in Constantinople, I dared not make a move. Even when he returned to the West, he would not stop at Ravenna but go directly to his headquarters in Arelate. I was on shaky ground and any attempt to assert my authority could mean my death. My best option was to lay low and make myself as inconspicuous as possible. So, for the next several months from late summer until the following spring, I faded into the background as Maximus strengthened his hold over the Emperor. I looked on helplessly as he strove to erode the Emperor's moral foundation, turning him into a confused, pathetic degenerate obsessed by his appetites and incapable of making decisions for himself.

But Maximus was creating a monster, and he was about to lose control of it. Before long it would cost him dearly.

# Chapter 23
May-August, The Year AD 454

It began, strangely enough, with the Huns. More accurately, it started with the Gepids who had rebelled against the Huns and gathered under their banner likeminded former vassals like the Rugi, the Suebi, and a large group of Goths unaffiliated with the Goths of Aquitaine. This second Gothic group comprised of those who had remained behind when their brethren had crossed the Danube into the Empire seventy-five years before, were known as the Eastern Goths, or Ostrogroths. The Goths who had migrated West and settled in Aquitaine were known as the Western Goths, or Visigoths. In the uprising of the vassal tribes, the Ostrogoths proved worthy allies. Together with the other tribes they successfully threw off the Hunnic yoke and killed Ellac, Attila's oldest son. In so doing, they removed the threat of a marriage between Ellac's daughter and Aetius's boy Gaudentius.

In an instant, Aetius's stranglehold on the succession was broken. Without the threat of an alliance with the Huns to compel the marriage of Placidia and Gaudentius, the wedding was called off permanently. Furious, Placidia went to her father and demanded it be restored. Her father consulted Maximus who calmly informed Placidia that her request would be taken under advisement then left the room before she could castigate him.

Placidia shook her father. She shouted in his face and accused him of being a tool in the hands of Maximus. His head lolled around on his shoulders, and he smiled in a drunken stupor. With a cry of frustration, she stormed out.

Aetius was in Servitium inspecting the troops when news reached him of Ellac's death – and the cancelled wedding. His response was silence. Earlier he had sent dispatches from Constantinople reporting on a mutual security pact he had reached with Marcian—without input from Ravenna. It was an agreement to support each other in the event of war. There was one proviso. The leadership in Ravenna had to be stable enough for the East to commit its resources. Aetius had signed the pact and sent a final dispatch from Constantinople before riding west. It was the last official correspondence anyone had received from him before news broke of Ellac's death. His silence after that made everyone in Ravenna on edge.

Message after message was sent from the palace demanding to know his army's disposition and when it could be expected to return, but there was no answer. Maximus railed at the Emperor and demanded Aetius's immediate arrest. At first Placidius agreed but reversed himself at the last minute. He feared Aetius's reaction. Maximus dropped all pretense of deference and ridiculed the Emperor for his cowardice in front of the whole court. Had it been any other crowned head, such insolence would have cost Maximus his life, but Placidius brushed it off with a laugh. Only later did it come to light that the Emperor was plotting his revenge by a more devious method.

All through this difficult time, the Emperor and his chief advisor remained avid followers of the chariot races, often attending events together. As members of the ruling class, they both backed the blues, the racing faction most aligned with the aristocracy, but Maximus often agreed to support the greens for purposes of wagering. It must have been hard for him for it required him to wager against the faction he loved most. Indeed, he held part ownership in the blues. Still, Maximus knew the value of a long-term investment. In cultivating the comradeship of the Emperor, he was speculating on a much richer return. As a result, Maximus lost a good deal of money to the Emperor, so much, in fact, it was presumed Maximus was deliberately losing to curry the Emperor's favor.

At one outing in the week following Maximus's intemperate outburst in the council chamber, his losses were so great he lacked the funds to settle with the Emperor on the spot. Thinking the Emperor would allow him to pay up later, he was surprised when Placidius, in a moment of sober lucidity, demanded a surety against the debt. Maximus asked him what would suffice. The Emperor pointed to Maximus's wedding ring.

I was present at this exchange having been called upon in my role as an imperial ornament to provide a show of domestic accord to a populace riven with rumors of the Emperor's infidelities. Also present on this occasion was Agnus who I had not spoken to since our encounter in the pearl shop six years earlier, and who I now regarded as little more than a doormat for Pertonius's ambitions. She looked haggard and worn. Between us was a distance attributable not only to her discomfort with me but also to my distaste for all she represented. We exchanged pleasantries and barely spoke the entire day.

Agnus had stepped away for a moment when Maximus asked for the wedding ring. She wasn't there to see the look of incredulity on her husband's face nor Placidius's self-satisfied grin as he pocketed the jewelry. But she did hear Placidius's drunken boasting when she returned and sat passively by with a stupid grin on her face as he rattled on about how he done what no other man had been able to do, which was to so empty Maximus's purse that he had been compelled to hand over things he held dear. Maximus gave his wife a pained look, but at no time did he explain to her what he had surrendered to the Emperor, nor did she, in her role as dutiful, subservient wife, ask. Her ignorance was about to cost her.

* * *

What happened next was related to me weeks later by an Agnus so shaken and traumatized by events that she spoke in a flat voice while staring blankly into the middle distance like someone who had witnessed a catastrophe.

The night after the races she was summoned to the palace by Maximus. It was late and more than a little suspicious. Maximus had never summoned her to the palace at such a late hour before. When she asked the messenger if he was quite certain the summons had come from her husband, he answered by showing her the very ring she had given Maximus on their wedding day. So, she went.

When she arrived, she was directed not to Maximus's offices, but to the apartments of the Emperor. Thinking Maximus was enjoying a late night repast with the Emperor, she followed the instructions. But upon entering the room, she found herself alone with the Emperor. He was reclining on a couch with a pitcher of wine and two goblets. She heard the door close behind her…

…and lock.

On catching sight of her, Placidius smiled and beckoned her forward.

She asked where Maximus was.

"He cannot be with us," Placidius said. "He has other matters to attend to."

"So late?"

"Oh, you know how he is," Placidius said. "He insists on attending to every detail. You would think he intends to run the Empire all by himself. He forgets what's most valuable—what's most precious and dear. Come here. Join me in a drink."

She hung back, a wary look in her eyes.

"Don't be afraid," he said. "I won't hurt you." He got up and took her by the hand. He drew her to the couch. "Have some wine," he said. He poured a draught and pressed the goblet into her hand.

She took a tentative sip and eyed him over the rim of the cup. "Why did you summon me, if I may ask, Your Excellency?"

He smiled. "I have something I want from you." He hesitated for a moment. "If I am to be honest, I have been meaning to ask you this for a long time." He reached out and took her by the hand. "Divorce Maximus. Be my wife."

Agnus recoiled as if she had been slapped. She tried to pull her hand away, but he held it tight. "But, Imperator," she said, "it's impossible. You're married to another."

He laughed. "You needn't trouble yourself with that. Licinia and I are estranged. For all intents and purposes, we are divorced. I have only kept her around for the children who are practically grown now. I have no further use for her. It will be a simple matter to put her aside."

"But what about the Church? The Church frowns on divorce."

"You needn't trouble yourself with that. Pope Leo is a reasonable man. He will endorse whatever the civil authority grants me. Besides, he knows there will be something in it for him."

Again she tried to jerk her hand away, but to no avail.

He leaned in close. "I'm in love with you," he said. "I've never wanted anything so much in my life."

"Please," she said. "Let me go. This is most unseemly. I'm married to Maximus, and he will never forsake me."

"Ah, so that's your objection. Fair enough. But tell me, if Maximus were to divorce you, would you marry me and rule the Empire by my side?"

"He will never divorce me. He adores me."

Now he had her by the elbow. "Humor me. Answer the question."

There was a trace of ugliness in his voice. To make him relent she said, "You are the Emperor. I must do whatever you command of me. But Maximus will never divorce me."

It was the wrong answer. He smiled, a wolf eying a lamb. "I command you!"

He lunged at her, grabbing her by the waist and pulling her to him. She spilled her wine. She wedged her forearm against his chest and tried to wiggle free. Her voice came out in a breathless gasp. "I can't!"

"You must," he said. "You belong to me now. I won you in a bet."

The words struck a chill into her heart.

"I summoned you here with this ring," he said. "My having it is no accident. Maximus paid me with it because he wants you to become the Augusta. He wants you to become the most powerful woman in Rome. He has given you wealth, yes. But I can give you power. He wants you to have it. It's the greatest gift he can give you."

The scenario was depressing in its plausibility. Maximus had always said he wanted her to have everything and would stop at nothing to get it. It was part of the promise he had made to her when he had lured her away from his son, when he stole her from Junius and made her his own. She began to weep.

Placidius loosened his grasp. "Don't be sad," he said. "Be happy! It's a good thing! It's every woman's dream to become Augusta."

"It didn't work out so well for Licinia," she muttered under her breath.

"What did you say?" There was an edge in his voice.

"I want to go home," she said. "Can I go home?"

He took her by the shoulders. "Look at me."

When her head came up, she was meek and afraid.

"I have always loved you," he said. "From the first time I saw you I thought you were the most exquisite thing I had ever laid eyes on, better than silver or gold, better than jewels."

Her eyes brimmed with tears.

"Why are you crying? You should be overjoyed."

"I want to go home."

He cursed under his breath, took half a dozen steps in a small circle, and then dropped to one knee and took her by the hands.

"You're torturing me. I cannot endure it. Tell me what you want, Agnus. Anything. You shall have it."

"I want to go home."

He walked across the room and leaned his forehead against the opposite wall. He let go a long, ragged sigh.

She rose and made her way with stiff and tentative steps to the door. She turned the latch. It was locked. She tugged at it and began to sob.

He never took his head from the wall. His voice carried all the warmth of a chill winter wind.

"Take off your clothes."

Her stomach sank. Her mouth went dry.

"Now!"

The floor beneath her feet appeared to tilt and shift. She staggered to one side and collapsed. Her flailing arms overturned a small table. An ornamental urn crashed to the floor.

He was on her in an instant. He seized her wrists and pinned her down. She fought and kicked. He straddled her. She bucked and squirmed. He tore away the top of her gown and fell on her nakedness like a slobbering beast. She redoubled her efforts to throw him off, which only seemed to goad him on. He ripped away her clothes, pulled up his tunic and drove himself into her. She screamed. He pounded away at her, tearing her with his repeated thrusts, grunting and snarling like a beast.

When it was over, he collapsed on top of her slick with sweat.

A moment later he got up, went to the door, and knocked thrice in rapid succession. He said something to the guard who opened it. Moments later, the soldier handed the Emperor a robe. Placidius crossed the room and tried to place it over Agnus's naked body. She whimpered and scrabbled away.

"There, there," he said with a guilty smile. "I'm only trying to help you."

She stared at him with the terrified look of a cornered animal.

He shrugged. "All right. Be like that." He threw the robe at her then drained the wine from his goblet. He wiped the back of his hand across his mouth without regard to the purple stain it left on his sleeve.

"I really do love you," he said.

He left her there – the remains of a shattered woman amid the remains of a broken vase.

✱ ✱ ✱

Agnus told me this in a daze, hollow-eyed and distant. And there was more.

That night she went home to Maximus and confronted him. She demanded to know if he had sold her like a whore. It was out of character for her to shout at him. Her words sounded non-sensical and distraught. He thought she had gone mad and called the guards to restrain her. The touch of their hands made her frantic. She thrashed and screamed, which only reinforced his suspicions about her mental state, so he ordered her taken away and confined to her room.

It was there, much later, after she had settled down, that he was able to approach her. In a hollow tone she told him what had happened.

He didn't react. He was cold and distant. To her, his behavior confirmed everything. Maximus left the room without a word. She spiraled deeper into despair.

When Agnus didn't appear at dinner the next day, Olybrius inquired about her. Maximus gave a terse, one word reply and refused to discuss it further. Questioning the servants, Olybrius learned about the scene between Agnus and Maximus. Concerned, he went to see her. She was in a stupefied state, vacant and uncommunicative. She faced him when he spoke but looked through him with the unfocused stare of insanity. Alarmed, he went and got Junius.

Junius suspected his father of having taken some gross liberty with her, some awful depravity that had broken her spirit. He was angry and wanted to confront Maximus, but Olybrius held him back. There was no reason to jump to conclusions, Olybrius said. They needed to find out what had happened. He suggested they find someone who could get through to Agnus, someone who would not frighten her, a woman, a friend. Naturally, Junius thought of me.

It was not ideal. Not only was there a chill between us, but I was also the wife of the man who had attacked her. Of course, I didn't know anything of the incident at the time. At the beginning I figured Junius was right; I assumed Maximus was responsible. We both knew him to be capable of terrible cruelty, so I agreed to meet with my former friend and try to draw her out. I succeeded only too well.

What she told me was deeply disturbing, not because I considered Placidius incapable of such barbarity, but because of the cold-hearted way he set about to avenge himself against Maximus. It was so self-centered it was monstrous.

I should have been more empathetic toward Agnus. I should have shared with her my own experience. I should have reassured her that the worst would pass, and a sense of purpose would ease her pain, but I did none of those things. I don't know why. Maybe I was still angry at her for being so naïve, so willfully ignorant, refusing to see things as they were, stubbornly denying the truth and clinging to lies. I only know that I felt a coldness toward her, which made empathy difficult. I told her to get some rest and promised to see her later.

I never did.

Instead, I demanded an audience with Placidius. He refused. I sent him a note telling him I knew what had happened and warning him that Maximus knew as well. My message never reached him. Maximus approached me as I was looking through my correspondence and dropped the crumpled paper in my lap. He whispered in my ear.

"Mind your own business."

He put his hand on my shoulder and left it there for a moment.

I didn't know what to do. I was without allies. I couldn't write to Aetius. Any message would be intercepted. I couldn't go to him either. My absence would be branded an abduction and the whole countryside would be called out to find me and bring me back. I thought about involving my daughters, but it was too much at their young ages to entangle them in such sordid affairs. Besides, what could they do? They were as trapped as I was.

Then, an opportunity.

Avitus, the retired general who had helped us in Aurelianum was in Rome to report the death of Thorismund, the young Gothic king who had been so instrumental in the defeat of the Huns. His death was unexpected; foul play was suspected. Thorismund had been succeeded by his younger brother, Theodoric, who was rumored to have slain his older sibling when Thorismund decided to break his alliance with Rome over suspicions that the Goths had been exploited by the Empire in the battle against the Huns. Avitus wanted to assure us that Rome still had a friend in the Goths and their new king, young Theodoric II.

Maximus had no idea I knew Avitus personally and made no attempt to keep us apart. Consequently, when I saw Avitus coming out of a meeting, I pulled him aside to thank him again for the great contribution he had made to our defense in Aurelianum, but also to whisper in his ear that the Emperor was in danger. He evinced surprise. He was of the opinion the Emperor was in good hands. I told him nothing could be further from the truth. I told him Maximus and his other co-conspirators were plotting to assassinate the Emperor. I had to get a message through to Aetius. Would he take it?

Avitus looked me up and down with a wry, half smile and said, "How is it that every time I see you you've gotten yourself into a fix?"

"This is serious," I said. "Will you take the message?"

He thought it over for a moment and shrugged. "Sure," he said. "Give it to me."

I handed it over.

Two days later there was a knock at my door. It was Heraclius. He was holding the message in his hand. "Maximus requests an audience with the Augusta on a matter of state security," he said. "Will you attend?"

What choice did I have? I answered yes.

"Good girl," he said with a smirk.

Then he reached out and stroked my head.

* * *

Maximus was waiting for me in the audience chamber. He sat on the throne as if testing it for fit. On seeing me, he dismissed Heraclius, then shifted forward. He placed his forearms on his thighs and studied his hands.

"You are an obstinate creature, aren't you?"

I didn't dignify that with a response.

He shook his head and sighed. "I don't know what to do with you. I really don't. I tried being reasonable. I tried being your friend, but you refused. I simply expected you to keep your place and not interfere. Even then, I expected too much. Please, can you tell me what to do because I'm at a loss?"

It wasn't really a question. He rambled on.

"I thought maybe you were upset over that unpleasantness between us in the garden of the hospitia. I don't mind telling you that, taken altogether, I think I got the worst of it. I mean, you hit me with a statue. Do you realize you could've killed me? At any rate, I figured maybe you were shaken up about what happened, maybe it had disordered your senses. But you were perfectly sensible when it came to Junius. You were quite rational with him, very open and forthcoming, one might even say persuasive, so you had *not* been traumatized. On the contrary, you were quite resilient by all accounts, rallying the citizenry at Aurelianum to repel the Huns. I mean, really, this is not the behavior of someone who is distraught. If anything, it appears my failed attempt to seduce you had a salutary effect. It seems to have motivated you."

"I suppose you want me to thank you for what you did."

He threw up his hands. "Such hostility! You see? That's what I'm talking about. You are bound and determined to make me your enemy. Tell me, Licinia, what must I do to win you over?"

"I want you to leave my husband alone."

He laughed. "If I left Placidius alone, he would be dead within a month. You know that as well as I do. He is too debased and vulnerable to rule without assistance."

"Yes, and you're the one who made him that way."

He chuckled. "Oh, I see. It's all my fault. And what about you? Where were you when he was seeking gratification outside the bounds of marriage? You are his wife. You should have been in his bed giving him what he needed, keeping him satisfied. Instead, you were off in Aurelianum playing house with my son, living with him, sleeping with him, becoming pregnant by him. Don't give me that look. Do you think Junius can keep a secret from me? Let's stop playing games. We both know the truth. Placidius's days are numbered. Someone must succeed him, and you have failed to give him an heir. So, who will it be? The eunuch Heraclius?"

"I detest you."

"Be that as it may, the world is full of people like me, people who refuse to stand idly by while a thousand years of greatness are squandered by a lifetime of selfishness and stupidity. I'm not about to allow Placidius to destroy the Empire by letting him rule indiscriminately without a firm hand to guide him."

"Who chose you to be his keeper?"

"He did."

"But he is not competent to make sound decisions. Didn't you just say so yourself? Correct me if I'm wrong, but I detect a flaw in your logic, Petronius Maximus."

He shook his head. "You think you're clever, Licinia, but you're playing a dangerous game with me. I warn you I won't stand for your insolence. And what happened to Agnus is none of your business. Stay out of it."

"Your wife was attacked by my husband. It would be un-natural for you not to want revenge. If anything, your restraint bespeaks a certain coldness on your part, an insensitivity to Agnus's suffering in an effort to remain inscrutable. But it won't last. I'm not stupid. I know that. You will have your revenge, Maximus, and when you do, others could get hurt as well. Which is why I have to take precautions. I have to think about my daughters. I have to protect them, which is why I reached out to Aetius."

"Don't insult my intelligence, Licinia. I know why you reached out to Aetius. You are no more confident in your husband's ability to rule than I am. It's just that you prefer someone else to control him."

"I prefer someone who doesn't intend to kill him."

"So, he should be allowed to go on ruling indefinitely? Don't be ridiculous. Rome can't survive much more of him. The reign of Valentinian III has already gone on far too long."

"You and I see things differently. From where I sit, things could have turned out much worse than they did. With Aetius's help, Placidius has survived invasions by the Huns and the Vandals. In spite of everything, the Empire remains mostly intact. I doubt you could have done better."

Maximus smiled. "Oh, Licinia your loyalty is something special, and this from a woman who has been banished from his presence, a woman who has been made to stand by and watch as he commits multiple adulteries, a woman who has been so eclipsed in his estimation by a mere eunuch that she has become a public embarrassment. Apparently, no amount of abuse or humiliation is enough to make you surrender your allegiance to this wastrel. But should you ever change your mind, I'll have a place for you in my new administration. You're not easy to get along with, granted, but you do have spunk, and I like that."

I scoffed. "You will have to excuse me if I decline your offer. As you point out, I'm just about at my limits when it comes to accommodating monsters."

He glowered at me. "Don't tempt me, Licinia. You're not negotiating from a strong position. Your attempt to conspire against the Emperor with Aetius is an act of treason. I could have you imprisoned for that."

I put my hands on my hips. "Are you threatening me?"

"I'm warning you."

"And I'm warning you, Maximus. I'm still the Augusta of Rome. You may think me weak and ineffectual, but if you try to hurt me or my children, I'll make you answer for it."

We glared at each other for a long moment. Then there was a knock at the door. It was a messenger with urgent news.

"What is it?" Maximus asked.

"It's about your wife," the messenger said.

Maximus took the message and read it. His face went ashen.

Agnus was dead—by her own hand.

# Chapter 24
September, The Year 454 – March, The Year 455

Agnus's death hit me hard; I considered myself responsible. God knows, I could have done more to relieve her suffering. I could have put aside my petty animosities and acted as a friend. My lack of empathy for her—especially considering that I had been through something similar—was inexcusable. What had come over me? What kind of person had I become?

I took the amulet off and put it away. I don't know what I was expecting when I did it; I felt no different. Within a few days, the anxiety I had been feeling over Agnus's death broadened and deepened. It resolved itself into a general sense of foreboding, a feeling that was not helped by the march of events.

In September, out of the blue, Aetius responded to the government's repeated requests to report his disposition. He had returned to Servitium after Constantinople and had remained there to keep an eye on things. The fracturing of the Hun coalition was causing instability across the region. Western Pannonia was particularly vulnerable. He was there now to shore up its defenses. His troops were working along-side the Eastern Roman army, a joint enterprise approved by Emperor Marcian. They were working together to make both halves of the Empire safe from yet another barbarian invasion.

Maximus wrote a testy response. He reminded Aetius of his required allegiance to the West, not to the East, and that his failure to respond to repeated requests to report his disposition could be interpreted as insubordination. Maximus ordered Aetius to return to Ravenna at once. Aetius wrote back to say he was on his way.

On hearing this I was overcome with a dreadful premonition. Maximus despised Aetius. Should Aetius try to talk down to him as he had to Placidius all these years, the consequences could be disastrous. The foreboding robbed me of sleep. I could not get the thought out of my head, and it was made worse by a growing sense of melancholy. I fought back tears, and occasionally surrendered to wretched bouts of weeping. Eudocia came upon me during one of these occasions and expressed alarm. She had never seen me so pitiful. She wanted me to call a physician. I told her it was nothing a physician could cure; it was a sickness of the soul. Accordingly, we went to the chapel.

I threw myself into my devotions. I begged God to forgive me. I promised to fast and do penance. Eudocia stood behind me and watched my supplications. When she suggested I had prayed enough and ought to come away, I resisted. Concerned, she went out and came back with a priest, a man Pope Leo had recommended. They stood in the shadows of the narthex and watched me. I was bent over on my knees, beating my head on the stone floor. My brow was swollen and red; my nose was bleeding. The priest crossed silently to the side aisle and returned with a flagellum. He handed it to me.

Eudocia was incredulous. "What are you doing?" He ignored her.

I considered the implement in my hands. It was two feet long with a thick woven handle and twelve leather thongs tipped with lead. I looked up at the priest. He nodded. Knowing what was expected, I began to lash myself, mildly at first, and then with increasing vigor. Eudocia turned away.

The thongs ripped through the fabric of my garment and bit my flesh. Before long, my tunic hung in tatters from my shoulders. The slap of leather on flesh echoed through the chamber. Blood and bits of tissue leapt from the lacerations as the whip slashed my skin. I wept and wept. The priest stood over me, a hungry look in his eyes.

Then everything shifted. A hand shot out and stopped the whip in mid-stroke. The flagellum was twisted out of my hand and held beyond my reach.

"No, Mother! Stop!"

It was Placidia. She turned on Eudocia.

"Why are you permitting this!" She reproached her sister with eyes of fire. Then she whirled on the priest. "You son of a bitch. Turn around."

The priest was speechless. Here was something new. A congregant refusing his order, a teenager girl who had appeared out of nowhere and was bearing down on him with daunting fury. He began to stammer out his answer, but she raised the whip.

"Turn around now! I'm not going to say it again."

He did as she said.

"Down on your knees."

He sank to his knees.

"Lift up your shirt."

He hesitated.

The whip whistled through the air and bit off a piece of his ear. He doubled over in pain.

"Do it now!"

He pulled up his shirt. His pimpled back was obscene in its milky pallor. She moved in front of him and handed him the whip. He glared up at her. She was not intimidated.

"Now it's time for *your* penance," she said. "Go ahead. Show us how it's done."

It was all too much for Eudocia. "Placidia, please stop."

Placidia ignored her. She took a step closer to the priest and slapped him across the face. "Do it!"

The priest reluctantly lashed himself.

"Harder!"

He lashed himself again, this time with a little more ardor.

"Is that all you can muster?" Placidia taunted. "You must not be very repentant."

Eudocia was crying. I was strangely detached, as if in a dream.

Placidia spit on the floor. "Coward," she said.

She took me by the arm and helped me to my feet. She led me out of the chapel to my rooms. Eudocia trailed behind us. They helped me into bed and stood beside me as I dozed off, which was very fast.

When I awoke sometime later, they were gone, and I was alone. Suddenly the recollection of what had happened flooded over me, and my emotions began to careen wildly.

I laughed, then cried hysterically. A servant peeked in at the door, and I waved her forward. When I was able to get control of myself, I asked her to bring me my lyre. She did so immediately, and I sat up in bed and plucked the strings as I looked past my outstretched feet to the chest at the end of my bed where the amulet rested.

* * *

When Aetius returned to Ravenna, I was ordered to attend the audience that would receive him. I was wary. A request for my attendance was rare these days. Only when the Emperor's handlers wanted to impress a foreign dignitary with the Emperor's domestic stability did they bother to include me. This directive hinted at something different: a point to be made, perhaps, or a punishment. As I sat down next to Placidius I was anxious. My hands were trembling. He was drunk as usual. He leaned over and patted my knee.

"This should be fun," he said.

Maximus stood behind us, his hand resting on the Emperor's throne. Heraclius stood to one side, his high conical cap tipped slightly back on his head, his leg thrust forward cockily. He seemed to be concealing something in his robes.

Aetius came in flanked by his guards. He stopped and stood dead center in the middle of the colorful mosaic that reached from wall to wall, an image of the good shepherd surrounded by his flock. The Emperor ordered the guards to step out. The guards looked to Aetius for confirmation. He nodded his approval, and they withdrew.

"They're very obedient," the Emperor observed. "They've been instructed in deference—at least as far as it involves you." He smiled idiotically as if he had made a clever point. Aetius did not smile back.

"Come forward," Maximus said. He beckoned with a cordial hand. "Let's have a look at you. It's been a long time since we've seen you. Longer than we would have liked."

Aetius stepped forward as self-possessed as ever. He was dressed in ceremonial garb, a thigh-length embroidered tunic belted at the waist, trousers and boots, and a cape slung over his shoulder. He held his helmet under one arm. He had no weapon. He stood before the company, looking up at the Emperor, his face devoid of expression. For a man who had always seemed so ageless, he looked much older now. Perhaps it was the way the light fell on him, narrow shafts of light from the high clerestory windows. His face seemed drawn. His lips, which had always been thin, were almost non-existent. He had deep lines at the corners of his eyes. His hair was thinning. There was about him an uncharacteristic weariness. And why wouldn't there be?

He had spent the better part of the last twenty years saving Placidius from one crisis after another only to be accused of treachery and threatened with arrest. The cancellation of the wedding was the last straw. He was sixty-four-years-old. Letters between himself and Gaudentius, which came to light later, communicated his longing to retire. Whatever dreams he had once had of resurrecting the Empire were behind him now, the optimism of his youth had vanished, the aspirations he had shared with Galla of restoring Rome to its former glory were a distant memory. He was done.

"I was trying to protect you," he said.

Placidius said, "I wrote asking for your disposition and you ignored me. That's not the way a Master of Soldiers should treat his Emperor."

"Our communication lines were disrupted. Gepid agents were working in our rear. My messages were intercepted."

"He's lying," Maximus said.

"I'm telling the truth," Aetius said.

The Emperor called for more wine. A servant brought him a cup. He swept it back in one gulp. Then he called for another.

Aetius waited.

"The Augusta has been working feverishly to contact you," the Emperor said. "Do you realize that? Apparently, she has something to tell you."

Aetius looked at me, and then back at the Emperor. "I don't know what you're talking about."

"Don't lie," The Emperor said. "Tell the truth. For once in your life, tell the truth, Flavius Aetius."

Aetius looked directly at the Emperor. "I've been trying to protect you."

Suddenly Placidius vaulted from his throne and drew his sword. "Liar!" He dropped to the floor and landed in a crouch. For a moment it seemed he might remain there, crouched, waiting, but then he flung himself forward and stabbed Aetius with a single well-placed thrust to the gut.

Aetius doubled over with a woof.

Heraclius came up behind the Master of Soldiers and stabbed him in the back.

Aetius collapsed to his knees.

My hands flew to my mouth.

Heraclius stabbed him again, driving the knife into his neck.

Aetius toppled over. Blood fountained up splattering the brightly colored silks and high conical cap of the snarling eunuch.

Placidius was wild-eyed and exhilarated. "There!" he cried. "That's what you get! That's what your arrogance has bought you!" He turned to Heraclius and nodded.

Heraclius bent over and stabbed Aetius several more times, short, chopping blows to the head and neck like a man butchering an animal.

I screamed.

Maximus had not moved. He was standing behind the throne with a satisfied expression, his hand resting on the back rest. The others in the room, the counselors, guards, and dignitaries had gone white.

Placidius raised his sword and gave a whoop. He capered from foot to foot, waving the sword over his head.

"He's dead! I killed him! I killed him!"

Heraclius faded back and resumed his place among the others.

Maximus came forward and clapped the Emperor on the back "Brave work, Your Excellency. This is a great day for Rome."

Placidius threw back his head and laughed. He turned to his counselors. "Did you see that? I killed him. I killed the Master of Soldiers."

They nodded grimly.

Then he turned to me. "Now who's the hero? Now who's the champion?"

I looked at him in horror.

He danced around in unrestrained delight.

Aetius's body lay face down in a pool of his own blood. The blood spread out onto the surrounding mosaic, finding its way into the grout joints, forming tiny rivulets that followed the shapes of the tiles.

Again, Placidius turned to his counselors. "I've done well, haven't I? Speak the truth, I've done well." Even now, the first hints of misgivings were beginning to creep up on him, but he tried to quash them with more rejoicing, which seemed increasingly forced.

I felt sick to my stomach. I broke out in a cold sweat. More than anything I wanted to get out of there.

Then there was a voice behind me. One of the counselors leaned in close. His lips practically touched the helix of my ear. He pronounced his words very carefully. He said, "Whether well or not, I cannot say. But he has cut off his right hand with his left."

It was true. From that day forward Placidius's days were numbered.

* * *

News of Aetius's murder was met with stunned silence. If Placidius had been hoping for congratulations, he was sadly disappointed. The Senate said nothing. The Church said nothing. The public muttered behind his back, calling him a drunkard and a fool. The army was a concern. Whether or not they would rise up and revolt was an open question. Had one of the barbarian tribes chosen to attack at that moment, the

Empire would have collapsed like shepherd's hut in the wind. As it was, the Vandals seized Melita, a brazen violation of a treaty they had honored for more than a decade. The provocation went unanswered. All was hesitancy and confusion. No one knew what to do next.

Fortunately, the army did not revolt. Placidius sent a gratuity to the new commander in Servitium, Majorian, the selfsame Majorian who had been proposed as a spouse for Placidia, and who had now been restored and promoted by the Emperor. Majorian understood the gratuity for what it was—a bribe to keep the peace—and it worked. The army was kept in check although Majorian's request to be promoted to the rank of master of soldiers was rejected. A replacement for Aetius was not immediately chosen.

The money sent to Majorian was Heraclius's idea. Maximus was not consulted. When he got wind of it, he was indignant. He upbraided the Emperor, accusing him of missing the point of getting rid of Aetius, which was to stop the drain on the treasury the army represented. If they were going to reestablish the precedent of buying the army's restraint, the whole exercise had been pointless. Then Maximus directed his anger at Heraclius. He chastised him in front of the whole court. As always, the eunuch took the tongue lashing stoically, but his stone-faced visage concealed a viperous malevolence I knew only too well. Aetius's killers were already turning on each other. Far from pleasing me, it filled me with foreboding.

In the aftermath of Aetius's death I was afflicted by a near constant dread. With Aetius out of the picture, the last hope of achieving long-term stability was gone. Given Maximus's antipathy toward the Emperor, and Placidius's vulnerability, the Emperor's assassination seemed imminent, but day after day, week after week, things went on as usual. It was like the constant drip of water through a crack in a dam. Sooner or later, the dam was going to burst, and when it did, everything was going to be swept before it.

My daughters saw what my constant fretting was doing to me. I was pale and drawn. I had begun biting my nails. I had developed a strange obsession with the number 17, whose numerals (XVII), when rearranged, spelled out the Latin word VIXI: "Life is over." I began to see the number everywhere: on mileposts, on stable doors, in the handbills posted on the public boards.

Eudocia suggested I get away from Ravenna and go out to the country, but Maximus forbade it. He had made me a witness to Aetius's killing for a reason. He was trying to break my resistance, to cow me and make me obedient. His refusal to let me leave the city was part of his plan and he was succeeding. This brute now held my life in the palm of his hand, and I lacked the will to oppose him.

Placidia was not so meek. She stormed into his office and rebuked him for his treatment of me. He listened to her with an amused expression, nodding as she ranted. When she finished, he jutted out his lower lip and pretended to contemplate her argument.

"Very well," he said, "your mother may go. But you, young lady, must remain in Ravenna. I have plans for you, wedding plans."

"I'm going to marry Gaudentius," she said, "and that's all there is to it." She folded her arms and tossed her hair.

He laughed. "My, my, Placidia, you are spirited. You're just like your mother. Sadly, your mother's defiance has brought her nothing but grief. She needed a strong hand to guide her, and she never got it. Now look at her. She's miserable. I would hate to see the same thing happen to you. You should do as I tell you. You'll be better off."

"Like your wife Agnus was better off?" she threw back at him.

He raised his hand to strike her.

She held her ground. "I'm not afraid of you."

He lowered his hand.

She laughed in his face. "Okay, so if not you, then who? Who do you have in mind to beat me? Somebody who will whip me like a dog? Somebody who will bring me to heel? I had no idea Majorian possessed such talents."

"Majorian is no longer under consideration. He has gone to Servitium to oversee the army. To call him back from such an important duty would be an error. No, I have someone else in mind, someone who also has some experience in taming unruly beasts: my adopted son, Olybrius."

She rolled her eyes. "Olybrius? You must be joking. He's a tool. He exists only as an extension of you, like a wooden appendage for a missing limb. He's a man without character or volition."

Maximus scowled. "Olybrius knows enough to respect his superiors. Something he will teach you, and you'll find he has volition enough to wipe that sneer off your face."

Placidia squared her shoulders. "You have no right to choose a marriage partner for me, much less speak to me in such a tone. I'm a princess of Rome. You're a mere subject. I could have you punished for your insolence."

He shook his head. "Oh, Placidia, you're so young. How old are you now? Fourteen? Someday you'll learn there's a difference between ceremonial power and real power. Yes, you outrank me, but in reality, I'm your superior. Get used to do it."

She glared.

Maximus arranged the papers on his desk. "Will that be all, Princess?"

She ground her teeth.

"You will be married after the first of the year." He got up and brushed past her as he left the room.

When he was gone, she overturned a brazier in a fit of pique. The coals spilled onto the floor. One was still burning. She ground it underfoot until nothing remained but a smoldering black smudge.

* * *

Maximus didn't wait. His row with Placidia convinced him there was no advantage to putting off the wedding until after the first of the year. So, one morning a contingent of soldiers dragged my defiant daughter out of bed and compelled her to get dressed. Twice she tried to bolt, and twice they dragged her back. When she swung her fists at them, they hit her. Disheveled and weeping, she was hauled before the court and forced to sign a marriage contract. She spat on it, but the soldiers grabbed her hand and forced her signet ring onto the wax. It took three of them to do it.

Olybrius was not present.

There was no ceremony, and she refused to allow Olybrius into her bed. Wisely, he did not force the issue. They remained apart and did not speak to each other, but legally Olybrius was now the heir apparent.

News of Placidia's marriage plunged me into despair. Once again, I had failed someone who needed me. This time it was my daughter, and I was ashamed. I receded further into myself and became withdrawn. Weeks slipped by.

One day in winter as the snow was falling, I was sitting before the fire in my bedroom, plucking the lyre when I heard Eudocia behind me. She had been reciting some scripture but had grown tired of it and was poking around among my things. She did that sometimes; we were about the same size, and she liked to try on my clothes and pose in front of the mirror. I heard her open the chest at the foot of my bed. A moment later she was standing beside me with the amulet in her hand.

"Mother, why don't you wear this anymore?"

I looked at it in trepidation. "I don't like it. It doesn't become me."

She turned it over in her hand. "Oh, I don't know," she said. "It's kind of interesting. Where did you get it?"

"It belonged to your grandmother."

"It looks so old."

"Please put it back."

She looked at the back of the disk. "There's something written in tiny letters here."

"No there isn't."

"Yes, there is. Look." She held it out to me. Sure enough, in a semi-circle that followed the shape of the medallion was a line of script I had never noticed before.

"What does it say, Mother?"

"I don't know," I said. "It's neither Latin nor Greek."

"We should have it translated," she said.

"I don't think so."

Just then the logs in the fire shifted and collapsed, startling us both. We looked at each other in surprise and laughed.

Eudocia crossed to the chest and put the amulet back. Our conversation turned to other things. We avoided the topic of Placidia's marriage. Instead, we discussed the twelve convents in Antinoe and the estimable Amma Talis and her disciple named Taor who remained inside the convent for thirty years and worked without ceasing.

"Can you imagine that kind of devotion?" Eudocia asked.

"Never," I said. "It sounds miserable to me."

"Oh, I don't know," Eudocia said. "It's all in how you look at things."

"Maybe," I said, "but I don't have the capacity for that level of self-delusion."

Eudocia gave me a funny look then left me to sit by the fire. I strummed my lyre for a few minutes before I got up and went to the chest.

I lifted the lid and looked down at the amulet. Eudocia had placed it on top of the garments and blankets within. I picked it up and looked at the tiny lettering on the back.

*How have I never seen that before?*

I tucked the amulet away and closed the lid.

★ ★ ★

At the first signs of spring the Emperor demonstrated an uncharacteristic vigor. As a young man he had shown a passion for archery, but across the years, his interest had waned and been replaced by drinking, whoring and chariot racing. For reasons I didn't understand he determined to see if his old skills remained intact. He ordered the butts to be erected in the forecourt of the palace, he pulled on his boots and gloves and headed down to try his hand.

Maximus, always in the know, was notified of the Emperor's sudden caprice. He intercepted Placidius in the corridor and reminded him that the ground was still damp.

"Your boots will be muddied," Maximus said.

Placidius sniffed with contempt. "Stand aside," he said. "I can still hit a target."

Two women were lingering nearby. Hearing what was about to unfold, they rushed upstairs to the second floor of the palace to watch the sport from a window overlooking the forecourt. Later they reported what happened.

In the forecourt Placidius was accompanied by several of his retinue including Heraclius and two guards. The guards were unknown to the women. They had been sent at the last minute, presumably by Maximus, to replace Placidius's regular guards. The women observed the substitution. They watched as the new guards approached the regular guards, spoke briefly to them, and pointed to the palace by hooking their thumbs over their shoulders. The regular guards withdrew, and the new guards replaced them.

Placidius didn't notice the switch. He was too busy boasting about his prowess as an archer to anyone who would listen. Heraclius feigned great interest. Then Placidius warmed up. Every shot sailed wide of the targets. He laughed it off and swung his arms in large circles as if stretching would restore his lost skill.

Now the time had come to prove his talent. He picked up the bow and nocked an arrow. He drew the string and sighted down the shaft. All the while he provided a running commentary, the content of which went unheard by the women at that distance.

The attack came out of nowhere, a sudden downward blow with a rock that took the Emperor by complete surprise. He wavered uncertainly on his feet. The bow dipped and weaved, the string went slack, and the arrow fell impotently to the ground. A roundhouse wallop snapped the Emperor's head around. Spittle flew from his mouth. He dropped to his knees. His eyes swam in his head, but he did not fall forward. He remained on his knees, stunned and woozy, until the second guard brought a large stone down on his skull with an audible crack. The Emperor slumped over and lay motionless in the grass.

Heraclius panicked and tried to bolt. He scuffled across the forecourt, his silk robes swishing around his legs, his slippers slipping in the mud. The guards overtook him and struck him with rocks. He fell to the ground; his conical cap rolled away. The guards took turns pummeling his skull until the eunuch's head was nothing but a mash of blood and brains.

A moment later, Maximus strode up to inspect the carnage. He kicked at Heraclius. When there was no response, he nodded and went to inspect Placidius.

Somehow, the Emperor was not dead. He was dragging himself across the lawn on his belly. Maximus shot an irritated look at the two guards then planted himself in the Emperor's path. Placidius lifted his eyes. Maximus sneered and pressed his foot down on the Emperor's neck. Producing a knife from his robes, he slit the Emperor's throat with a single, rapid stroke.

Maximus wiped the blade on the tail of his tunic. Then he glanced up at the women in the window. They shrank back into the shadows, worried he would come after them, but he never did. It was almost as if he was glad they had witnessed the assassination – them and the others. No one was ever reproached for reporting what they had seen. Maximus seemed content to have it advertised far and wide.

I got word of the killing before the end of the day, but it wasn't until after my arrest and detention that I heard all the details. The women told me the story as I sat waiting for an audience with my new lord and master, the man destined to become the next Emperor, the murderer of my husband and manipulator of my daughter, Petronius Maximus.

# Chapter 25
March – June, The Year 455

Maximus's proclamation as Emperor was not a foregone conclusion. There were many in the army who believed he was complicit in the slaying of Aetius and despised him for it. Among them was a former bodyguard of the general's named Maximianus. He immediately announced his candidacy for the purple. Majorian, the former cavalry officer turned military commander who had once been proposed as a spouse for Placidia, also seized the opportunity. Under ordinary circumstances, neither man would have dreamed of taking such a risk, but the army was in the best position to determine who would succeed Placidius since it was the only institution possessing the ability to enforce its will. If it came down to it, the Senate, the Church and the people would have to accept whatever decision the army made, and Maximus was not their first choice—not yet anyway.

To win the army's favor, Maximus was forced to do the one thing he had been loath to do when Aetius was the master of soldiers, to pay them off. Although he resented having to distribute bribes, he doled them out with maximum effect, and within a fortnight, he was proclaimed Emperor.

The Senate and Church didn't object to Maximus becoming the new emperor in spite of the violent way he had taken the throne. They were optimistic, thinking he would be as generous with them as he had been in the past. But the people were not so sanguine. They had seen what could happen when the throne was taken by force—Roman history was riddled with such instances—and it usually led to war, the cost of which inevitably fell on them.

The first time Maximus met with me a few days after the assassination, he was humble, even apologetic. He was sorry for the turn of events. It was regrettable, he said, that Placidius had become so unfit as a leader his removal had become unavoidable. The Vandals were on the move, he reminded me. Since taking Melita, they had rolled up other territories in a blatant violation of longstanding treaties. They were going to have to be dealt with, and Placidius had been too distracted by his appetites to respond with any effect. Now Rome could focus on vital matters of state interest that had been neglected for too long.

I said nothing.

He watched me for a moment. "I want you to know I have nothing against you personally," he said. "The friction between us has all been because of other people. But that's behind us now. Let's start fresh. Let's be friends. I'm releasing you from detention. You're free to go. I hope you will not hesitate to ask if there's anything you may require. I still consider you the Augusta. I will honor you in that role."

I had no illusions. At that time, he had not yet been proclaimed Emperor and the attitude of the public toward him was plain to see in the graffiti scrawled on the city walls. But as soon as the imperial diadem was on his head, he changed his colors. He ordered me before him to answer for my offences.

I found him sitting back smugly on the throne, his fingers knitted behind his head, his legs thrust out in front of him and crossed at the ankles. Behind him were his two sons, Olybrius and Junius. Both looked awkward and embarrassed. When I tried to make eye contact with Junius, he became very interested in a thread hanging from his tunic. Maximus laughed.

"He won't save you this time," he said. "He may be impetuous, but he's not stupid—at least not stupid enough to make the same mistake twice."

I didn't try to defend Junius. I wasn't going to hang myself. I was only thirty-three and not yet ready to die. I wanted to see my daughters grown up. I wanted to meet my grandchildren. I felt an upwelling of sorrow. I bit my lip and fought the urge to cry.

Maximus cocked his head. "Oh, such a tender flower. Where is the defiant firebrand now? Where is the woman bold enough to attempt to kill a man with a heavy statue?"

I kept my mouth shut. Tears rolled down my cheeks.

"How dare you play the shrinking violet with me," he said. "I know you, Licinia Eudocia. I know who you are. I know what you're capable of. I ought to put you out of your misery before this goes any farther. But I won't. I have plans for you."

His countenance grew dark. "Let's be honest. The circumstances of my ascendancy are not ideal. The public knows how I got here, and they are not pleased. You would have thought they would be grateful. They despised your husband. I did them a favor. But instead, they whine and complain. No matter how many sermons the Pope gives telling them I'm the rightful Emperor, they shout and moan. They call me all kinds of horrible names. I ought to let the Vandals tear them apart. Then we'd see where their loyalties lie. But, alas, I must think of Rome. And without their support it will be difficult to achieve my goals."

He gave me a condescending smile full of spite and arrogance. He seemed excited like a small boy who had set a trap for some helpless creature and was eager to see it snap. "Something must be done to bring them over to my side," he said, "and that's where you come in. My reign needs legitimacy. My throne must be associated with the House of Theodosius. By marrying Olybrius to Placidia I've made a start, but it won't be enough. The next step is obvious. You will become my wife. It's as simple as that."

My flesh turned cold. A wave of nausea swept over me.

He threw his head back and laughed. "No one has ever met such good news with such a sour expression. I just saved your life. Everything that's been taken from you will been returned. Better yet, you will have a husband again, a real man who actually wants to share his bed with you. You should be celebrating. Instead, you're crying. Oh, Licinia, if you're not plotting and scheming, you're moaning and whining. I don't think I've ever met anyone so selfish and spoiled, not even your daughter."

I refused to meet his eyes.

"Oh, well. It's up to you. Think about it. You have two days. If you refuse, I will gladly put you out of your misery."

He nodded at the guards who seized me. But before they led me off, he got in one last word. "Never say I wasn't fair to you, Licinia. Never say I didn't give you a chance. I always give people a chance. It's their fault if they make the wrong choices."

The guards held me tight as if worried I might try to run, but escape was the farthest thing from my mind. My days of running were over. I was trapped, and my cage was the size of the Empire.

* * *

I took my elder daughter aside and urged her to flee to the Vandals. She was still betrothed to Huneric, and Maximus had no immediate designs on her. This was her one chance. If she could get to Carthago, Huneric would take her in and protect her. I could arrange the passage. I would do this for her, although it risked everything.

I was with my daughters in our apartments. They had just gotten news of my betrothal. They were upset, but the guards at the door were watching us, so we had to be careful.

Placidia called me over to the window and spoke under her breath. "So Eudocia gets to leave while I have to stay here? That's not fair."

I took her by the shoulders. "Be strong, Placidia. We have to deal with things as they are. We have to accept them. It makes no sense to resist when we know we can't win."

She sulked. "I don't believe it. This can't be happening. There must be someone who can help us. Maximus has enemies everywhere. Gaudentius, for instance. All I have to do is reach out to him."

I gave her a forbidding look. "Don't even think about it. They have spies watching us. If you try to contact him, you'll condemn him. Do you understand me? Do you want his death on your conscience?"

She bit her lip and seethed.

Eudocia came over to us. "I won't go to Carthago. I'll stay here with you. Oh, Mother, this is horrible."

I touched her cheek.

"You don't have to do this, Mother," Placidia said. "Stand up to him. Tell him you won't marry him, not in a thousand years."

I shook my head and spoke in a tight whisper. "I owe it to you to stay alive. If I refuse him, he'll execute me. You'll lose your mother. Do you want that?"

"But he murdered our father!" Placidia practically shouted.

I looked at the guards. They seemed indifferent, as if they would rather be somewhere else.

"Look," I said. "I have to get through this. God knows I've endured hardships before. I have to get through this and figure it out."

"But what about the Empire?" Eudocia asked.

Her artless simplicity caught me off guard.

Somewhere deep inside me the question begged to be answered, but at the moment I sought rationalization. It wasn't up to me. If the institutions of the Empire—the government, military, and Church, along with the people—lacked the will to rid themselves of a usurper like Maximus, if the corruption had eaten so deeply into their foundations that a man like him could be accepted and embraced, maybe the Empire didn't deserve to survive.

I pulled my daughters against me, and we wept.

* * *

I married Maximus the next week. There was no celebration, just a general announcement posted on the signboards declaring that the right and honorable Augusta had given herself in marriage to the right and honorable Emperor, and that was the end of it. The aristocracy applauded. The Church sang our praises. The public was ominously silent.

That very night Maximus came to my room and took what was his. I lay perfectly still, as cold and impervious as a sculpture. My frigidity didn't deter him. When he finished, he got up and walked away without a word.

I lay as if obliterated and reflected on all I had lost, of Agnus and the destruction of her innocence, of Aetius and his final jaded surrender to hostility and disparagement, of Junius and his powerlessness, and of Placidius and his inability to rise above his flaws no matter how much power had been granted to him. I thought of the Church whose answer to my suffering was to tell me to hate myself. I thought of the senators who had gotten what they wanted, an Emperor who permitted them to indulge themselves like termites in wood until the structure supporting them grew weak and collapsed. Then I thought of the amulet at the bottom of my chest a few feet away. I felt the seed of my enemy leaking out of me and soiling my bed.

I was beyond anger. I was beyond despair. I remembered the image of Nemesis whose figure had graced the wall over my wedding bed in Thessalonika eighteen years before, a woman with the power to judge, a woman with the license to punish, a woman whose fate was to be painted over and eradicated, an expendable god. Or was she?

Above all, I thought of my daughters. My sole duty now was to keep them alive. I could not be tempted. I put thoughts of vengeance out of my head.

And the days dragged on.

*　*　*

News reached us of Vandal incursions along the Mediterranean coast. Chagrined, Maximus sent an envoy to Carthago to protest the violation of the treaty. He received a curt reply from the Vandal king. As far as Genseric was concerned the treaty had been nullified the minute Placidius had been assassinated. His arrangement had been with Placidius, not with Rome, and it had always been tenuous since Placidius had never fulfilled his promise to wed Eudocia to Huneric. If Maximus wanted to restore the treaty, he could begin by fulfilling the original terms and sending the sixteen-year-old girl to Carthago without delay.

If he had assumed ruling the Empire would be any easier with Placidius out of the way, Maximus was disappointed. If he wanted to prevent the Vandals from stripping away Roman territory, he was going to have to act militarily despite being saddled with an army that was underfunded and unreliable. He summoned Avitus.

The retired general had remained in Rome after delivering the news of Thorismund's assassination. Now Maximus had an offer. If Avitus would head an embassy to the Goths with an appeal to the Theodoric II for assistance, Maximus would make him the new Roman military commander in Gaul.

Maximus must have recognized he was inviting exactly the kind of rivalry he had hoped to escape of by orchestrating the murder of Aetius. What's more, he was setting up the conditions by which a foreign power would become the main line of defense within the borders of the Empire. Should the Goths have to occupy Rome to defend it against the Vandals, there was no guarantee they would ever leave it again. But like Placidius before him, Maximus lacked the courage to force the aristocracy to finance a Roman military strong enough to protect its own interests, so he turned to the Goths.

Theodoric II had sat on the Gothic throne for nearly two years now. The rumors suggesting that he had murdered his brother were accepted fact. The Gothic king was a man willing to murder his own kin to seize more power for himself, and Maximus was yoking the future of the Western Empire to this person. I was appalled, but impotent. Like many Romans I had become resigned to the inevitability of poor leadership. I tried to put it out of my mind until I received a letter from Huneric. He had never written to me, so I knew the message was of great importance.

He begged me to intercede with the Emperor to prevent a war. His father the king was determined to strike Rome when she was at her weakest. The only way to prevent conflict was to bring about the long delayed marriage between he and Eudocia. There could be no further delay. We must send Eudocia to Carthago at once.

But I could not approach Maximus with such a demand. Maximus was not Placidius. He would not take my counsel. He would not tolerate my offering it. Should I attempt to pressure him, I would be punished—severely. The only option was to smuggle Eudocia out of Ravenna without his knowledge. Yet what had been possible just a few weeks before no longer was. Back then Maximus had been distracted by other things, chiefly his marriage to me as a way to shore up his claim to the throne; Eudocia was the farthest thing from his mind. Had we acted sooner we might have accomplished it. Now he was eyeing her as a bargaining chip of a different sort.

Avitus had not yet agreed to accept the Emperor's offer to become the next Roman military commander in Gaul. Before the war against the Huns, Avitus had been enjoying a comfortable retirement. In that instance he had agreed to act as a diplomat and had lent a hand militarily when called on to do so, but he was not eager to take on the responsibility of full military leadership. But Avitus was a widower, and Maximus assumed his appetites were similar to his own, so he hit on the idea of offering Eudocia as an inducement to bring him on board.

Fortunately for us, Avitus accepted the position before Maximus was able to make the offer, so it was no longer necessary to bribe him, and Eudocia became an afterthought again. This was my chance. I dashed off a letter to Junius and asked him to help me find a reliable sea captain who could take her aboard a ship to Carthago. I didn't mention the reason for her travels, but the intent was obvious. I awaited his answer.

Three days later I was called before the Emperor. He had my letter in his hand. Junius was standing by his side.

"I'll decide when and whom Eudocia will marry," Maximus said.

He crumpled the letter and threw it at my feet. He pulled me close. His teeth were clenched. "I am not Placidius," he said.

He hit me with his open palm.

* * *

I made no attempt to conceal my bruises when I confronted Junius.

"How could you?" I demanded.

We were standing in the concourse of the Colosseum where he was assisting Olybrius in the staging of a pageant honoring the Roman Senate.

He hustled me behind a pillar. "What are you doing here? Are you mad? We can't be seen together."

I pulled the stola off my shoulder and showed him the scratches on my back.

"Satisfied? That's what your cowardice has gotten you." I shook my head in dismay. "I can't believe I ever trusted you."

A moan escaped him. "Oh, Licinia. I'm so sorry. I didn't want this. I swear."

"What were you thinking? That by letting him put his boot on your neck he would love you? That he would embrace you as his son? He never will. He's incapable of loving you—or anyone else for that matter. We're all just wedges and levers to help him get what he wants. You understood that once. But apparently you've forgotten. Now it's going to cost you."

He looked frightened.

"Eudocia is betrothed to Huneric," I said. "The Vandals expect the marriage to take place. They've been waiting for fifteen years. Their patience has run out. They're preparing to attack. The only thing that will restrain them now is the wedding. Your father needs to know that, but I can't tell him. If I try, I'll get more of this!" I showed him an ugly bruise on my thigh. "So, I was trying to smuggle Eudocia out. To stop the invasion. To save Rome. That's what you thwarted when you decided to betray me."

He declined to meet my furious gaze.

"You must make this right, Junius. If you have a shred of decency left, if you love Rome, you have to help. You must warn your father. Tell him what will happen if Eudocia is not sent to Carthago. Persuade him to honor the treaty. Don't take no for an answer. Insist on it."

He muttered something under his breath.

"What did you say?"

"I can't help you," he said. "Leave me alone. And don't contact me anymore." He started away.

I caught his arm. "There's something you're not telling me."

He shook me off. "Stop it. You're putting us both in danger. Listen, we fought, and we lost. It's over. As painful as it may be, we have to face facts. My father is in charge. He makes the decisions. Not you. Not me. And certainly not the Vandals. We have to do it his way."

In his cowardly evasion I recognized the same thing I had told Placidia: to surrender, to give in, to quit fighting. It was shameful. The future of the Empire was at stake. If Galla Placidia could see me now, she would be ashamed. She had put her faith in me, and I was failing.

I blocked his path. I made him face me.

"Listen to me. Your father is not the kind of man who should be allowed to dictate the lives of others. He was in charge of Agnus life and look what happened to her. Will you deny it? Will you pretend it didn't happen? You loved her once. She was yours before she was his. But he took her from you and destroyed her. And now he's doing the same to me. Are you so craven that you would let him do it again?"

I could see the pain and confusion in his eyes, but it wasn't enough to make him change course. He brushed past me and stalked off. I looked after him in disbelief.

I made my way back to the palace alone. I came across a signboard and stopped dead in my tracks. My head pounded. My knees buckled. Before me was the public announcement of a royal betrothal. Junius was to wed Eudocia before the end of the week.

Maximus was making it known. The agreement with the Vandals was dead. He had other ideas about the future of Rome. My daughter would be marrying my former lover, and, in so doing, the formal ties of Petronius Maximus the usurper and assassin to the House of Theodosius would be reinforced. There was also a certain vindictive twist of the knife meant especially for me.

* * *

The amulet felt heavy in my hand. But when I hung it around my neck, it felt as light as a feather. I looked at myself in the mirror and saw a woman who had been beaten down, sallow and weary, but with a certain tenacity of purpose clawing its way to the surface again.

I went to Maximus.

He was his usual disdainful self. "What? Did you think there would be no consequence for turning my son against me?"

"The Vandals are going to invade," I said. "They're not going to sit quietly by and accept this. When they hear you've betrothed Eudocia to Junius they'll send their ships."

"Silence! You do not advise me!"

I took a step closer. "Be reasonable, Maximus. Rome is not prepared to withstand an attack of this magnitude. Avitus has not yet enlisted the aid of the Goths. If the Vandals strike now, Rome will be destroyed."

He raised his hand to me. I held my ground. He knocked me to the floor. I scrambled out of the way, and he came after me. I backed up against the wall, teeth bared in defiance. For eighteen years I had stood by and watched the fortunes of the Empire squandered by fools. I wouldn't do it any longer.

His eyes widened in anger, and he lunged at me. I tried to escape, but he caught me by the tail of my stola and jerked me back. He wrestled me to the floor and began to strangle me. His thumbs pressed into my windpipe. I struggled to breathe. The amulet fell out of the neck of my garment. He saw it, but it didn't faze him. He bore down.

Then someone pulled him off.

Air rushed back into my lungs. My breath exploded out of me in a series of convulsive gasps. Olybrius pushed Maximus up against the wall and held him there. Maximus reviled me with curses and jabbed his finger at me over Olybrius's back.

I got to my feet. I read Olybrius's look. It urged me to get away while I still could. I backed out of the room and went to my chambers. I took out a piece of parchment and wrote to Huneric.

The note was brief and to the point. It explained the situation. Eudocia's betrothal to him had been cancelled over my strong objections. There was nothing I could do. Rome was enthralled to a tyrant. Even now this brute was scheming to make an alliance with the Goths. It could only be prevented if the Vandals got to Rome first. I ended with a personal plea.

> Huneric, you once said to me that,
> should I ever need you, I need only
> ask. Well, I'm asking now. Will you
> come? Will you save us?

I put the letter in a pouch and included my signet ring as proof of my identity. Then I put my mind to the tricky problem of how to send it.

* * *

Help appeared in the most unlikely of places, among the Emperor's own family. It was not Junius. It was Olybrius. He came to me in my rooms following the altercation with Maximus to apologize for his father's atrocious behavior. He tried to explain it away by claiming that Maximus had been under a lot of stress. I told him I appreciated his concern and was sorry to have involved him, to which he responded with a sincere humility I found interesting.

Olybrius was a handsome young man of twenty-five, tall and well-built with a softness in his eyes and a gentleness in his manner that made him the superior of Gaudentius for sheer masculine appeal, although it would have been useless to tell Placidia so. Even though he never pressed her to honor her duties as a wife, remained well away from her, and had never done anything to offend her, she was sure Olybrius was a monster and was determined to divorce him as soon as she got the chance.

Olybrius was preparing to withdraw when he saw the amulet, still hanging below the neckline of my stola where it had fallen after Maximus's attack.

"That's remarkable," he said. "Where did you get it?"

"My mother-in-law, Galla Placidia."

"It's extraordinary," he said. "May I touch it?"

"Yes."

He put his index finger to it.

"May I hold it?"

I took it off and handed it to him.

He took the medallion between his thumb and forefinger and rubbed it.

"What's it made of?"

"Lead, I think."

He weighed it in his hand. "It's too light to be lead."

He laid it against his breastbone. He blushed slightly. "Sorry," he said. "I was just wanted to see what it would look like if I wore it. It's beautiful."

"You know, it's funny," I said. "Some people see nothing in it."

He shook his head. "I can't believe that."

He was still holding the amulet when a thought occurred to him. "Do you suppose you could put in a word with Placidia for me? I know she didn't want to marry me. But we *are* husband and wife, and I would just like the opportunity to get to know her better."

I took a moment to gather my thoughts, which he must have read as hesitation. He hastened to add, "Of course I don't want to push her if she's not ready."

I assured him I would put in a word for him, but I cautioned him that Placidia was a headstrong girl and would not respond well to pressure. One had to be delicate with her. Her first impulse was to resist. But I would help him, if he liked.

He was excessively grateful like a man who had been holding his breath under water and had finally shot to surface. He handed the amulet back.

"No," I said. "Hold it a while longer. Try it on if you like."

He smiled awkwardly and slipped it around his neck.

"You know, I can think of one way you might win your way into Placidia's good graces," I said. "She's very fond of her sister. She hates to see her hurt." I left it at that, waiting for him to ask the question.

"How is she hurt?"

"Oh, I think you know. It's this betrothal to Junius. It was quite unexpected. She's been betrothed to the Prince of the

Vandals since she was a child. She always expected to marry him, and now, overnight, she is to marry Junius. It's confusing and upsetting and made worse by the fact that the Vandals are threatening to attack us over it. She feels responsible."

"I can see how it would be upset her," he said. "It did come out of nowhere."

"Yes, and now Placidia is upset too."

He thought it over. "Do you want me to speak to Maximus? Maybe I can get him to change his mind about the wedding."

"No. I don't think that would be wise. It would only make him angry and cause him to dig in harder. I think we've gone as far as we can go with him."

I said no more. I let the moment drew itself out.

At length he said, "Is there something else I can do?"

I feigned embarrassment, equivocated. "No. It wouldn't be right. I'm sorry I brought it up. It would be asking too much of you."

"What would be asking too much of me?"

I looked both ways. There were guards at either end of the corridor. I motioned him into an alcove by the window. I pretended to hedge and dither.

I said, "Believe me, you don't want any part of this. It's the kind of thing that could be easily misinterpreted. I'll find someone else. I know someone who might do it, a young man who would be willing to do anything for Placidia, someone with less at stake than you." I meant Gaudentius, of course, and he understood that.

He rubbed the amulet with his thumbs. "Well, I can't give you my answer if I don't know what you're requesting of me."

I stole a furtive glance at the guards. "No," I said. "Forget it. Forget I brought it up."

"Listen," he said, "I know it's not what you intended, but I am your son-in-law now. You can confide in me. I won't betray you."

I saw something in his eyes, something good and decent. Somehow, I believed him.

"It's about the way this is being handled," I said. "We're losing an opportunity. Granted, this is coming from a woman, but I've been around powerful men my whole life, and I've observed a few things. I hope you don't think I'm being too presumptuous by talking about this."

"Not at all," he said. "Go ahead."

I drew him deeper into the alcove, out of sight of the guards.

"Avitus has not yet reported back on his mission to the Goths. We don't yet know if they'll agree to an alliance. We don't yet know if they'll come here and defend us. In the meantime, the Vandals are stepping up their attacks. Their coastal raids are increasing. We need to buy time. But the betrothal of Eudocia to Junius is being presented as an accomplished fact. It gets us nothing when, instead, it could be used as leverage."

He was interested, and his interest was sincere. I could see it.

"Why not use the betrothal as a bargaining chip?" I asked. "Why not tell the Vandals that Eudocia can still be wed to Huneric, but only if they stop their aggressions? Otherwise, she'll be wed to Junius."

"Do you think they'll respond favorably to that?"

"They might. I know Huneric personally. He was a hostage here as a boy. We're old friends, and he values our relationship. If I reach out to him personally, there's a good chance he will agree."

"But what if Maximus won't honor the agreement? What if the Vandals agree to stop their raiding, and then Maximus still doesn't hand over Eudocia? Then they'll be angrier than ever."

"Yes, but we'll have bought the time we need to get the Goths here. By then we'll have a fighting chance. Without that time, however, we're doomed. The Vandals will overrun Rome and destroy it."

Olybrius brooded. "I can see why you think Maximus would misinterpret this. If he found out what we're planning, he would consider it treason."

I let him think about that for a moment.

"And you think this will win Placidia's approval of me?"

"How could it not?" I asked. "To take such risks to help her sister and save Rome, it's undeniably heroic. Placidia responds to such things. Believe me."

"But it could still go wrong," he said. "Maximus could still force Eudocia to marry Junius."

"True. But at least we'll have tried something. And Placidia will know about it."

He scratched the back of his neck. "If we do this, we have to be careful. Not a word of it can be breathed to anyone."

"I agree. We have to take every precaution. I'll write the letter to Huneric and put it in a pouch with my signet ring. That way he'll know it's me. I'll seal the drawstrings with wax. If the wax is broken, he'll know the message has been tampered with."

He nodded.

"In the garden below this window there's a loose stone in the terrace wall. There," I said. "Do you see it? The gray one."

"Yes."

"As soon as it gets dark, I'll sneak down, remove the stone, and conceal the pouch behind it. Later, when you look, you'll find it there. Take it to the proper people in Ostia. Tell them it's a top secret diplomatic pouch bound for Carthago and not to tamper with it. Give them this to ensure their cooperation." I put a dozen silver coins in his hand. "Tell them there's more where that came from if everything goes right."

He took the coins without hesitation. There was a keenness in his demeanor. He was all in. He was going to do it.

I hated to deceive him; he seemed like such a nice, friendly young man, but I had to get the message out to Huneric, and Olybrius would be above suspicion. It was perfect.

Before going, he took the amulet from around his neck and handed it back to me. "Thank you," he said. "It's beautiful."

I gave him a warm smile. "Maybe when this is all over, I'll give it to you."

## Chapter 26
May 24 – June 16, The Year 455

When the invasion came, it was so sudden and unexpected it was as if the Vandals had been chomping at the bit all along and my letter had been the spur to propel them to action. Within fifteen days of sending the diplomatic pouch and the signet ring, reports began filtering back of a large Vandal fleet crossing the Mediterranean from Carthago.

Maximus was thrown into a panic. Avitus had just begun negotiating with the Goths, and Theodoric II was driving a hard bargain. He was demanding Roman cooperation in a scheme to oust the Suebi from Hispania in exchange for Gothic assistance against the Vandals, and no amount of pleading or cajoling by Avitus could change his mind. In any case, the Goths were a long way from coming to Italia, and the Vandals were just two days away.

Maximus dropped any pretense of preparing a defense and tried to flee from Rome. As word of his cowardice spread, public outrage against him intensified. It reached a fever pitch unlike anything Placidius had ever known. While the public had long detested Placidius, there was never any doubt about his legitimacy. He was the only son of their beloved Galla Placidia, and the grandson of the legendary Theodosius. Petronius Maximus, by comparison, was nothing but a money-grubbing aristocrat who had purchased the backing of his supporters. He was suspected of having a hand in the death of Aetius and had assassinated the rightful emperor. Worst of all, he was incompetent as a ruler.

The people of Rome were not stupid. They could see that by refusing to finance the army and relying on the Goths, he risked putting all of Italia under the bootheel of the barbarians. Worse yet, he had unwittingly sent a signal to the Vandals that the time to invade was now, before the Goths could arrive. In the minds of many, the reckless policies of an illegitimate usurper had brought on the crisis, and now he trying to run away. They were not about to let him.

The Emperor was standing at the city gates angrily demanding they be opened when an angry mob descended on him. Frightened, he escaped back into the city and took refuge in the Palace of Domitian. The mob gathered outside and called for his head. Frantic, he turned to Olybrius and Junius and demanded they save him. Flustered, his two sons began canvassing the household staff. Were there any secret passageways out of the palace?

No.

At least not any the servants would reveal to save Maximus.

There was a tremendous pounding. The mob were trying to break down the doors. Junius went to the kitchen and found a fishmonger's wagon near the service entrance. He suggested his father smuggle himself out beneath a load of rotting mullet. Maximus was indignant. What kind of a fool would suggest such a disgrace? He demanded they find a different way.

The mob was growing more emboldened. They were trying to scale the walls and setting fire to the wooden palings around the livestock pens.

Maximus whirled in circles of fear and incompetence. "Where are the guards! Why are they not defending us?"

He soon had an answer. Over half of the palace guards had deserted. Some were even now trying to break down the palace doors alongside the mob. If Maximus didn't escape soon, he would be set upon and killed.

Grumbling, he accepted the only available option. He held his nose and slid beneath the stinking, gelatinous mass of rotting fish. The doors opened and the wagon went out through the back gate and down a winding cobblestone street into the heart of the city.

Thinking no one would recognize them, Junius and Olybrius trailed the wagon by some distance. They walked like monks at prayer, eyes to the ground. They were wrong. Both men had served in the office of praetor and been responsible for the games. Everyone knew them.

When a gust of wind snatched Junius's hood off his head, a shout of recognition went up and the mob gave chase. The two men abandoned all pretense and fled down a narrow passageway. They scaled a wall to a rooftop, jumped to an adjacent building, and shinnied out onto the roof of a third where their pursuers could not see them.

As it happened, they were on top of the chapel of Saint Stephen, which had once been a shrine to the goddess Vesta, the virgin goddess of hearth and home. In its former incarnation, the building had been restricted to consecrated priestesses, the Vestals, who had tended the sacred fire. The fire was said to be essential for the preservation and continuity of the Roman State. Should it ever go out, legend claimed, Rome would fall. But these were pagan ideas, and when Christianity spread over the Empire, the Vestals were ejected from the temple and the fire extinguished. The building was repurposed as the chapel of Saint Stephen, the first Christian martyr who had been stoned to death by a Jewish mob for accusing Israel of being disobedient to God. Junius and Olybrius lay on their bellies on the roof and peered down into the street. From their vantage point they were able to see what happened next.

After chasing Junius and Olybrius away, the mob gathered around the fishmonger's wagon. Sensing a ruse, they overturned it, spilling Maximus into the street atop a cascade of putrid fish. Seeing he was caught, he raised his hands and tried to reason with them. He demurred, disputed, objected, all the while backing away. With a menacing growl, they advanced on him, stones in hand.

His voice trembling, he swore he was the rightful emperor, the legitimate heir to the Theodosian dynasty because he had married Licinia Eudocia.

"She married me!" he said. "Willingly!"

They rushed at him with a roar. He turned and ran. They poured after him like water down a drain, chasing him through the streets until they caught him with his back against a wall. He begged for mercy. He wept. He clasped his hands.

The first stone missed him altogether. It took a chunk out of the wall. Maximus stared at the wall as if it had exploded of its own accord. Then the next stone came, glancing off his hand. He shook his fingers like a child who had touched a hot stove. The next rock plunked him on the thigh, and he bent over with a shriek. The next struck him on the shoulder. Two more pelted him in rapid succession, striking him on the shoulder and chest. After that, they came like the driven rain, a shower of projectiles, bombarding him with malicious violence until he fell face first in the street and lay still. Even then, the stoning didn't stop. Stones continued to pound his prone body like a vigorous butcher tenderizing a piece of meat.

Eventually, the onslaught slackened. Someone crept forward and inspected the body. "He's dead."

A few cheers greeted the announcement, but the prevailing mood was one of disappointment. The mob had swelled to twice its original size since the assault on the palace and many of the recent arrivals felt they had not gotten in on the fun. A grumble of frustration rippled through them. Some rushed forward and tried to shake him awake. Others slapped him. One man punched him with his fist. Another stamped on his leg. Two men grabbed him by the arm and tried to pull him away from the others. The others pulled back. There was shouting and laughter. The Emperor became the object of a grisly tug-of-war.

Then the most extraordinary thing happened. Maximus regained consciousness for one brief moment. His eyes bulged and his mouth distorted in an excruciating howl. Then one of his arms was pulled from his body. A geyser of blood showered his assailants, but rather than recoil in horror, they jumped about and pumped their fists in jubilation. It was just the start. They pinned his torso underfoot and with great effort pulled away the other arm. Then they set to work on his legs.

Junius and Olybrius looked on from the rooftop, mortified but transfixed by the mob's mindless violence. The unhinged participants tore the body apart, then cavorted around with the dismembered limbs. Someone brought an ax and hacked off Maximus's head. Someone else cut away his genitals and used them to torment a pair of young women before tossing them to a pack of starving dogs. In the end, the decapitated head was stuck on a pike and paraded through the streets amidst cheers and applause.

When the mob had gone, Junius and Olybrius climbed down from the roof and stood in their father's blood. Junius's face was drained of color. He knelt down and touched the stain.

"They were like jackals," he said.

Olybrius said nothing.

The distant sound of the mob rose and fell in the city. At times it sounded like it was coming back around, which shook the two men from their reverie and prompted their flight. But on the way to the Porta Metronia where Junius thought they could still board a departing ship, Olybrius stopped.

"I'm going back," he said.

Junius was incredulous. "You can't go back there. They'll kill you."

"I'm responsible," he said. "It's my fault."

Junius demanded an explanation, but Olybrius declined to give him one. "Go to Ostia," he said. "I'll meet you there later."

Olybrius stood in the street and watched him go.

It was the last time anyone saw Junius. He was never seen or heard from again.

* * *

We fled Ravenna as soon as we got the news. We traveled to Rome on horseback as fast as the horses could carry us. We wanted to reach the city before the Vandals made landfall. As we headed south, we encountered a steady stream of refugees heading north. Before long, the road was clogged with wagons and carts all piled high with personal belongings. Panic was written on every face.

We did not pass unmolested. We were recognized. Fingers were pointed. Someone issued a threat. Someone else refused to make way. One ruffian took hold of the reins of Eudocia's horse. Another grabbed at my cloak. Placidia swatted an outreached hand. Several men came forward to defend us. Arguments broke out. Punches were thrown. Seeing our chance, we broke free and rode hard across the open country.

We reached the city gates just as they were closing. We slipped inside at the last possible moment. What we saw was shocking. The city's defenses were in disarray. The command structure had fallen apart and the few soldiers we saw were disorganized and confused. When I heard the news, I couldn't believe my ears. I asked to have it repeated. Maximus had been killed by the mob.

My daughters looked at each other with a mix of fear and satisfaction. The soldier who made the reported kept his head on a swivel. He was on the verge of panic. Anything could happen.

"You'd better get out of here," he said. "The Vandals are coming."

I tried to determine where Huneric would come to look for us. I had neglected to provide a precise location in my message. Lacking specific guidance, he would go to the Palace of Domitian atop the Palatine Hill, the traditional residence of the Imperial Family. So, that would be our destination.

I tried to persuade the soldier to escort us, but he refused. The situation was risky enough. Guarding three women struck him as ludicrous. Mobs roamed the streets, taking advantage of the general lawlessness to settle old scores. We heard shouts and grunts. We heard cries and screams. It was chaos. I tried to pay the soldier, but his eyes darted about so fast, I doubt he even saw the coins. Before I could make another appeal, he was gone.

"Come on, girls," I said. "Follow me."

We made our way through the old Forum, heads down, hoods up. Ahead of us on a hill between the columns of the Basilica Nova a lone figure appeared. He disappeared inside and reappeared a few moments later. We saw him again along the Agriletum near the corner of the Curia Iulia. He watched us pass.

"Who's that?" Eudocia asked.

"I don't know," I said. "Just keep walking."

We quickened our stride, but he kept pace with us. He dodged between the buildings. When he finally approached, I picked up a stone and gathered the girls behind me.

He came closer. His eyes widened. "Is that you, Excellency? What are you doing here?"

I finally recognized him. He was a minor secretary for the Pope. He had been sent by the Pontiff to see if he could locate any officials who could update him on the crisis and inform him of measures being taken to confront it.

"I have learned nothing," he said. "Everyone has fled. All order has dissolved." A momentary pause. "Where are you going?"

"To the Palatine Hill," I said.

"That's a bad idea," he said. "That's the first place the invaders will look for you. Come with me. The Pope will give you refuge at the Lateran Basilica. They won't dare to break in there."

He seemed confused when I turned him down.

"But the Pope will ask the Vandals to honor the sanctuary of the basilica. As Christians they are obliged to grant it. You will be safe there. Come with me."

Again, I refused.

He looked at me as if I were crazy.

Placidia weighed in. "Please, Mother. Can we go with him? Pope Leo will protect us."

"Be quiet," I said.

But she would not be silenced. "Be reasonable, Mother. If his warriors get here first, they won't wait for instructions. They'll kill us."

Eudocia hissed from my other side. "Shut up."

The man's brows lifted. "Instructions? What instructions?"

I glared at Placidia and then turned my attention to our do-gooder with a calm expression.

"If you must know, I sent a message to the Vandal prince. I asked for mercy. I have good reason to believe he will grant it. After all, he is betrothed to my daughter."

I pointed to Eudocia.

The man cut a glance at her. "It was my understanding she was to wed the Emperor's son, Junius."

"The Emperor is dead, murdered by a mob. The situation has changed."

"Perhaps. But you could not have known that before sending a message to the Vandals."

I fixed him with a hard stare. "You are very perceptive—perhaps more than is good for you."

I watched his hand. He had a dagger in his belt. The moment seemed to stretch itself out.

"Have it your way," he said. "I was only trying to help." He excused himself and hurried off.

"Come on," I said to the girls. "Let's get to the palace. There's not a moment to spare."

* * *

I was right about the brevity of time. As we climbed the steps to the Palatine Hill the invaders come pounding into the Forum on horseback. We ducked behind a bush and looked on as they cantered up and down in search of resistance. A man wandered into the Forum looking confused and frightened. Seeing the Vandals, he tried to get away, but they rode him down and beat him senseless. Soon the sport lost its luster, however, and they turned to wanton acts of destruction. They pushed over statues and uprooted plants. They smashed down the doors of the House of the Vestals and swarmed inside emerging a short time later with anything they could carry: lamps, furniture, statuary, amphorae. They smashed some of it and loaded the rest into wagons. More Vandals arrived. They broke into other buildings, set fires, and scratched their names into walls with nails and knives.

"Is Huneric down there?" Eudocia asked.

"I don't think so," I said.

Placidia groaned.

With the Vandals distracted by their looting, we made our way up the hill and into the palace. The gates stood open. The guards had run away. The place was ripe for the picking. In the interior courtyard we were met by an eerie silence. Placidia began to tremble as if with a violent fever. I put my arm around her; Eudocia followed suit. Together we led her up the main portico and into the palace.

The main entry hall was empty except for the statues of our forefathers, Caesar, Pompey, Scipio and Agrippa, heroic men with manly physiques who stared off into space. Their somber expressions reflected on the disgraceful cowardice afflicting the city. We hurried into the cavernous audience chamber. The golden throne sat unoccupied and forlorn upon its raised dais. A smaller throne for the Augusta had been overturned. I righted it and sat down.

Placidia looked up at me with tear-filled eyes. "That's it?" she demanded. "You're just going to sit there and wait for him?"

Eudocia snapped a response. "What do you want her to do?"

Placidia rubbed her eyes. "Maybe someone should go and find him."

"Do you want her to go out there and leave us alone?"

"No," Placidia said. She gnawed her thumbnail as her father used to do.

A sudden clap like a plank of wood slapping to the floor made us all jump.

"Stay here," I said and went to investigate.

In an adjoining room a large timber truss had broken loose from the roof and sent a plank through the rain aperture and onto the mosaic floor by the pool. I walked over and gazed up through the aperture. Then I saw him, a Vandal warrior with his back to me. He was prying up the gilt-edged roof tiles. I stepped out of his line of sight and hurried back to the girls.

Eudocia met me at the door. Her face was ashen. "Placidia's gone," she said. "I tried to stop her, but she ran off. She was scared, Mother. She didn't believe they would know us. She thought they would kill us before they bothered to find out."

"Stay here," I said. "Get out of sight. The Vandals are up on the roof. Don't let them see you. I'm going to find her."

Eudocia grabbed my arm. "Wait, Mother. What if she's right? How are they to know it's us and not just three aristocratic women trying to hide?"

"That's why you have to stay hidden until Huneric shows up."

"But Huneric has never seen me before. He doesn't know who I am." Her eyes were wild with fear. "Oh, Mother, please don't leave me alone. Let me come with you."

All of my motherly instincts yearned to do as she wanted, but if we all left the palace and Huneric arrived, we would miss our one chance to escape. I knew what I had to do, but it would require something of me I had hoped to avoid.

I slipped the amulet from around my neck and handed it to her. "Put this on."

She took it gingerly as if it was something fragile and priceless.

"Huneric will recognize it," I said. "He'll know who you are." Then without another word I hastened away and left her.

I hurried down to the end of the hallway where a servant's corridor led to a rear exit. The door was open. I poked my head out and saw a winding path that led through a vegetable garden to a gate at the back. Taking a cautious glance up at the roof, I stepped out and followed the path. Beyond the gate the path descended down a flight of steps to a promenade that ran atop the defensive walls surrounding the grounds. At the far end I glimpsed the swish of Placidia's dress as she disappeared through a doorway into a stone keep.

I started to go after her but caught myself. The top of the promenade was visible from the rooftop. The looter I had come upon earlier was not alone. He was accompanied by a half dozen other men who were denuding the roof of its valuable, gilt-edged tiles. How many other Vandals were inside the palace I didn't know. I could only hope that Eudocia would remain hidden until I got back.

I looked up at the roof. When most of the men were preoccupied and tugging at some cladding, I started out, only to shrink back when one of them turned in my direction. This happened several times until I felt like I must take the plunge or lose Placidia forever. The men bent to their work. I raced down the promenade and ducked through the doorway, feeling every instant as if they had seen me. Whether or not they had, I could not say, but I ran as if they were pursuing me. I flew down the steps and emerged onto the street.

I saw no sign of her or anyone else. I did not have time to search every nook and cranny. I had to stop and think. A moment's reflection told me she had gone to the Lateran Basilica to seek the sanctuary of the Pope. So, I went there.

My passage was not easy. I turned a corner and came upon a pack of Vandals tearing the bas-reliefs from the architrave of a ceremonial building. Fortunately, they did not see me, but they were not the only invaders I encountered. The city was teeming with roving bands of plunderers. Every turn brought new surprises.

I saw shop after shop broken into, their goods strewn into the street. I saw oxen and donkeys with their throats cut and left to die. I saw wells and fountains fouled with urine and feces. I saw vile imprecations scrawled on the walls. I saw fire. I saw death.

Suddenly it occurred to me that these were the same people I had entrusted with our liberation. Was there no decency left in the world? Was there no one who could restrain himself out of a sense of moral duty? What had the world come to? And where was the God I had once believed in with such fervor?

* * *

The Lateran Basilica was untouched. The Vandals were Christians, albeit of the Arian sort, but when it came to respecting the law of sanctuary, they demonstrated restraint. As pillars of smoke rose from conflagrations across the landscape, the Pope and his retinue watched and prayed, complacent in the knowledge that God had spared them. They gave no credit to the mercy of the enemy. Their arrogance unbowed, the Holy Father and his cronies were not given to complimenting heretics.

I knocked at the door. A head popped out of an upstairs window and looked down at me. A moment later the door opened, and I went in.

The basilica was jammed with people, most of them poor, ill, and weak. They huddled together on the floor, which stretched before me the length of a city block and terminated at a series of steps leading up to a golden altar. The Pope was nowhere in sight.

As I came in, numerous faces turned to me, frightened, haggard faces. I walked among them looking for Placidia but saw no sign of her.

I went to a man dressed in a richly embroidered dalmatica and a jewel encrusted necklace who was standing beside a fluted column in the northern gallery. I told him I wanted to see the Pope. He informed me it was not possible. I told him I was the Augusta. He refused to believe me.

"Show me your signet ring," he said.

"I don't have it," I said.

He told me to get away. When I objected, he raised his hand to me.

Someone stepped in front of him. It was the man who had confronted us in the Forum. He smiled thinly. "So, you've come to seek sanctuary after all."

"My daughter is missing," I said. "I have to see the Pope."

"I'm afraid he's indisposed at the moment. Too bad you didn't come earlier; he might have seen you then."

I gave him a withering stare. "Stand aside."

He made as if to obey.

The first man looked at him in astonishment. "Is she really the Augusta?"

"She *was* the Augusta," the second man clarified. "Now she's nothing. The Emperor is dead. The Pope is the highest civil authority in Rome, and he's not seeing anyone."

I started to go around him, but he blocked my path.

"You should be careful," he said. "I know what you're up to." His hand went to his dagger. "Contacting the Vandals. Would you care to explain?"

I looked him up and down with contempt. "If you think you have a weapon with which to threaten me, take it out. Brandish it… and then fall on it, for by such an act you will have sealed your doom."

The man tried to maintain a stern front but lost his nerve and looked away.

I pushed past him and went up the steps to a gallery overlooking the main floor of the basilica. I hastened down the gallery to the Pope's private quarters and burst in. I found myself in a large ornate room trimmed in gold and adorned with bright frescoes, lush draperies, and precious furniture. Leo was cowering in the corner with his back against the wall and his knees drawn up to his chest. His eyes were bloodshot and furtive. He looked like a trapped rat.

"What are you doing?" I demanded of him. "Get up. Go out there. The people are waiting for you. They're frightened, and they need someone to reassure them."

He held his head in his hands and moaned. "It's no use. We're finished. They'll kill us all, the weak and the strong."

"What are you talking about? The Vandals have granted you sanctuary."

"I don't trust them," he whimpered. "They're Arians, the worst kind of people. They're savage barbarians. They're animals."

"They're Christians," I reminded him.

"They're heretics!" he shot back. He practically spit the word from his mouth.

Now I saw things as they were.

"So, what you're telling me is that if the situation were reversed, if they were asking for sanctuary from you, you wouldn't grant it."

"The Arians are an offence to God," he said. "God wants them dead."

"And yet they're not dead," I pointed out. "They're very much alive. But death hangs over *your* head at this moment. Is this also the will of God?"

His brow creased. He scowled through his tears. "Your womanly lies are like the slithering of a serpent's tongue. Get away from me, lest God's wrath fall on you."

"She's not to be trusted." The voice came from across the room. It was the man who had confronted us in the Forum, the man with the dagger in his belt. He had followed me up to the Pope's quarters.

"She's guilty of treason," he said. "I have reason to believe she conspired with the Vandals to bring them here. She's counting on them to rescue her and her daughters."

Pope Leo fixed me with a malignant stare.

The man drew the dagger from his belt. "Would you like me to chastise her, Pontiff?"

The Pope considered him for a moment. Then he looked back at me. "Leave her with me," he said. "I'll deal with her."

The man was confused. "But—"

"Go," the Pope said, "and close the door behind you. Like I instructed you before, I am not to be disturbed."

The man bowed and withdrew.

Pope Leo waited until he heard the door close, and then he turned to me. "Help me," he said. "I've got to get out of here." His whole demeanor had changed. He was no longer a smug, self-righteous man of God but a mewling supplicant. "Take me with you," he said. "I won't be any trouble."

"But they're Arians," I reminded him. "Heretics."

"I can be openminded," he said. "As long as they're willing to meet me halfway—as long as they're willing to listen." He crawled across the floor and looked up at me like a whipped dog. "They're not beyond redemption," he said.

I regarded him with disgust. "Half the city is in flames. People have lost everything. And all you can think about is yourself."

He got to his feet and drew himself erect. He lifted a finger into the air. "But I know the will of God!"

I shook my head. "Cowardice, selfishness and arrogance. That's not the will of God. That's the will of man."

The exuberance drained out of him, and he sagged.

Suddenly there was a commotion from outside. I went to the window and looked out. Vandal raiders were riding into the plaza. I was running out of time. "I have to find my daughter," I said. "Obviously you have no idea where she is."

He chased after me. "Wait," he said. "Let me help. I can enlist the aid of my prelates."

He followed me down the gallery. He scurried to keep up. "We'll find her. Don't worry."

As we descended the steps, we met a man coming up. "They're in the plaza!" he wailed. "Hundreds of them!"

Down on the main floor the basilica was in an uproar. Terrified people were rushing to and fro. Some were screaming. Some were crying. Others were on their knees in prayer. Pope Leo looked around in fear and consternation. I grabbed his shoulders and shook him.

"Pull yourself together, man! Go to the altar and speak to them. Calm them. They believe in you."

He looked befuddled. Tears spilled down his cheeks. He wouldn't budge.

I went to the massive doors and began to pull them open.

Someone shoved me aside. It was the man with the dagger. He pulled the weapon from his belt. "Back away, Augusta."

I ignored him and hauled the doors open with all my strength.

The man's mouth fell open. The dagger dropped from his hand and clattered to the floor.

A hush fell over the basilica.

On the other side of the doors stood the Vandal prince, my old friend, his fist raised to knock. A smile spread across his face when he saw me.

"Augusta," he said.

"Huneric," I said.

Behind him on horseback was the Vandal king Genseric. Beside him was Eudocia astride a white pony and wearing the amulet.

"Mother!" she cried and swung down out of her saddle. We threw ourselves into each other's arms.

Arrayed around the plaza were mounted Vandal war-riors, weapons drawn, facing the basilica. In the doorway of the church, stood the man with the dagger, frozen in fear, his weapon at his feet. Further back in the shadows stood the crowd of frightened supplicants. The Pope was not among them.

And neither was Placidia.

# Epilogue
## August, The Year AD 455

I am writing this to clear my name and relate the circumstances that drove me to act as I did. I began my journey as a pious young woman with dreams of a fruitful marriage. I shared my husband's ambitious hopes of reuniting the Empire and reviving its glory. But I soon learned those close to me were flawed beyond imagining and I recognized malevolent forces moving to take advantage of every weakness.

In every instance I strove to maintain my dignity and to hold onto the tattered shreds of decency and morality, the foundations of my upbringing. In the course of things, I saw models of virtue like my aunt Pulcheria exposed as malefactors, and I saw miscreants like Justa partially redeemed. My understanding of what constituted a good person changed, and I came to realize that no person, place, or institution is morally infallible. All are vulnerable and many have been corrupted. In the end, it was all I could do to save my daughters from the wickedness closing in around them.

Eudocia and I escaped to Carthago with Huneric. We took up residence at the royal palace. We were given comfortable quarters and granted every privilege. We were not prisoners. We were dignitaries. It might be supposed I spent my days pining for Placidia. After all, I had not seen her since she ran from the palace. But Vandal agents working in Rome assured me she was alive and well, and in safe hands.

Days passed, and then weeks. I began to work on this chronicle. I poured myself into it. I took as inspiration the long letter Galla had written to Placidius. Though hers was meant to guide him, it was never my purpose to advise anyone, only to relate how a hopeful young woman could become so beaten down by circumstances that she could do something as traitorous as I had done. I wrote and waited.

One day a servant came to me and said there were a pair of visitors waiting for me in the atrium. I wondered who would have come all this way to speak to me. Were they agents from the new regime in Ravenna? Were they representatives of the Pope? Did I harbor any hope?

I went down to the atrium with my heart in my throat. Eudocia joined me on the way. We waited together. The doors swung open and Placidia entered. We flung ourselves into her arms. She had arrived accompanied by Olybrius. He looked on with a gentle smile as we greeted each other with tears of relief.

As the story came out it became clear that Olybrius had done a heroic thing. As the city burned and bloodthirsty mobs roamed the streets, he parted from his brother and went in search of his wife. With only his intuition to guide him, he sought her out. He believed she must have come to Rome to seek the protection of the Emperor, only to find the Emperor dead and the city in chaos.

He skirted the mob and sidestepped the Vandals. By some miracle he came upon her en route to the basilica with a group of nuns who had fled their abbey when it had been set on fire. Not trusting the Vandals to honor the sanctuary of the basilica, he had whisked her away to the port at Ostia where they hid out until a merchant ship took them to Sicilia.

Now, three months later, we were reunited. All of Placidia's resentment over being compelled to marry Olybrius had vanished. They appeared to have a real affection for each other. Later Placidia told me she believed, as he did, that they had found one another via a miracle. All the credit was due to God, they said. They prayed in the chapel three times a day and were generous with the Church. It seemed out of character for Placidia to submit herself to a higher authority, and I didn't quite believe it, but I held my tongue. Far be it for me to discourage anyone in their devotions.

When Placidia asked for the gift of the amulet, I refused her. I had already done the same with Eudocia when she asked if she could keep it. I took it back from her and put it away where neither of them could find it. Later, when I went to look for it, it was gone. Perhaps one of the servants took it. I didn't investigate. Its mysterious power was worrying, and I was thankful it was gone.

Eudocia married Huneric near the end of the year and sealed a long-sought alliance even though it hardly mattered any more. The House of Theodosius no longer factored into the question of who ruled the Empire. Following the death of Maximus, the Roman military commander in Gaul, Avitus, was proclaimed Emperor by the Gothic king Theodoric II. A month later Avitus was endorsed by the Roman Senate when he arrived in Ravenna backed by a Gothic army.

While the marriage of Eudocia and Huneric strengthened the claim of Huneric as the rightful heir, the Vandals knew the Roman people would never accept a Vandal as their Emperor and that the Goths would oppose him with arms. In any case, the reward of taking the throne was no longer worth the risk as Avitus himself found out a year later when he was deposed. The Vandals were content to control the trade routes in and out of Italy. The ensuing chaos after Avitus's ouster was somebody else's problem, and they were welcome to it.

Thus, a new status quo took hold, one in which my daughters and I played a negligible role, and I was grateful for it. From the day I had married Placidius, my life had lurched from one crisis to another. I was tired. I wanted to rest. Carthago was the perfect refuge.

When Pope Leo began denouncing me from the pulpit, I hardly even noticed. His accusations of treason barely registered. Of course, it meant I could never set foot in the Empire again on pain of arrest, but I had no intention of doing so. I was content to write and reflect, to play my lyre, and enjoy the company of my daughters.

For those who may read this in the future, make no mistake. The Pope is right. I did commit treason. I called upon the Vandals to invade Rome and rescue us from the tyranny of Maximus, but, as always, there is more to the story than it appears on its face, and I hope these words will help people understand the truth of what happened.

When all is said and done, I hope I will be remembered as a simple, well-intentioned woman who was trying to do her best in a world that was crumbling all around her.

May God forgive me.

The End

# Afterword

As always with a work of fiction based on historical facts, the question arises, "How much is true?" When working with a period like the mid-fifth century the sources are sparse and fragmentary. Much of the information is incomplete and disputed. To make matters worse, the Church historians of the time had a naked political agenda. They aggrandized those they favored and vilified those they didn't. Objectivity never came into it. Consequently, people and events must be considered from multiple perspectives; personalities must be cobbled together from a rough consensus.

To begin, the historical record has little say about Licinia Eudocia (alternatively fashioned Licinia Eudoxia). She was the daughter of Theodosius II and the wife of Valentinian III (Flavius Placidius Valentinianus). She bore two daughters, Eudocia and Placidia. After the assassination of her husband, she was forced to marry the man who had orchestrated his murder, the usurper Petronius Maximus. So objectionable did she find the union that she followed the example of her sister-in-law, Justa Grata Honoria, and reached out to the enemies of her country for help. As a consequence, she triggered the Vandal sack of Rome, which lasted for two weeks.

Her depiction as a well-meaning but naïve young woman transformed into a dauntless heroine by circumstances is my invention. Her inspiring presence at the Siege of Aurelianum (modern day Orleans) is made of whole cloth as is her audience with Attila the Hun a few weeks prior to his death. As far as I know, the real Licinia was not present at the Battle of the Catalaunian Plains, nor was she in Constantinople when an earthquake struck and created the breach in the walls that was miraculously reconstructed in 60 days as the Huns closed in.

The record has more to say about her husband, Flavius Placidius Valentinianus. Among scholars, Placidius is widely reckoned a weak and feckless ruler who was easily manipulated, first by the eunuch Heraclius and later by Petronius Maximus. His distaste for his Master of Soldiers Flavius Aetius is well documented. The shocking murder of Aetius by Placidius is a matter of historical record.

The condition of Placidius's marriage to Licinia Eudocia can only be speculated, but his drunkenness and infidelities were noted by his contemporaries, and his rape of Maximus's stunning young wife, Agnus, is a historical fact, which has been posited by scholars as a motive for his assassination by Maximus. While an avowedly religious man, Placidius's indulgence in asceticism (to the extent that he contemplated becoming a eunuch) is exaggerated. Licinia's influence on him as an exemplar of Christian piety is a dramatic invention, albeit entirely plausible.

The misogynistic tilt of the Nicene Church in the fifth century is as authentic as it is appalling. The theological writings of men like Tertullian, Origen, Augustine, and Jerome were much in vogue during this period, an interesting irony given the ascendancy during this same time of powerful female figures like Pulcheria and Galla Placidia. That Licinia would have been influenced and oppressed by this theology is certainly likely but not backed up by any written sources.

The basic narrative of the rise and reign of Pope Leo I accords with history. Dispatched by Pope Sixtus to mediate a dispute between Aetius and Albinus, his subsequent success was used as a springboard to secure the Papacy. The early years of his reign were characterized by a series of persecutions against rival sects and a persistent effort to establish papal authority over other bishoprics. To the extent that a man's behavior can tell us something about his character, I believe it is safe to describe Leo as power hungry.

During the latter part of his ascendancy, Leo claimed credit for dissuading Attila from invading Italy. Yet the contemporary sources are in dispute as to why Attila withdrew, and modern scholars downplay Leo's influence. Regardless, the Roman Catholic Church is sticking by Leo's version of events.

In any case, Leo was not finished. He subsequently claimed to have discouraged the Vandals from destroying Rome during the sack of 455. If these assertions are suspect, it points to a man who was not only greedy for power but also willing to use falsehoods and exaggerations to achieve it. I have drawn Leo as such a person.

Virtually every character in the novel is an actual person, someone who lived and breathed in the fifth century and did something noteworthy. In some cases, as with Leo, I had a good deal to work with in presuming character and motives; in others I had little more than the name.

A figure like Petronius Maximus stands out for the terrible things he did to secure the throne. He comes across as a villain even in the contemporary records. But someone like his son Junius (real name Palladius) is a cipher. We know he held the title of praetor during his father's consulship and was subsequently tapped to wed Eudocia, thus requiring the cancellation of her betrothal to Huneric. His fraught relationship with his father and his love affair with Licinia are devices employed for the purposes of storytelling.

Huneric was indeed held hostage in Rome during his youth and may have resided at the imperial palace. Proximity in age and environment may well have thrown Huneric and Licinia into each other's path, but there is no record of this. Huneric's subsequent betrothal to Eudocia may have been for purely political reasons, but the fact that Licinia later reached out to the Vandal prince for help suggests there could have been something more personal in their relationship.

In crafting this story I began with the characters, researched their histories, deduced their motives, and then placed them in the context of the times to see how they might interact. Out of this grew the web of relationships at the heart of the story. But that network had to be confined within the framework of known events: the Vandal menace, the Hun invasions, the ascendancy of Pope Leo I, and the murders of Aetius and Placidius. These events further shaped the characters while at the same time being shaped by them and resulted in a coherent whole that I hope you have found entertaining.

As is true of all history, the fifth century and the Fall of Rome are compelling not only for what they tell us about the past, but also for what they reveal about the present. Too often, however, readers get caught up in the broad strokes of events and draw parallels between past occurrences and current events. They love to note similarities and make predictions. Unfortunately, this tendency overlooks the true driving force behind history, the intimate details of character, the virtues and flaws we all share, and the reasons we act as we do. By tightening the focus from the broad narrative of fifth century history and zooming in on individuals and their motives, I have tried to breathe life and color into the period.

I hope I have succeeded – and I hope you enjoyed the book.

Malcolm David Logan
February 3, 2022

# Author's Bio

Malcolm David Logan is the author of *The Wind in the Embers*, the first book in the Amulet Series about the Fall of Rome. He is a writer, teacher, blogger, and student of history. He lives in Chicago.